Seduced

Seduced

Virginia Henley

Island
B O O K S

ISLAND BOOKS
Published by
Dell Publishing
a division of
Bantam Doubleday Dell Publishing Group, Inc.
1540 Broadway
New York, New York 10036

ISBN: 0-440-21135-2

Printed in the United States of America

Published simultaneously in Canada

For Jay Acton, my magic man.
Hocus pocus, fish bones choke us!

Seduced

Chapter 1

Lady Antonia Lamb stood before the oval cheval glass, a worried frown marring her lovely brow. She was classically beautiful with black-fringed, wide green eyes above delicately sculpted cheekbones and full, generous mouth. With impatient hands she swept the cloud of dark hair that fell past her waist back over her shoulders to reveal high, young breasts thrusting up from her lacy corset.

"They're so small!" she lamented.

Her maternal grandmother, Lady Rosalind Randolph, put down her chocolate cup and said dryly, "It isn't size that counts, it's firmness. The champagne glass was molded from Marie Antoinette's small breast, which was declared perfection. Much good perfection will do her with the rabble of Paris," Roz added irreverently.

Her eyes assessed the tall, slim figure of her granddaughter, noting with satisfaction the nineteen-inch waist and the lovely long legs. It brought back memories of her own debut when she had been sixteen.

"The men will be at your feet, Antonia, you haven't a thing to worry about. The last ball I attended looked like a competition for hideousness. Lady Denham, who's as thin as a damned lat, wore an exaggerated bosom of stuck-out gauze. She looked exactly like a pouter pigeon and had the absurd idea it was becoming. The Duchess of Bedford was aiming, I think, to copy the Navy's new colors of blue and white, but her gown was a screaming shade I can only describe as *woad*. Fortunately no one noticed because they couldn't take their eyes off her blue, powdered hair, replete with battleship. Damned woman held court for an hour repeating the unedifying eloquence of her hairdresser, Legros, no pun intended." Roz struck a pose to mimic: "Three weeks is as long as a head can go well in the summer without being opened."

Antonia's eyes brimmed with laughter. She flicked a snowy curl on the creation sitting on her dressing table, made a pretty moue with her mouth, and said, "Oh, Roz, I was so looking forward to wearing my first wig, but you've quite put me off."

"Good! They are nothing but monstrous germ gatherers of horsehair, hemp-wool, and powder. I shall thank God when they go out of style, for daytime wear at least."

"I suspect you are trying to build my confidence. The Duchess of Devonshire is such a renowned beauty and I know her preseason ball next week will overflow with beautifully gowned and bejeweled ladies." Antonia had little confidence in her looks, in fact she had no idea she was beautiful. All her life whenever anyone had met her they had said things like "How unfortunate you don't have your mother's coloring," or "You are tall as your brother, yet I remember your mother being dainty as a kitten."

"Not all of them are ladies, darling," Roz drawled dryly. "Least of all Georgiana herself! Besides, it isn't the women you'll have to compete with, it's the men. 'Skiffy' Skeffington's face was painted with white lead, he reeked of civet cat, and the raffish Carlton House set wore red high-heels to a man."

"Skiffy, what a preposterous name," Antonia said, "I can't wait to see him."

"Not nearly as preposterous as his real name, poor devil. It's Lumley," Roz confided. "I swear he carried a snuffbox, sword stick, handkerchief, fan, head scratcher, patch box, and a muff. He resembled an infernal juggler from the circus!"

"You're exaggerating again. I'm sure he only carries a muff in winter."

"Oh, no. The very latest fashion in the *London Magazine* is a summer muff of swansdown. We must get you one when we go up to town next week. It's all the rage to be eccentric, but then is it any wonder when King George himself is raving mad?" Without seeming to pause for breath Roz said, "Now let's get Molly in here. I want to see what the new ballgown looks like."

Antonia could feel excitement beginning to build inside her. Until a few weeks ago, leaving Stoke behind for the London town-house had meant only an opportunity to haunt the bookshops for volumes on stately homes, their furnishings, and gardens that Antonia found fascinating. Then her grandmother, Lady Rosalind Randolph, and her grandmother's great friend, Lady Frances Jersey, had decided Antonia was old enough for her first season. Suddenly, instead of spending her days riding and sailing with Anthony, her twin, she stood for endless hours being fitted for ballgowns, took dancing lessons, and listened to advice on how to bludgeon eligible young lords into offering for her hand in marriage.

The maid was summoned, the white-and-silver tulle creation was settled over Antonia's petticoats, her own hair was tucked beneath the fashionably curled wig, the glass cone was held to her face while the white powder was applied, then a patch was selected and carefully placed near her lips *à la friponne.*

All three heads turned to the doorway of the bedchamber as the unmistakable tread of a boot told them Anthony was returned from riding. With hands thrust into his pockets, the tune on his lips died away as the tall, dark young man stood upon the threshold.

"Tony, is that you?" he asked his twin in disbelief.

His sister dimpled. "Tony, indeed it is me. What do you think?"

They called each other Tony, which confused others but never themselves and was precisely the reason they'd done it since they were children.

"I don't like it," he said bluntly and without apology.

Antonia's face fell, her confidence shattered.

"You look like a damned wedding cake!"

"Oh-ho," Roz teased, "you hear wedding bells and that will deprive you of a first mate to order about on the sailboat. Well, let me remind you, Anthony, that's a decidedly selfish attitude."

"I'm a male." He grinned. "I'm supposed to be selfish."

"It's all very well for you, darling. You'll inherit all this without so much as lifting a finger, but your sister must marry and marry well if she wants a home of her own and a title for her firstborn son."

He protested, "Roz, we're only sixteen! The mere thought of marriage terrorizes me."

"And so it should, you silly boy. You won't be ready to be shackled for years, whereas Antonia is ripe for the marriage market."

Antonia did not feel ripe. She felt totally inadequate. Both her grandmother and her mother had captivated titled lords who had whisked them to the altar when they had been her age. She knew she had little chance of meeting anyone here in the country and gave a prayer of thanks that she was being given the opportunity of a London season.

Wide green eyes looked into identical wide green eyes. "The thought terrorizes me also, Tony. I'm nowhere near ready for marriage, although I'm breathlessly excited about all the fêtes I'll be attending."

"You don't take after your mother. Eve was more than ready at your age. Set society on its backside and caused the devil of a scandal." Evelyn had been engaged to Robert Lamb but when his father died and Robert's elder brother Russell inherited the title and Lamb Hall, she immediately eloped with him and became the talk of the *ton*.

"I wish our parents would return from Ceylon," Antonia said wistfully. "I've almost forgotten what mother looks like, except that she has blond hair and is very beautiful."

"That was ten years ago. Females go off in the heat of the tropics," Anthony said irreverently.

"Not Evelyn," said Roz. "Her ability to take good care of herself is tantamount to a holy crusade."

"Roz! Sometimes you give the impression you don't like mother," Antonia admonished.

"Mmmm," her grandmother replied noncommittally. "Molly, you may pack the wig and gown with the rest of Antonia's new wardrobe. I think we'll go up to town a day early so you may have twelve hours of rest. Once the season starts you won't see your bed before dawn each day."

The summer day was absolute perfection. The warm sun had opened up the profusion of roses and lupins and the light breeze from the south wafted their perfume through the open casement windows of Lamb Hall. Antonia was humming happily, caught up in daydreams of the social whirlpool that awaited her in London. A small bubble of excitement seemed to be expanding in her chest now that her debut approached, and she realized she probably was ready. At least she was ready for powder and paint, high-heeled slippers, and fashionably low necklines. Her very existence was about to undergo a metamorphosis with balls, routs, plays, soirées, galas, masquerades, and ridottos.

Her grandmother had made sure she had had a sheltered upbringing, rather like a country caterpillar, but now the time had come to spread her butterfly wings and attract the attention of suitors. Her parents had set aside money for her dowry and she knew this added to her attraction as did her father's title, so she was not without hope.

Her eyes fell on the verse she had cut from *Le Beau Monde*, the fashion periodical, and Antonia read Luttrell's witty lines again, entitled "Advice to Julia":

"All on that LIST depends;
Fame, fortune, fashion, lovers, friends:
'Tis that which gratifies or vexes

All ranks, all ages, and both sexes.

If once to Almack's you belong,
Like Monarchs you can do no wrong;
But banished thence on Wednesday night,
By Jove, you can do nothing right."

Antonia laughed out loud. She could afford to. Thanks to Lady Jersey, she had her subscription to Almack's, the exclusive establishment where society's debutantes met prospective husbands. From her window she could see the boathouse where the lawns sloped down to the River Medway. She caught her breath as a heron winged through the trees, then waded out into the water. She would be gone all autumn and winter. There was much she would miss here in the country.

Antonia loved Lamb Hall with a deep and abiding passion. She had been born here and it was more than just a home. Up until now it had been her whole life. When her parents had gone to Ceylon, the beautiful country estate had represented security to her. The warm red brick covered by dark green ivy had stood there for a century and she knew it would always be there for herself and her brother, and would pass down through generations to her brother's son, then his son. It was a comforting thought that though people might come and go, the hall would remain a bastion against the storms of life for at least another century.

She knew how much she would miss her wild rides over the meadows and the exhilarating sea when they took out their sailboat, but she knew as well that she would be far too busy for homesickness and wouldn't give up this opportunity for anything in the world.

A carriage was being driven up the gravel driveway and Antonia watched with curiosity as a gentleman stepped from it and approached the front door of Lamb Hall. She didn't recognize him as one of her grandmother's frequent callers, so she went along the landing to the front staircase and was descending just as Mr. Burke opened the door to the stranger.

Her step was light, her spirits high; she had not one hint of foreboding. When she and her twin were ushered into the library, however, and she saw the pinched look in Roz's face and watched her hands holding the paper tremble, she sensed the stranger was from London and the news he had brought would burst her small bubble of happiness.

"Anthony . . . Antonia . . . this is Mr. Watson of Watson and

Goldman, your parents' solicitors. He has brought us some dreadful news . . . oh dear, I don't know how to tell you." Roz's hand went to her throat.

Icy fingers clutched Antonia's heart, while Anthony glowered at the man who had dared to cast a shadow over the sunshine of Lamb Hall.

"Father's ill." Antonia voiced her premonition.

"Yes, love," Roz said gently, "his heart . . . but his illness was fatal, darling. I'm afraid he has died."

"When?" Anthony demanded, rejecting the unwelcome news.

"Apparently in April. It has taken some months for the letter to arrive from Ceylon."

Anthony held out his hand for the letter. Roz saw the blood drain from Antonia's face until her pallor was alarming.

Mr. Watson cleared his throat and turned his attention to the new Lord Lamb, who was desperately scanning his mother's delicate script. "My lord," Mr. Watson said with great deference, "I have taken the liberty of having copies made of the papers granting you the title and of course the deeds to Lamb Hall. Because you don't come of age for almost a year and a half, your money is in trust. Before the late Lord Russell Lamb passed away, he appointed one Adam Savage as your legal guardian."

"Who?" Anthony asked, a dull ache beginning to fill his chest.

"Mr. Savage was apparently your father's friend from a neighboring plantation in Ceylon." Mr. Watson again cleared his throat. "Your allowance will continue as before, but the rest of your money, my lord, I regret to inform you is in the hands of your legal guardian, Mr. Savage. It will be entirely up to him whether or not your allowance will be increased to cover the upkeep of Lamb Hall and its tenant farms."

The last thing Anthony seemed to be thinking of at this moment was money, so his grandmother spoke up for him. "That seems a decidedly inconvenient arrangement. Surely it would have been better in his solicitors' hands, here in London?"

Mr. Watson of course agreed with her, but everything was scrupulously legal and without loophole. "Mr. Savage is presently having a house built at Gravesend and is returning from Ceylon when it is completed, so perhaps the arrangements will not prove inconvenient. Lord Lamb, if you will be so kind as to put your signature upon the deed to Lamb Hall so it may be registered in your name, and of course the deed to the Curzon Street town house."

Anthony complied with the legalities and Mr. Watson seemed disinclined to linger in a house of mourning. "Lord Lamb, Lady Randolph, permit me to offer the condolences of Watson and Goldman. We will continue to serve you in any capacity you wish, as we served the late Lord Lamb. A death notice has been placed in the *London Gazette.*" Mr. Watson tried not to stare at the remarkable similitude between Lord Lamb and his twin sister. He bowed to the ladies and took his departure.

Antonia looked helplessly at her brother and whispered, "Will mother be coming home?"

"Apparently not," Tony said, handing her their mother's letter, then shoved his hands deep in his pockets.

Antonia read it, then handed it to her grandmother. The tears gathered in her eyes and spilled over. She moved toward her twin and they stared at each other in mute misery. Communicating without words, they left the library together and sought the privacy of the outdoors.

Through the window Rosalind watched the two dark heads disappear toward the river. "God damn the tropics!" She immediately took Mr. Burke into her confidence. The butler had always been with them and was indispensible to the workings of Lamb Hall. He placed a footstool beside a comfortable wingchair and indicated that Rosalind should sit down. She sighed.

"Shall I make you some tea, my lady?"

"Brandy . . . brandy," Roz said decisively, "and pour yourself one while you're at it, Mr. Burke."

In the boathouse the twins busied themselves coiling rope and tidying the careless disarray of their sanctuary; then, when they had exhausted every chore, they climbed aboard and sat down listening to the water rhythmically splash against the side of the boat.

"What you said this morning is true," Anthony lamented. "I can't remember what either of them looks like."

"Poor mother, out there all alone. I wonder how she's coped these last months?"

"Damnation, I should be there with her," Anthony swore in frustration. "Christ, only this morning Roz said I'd inherit all this without so much as lifting a finger." His shoulders began to shake and he looked at Antonia with raw pain in his eyes. "I swear I don't want to be Lord Lamb and inherit everything . . . not this way!"

Antonia reached out her hand to comfort him. "Your grief is all mixed up with guilt, Tony." The lump in her throat threatened to choke her. "It isn't your fault."

He turned to her gratefully, as if she were his lifeline, and rubbed an impatient sleeve across his eyes. "I'm a selfish bastard. I'm glad you won't be going up to London for the season."

Antonia had completely forgotten about London. It was out of the question now that they were in mourning. She felt a pang of guilt at the money that had been wasted on gowns she might never get to wear. Perhaps they wouldn't be too out of style next year when she made her debut. She pushed thoughts of herself away and concentrated her attention on easing her twin's pain. "We're lucky we have each other. Sorrow shared is sorrow halved. I've never told you this before, but this house is my security. It makes me feel safe. When things go terribly wrong, like this, I feel the very walls draw about me to protect and comfort. The house will be our bastion and we'll be strong for each other."

"What the devil was father about, making me a ward of this Savage fellow like I'm a snot-nosed schoolboy!"

"It's not just you, Tony. Adam Savage is my guardian too," she pointed out.

"Who the devil is he? We know nothing of him!" Anthony complained bitterly.

"Yes, we do. We know he's building a house at Gravesend. That's only ten or twelve miles off. Let's ride over there next week."

The plan to do something constructive alleviated the feeling of helplessness that almost suffocated them. They remained outdoors until the shadows lengthened and the chill off the sea drove them indoors. They both excused themselves from the light meal Mr. Burke had had prepared, and Antonia retired to her bedchamber.

Roz came in to make sure she was all right.

"I can't understand why mother didn't come home," Antonia said, at a loss.

"Can't you, darling?" asked Roz quietly. "Lamb Hall belongs to Anthony now. Eve couldn't be lady of the manor here. In Ceylon she lives like an empress, her servants are almost like slaves to do her bidding. She is one of a unique and very select group, a white woman in a primitive culture. Society in Ceylon likely gravitates about her as if she were the sun, the moon, and the stars."

"You make her sound shallow," Antonia said sadly.

"In some ways your mother is shallow; in others very deep. However it isn't easy being a woman, Antonia. It's a man's world and always will be. Did you not notice today that Mr. Watson almost ignored your very existence? Does it not strike you as slightly unfair that though you and Anthony were born the same hour, the same day, to the same parents, he inherits all; you nothing? This is based on the simple fact that he is male and you are female."

"But titles can only pass through the male line," Antonia said without rancor.

"And titles usually entail property, land, and wealth. Quite a system, created to ensure power remains in male hands," Roz said bluntly.

"I never questioned the system before," Antonia said solemnly.

"None of us do until it affects us personally. Because I gave Lord Randolph a daughter rather than a son, his heir became a nephew who got the title and my home when your grandfather died. I was dispossessed except for a dowager's cottage on the grounds of my own estate."

"Oh, Roz, how unfair! I often wondered why you took on the burden of twins; you had little choice."

"You've brought me nothing but pleasure, darling. I could have married again, but somehow I couldn't bear to give another man control over my life."

"I suppose that's what marriage means," Antonia said thoughtfully.

"Some women are happy married to dominant men. Others prefer to rule the roost and wear the breeches in the family, so to speak, but those women have little respect for a husband who can be bullied and so once again women are placed in a cleft stick; damned if they do, damned if they don't!"

"Oh, Grandmother, you do make me laugh, and it's so dreadful of me to laugh today."

"No it isn't dreadful, darling. *Carpe diem . . .* seize the day! It's so very unfortunate that you can't go up to London for the season." Roz heaved a sigh of resignation. "A Georgian woman requires two things, beauty and money. If she has the first she can marry the second. If she has the second, she doesn't need the first."

Antonia smiled through her tears. "What a choice, marriage or 'leading apes in hell.' Isn't that the unenviable fate of spinsters in the afterlife?"

"I'm glad you can smile. When Anthony sees his father's death notice in black and white in the *London Gazette* he's going to be desolated."

Antonia lay in the dark trying to remember her father. She couldn't see his features distinctly, but her memories were of a tall, dark man who was always kind and gentle with her. Whenever she had fallen or hurt herself he had cradled her in his arms and wiped away her tears. He'd taught her to ride and to sail and never shown any preference for her twin brother. Her mother, conversely, could never hide the fact that her favorite was her son, Anthony. Her mother's sharp reprimands had often sent Antonia to seek out her father and climb into his comforting lap. She turned her face into her pillow, knowing she would never again know the comfort of his arms. A voice from within told her she would have to get all the tears out tonight. Tomorrow she would have to be strong for Anthony's sake.

Her time for growing up was upon her. Suddenly she felt years older than her twin. Though Tony was now Lord Lamb and owned the estate, in reality he was still an immature youth. Antonia, on the other hand, felt as if today she must leave her girlhood behind. She realized that becoming a woman meant being mature and taking responsibility for oneself. Men could afford to be the dreamers, while women must be the practical ones.

The tears were still seeping beneath her lashes when she fell into an exhausted sleep, and her dreams transported her back to her childhood. She was riding her pony, showing off for her father and the other men who were guests at Lamb Hall. They were laughing at her antics and the look of love and pride and approval on her father's face made her almost giddy with joy.

She dismounted and ran into her father's outstretched arms. She laughed down into his dark face, smelling his shaving soap, feeling his strong hands lift her high in the air.

"Toss her to me," laughed one of her father's friends.

She squealed with glee at all the lovely attention she was getting, then suddenly saw her mother's face as she came across the lawn. It was cold with disapproval. She did not want her father to play with Antonia or cuddle her, even when they had no guests.

Antonia was thin and dark like her father, and her mother said she was too boyish and ran wild. Antonia stiffened in her father's arms and he lowered her until her feet touched the ground. All the sunshine had gone out of her day.

"You shouldn't encourage her to be pert, darling. If she were a pretty child her pertness would be forgiven by everyone." Her mother linked arms with two of her father's friends, dazzling them with her beauty. The others trailed after her across the lawn, Antonia totally forgotten. She wasn't forgotten by her father, though. He blew her a kiss, which she caught and tucked into her pocket. She felt a penny inside and dropped it down the wishing well.

"Let me be as beautiful as mother when I grow up."

Antonia awoke with a start. Then she remembered that her father had died and she would never see him again, except in her dreams. Her memories of him were happy ones, filled with love and laughter, and those could never be taken away from her.

When her brother Tony read the death notice, she would be strong enough for both of them!

Chapter 2

Thirty miles away in his cramped bachelor's lodging in Soho, Bernard Lamb read the announcement of his uncle's demise with what could only be described as joy. Up until this morning his prospects had seemed very dim indeed.

It had taken him exactly a year to run through the money his own father had left him, which was little enough due to the addiction to gambling that Bernard had inherited from his sire along with his pittance. The small house in Clary Street was long gone, he was up to his handsome eyebrows in debt, and the rent was overdue on his dingy flat here in Tottenham Court Road.

The notice in the Gazette, however, filled him with elation. Bernard narrowed his eyes and allowed his imagination to take flight. It didn't have to soar too high to see himself a landed baron. Now that his uncle, Lord Russell Lamb, had stuck his spoon in the wall, only his cousin Anthony stood between himself and the title. "Lord Bernard Lamb" had an irresistible ring to it.

He laughed out loud as an amusing picture flitted through his head. Angela, the delicious little actress who'd been on the point of abandoning him to the gutter, could now be lured back. The aroma of future money would linger about him, attracting the fair sex like steel filings to a magnet. Money was power. He would revel in the power it would give him over the girl from the stage with the face of an angel.

She was an opportunist like himself. The mere hint of his prospects would bring her down to the mattress. His promises would turn her into his own private wanton angel. How he would enjoy punishing her for her indifference these past months. How he would savor watching her perform erotic little acts to ingratiate herself with him again.

Bernard decided it was high time he traveled to Stoke so he could assess Lamb Hall. He licked his lips in anticipation. Suddenly he was heir to a title and a small fortune and would borrow on his prospects immediately.

The day Bernard chose to present himself at Lamb Hall to offer his condolences was precisely the day the twins had ridden off to Gravesend.

Mr. Burke alerted Lady Randolph that one Bernard Lamb was in the library and they put their heads together and decided he could only be the son of the late Robert Lamb, to whom Evelyn had been engaged when she up and eloped with the more eligible Russell.

Rosalind, a small, pretty woman who hid her age as successfully as she hid her shrewdness, swept into the library with a rustle of black silk skirts. She caught young Lamb surveying the room with a specula-tive eye. He introduced himself immediately, brought her hand to his lips with an easy manner, and offered his condolences.

It took her perhaps thirty seconds to dissect him. Bernard Lamb was fashionably dressed, had pretty manners, and a handsome face. He was of an age with her grandson Anthony, yet he was worldly and far too smooth for one of such tender years. Roz summed him up with one word. *Vulture.*

She gave him a dazzling smile and said in a glacial voice, "I shall convey your condolences to Lord Lamb. He is in deepest mourning and not receiving callers."

The butler came into the library, but Bernard was surprised that he did not offer the usual obligatory wine and wafers. Instead, Lady Ran-dolph said, "Mr. Burke, would you show the young man to the door."

Bernard Lamb seethed with humiliation and he instantly vowed revenge. The old strumpet thought she had dismissed him, but Ber-nard Lamb did not dismiss quite so easily, as she would one day learn.

When all this was his, he would take particular pleasure in putting her belongings in the road.

The twins had no idea where Adam Savage was building his house, but they soon discovered everyone else in Gravesend knew exactly where Edenwood was located. The estate covered a thousand acres of wooded parkland beyond the town in the countryside. The property's northern boundary was the River Thames.

In a spacious clearing rose a three-story neoclassical house, easily the most beautiful Antonia had ever seen. Workmen were everywhere, carpenters, masons, and painters labored under the direction of a man who carried what looked to be a set of plans.

The twins dismounted and Antonia strolled up to the man while Anthony tethered the horses.

"Please excuse our interruption. I understand this home is being built by Mr. Savage of Ceylon. He is our guardian and we are naturally curious. Would you mind if we had a look around?"

The man smiled at the beautiful young woman. "Not at all," he said, then stared frankly as a youth who was her double joined them.

"Is that great building the stables?" the young man asked incredulously.

The man nodded. "Be my guest."

Anthony strolled off in that direction and Antonia said, "How rude of me. I'm Antonia and that's my twin, Lord Anthony Lamb."

"How do you do, my lady. Permit me to introduce myself. James Wyatt, at your service."

Antonia's mouth fell open. "Not *the* James Wyatt?" She gasped.

"James Wyatt, Architect," he said, both pleased and surprised that such a beautiful young woman knew of him.

Antonia tried not to gush. "Mr. Wyatt, I can't believe it. I'm such a great admirer of your work. I have your *Book of Architecture* at home. You designed the Pantheon in the Oxford Road. Your central block linked to octagonal towers is a replica of the Tower of the Winds at Athens!"

He bowed. "I'm vastly flattered. What do you think of this house?"

"It's magnificent. Mr. Savage must have perfect taste."

"It isn't his design, it's mine. He bought the land and instructed me to build him a stately home that would *add* beauty to its setting rather than detract from it. Edenwood is an apt name, I think."

"He instructed you to build whatever you fancied without regard to cost?" she exclaimed, then blushed at the rudeness of her question.

Wyatt only smiled. "This is a new design . . . a semicircular, bow-windowed bay rising through two stories in the south front. It forms a balcony or small terrace above from the master bedchamber. The west front has a simple Roman portico."

"I quite agree with your theory that the main rooms should be in touch with the outside world by views through the windows and accessibility to the gardens through French doors opening onto the lawns. Will it have a conservatory?" she asked with enthusiasm.

"I'll let you decide," James Wyatt replied.

Her green eyes widened with pleasure. "Then, yes, by all means let's bring the outside indoors." She thought Mr. Savage must be rich beyond reason and have a very large family to need a home this size. When she commented on the need for so many rooms, Wyatt smiled at her innocence.

"It's a power house. A house of the ruling class. Owning broad estates is power based on ownership of land. An estate this size will rule the county. During the last century the tenants and neighbors would fight for the owner; nowadays they will vote for him. Land leads to the peerage and establishment of a dynasty. It puts one in control of patronage and legislation." She grasped everything he told her, so he continued.

"A stately home is an image-maker that projects an aura of power, glamor, mystery, and success. When a new man buys an estate, the kind of house he builds shows exactly what level of power he is aiming for."

"Then I would conclude that Mr. Savage intends to rule the world." Antonia laughed. "Tell me, Mr. Wyatt, what rooms make up a power house?"

James Wyatt was enjoying himself. It was rare to find a young lady with intelligence combined with humor. "Morning room, dining room, ballroom, smoking room, billiard room, library, card room, office, music room. The center of the house will have a top-lit staircase with reception rooms all the way around on the first floor. Each room could have a different color scheme or different style of decoration so that guests can climb the splendid staircase, make their way about the circle enjoying the various distractions provided for their entertainment, then make their way down the stairs and out."

"Good heavens," Antonia whispered, lost in the picture he had painted. Her eyes wandered over the entire property and the corners of her mouth went up as she said mockingly, "There must be a lake, of course, and a bathing pool, a chapel, a temple, and a folly."

"I expect so, but that will be up to William Kent, who is designing the gardens."

"William Kent!" Antonia exclaimed, "Oh, I don't believe it. I have studied all his books on landscaping."

James Wyatt thought such interests an oddity in a young lady.

Her twin joined them and said, "It's unbelievable. The stables must have forty or fifty stalls."

"Mr. Wyatt," Antonia asked, "I would love to come again to see your progress, if it wouldn't be too much of an inconvenience for you?"

"It would be my pleasure, Lady Lamb. I'm not here every day, but there are always workmen here. Your looking about the place won't interfere with their progress, I'm sure."

"Thank you, sir. I am honored to have made your acquaintance."

James Wyatt stared after them as they rode off, wryly thinking his name and reputation had been totally lost on young Lord Lamb. Stables interested him far more than houses.

Back at Lamb Hall the stables seemed to interest Bernard Lamb, now that he had been summarily dismissed from the house. He concealed himself and watched to see how many servants worked there. He saw a man enter the carriage house and pull a small coach by the shafts out into the yard. He was about to wash the mud from the carriage and polish its lamps.

Bernard shrewdly observed that he fetched the bucket and water himself rather than calling for a stableboy and concluded he was alone. When the stableman was absorbed in his task, Bernard slipped inside. He saw a handsome pair of coach horses, two empty stalls, then what looked like a dam and her colt. His eyes narrowed as his quick mind went over his choices. His goal, of course, was for the new Lord Lamb to come a cropper. A riding accident was an ideal solution to his needs.

He considered driving a nail into the tender part of the mare's hoof, but it would take too long to find a horseshoe nail and a mallet. He cursed himself for not having thought to bring along a sharp needle that would have been even better. He took out a pocket knife and moved toward the mare, but she whickered nervously and moved to protect her colt. Bernard quickly moved away from her lest she give him away.

Instead he reached for a halter and bridle and cut partway through the leather that held the bit. Then he pried the studs on the inside surfaces so that they would be sharp and irritating against a horse's face. Finally he cut partly through a stirrup and the belly strap of one of the saddles. He reached for the other saddle, saw it was a woman's sidesaddle, and left it alone. He didn't want to harm his *female* cousin, at least not yet. Perhaps her father's death had left the girl wealthy. Marrying money was second best to inheriting it. He'd never seen her, of course, but face and figure were of small account when fortune was involved.

Bernard Lamb decided against taking the coach back to London. He did not delude himself that the chicanery in the stables would bring about the probable demise of his cousin; it was only a hoped-for possibility. The town of Gravesend was a port, and down by the wharf were many inns where he could put up for a few days. This would give him an opportunity to visit Lamb Hall after dark, prowl about undetected, observe his twin cousins on a daily basis to learn their habits and activities, and allow him time to come up with a more diabolical plan whose results would be guaranteed.

Rosalind wrestled with her conscience, then decided not to tell the twins of the visit from their cousin Bernard. They might welcome him with open arms in their naïveté, but Roz knew instinctively he was nothing more than a fortune hunter in spite of his fashionable clothes and polished manners.

She remembered how his father, Robert, had had a passion for gambling and the fast life, which is, of course, what had attracted her daughter Evelyn. She and Robert Lamb had been inseparable in spite of, or perhaps because of, his reputation. No one had been more relieved than Rosalind when Eve eloped with Russell, even though she was cynical enough to see that his new title had been the deciding factor.

Roz sighed. Best to keep young Bernard Lamb at arm's length. Fraternization could only produce jealousy and greed, or at the very least lead Anthony into the disreputable habits of drinking, wenching, and that most debauched addiction of all, gambling. Roz shuddered. By the time the twins had reached their fifth birthday, Evelyn had accumulated so many gambling debts, they couldn't be calculated.

Nowadays, Georgiana, Duchess of Devonshire, had set a fashion for such behavior, but unlike the Duchess, Eve's husband had not been one of England's wealthiest dukes.

For a year she had lived on the edge, accepting jewels from gentlemen admirers to appease those she owed, but when Lord Russell was offered an administrative post with the East India Company she encouraged him to grab it and off they had sailed to Madras, India, ten years ago, deftly avoiding another scandal. The tropics was no place for children, however, so she had jumped at her mother's offer to move to Lamb Hall to look after the twins and run the house until they returned to England.

Over the candlelit supper-table Antonia described to Roz what they had seen that afternoon at Edenwood. "This Adam Savage must have a great deal of money. He'll be able to hunt on his own property. There must be a thousand acres of woods. The outside of the house is almost finished, but not the interiors. Its grandeur is breathtaking, isn't it, Tony?"

"The stables will hold fifty stalls," Anthony added negligently, more interested in slicing off a pink slab of beef than describing a house. "I don't think I'll have any trouble getting this Savage fellow to increase my allowance. He spends money like water."

"Mmm, must be one of these nabobs I've read about in the *Tattler*. They make fortunes in the Indies, then return to England with their houris and pet monkeys. They wear voluminous, brocaded pantaloons and turbans. They buy up all our treasures while royalty fêtes them and society in general falls over itself to kiss their bottoms."

"I wish Mother's letter had told us more about him," Antonia said wistfully.

"Perhaps she doesn't know much about him," offered Anthony. "He was probably a business associate of Father's." Anthony could not yet speak of his father without choking up.

Antonia's imagination had taken flight over the picture Roz had painted of the nabob, while Roz thought cynically, *If Savage is as wealthy as you surmise, Eve will make it her business to learn everything there is to know about him!*

Chapter 3

At Leopard's Leap plantation in Ceylon, Adam Savage stood in the heavy shadows of the eucalypti and bamboo, absorbing the haunting beauty of the night. He often came to this spot, which gave him a clear view of the lake. In reality it was a holding tank for water, but it drew wild animals as if it were a natural watering hole.

He stood absolutely still, waiting with infinite patience, as the moonlight flooded down with blue-white intensity to reveal a leopard standing reflected in the oval pool. It was breathtaking in its beauty and grace. Leopards had a trick of appearing with no perceptible approach.

His strong brown hand went to the pistol tucked in his belt, but it was an unconscious gesture to reassure himself it was there if needed. To Adam Savage shooting animals who came to drink was murder. High leather boots reached to his well-muscled thighs to guard against scorpion, centipede, and snake.

A half-smile touched his lips as he recalled how wary he'd been of snakes when he first arrived in the Indies. He'd worked his way on an East Indiaman to buy wood for his father, who was a cabinetmaker. He'd sent back satinwood, ebony, teak, mahogany, sandalwood, and he had discovered calamander, stronger and finer than any rosewood. In those early days he'd seen pythons on every trunk, cobras beneath every fern, but there was an Eastern saying, "Only he who fears snakes sees them," and it was true. Now, he never saw them. They were there. He'd hear them slither through the rafters, hear them thrash about catching rats, and hear the rats squeal when they became a meal, but once he accepted snakes as necessary to keep down vermin, he never noticed them again.

One of the things he would truly miss when he returned to England was the fantastic wildlife. In the distance he heard the banshee wail of a pack of jackals. Every hour of the day and night was filled with the sights and sounds of Ceylon's exotic fauna. Twilight was the hour of winged creatures. At sunset the caves disgorged their hordes of fruit bats. Some, called flying foxes, had four-foot wingspans, others no bigger than a bumblebee would fly to his bungalow as if they were invited dinner guests to feed on the swarms of insects that were attracted to the glow of the oil lamps. Anything like the gekko or house lizard that dashed about everywhere and devoured flies and mosquitoes was devoutly welcomed.

Suddenly Adam's nostrils were filled with the sweet, heavenly perfume of the iron tree. Hindus believed that the God of Love tipped his arrows with this blossom. Savage closed his eyes and thought of Eve. He finally admitted to himself that he wanted her. Now that she was a widow, no barrier prevented him from taking her. She liked to flirt, she liked to have men at her feet, but that was a game many pretty women played. It was important to him that their attraction was mutual. His hand went to his face to finger the scar that marred him. Not that he'd had any claim to beauty before the knife had carved a deep gash that ran from the side of his nose right through his top lip. But now his strong, masculine features had taken on a dark, sinister look that hinted at an unsavory past.

He knew Fate had marked him as a grim reminder of his sins, and as Omar Khayyam had written, not all his piety could cancel half a line. His looks frightened off young women, yet ironically, older women, especially married ones, were attracted to his saturnine face almost irresistibly.

Sometimes he thought Eve sent him subtle invitations, but he had never acted upon them. Not that it was against his code to seduce a married woman, it was only against his integrity to dishonor a trusted friend by sleeping with his wife. And Russell Lamb had been a trusted friend.

One more white devoured by the tropics. The Indies did that with relentless frequency, yet he had always thrived here. He respected the country and its climate, realizing from the beginning that large meals accompanied by flagons of wine at midday would kill off a white man quicker than disease.

Tomorrow, Lady Evelyn Lamb was coming to Leopard's Leap to dine with him for the first time. Previously he had always dined with Lord and Lady Lamb at Government House, their palatial home on the next plantation. Though the house was imposing, the plantation was insignificant when compared with his twenty thousand acres, but the paperwork of the East India Company had kept Russell chained to his desk and allowed him no time to cultivate crops.

Eve was a fair English beauty as tempting as her namesake. She was in her early thirties, perhaps even a year or two older than himself, but this only added to her allure. There was a coolness about her beauty that made him wonder if she had ever been fully awakened sensually. Or ever been fully satisfied. Nevertheless, she was far from virginal and he hoped his sexual experience could teach her to be rewarding in bed. Eve had that "look-but-don't-touch" aura about her that challenged him.

Ordinarily she would have been far above his touch, if it had not been for that great equalizer, wealth. Anticipating their encounter tomorrow he could see her flawless white skin, feel her golden hair brush against his cheek, hear her cultured voice banter a sophisticated witticism, taste her—Adam's balls tightened pleasurably and he stepped from the shadows toward his comfortably spacious bungalow, where his servants would be waiting with his bath and his evening meal. A bandicoot that looked like a cross between a small pig and a large rat scurried from his path.

Adam Savage dwarfed his manservant, who stood at the door with bootjack in one hand, slippers in the other.

"Good evening, John Bull," Savage said, sitting on a stool while his servant removed his boots.

"Good evening, Excellency," John Bull said, bowing his crimson turban until it almost touched his white pantaloons.

Savage's dark brow cocked. "Excellency?" he questioned.

John Bull said solemnly, "When we are in England—"

Adam held up a protesting hand. "Must you preface every sentence with 'When we are in England'?"

"Yes, Excellency, when we are in England, it will be a fitting title. You do not like it when I call you master, and sahib will sound too foreign, so I have ruminated long and think Excellency will be good . . . when we are in England," he added unnecessarily.

Adam had learned to keep a straight face when conversing with John Bull, a nickname he had given him because the man worshiped everything English and lived for the day he would finally set foot in that haloed land.

"John Bull, we are not yet in England," Adam reminded him.

"Ah yes, Excellency, but tomorrow when the memsahib Lady Lamb comes to dine, it is very, very important that she not think us uncivilized."

Adam rolled his eyes. "Give me strength," he murmured.

"You are the Leopard, the strongest man in Ceylon. Why do you waste prayers asking for more strength, Excellency?"

Adam knew from experience it was better not to answer him. He crossed the hall and offered the mynah bird a piece of pawpaw fruit. "Hello, Rupee."

"Sinner! Hellfire!" replied the flame-crested bird.

"When we are in England, I think it would be best not to take this accursed bird. His vocabulary is defaulted and could prove harmful."

Adam thought wryly that if the English survived John Bull's vocabulary, it would be a miracle. He picked up some charts from his desk then his eyes scanned a map of the plantation that covered the wall behind. Tomorrow morning he would have to arise at four to organize the tappers before daylight. Latex only flowed readily from the rubber trees before the heat of the day. It coagulated in warm temperatures.

Kirinda, Adam's Sinhalese woman, entered the room on silent feet. In her soft voice she told John Bull that the Leopard's bath was ready. All his people thought and spoke of him as the Leopard. He thought cynically that the name came more from his resemblance to a scarred beast, than from owning Leopard's Leap.

John Bull remonstrated with her in a stage whisper. "When we are in England you will not order the master about. When he is ready for his bath he will come into the bathing room. At the moment he is not interesting!"

Adam Savage put down the charts. "I resent that remark, John Bull," he said lightly. "Lead the way, Lotus Blossom."

She never walked before him, always behind. When Adam had passed her on his way to the bathing room she raised downcast eyes and pulled an impudent face at John Bull.

He said scornfully, "A lotus is nothing more than a common water lily!"

In the center of the room was a sunken, tiled bathing pool steaming with warm scented water. Adam pulled his white cotton shirt over his head and allowed Kirinda to help him peel off his riding breeches, then he walked down the steps into the water that came up to his hips. His broad chest was heavy with sleek muscle from years of hard physical labor. The tropical sun had tanned him to a dark mahogany above the waist, while below, his taut buttocks and strong legs seemed startlingly pale in contrast.

Kirinda loved to look at the master's body, though she always appeared to keep her eyes modestly downcast lest he think she stared at his scars. He was deliciously different from the men of this land. His chest and manhood were covered by black curls and he was wonderously large. His hair fell to his shoulders and was as dark as any native's, but his eyes were a startling ice-blue and they could freeze a person with one glance if he was displeased.

She stole a look at him and saw that his elbows rested upon the tile ledge, his head was thrown back, and his eyes closed as the sensual feel of the water relaxed his tired muscles. As Kirinda bent to pick up a sponge her black hair swung forward like a silken waterfall. She straightened, slipped off her richly embroidered sari, and walked gracefully down the tiled steps into the water.

When Savage bought Leopard's Leap from its Dutch owners it had been a failing plantation. He had worked twenty hours a day to make it thrive. In those days he had literally been too tired to bathe and so one night she had done it for him. The experience had proven so pleasurable to both that now it was a ritual.

Kirinda had to reach high on tiptoe to lather his neck and shoulders, then she held up her palm with the cake of soap upon it. Adam took it, washed his face and hair, then ducked beneath the water to rinse off the suds. She soaped his back, chest, and belly, then again passed him the soap so he could wash his own intimate parts. Their relationship was nonsexual and completely matter of fact. Adam, now totally relaxed, closed his eyes and leaned his head back. He felt as if his very bones might melt.

When he opened his eyes a minute or two later, Kirinda was standing patiently with his towels. The ritual time spent with Lotus Blossom was soothing to a man. She never chattered. She never recoiled from his scars. His blue eyes smiled into hers as he slipped on a robe and went to eat his evening meal.

When he had eaten he went out onto the screened verandah to catch the breeze and enjoy a cheroot rolled from tobacco grown in the dry zone of Jaffra. His thoughts drifted about, lulled by the nocturnal symphony of tree frogs.

It was still pitch-black when he arose and made his way to the sheds beside the smokehouse. Over the years his tappers had become highly skilled, learning the importance of cleanliness in gathering the snow-white liquid. Savage handed out knives, cups, coconut shells, and buckets. Then he began to pour acetic acid into molds, knowing the tappers would quickly start returning with latex. After setting for eighteen hours the sheets would be put through rollers to press on a rough pattern to prevent adhesion, then hung in the smokehouse for several days to dry.

The men who had become proficient in English were promoted to overseers and given an umbrella as a badge of office. The Leopard, as the plantation workers also called him, was a hard taskmaster who ruled with an iron hand. He would put up with nothing that displeased him. Punishment was both swift and harsh. He was never lenient, there were no second chances. Mixed with their fear of him, however, was a healthy dose of respect. There was not one task on the entire plantation that he could not do himself and do it better than any other.

When the Dutch owned the plantation, the workers had all been native Sinhalese. They were an attractive people but extremely cunning and indolent. If they did not wish to work on a particular day, no power on earth could make them. When Adam had been in India he had witnessed how the natives manipulated the English by their own form of blackmail. They would sit on a step and fast to get their own way or threaten to disembowel themselves or even dash out their childrens' brains.

When Savage took over he dismissed the Sinhalese workers and replaced them with darker-skinned Tamils, who were far more industrious and willing to do labor. Savage allowed them their own customs unless those customs offended him, in which case he forbade them. In the East a woman was barren until she bore a son, then her husband was permitted to take a second wife. Concubinage was normal, so he did not interfere. A female must marry as soon as puberty was reached or she became the prey of all males in her caste.

Kirinda was the only Sinhalese woman on the plantation. She became a twelve-year-old widow during his first week and marked for sati. He saved her from burning on the funeral pyre by taking her as his personal body servant.

The other practice he abolished immediately was the murder of female children at birth. Savage insisted they could be taught to work for paid wages.

At the first blush of dawn he left the rubber trees and walked swiftly to the mustering grounds where all the workers gathered each morning to receive their daily tasks. With the aid of a multilingual banyan the day's tasks were allotted to the work force of fifteen hundred Tamils.

Each day after the mustering Adam Savage returned to his bungalow for breakfast. Then he saddled up and rode over the entire twenty thousand acres to supervise the various harvests that he exported to Britain. His homeland had developed an insatiable demand for anything and everything the tropics could produce.

As he cut through a coconut grove on his way to the house he heard the pitiful whimperings of a monkey. It lay in his path, its small body at a peculiar angle. He saw immediately that it had broken its back in a fall from the top of a high palm. Its eyes looked up pleadingly from its small orange face. Already there was a trail of red ants swarming toward the helpless creature. He could tell it was in great pain but knew that within minutes its suffering would increase a thousandfold. He took his gun from his leather belt and shot it. It was a far kinder death than being devoured alive by a million red ants. Leopard's Leap was surrounded by jungle on three sides. In the jungle death was the most common occurrence of the day.

Adam was subdued at breakfast, so John Bull thought he had better remind him of something. "Do not forget about Lady Lamb's visit. I will have fresh clothes and a bath ready at four of the clock sharp."

"I'll be here," Adam reassured his man, refusing more fruit and coffee. "No time. I have a lot to do before four." He did not need to check on details of the dinner to be served to his guest; John Bull was a perfectionist.

Savage saddled one of his Arabs and rode toward a hilly region planted with tea bushes. Men and women and older children of both sexes were pluckers. They made an exotic picture in their gaily colored cottons, their bamboo baskets slung on their backs, fastened by a rope around their foreheads. Young runners went up and down the rows carrying sacks so that the pluckers could empty their filled baskets.

Mature tea bushes yielded a crop of flush every two weeks. Flush was the tender closed tea bud and two leaves. The overseers with their umbrellas checked continually to make sure the bushes were cleaned of unproductive stems, but that the coarse leaves did not go into the baskets.

As Savage tallied the pounds of tea that had been picked, he watched the women with pride. They made much better pluckers than men. Their hands were superlative, darting over the bushes with dainty movements, gathering handfuls of flush, then lithely throwing them over their shoulders into the baskets without crushing or bruising the tender buds.

Savage moved on to farther acres that were being pruned. Pruners were paid higher for their services because of their know-how. Tea bushes must be pruned in strict rotation to ensure they produced for eighteen months before needing to be pruned again.

Scores of other laborers were needed for cleaning drains, culverts, and silt pits. The plantation boasted a timber reserve of quick-growing fuel trees where men chopped, split, and hauled wood to the latex smoke houses and the four-level tea factory where five processes were carried out: withering, rolling, fermenting, firing, and grading.

For the thousandth time he thanked Providence that on his nefarious runs to China importing and exporting illicit cargoes, he'd also taken an interest in the licit crops the Chinese produced. Once he learned how much tea could be packed into the hold of a ship, and the ridiculous prices the English were willing to pay for this newly fashionable beverage, he had taken immediate advantage. Then later when he had scraped together enough to buy the plantation in Ceylon, he had bought hundreds of the fragile seedlings, transplanted them with gentle hands, then labored and worried over each as if it were a child of his loins to be cared for with infinite tenderness and love. The care he had lavished upon these first delicate tea bushes in Ceylon had paid off a thousandfold. The following year he'd done the same with rubber plants he brought from Burma.

Any number of afflictions could cause havoc on a plantation. Early in the afternoon as he was examining some groves for root and stem disease, Adam was distracted by the birds. The sight and sound in the treetops played hell with his emotions. The swallows were gathering to return to England and such a wave of nostalgia for his homeland swept over him that he knew he must soon return or go "doolally," a condition bordering on madness from being in the isolation and heat of the tropics overlong.

Savage thought of the house he was having built. It was a culmination of all his dreams and all his hard work. With the naive hopes of youth he had come to the Indies to acquire wood so that his father's business would increase. Visions of prosperity danced in his head along with a plan to buy a small house in a respectable neighborhood away from the unhealthy, damp yard where his father's cabinetmaking business was located by the Thames.

His father's death had snuffed out all his hopes and covered him with guilt. To this day he believed if he'd been there to nurse his father through his chronic bronchitis and do all in his power to fight the insidious conditions of poverty, his father might still be alive.

Savage had emerged from the grief and guilt with an iron determination to acquire wealth. If his resolve was fixed strongly enough, and he let nothing stand in his way, and he swore to do anything to attain his goal, including kill, nothing on this earth could keep him from that goal. And he'd done it. Oh, it hadn't been easy. His driving ambition had led him down paths of iniquity and he'd paid dearly for every mistake he'd made. But gradually, slowly, a plan had been forged.

It was an ambitious plan, a glorious plan, and most importantly a worthy plan. That was the secret of success, probably. It wasn't enough to need something and want something. Until you also deserved it, you didn't begin to get it.

The stately home in England was only part of his plan. It was a means to an end. Without the trappings he could never achieve the worthy goal he'd set himself. A woman such as Evelyn Lamb would be the crowning touch for his English estate. She was even titled. With a gracious hostess like Lady Lamb at his side, his ambitions could be realized in half the time.

He decided to waste no more time. He'd begin his wooing today. It might take a little time. She wouldn't fall into his bed like some chee-chee girl, he wouldn't want her to, but he must breach the barriers of class between them that would impede a more intimate relationship.

Savage returned to the bungalow early to bathe and change, so that by the time of the appointed hour of five, he was on the verandah steps when her open carriage arrived, driven by a Company sepoy. She was dressed in black silk, her beautiful blond hair swept into elegant coils and fastened by tortoiseshell combs.

"Good evening, Mr. Savage," she said formally before the soldier.

"Good evening, Lady Lamb." His slow smile belied the formality of his tone. He smiled rarely, but when he did, his scarred lip gave him a look that was both dangerous and deadly. "I promised to show you the tea factory. There is still an hour before sunset."

She nodded her acceptance and the sepoy stepped down and handed the reins to Savage. Adam had changed into fawn riding breeches and cream shirt and jacket. The coat was a special concession to his guest. The most he usually ever wore was a shirt.

He handed her from the phaeton and saw she was wearing high

leather boots beneath her whispering silks. "I have a horror of creeping things," she explained, her mouth curving deliciously. He took her arm and led her through the factory.

"The top three floors are simply withering lofts. These fans keep the air moving until the leaves become dry." As they descended to ground level he kept a strong hand at her elbow. "Four rollings extrude the oil, which is a sticky golden green. This floor is kept continually cool by having water run down the walls. Your nose tells you when the tea has fermented enough to be put in the ovens and fired."

He led her into an airy building adjacent to the first where the pleasantly pungent fragrance rose up from the heaps of black, crisp tea. "It's ready for sorting, cutting, sifting, grading, and packing."

Evelyn touched the tea chests stacked against the wall. "When the English sip their orange pekoe or souchong they haven't the vaguest idea how much time or labor is involved."

"They pay a high price for the privilege, so I cannot complain."

Money! It was the subject Evelyn was longing to pursue. She must be subtle, and yet she must waste no more time in breaching the barriers between them that would lead to a more intimate relationship.

Chapter 4

Adam handed Eve back into the open carriage and urged the horse toward the lake. Then he invited her to walk with him. The deep blue of the sky was turning to saffron with shafts of brilliant gold. A swarm of macaques with tufted faces gamboled in the branches, throwing fruit rind at submerged water buffaloes. Sapphire kingfishers and black and golden orioles darted across the water to catch gnats, while a flock of flamingos took wing.

As they strolled along the lake's edge the sky was turning into a deep red, making Eve's alabaster skin a blush-pink. From beneath her lashes she saw how Adam's cream shirt contrasted against his mahogany throat and her breasts began to tingle. Adam Savage had such an air of authority and command, which she knew came from having supreme confidence in himself and his own abilities.

Evelyn was used to having her own way in life. She had avoided marrying a dominant man and as a result ruled her own roost like an empress, but at the moment this virile, dominant self-made man was an unbelievable catch. He was attracted to her, he was still available, and most important, he was wealthy.

They stopped short as two wild water buffalo roared at each other a few hundred yards off. She watched in disbelief at the speed and ferocity of the charge. One bull hit the other so hard, it knocked it through the air and it lay in the mud as if dead. Then the victorious bull mated the waiting cow buffalo in a spectacular orgy of pure sexual pleasure. The man who witnessed it felt an atavistic thrill.

Eve gasped and drew back against Adam. He took her in his arms swiftly, decisively, and brought his mouth down on hers as if he were starving. Her belly felt like molten mercury and she stiffened as her breasts and mons felt the iron hardness of his chest and groin. He mastered her with his tongue and as her mouth filled with the feel and taste of him she moaned.

A wave of guilt swept over her. It had nothing to do with her recently deceased husband. Sex always made her feel guilty and dirty. She had thought the act of the animals disgusting and was fearful that the primitive mating, coupled with Savage's virile presence, might sexually arouse her.

She was on very dangerous ground here. Savage might make her lose control, and Eve did not want that to happen. She must retain control. She suppressed her body's physical response immediately.

Adam was surprised when she suddenly pulled from him and with cheeks flaming looked about to see if they had been observed. He noted with sardonic amusement that this would have horrified her. She retreated to the phaeton and her previous formality.

Adam drove to the stable and turned the horse over to a native groom. His instructions brought alarm to her face. "I cannot stay late—" She said low, "Servants gossip incessantly."

"As you wish," he said quietly, but no matter how much she wished otherwise, the kiss had wiped out a great many barriers that he would not allow her to reerect.

As they passed through the front hall Rupee retreated to the far end of his perch because of the stranger and cried, "Sinner! Repent!"

John Bull was relieved that the bird chose biblical words that did

not offend because there were many words in the white man's Bible
and Rupee's repertoire that were offensive. Eve, however, could have
stoned the mynah.

Though the windows and doors of the dining room had jalousies to
let in the breeze, a servant sat cross-legged on the floor pulling the
cord that turned the punka ceiling fans.

Beside Evelyn's plate Adam Savage had placed an exotic orchid. Its
black velvet petals were shot through with veins of gold and scarlet.
"Lovely," she murmured, and suddenly Adam wanted to see it against
the pale gold of her hair. He resisted for the moment and pulled out
her chair for her.

John Bull in immaculate white jacket and pantaloons served the
meal in his most unobtrusive manner, never uttering a word. Adam
knew how much restraint this took on John Bull's part and made a
mental note to compliment him.

Though the servant's manner was unobtrusive, Lady Lamb's eyes
fastened on his crimson turban, which was anything but. In its center
was a ruby as large as a man's thumbnail. She had suspected Savage
was a wealthy man, but she'd had no idea he was rich enough to
shower his servants with jewels.

The ruby made Eve change her tactics. The subject of money must
be broached, and in her experience a strong, dominant man responded best to a delicate, helpless woman.

Adam watched her make a pretense of eating. After a couple of
small bites she began to toy with the delicious food on her plate. Eve
found Indian food repulsive and she was thankful that it was so. Eating practically nothing was the only way she could retain her slim
figure. Adam assumed she had not regained her appetite since her
bereavement.

"Eve, do you need someone to talk with?" he asked quietly. He saw
the relief in her eyes.

"Oh, yes . . . I need your help . . . your advice," she amended
quickly. "I will no longer receive Russell's salary from the East India
Company. They will appoint another administrator."

Adam was not taken aback that she spoke of money. He was shrewd
enough to see through her pretensions. Perhaps she was more interested in a financial partnership than an emotional relationship. Perhaps he, too, wanted her more as a chatelaine for Edenwood than as a
real wife. "Russell explained that you own Government House outright. It doesn't belong to the Company."

Eve nodded and said helplessly, "Yes, but, you see, they paid us a very generous amount to use our home as Government Headquarters here in Ceylon. That money will stop now."

"Not necessarily," he said thoughtfully. "The Company will still need offices for the administrator and his assistants." Adam had no idea if she was knowledgeable about the business of the East India Company and how it was tied to politics. "You see, the Company and the Crown have dual control over India and Ceylon. Only two things interest them, profits and collecting taxes."

"But I thought Raja Singha was the ruler. I'm a frequent guest at the palace. I've seen you there occasionally. His wealth is beyond belief."

"I don't question his wealth, but he is a figurehead. Clive conquered the colonies for Britain thirty years ago. The Raja is allowed his golden palace and opulent life-style to keep him pacified, and just in case there's a hint of trouble, every plantation has its army of sepoys. India is owned lock, stock, and barrel by the British and as soon as she rids Ceylon of the last of the Dutch, I know it, too, will be made a Colony of the Crown."

Eve laid down her heavily ornamented silver knife and fork as a realization hit her. "That's why you have made plans to return to England within the next year. As a planter in a Crown Colony you would have to answer to the government and you prefer to answer only to yourself."

Adam smiled inwardly at her shrewdness. "Up until recently the Governors General of India have played cricket on Calcutta lawns, ridden to hounds to hunt the jackal as if it were the fox, and translated Persian classics into English. All at once the incompetent British Government fell and that genius Pitt became chief minister. As a result his India Bill has been passed by parliament, forcing the East India Company to accept a board of control." He hesitated a moment, then continued.

"Russell told me the Company's profits last year were in excess of three million pounds. The Government intends to investigate." Adam blamed Russell's heart troubles on the pending investigation, but he said nothing to Eve. "The Company controls the balance of power and the British Government intends to take it for itself. In the end everything comes down to money," Adam said cynically.

Eve was so absorbed, she didn't even flush at his remark.

"So," Adam gestured expansively, "it's bad for me, but good for you. I must get my gold out before anyone questions how the hell I accumulated so much and you can gouge them by renting a wing of Government House for their horde of tax collectors. You can also expect to be compensated for the army of sepoys billeted on you and odds are in favor of the new administrator being unmarried or at least not having his wife here with him and they will still have to rely upon you to run the social life of Ceylon, as you have for several years. In fact I think you should be on the Company's payroll. I'll see to it for you."

Adam was used to the system of bribes that oiled the machinery.

"Thank you, Adam." Her mind dashed about like quicksilver. Christ, he *had* said "gold" hadn't he? Surely it wasn't her imagination! The man was almost a complete mystery. She was about to say something but the presence of John Bull and the servant cross-legged on the floor made her hesitate.

Adam was aware of her hesitation immediately. He saw that she had no intention of eating her dessert, so pushed his chair back and drew her toward a private sitting room.

"Tell the servants to retire," he told John Bull, whose job it was to ensure the couple's complete privacy.

Eve picked up her orchid and allowed Adam to lead her into the adjoining room. She sat in a peacock chair of bamboo, knowing it would frame her beauty, while Adam poured them Madeira, one of the few wines that kept well in the heat of the tropics.

As if Adam were a priest and she at confession, she blurted, "I need money. I have gambling debts."

His blue eyes crinkled at the corners. "Such wickedness," he teased. "Gambling is an ingrained characteristic of the English. I, too, am a gambler."

Obviously he had no idea hers was a compulsion, an addiction. He thought it a mere peccadillo.

"The only difference is that I gamble on ships' cargoes and insurance rather than on cards."

"I've thought of that," she confessed, "but the risk is too high. If I insured a cargo and the ship was lost, I'd be wiped out."

Suddenly he realized she was very serious about money. "Good God, don't even consider it. I have a vast knowledge of ships and the perils awaiting them on the high seas. I'd never insure a cargo unless the ship carrying it was completely seaworthy, bristled with guns, and was manned by cutthroat sea-dogs who could outfight pirates."

"You own your own ships, don't you?" Eve was astonished the conversation had turned to shipping. She had thought it would take two or three visits before she could ask the favor she desperately needed.

"A few years back I had my first East Indiaman built in Bombay of finest teak. I have three smaller vessels for the India-China run. They make port in Burma, Sumatra, and Canton but not Persia. It's overrun with pirates."

"Adam, would you give me cargo space on one of your ships?"

"Of course. Forgive me for not offering it. Anytime I can fill one of your needs, I shall be happy to do so!" His blue eyes pierced her with a searing, intimate look that gave his words an unmistakable meaning.

He came to her and took the tortoiseshell combs from her hair so that it fell about her shoulders in pale golden waves. Then he took the exotic orchid and tucked it behind her ear. "I've been wanting to do that all night," he confessed huskily. He cupped her face with his strong brown hands and lifted it until her mouth almost touched his.

"Eve, I'll pay your gambling debts."

These were the exact words she wanted to hear, but she knew she must pretend otherwise. Over the years she had become a consummate artist at pretense. She stiffened and pulled away from him.

"I couldn't possibly let you do that." She knew that nothing was free under the sun, especially from men. She was prepared to pay his price, of course, she'd been doing it all her life, but up until now it had been on her terms and she wanted to keep it that way.

Savage was so unreadable, an enigma really. She knew he was dominant and strong-willed but his sex drive might be insatiable enough for her to control him. She allowed her stiffness to dissolve. She cast him a sidewise glance as a lure and said temptingly, "Perhaps I could *win* the money from you."

Adam knew she was showing him an acceptable way of letting her have his money. Though she had eaten little, he saw that she drank the Madeira. He refilled her glass, then opened the drawer of the games table and took out dice. Dice were quick. There was no way he was going to waste the remainder of their evening playing cards.

He lifted the lid of an oblong silver box and emptied its contents on the table. "We'll play for jewels," he said softly, his eyes on her mouth. He saw her gasp and lick her lips. He allowed himself the luxury of hardening in anticipation. He evenly divided the uncut gems between them until both sat before a small pile of rubies, emeralds, and diamonds.

Eve felt her pulses quicken. The very blood in her veins began to warm and flow faster. She caught her breath as she picked up the die caster and experienced a delicious rush as she flung the ivory cubes onto the table. She rolled double five. Adam's eyes never left her face. Almost negligently he rolled a five and a six, then reached over and selected the largest uncut emerald from her pile.

He saw her concentration increase, saw the intense look of triumph when this time it was Eve who rolled eleven. Adam leaned back indifferently and cast a double six onto the table. Very casually he took a diamond from her.

Her eyes became brilliant and she was short of breath as the game of chance took hold of her.

Adam's visage in the glow of the lamps was dark and inscrutable as a black leopard's, masking his thoughts and his intent, which were both blatantly sexual.

Eve's desire for the jewels was written upon her face. Just so would he like her to look at him when he was naked. It was a hungry look that said, *I must have them or die.*

Relentlessly he took back his jewels, one at a time. He knew Russell had let her have her own way about everything. He would teach her that if she was his woman she would have her own way about nothing, and he would teach her to like it.

As he took her last gem she stood up quickly clenching her fists and in a hurt, little-girl voice said, "I thought you were a gentleman. I thought you would let me win."

"I never let anyone win against me in my life, and I'm not about to start." He stalked around the games table like a raptor sure of its prey. His voice was like smooth, dark velvet as his hands cupped her shoulders. "Eve, you above all other women are acutely aware of the fact I am not a gentleman."

She shuddered as he brought his mouth down upon hers to drain her of her will. But her body was aroused by the high-stakes game, not by the presence of the virile man. When he touched her, she froze.

Savage had her gown undone and off her shoulders before she realized how bold he was. The gown and its petticoats fell to her feet and she stood before him clad in corset, drawers, and tall black boots.

Savage had undressed a thousand women in his lifetime. He was an expert at the game of seduction. At twenty when he left England he had considered himself highly experienced with women, having known servant girls, married ladies, and professional harlots, but once he arrived in India he realized he was almost untutored in the sensual arts and his education had begun in earnest. He had visited the secret temples erected to the goddesses of love and fertility, where even the statues were so sexually explicit, they could make a sailor flush with embarrassment. He had been entertained by rajas and nawabs whose nautch dancers knew tricks that would harden the cock of a corpse. He had seen and traded in priceless collections of Hindu and Oriental erotica that had broadened his mind, his taste, and his appreciation so that he explored and enjoyed to the full his own sensual nature without shame or false prudery inherent in Western civilization.

He thought she rejected his advances because he was a commoner. He tried to unthaw her by being deliberately suggestive. "I'm quite willing to wager that you've never allowed an untitled man access to your body," he whispered. "You are used only to noblemen, but you are about to experience a noble savage."

"Please, no, the servants will know . . . ohmigod, Adam, don't take off your clothes!"

"Eve, the naked state is the natural state. You've suppressed yourself to the point where you worry about servants. You won't allow yourself to become aroused and excited." As he held her at arm's length he imagined the enticing picture she would create naked. The cool English titled lady with alabaster skin and pale golden hair would look untouchable until he took into account the black leather riding boots.

"No, Adam," she said. Her eyes were pressed closed in a pretense that he was forcing her to this abomination. Eve was afraid that if she saw his magnificent body, more lithe, more rampantly male, than any animal's, she might lose control. She had never lost control in a sexual encounter in her life and it terrified her.

Savage thought better of removing his clothes. If he revealed his scars he would have to explain them. They would prompt too many questions about his unsavory past. He didn't like people to know the eels that lurked in the water beneath the surface. He had a private side he allowed none to explore. He drew her close and cupped her breast.

"Eve, relax and let me love you."

"Mmm, no, mmm, no," she breathed, almost incoherent. She was filled with revulsion for herself because Adam Savage was beginning to bring her pleasure, and she fought against the sensations valiantly.

Eve had never allowed a man to bring her to climax. She couldn't.

Her body didn't work that way. Unconsciously she had to stay in control. When she could not avoid the act she wanted it to be over with swiftly. Instinctively she knew Savage would revel in the slow, rhythmic dance of lovemaking, sustaining forever, never spending. He would be the kind of dominant man who would fuck her until she yielded herself to him. She stiffened, imagining the servants were outside the door listening. Suddenly she felt he was behaving like the animals they had seen. Savage was a bull who would wildly mate her. She pulled from his arms and snatched up her gown to cover her underclothes.

"You bastard, how could you make me feel so dirty?" she hissed.

Adam Savage realized Eve was frigid. If he ever hoped to unthaw her, he knew he would have to go about it in a different way. He gently took the gown away from her and dressed her. He pinned up her hair with the tortoiseshell combs, then gathered her in his arms. He told her how lovely she was, how beautiful, how exquisite. He began to kiss her face, trailing a fiery, sweet path from her temple to her eyelids, then on to her lips. He made her feel beautiful.

Suddenly he was giving her the kind of pleasure she liked. She loved to be told she was beautiful. Now that she was dressed she knew he would not spoil her delicious glow by wanting to have sex.

Savage hoped that if he left her slightly aroused, perhaps wanting more, she might fantasize about him when they were apart.

In that moment Eve knew she would be willing to marry him, if only he had a title. She stood on tiptoe to press a last kiss upon his devastating mouth. "You would make a savage Lord Savage, Adam."

Chapter 5

When Bernard Lamb returned to the Hall the next evening he wanted to see what his victim looked like, but he knew his curiosity must be secondary to caution. Under no circumstances must he be seen by any member of the household. If and when an accident occurred, it must be considered exactly that, an accident. If foul play was even surmised in the removal of Lord Lamb, the next in line would automatically be suspect.

Bernard concealed himself in the shrubbery some distance from the Hall to observe its inhabitants through the candlelit windows. He had the patience of a spider hidden beneath the leaves, lurking in the shadows.

He had no trouble identifying the old strumpet. She was a small woman who moved about quickly and used her hands with exaggerated gestures when she spoke. Bernard had no trouble identifying the servants by their uniforms, but from this distance it was difficult to distinguish one cousin from the other.

Both were tall, dark, and slim, both walked with casual, unhurried steps. He had thought he was watching his cousin Anthony as he sat reading at a desk in what Bernard assumed must be the library, but when the figure arose and crossed directly in front of the window, he saw skirts and realized it must be Antonia. Though he saw no features, he knew he could never be attracted to a woman who was not overtly ultrafeminine.

He thought of his little actress, Angela Brown, all deliciously rounded curves, her glorious, silvery-gilt hair dressed high in the latest fashion, her ripe breasts swelling from the frills and laces of her satin gowns.

Bernard saw the lights in the Hall being extinguished. They certainly retired early here in the country. When Lamb Hall became his, the lights would blaze until dawn, he vowed.

He was about to emerge from the shrubbery when he heard a heavy step crunch on gravel. A man with an oil lamp was coming from the stables. He watched him go to the back of the house toward the servants' wing. It was the same man who had been cleaning the carriage yesterday.

Suddenly a brilliant idea came to him, and his mouth curved into a self-satisfied smile. He made his way to the carriage house adjacent to the stables and slipped quietly inside. Bernard saw with satisfaction that there were no windows through which he could be observed and quickly lit a lamp. There was a toolbox on a shelf, from which he selected a mallet. He went to the rear of the carriage and hammered the lockpin from the hub of the tall carriage wheel and slipped it into his pocket.

How simple an act. He need do nothing more. The carriage would have to travel a few miles before the nut would loosen and fall, then the large wooden wheel would fly off, likely overturning the vehicle. The beauty of it was, there was no possible way they could connect him with a carriage accident.

His business in Stoke was completed for the present and Bernard could hear the siren call of London. To be precise, the voice of Angela Brown from the stage of the Olympic Theater.

Anthony Lamb had been withdrawn since he learned of his father's death two weeks past. He felt guilty that he had not been in Ceylon to take some of the business responsibilities from his father's shoulders or to console his mother in her loss. Anthony was frustrated that soon he would be seventeen and had never set foot out of England.

He was a little bitter that his parents had never sent for him to come to Ceylon and decided that, as soon as he came of age in just over a year, he would make the voyage. He wouldn't say anything to Antonia, but when this Adam Savage fellow arrived, he'd pick his brains and learn all he could about the Indies. Once he began to make plans for the future, he felt decidedly better.

Antonia was happy to see her brother had taken pains with his toilet this morning. He wore dove-gray riding breeches and a jacket of blue superfine. She saw that he was wearing a new tiewig and doubted he would go to so much trouble for his usual morning ride.

"I thought I'd ride over and speak to the tenants this morning. They will have heard about father by this time, and I think I should reassure them that I won't be making any changes now that they are my tenant farmers."

Antonia nodded and hid a smile. They had two farms on their land and both tenant farmers had pretty daughters, hence the new tiewig. "There's a wonderful breeze today, I'll probably go sailing."

He grinned at her and she was relieved that he looked like his old self.

"I don't suppose I could talk you into staying in the Medway?"

"No fear! What's the point in living on the coast if you don't sail in the sea? You are not hinting that I'm not as fine a sailor as you, are you Tony?"

"Oh, Lord, now you'll take my words as a challenge! Just be careful. You don't have to prove anything to me."

As Antonia was changing her clothes for sailing, she glanced out of her bedchamber window to see Anthony take off as if he were riding in a race. Wasn't it just like him to urge her to caution, then risk his own neck riding hell for leather! He was a superb horseman and she watched with pleasure as he soared over the hedge that took him from the park into the meadow. He made the jump cleanly, but then something happened and rider and horse separated company. She saw that the horse was behaving like a wild thing and that Tony had not gotten up from his fall.

Antonia ran down the stairs and called to Roz, who was in the breakfast room. "Tony's come a cropper. Get Mr. Burke!" She picked up her skirts, ran out through the garden, across the small park, and climbed through the hedge into the field.

Her twin lay still and pale as death upon the grass. Her heart was in her throat. He couldn't be dead! *Deaths come in three,* a voice whispered in her ear. "No! No!" she cried aloud to dispel her fear.

Suddenly Antonia could not breathe and a loud drumming in her ears threatened to deafen her. She glanced up and saw the sturdy figure of Mr. Burke cutting through the hedge. As he bent down to her brother, Anthony suddenly sat up, rubbed his head, and grinned foolishly. "Stab me, I must look a damned fool to fetch everyone running."

Antonia realized the drumming in her ears was her own heartbeat. "Tony, you great fool—I feared you were dead!"

Mr. Burke helped him to his feet and, embarrassed, Anthony brushed himself off and refused to be aided back to the Hall.

"Go with Mr. Burke. I'll get your horse," Antonia ordered in her most bullying tone.

Mr. Burke was more diplomatic. "Come back to the Hall and reassure your grandmother that you only took a harmless tumble."

By now the mare had quieted and stood trembling. As Antonia reached for her bridle she saw that her face was bloodied. "Venus . . . hush, darling. Let me see what's wrong."

The horse had been cut about the face by something on the halter. Antonia slipped it off and ran her fingers over the jagged studs. She saw that the bit had cut clean through the strap and it was lucky Venus hadn't choked on it. She smoothed her hand along the horse's neck and murmured soothing words to her.

When Antonia began to walk back to the stables the mare followed her. By the time they arrived, the saddle had slipped to one side and was hanging off.

"Bradshaw," she said to their carriage driver, "I had no idea the harness was in such bad shape. Don't use this again, and check all the other tack too. We'll have to buy new."

Antonia went to the stable supply cupboard and took down a cake of carbolic soap and a bottle of linament. She washed the cuts and dabbed on the oil of wintergreen linament while Bradshaw held the mare's mane. Venus whickered and rolled her eyes, but displayed none of the wildness that had been brought on by sharp pain stabbing into her cheeks.

By the time Antonia went into the Hall, Anthony had changed his clothes and she heard him downplay the fall to Roz. "The belly strap broke and the saddle slipped just as I took the hedge."

Antonia spoke up. "The tack you were using is worn out. We'll have to buy new. Poor Venus came off a lot worse than Tony."

"Is she all right?" he asked with concern as he headed for the stables.

"Cut her face a bit, but she'll be all right. Take a look at the sharp studs on the inside of that halter."

When he had gone, Antonia placed her hand over her still rapidly beating heart. "Oh, Roz, he was lying there so still and so pale, I thought he was dead, but he was only unconscious for a minute."

Roz looked at her keenly. "You've had a real fright, darling. Come, I'll give you a little brandy."

Antonia shuddered and coughed, for as the brandy went down it took away her breath, but it certainly gave her a warm feeling of confidence as it spread like a red rose inside her chest. "I was overcome with fear when I saw him lying there. I felt utterly alone without him, as if I'd been abandoned."

"Praise God it was only a little accident and not fatal. If anything happened to Anthony, we'd have more to worry about than missing him."

"What do you mean?"

"That wretchedly smooth, fortune-hunting cousin of yours, Bernard Lamb, would inherit not only the title, but the Hall and the property that goes with it. Even the town house in London. You and I would be out on our derrieres to put it crudely."

Antonia shivered as if a goose had walked over her grave, in spite of the brandy. She had lost all desire to go sailing. Instead she became thoughtful about how dependent women were upon their men. She picked up a book and wandered out to the garden, but it lay in her lap unread as one disturbing thought led to another.

Antonia didn't even have any money of her own. The new tack would have to come out of Anthony's allowance. She knew vaguely there was money for her dowry, but suddenly she felt humiliation sweep over her because she was going to have to find a husband to take care of her for the rest of her life.

How pitiful to be dependent upon a father, then passed on to a brother, then a husband. She had better find one before Anthony found himself a wife, or she would find her position intolerable. She would have a roof over her head on sufferance and her status would be no more than that of old spinster aunt to her brother's children.

Antonia was not a young woman who acquiesced helplessly to a situation. She decided to go up to London and question the family solicitors. She would insist on knowing the amount of her dowry. If she decided against marriage, she wanted to know if she could have the money once she turned eighteen. She would also demand to know if she had been left anything in her father's will, and if not, why not!

As children they had been treated as equals. Antonia had always assumed because they were twins, that they *were* equals. Now that they were no longer children, the rules of the game had changed. Apparently a male was far more equal than a female.

Because they had never had secrets from one another, Antonia spoke to her brother about her intentions. Anthony showed no inclination to go up to London.

"Find out when that Savage fellow is coming. I'm going to the saddlery at Rochester to buy new harness and tack, so I'll be in need of money soon."

Roz and Antonia, accompanied by Mr. Burke, set off for London. The town house had servants aplenty, so they needed no maids, but Burke was indispensable. Roz felt safer traveling with another man besides their driver, Bradshaw.

"This trip to London will do us a world of good. Even though we cannot attend any balls, we can visit with Lady Jersey. Frances will fill us in on all the latest gossip."

"How did you two come to be friends, Roz?" Antonia wondered out loud.

"Your grandfather, Lord Randolph, was a friend of the Earl of Jersey. I met her for the first time at her wedding, a very grand affair. Though she was a few years younger than I, we became fast friends because we seemed to have so much in common. We are exactly the same size and we both possess an acid tongue. When we attend the same function we are capable of terrorizing the assembly. She's also a grandmother now, which proves that age simply sharpens the wit."

Antonia and Mr. Burke exchanged amused glances. All were unaware that as the carriage gained speed, the large cast-iron nut holding the back wheel in place was gradually working itself loose.

Bradshaw was tooling along at such a rackety speed, Roz braced her feet on the seat opposite to keep her balance. "Bradshaw must think he's Hellfire Dick!"

Antonia laughed. "Who, pray, is Hellfire Dick?"

"You never heard of him? Oh, Lord, you are such an innocent little rustic, darling. He drives the Cambridge Telegraph coach. He has a great gap between his two front teeth through which he spits with amazing accuracy."

Antonia narrowed her eyes with skeptical amusement. "I'm not rustic enough to believe all your stories, Roz."

"Darling, it's gospel truth. Lord Ackers had his front teeth filed and paid Hellfire Dick fifty guineas to teach him to spit through them. London is chock-a-block with eccentrics. Coach-driving is one of the new 'passions.' Even women are dressing like coach-drivers and swearing at the horses, which are now called 'cattle' in fashionable circles."

The carriage began to slow and Bradshaw pulled into the yard of a coaching inn. He jumped down and Mr. Burke opened the carriage door and stepped outside.

"Summat's wrong. The coach is swaying about like a drunken lord," Bradshaw announced, keeping a firm hand on the reins of the sweating horses.

"No bloody wonder. You drive like a maniac!" Roz accused through the window.

Bradshaw touched his tricorn and looked inordinately pleased.

Mr. Burke said, "Drive across the yard while I watch."

Bradshaw climbed to the driver's seat and tooled the coach across the inn yard. The back wheel wobbled ominously and the heavy iron nut rolled from the hub onto the ground.

"Stop! Stop!" shouted Mr. Burke in alarm. "The back wheel is about to fly off!"

A shaken Bradshaw came to examine it. "The lockpin's gone. Christ, that was a close call!"

Mr. Burke suggested the ladies take refreshment while a new lockpin and nut were secured at the stables. The ladies didn't bat an eye at their close encounter with death as they alighted and went to sit in the inn's parlor.

The innkeeper muttered under his breath when Roz ordered a dish of bohea and Antonia asked for cider. Bloody tea would take the place of ale and spirits if it kept growing in popularity, and then where would he be?

When Mr. Burke came in and ordered small beer the frown left the innkeeper's face. Mr. Burke's brows were drawn together, however. "Two accidents in two days strike me as suspicious," he said quietly.

"It's just coincidence," Antonia replied.

"There is no such thing as coincidence," Roz scoffed.

"Do you think someone is deliberately trying to harm us?" Antonia asked jokingly.

"It's within the realm of possibility that someone is trying to harm Anthony."

Antonia said with disbelief, "You actually think that cousin you mentioned would come all the way to Stoke and prowl about stealing lockpins and cutting through saddle straps? He probably isn't aware of our existence."

Roz and Mr. Burke exchanged significant glances. They did not wish to alarm Antonia over what might be only a suspicion and carried on the journey to London without discussing it further.

That night, however, as Antonia slept in her bed in Curzon Street, a terrifying nightmare gripped her. She dreamed that while they were away in London, someone murdered her twin brother. She was shattered. The deep pain of Anthony's death was like losing a part of herself, an arm or a leg. When they rushed back to Lamb Hall they discovered that everything they owned had become the property of the new Lord Lamb.

They were not even permitted to set foot on the land to decently bury Anthony. An evil cousin, who was all the more terrifying because he was faceless, was in firm possession of the title, the Hall, and the property.

She and her grandmother had been dispossessed of everything—furniture, clothes, even keepsakes. They were destitute and about to be sent to the poorhouse. The nightmare was so real and so devastating, Antonia awoke in terror and huddled beneath the covers thinking it had really happened. Her arms were covered with gooseflesh and her feet felt as cold as if she had been trudging barefoot in deep snow. Dawn was creeping up the sky before she could stop shivering.

Chapter 6

By the time Antonia arrived at the chambers of Watson and Goldman, the terror of the dream had evaporated, but it had hardened her resolve to find out about her financial position.

She was ushered to a chair by Mr. Watson, who found her appearance quite changed today from the young girl he had seen in the country. In London, of course, everyone was bewigged. He himself now wore the new-fashioned tiewig, but his partner, Mr. Goldman, still preferred the full-bottomed wig that he insisted carried the authority necessary for their profession.

Young Lady Lamb was dressed in the height of fashion, with fitted pelisse and billowing silk skirts, even though they were in mourning black. And the saucy little hat with its black ostrich feather looked very smart indeed atop the fashionably powdered wig. Only her green eyes, exactly like her brother's, reminded him that she was a twin.

"Mr. Watson," she began, "there is absolutely no point in my being coy and beating about the bush. I have come to look into my finances." She had the most attractive husky voice with the hint of a drawl, and he found himself almost mesmerized. Her beautiful eyes widened in expectancy.

"Your finances?" he repeated blankly.

"When you came to Stoke you discussed only my brother's affairs. How does my father's death affect *my* finances, Mr. Watson?"

"My dear Lady Lamb, you have no finances. In the past you were your father's responsibility, at present you are your brother's responsibility, and in the future you will be your husband's responsibility."

Antonia bristled until green sparks flew from her eyes. "If this mythical husband you speak of does not materialize, may I use my dowry to help support myself?"

"My dear Lady Lamb, you will have no trouble attracting a husband, I assure you."

How dare he patronize her? "By that I take it *you* are willing to marry me, Mr. Watson?"

"I should be more than willing, my lady, if I did not already possess a wife."

Antonia almost shouted, *You cannot possess a wife,* but upon reflection she realized that men did just that. She took a deep breath to calm herself. "I'm sorry, Mr. Watson. I'm not usually so rude. Was I left anything at all in my father's will?"

"Nothing, I'm afraid, but of course your dowry is in trust and it won't be affected."

"How much is my dowry? And in the event I do not marry, may I use the money to help support myself?" she repeated.

"It is not my place to disclose the amount of your dowry, my lady."

"Whose place is it, sir?" she demanded.

"Why, your guardian's place, of course. Your father named Mr. Adam Savage as your legal guardian, and it is his permission you must seek on any and every matter. As must your brother."

"You mean this stranger on the other side of the world rules what we can and cannot do? That is preposterous! I shall write to my mother immediately and inform her this is intolerable."

"Your mother cannot alter the law, my dear. Your father's will would have to be contested to change the situation."

"I see," she said with quiet resignation. "This Savage person can interfere in my life any way he wishes. Lord Lamb needs money. Will he really have to go begging hat in hand to this Savage?" Antonia asked with distaste.

"My dear lady, Mr. Adam Savage is in total control of the purse strings, so much so that he could spend the money himself, if he so desired."

Antonia's mouth fell open. Well, if that was the case, she'd damn well spend his money and see how he liked it! A diabolical plan regarding Edenwood began to form in her mind.

When Antonia returned to Curzon Street, Frances Jersey was ensconced in the salon with Roz. "Antonia, I'm so sorry you've been deprived of your season. It's such an advantage to begin husband hunting at sixteen."

"Men! I'd like to shoot the lot of them," Antonia announced, removing her hat and stabbing it with her hatpin.

"Roz, you've prepared her beautifully for society. Men deserve to be treated like dogs."

"Speaking of which, what's that puppy, the Prince of Wales, been up to lately?" Roz asked.

"Well, you recall how he escaped from under the tyranny of the

King last summer by taking refuge with his uncle, the disreputable Duke of Cumberland?"

"Yes, at that seaside place with the peculiar name, Brighthelmstone," Roz said, nodding.

"Well, the Prince has taken a house for the summer and the place has become so popular that on weekends London is positively deserted. They have even changed the name to Brighton."

"Seawater is supposed to have therapeutic qualities, but it didn't do a thing for George's swollen glands. I hear he's taken to wearing high neckcloths to disguise it," Roz said.

"Yes, and wouldn't you just know it, high neckcloths have become the latest rage, just as Brighton has. The smart set rushes coastward to be cured like tongues dipped in brine," quipped Frances.

"We know the real attraction is the disreputable Cumberlands," Roz stated flatly.

"Why are they disreputable?" Antonia asked, becoming caught up in their conversation.

"The King's brother Cumberland has gone from one scandal to another all his life," explained Roz. "It all came to a head when he had an affair with Lady Grosvenor and Lord Grosvenor discovered the filthy letters he wrote her. Grosvenor brought an action against Cumberland and was awarded thirteen thousand pounds. It was the first time a prince of the blood appeared in divorce court."

Lady Jersey took up the tale. "Did Henry Frederick learn his lesson? Not a bit of it. He up and wed that young adventuress Anne Horton. She had a wide experience and eyelashes a yard long. She got him banished from Court. . . . It was because of her the King got the Marriage Act passed. No one in the Royal Family may marry without permission of the King."

"It's precisely because the Duke and Duchess of Cumberland are banished from Court that the Prince spends so much time with them. He hates and detests his father and will do anything to send him off into another fit of madness."

"Roz dear," said Frances Jersey, "it's no wonder he hates his father. The King raised his children in that abominable Teutonic manner. The boy's tutors were such cruel disciplinarians that the Prince of Wales's teacher used a dog whip on him. Is it any wonder his neck is permanently swollen and he escaped to his disreputable uncle!"

"The Princesses fare no better. None of them is permitted into society and none of them may marry. Wags refer to St. James's as the Nunnery," Roz lamented.

Frances Jersey laughed. "Too bad the girls aren't allowed a visit to their uncle. They'd soon learn debauchery as George did. Actually," Lady Jersey confided, "Henry Frederick is charming, witty, and deliciously amoral, no wonder the Prince is completely under his spell."

"How was the Duchess of Devonshire's ball?" Roz asked.

"The usual dice, dancing, crowding, sweating, and stinking in abundance! The Earl of Bristol's false teeth are made of Egyptian pebbles. They look positively squalid. No wonder he carries a fan."

"Ugh," Roz shuddered. "Why can't he wear the new porcelain with the paste from Wedgwood? How is dearest Georgiana? I must call on her before I leave London."

"You'll never catch her at home. You'll find her at that new toy shop in Fleet Street buying loaded dice. Her gambling debts are even higher than her bosom friend's, the Prince, though her beauty still has every beau in London at her feet. Everyone goes to the toy shop to make assignations."

"Was our friend Selina, Countess of Huntingdon, at Georgiana's ball?" Roz asked eagerly.

Antonia knew for a fact that both she and Frances disliked Selina intensely, so expected a deliciously catty reply.

"Dear God, her gown was embroidered with chenille in the pattern of a large stone urn crammed with flowers, no urns on the sleeves, but two or three on the tail. More suited to a stucco staircase than a lady's gown. But, oh, my dear, she has languor down to an art. Lisps Italian now!" Frances laughed.

"Her refined delicacy belies that she has to pour her three-bottle husband into bed every night," Roz added spitefully.

"Poor lady," Antonia said softly.

"Darling, I know disapproval when I hear it," Frances said with her eyes sparkling. "You'll have to sharpen your tongue before next season. Indulging in scandalous gossip is society's newest hobby. Well, I'm off."

"I've always known that, darling," Roz said dryly.

When Lady Jersey left, Antonia said, "What happened to the days when ladies discussed the latest fashions and beauty recipes?"

"Oh, now we can read about all that stuff in the *St. James's Chronicle*. Leaves us more time to malign our friends. I must buy all the latest periodicals before we leave London." She glanced shrewdly at

Antonia. "I take it your interview at Watson and Goldman proved unprofitable?"

"What I learned made me furious. A woman is entirely under the control of a father, a brother, or a husband with the added hindrance of a guardian in my case. Roz, I am going to be such a thorn in the side of Savage, he'll relinquish the guardianship!"

"Well, darling, since there's nothing you can do until he arrives in England, I suggest you put him out of your mind and we'll go shopping."

"Nothing I can do?" Antonia smiled, her wicked juices starting to bubble. "Watch me!"

They took a chair to the Exchange, which was filled with specialty shops. Roz spotted a five-foot stick with a hinged jade topknot to carry a message or snuff, and lusted for it.

Antonia said, "You must have it, only think how envious Lady Jersey will be."

"It's elegant but extravagant. I cannot afford it."

"Oh, Roz, we aren't paying. The bills can be sent along to Watson and Goldman. My guardian can attend to the dreary matter of settling accounts."

Before they left the Exchange, Antonia had acquired a petticoat with whalebone hoops, a quilted calico wrapper, a seed pearl pomander, and a fan painted with the loves of Jove. She couldn't resist a brimmed straw hat with cherry ribbons, especially designed for carrying rather than wearing, and a stomacher with matching cherry ribbons in rungs like a ladder. They each bought summer muffs, red high-heeled slippers, and a new dress. Roz chose a sky-blue, especially suited to her tiny figure. It had a long-waisted bodice, with side panniers looped back into a bustle, and a small train.

Antonia who had half a dozen ball-gowns as yet unworn, chose something for daytime. It was a pale green muslin sprigged with tiny violets. For Anthony she bought two pairs of the very modern pantaloons that went to the ankle, with the strap designed to go under the boot. "I must take a couple of these yellow oilskins. They'll be perfect for keeping us dry when we go sailing. Now all we need are your periodicals and I venture to say we've done enough damage for one day."

As they caught each other's eye, they couldn't keep straight faces. "Antonia, I am proud of you."

They had so many packages, they had to take two chairs back to

Curzon Street. As the sedans swung down the Strand, it was thronged
with uniformed soldiers, Life Guards in scarlet, Horse Grenadiers
with their sky-blue caps emblazoned in gold and silver, and Halberd-
iers still garbed in long coats and ruffs as they had been in the days of
Henry Tudor.

Fashionable ladies with their towering pomaded hairdos rubbed
shoulders with foreign adventurers, eye-patched Aspasías, pickpock-
ets, piemen, and barefoot beggar boys. When they turned into
Charing Cross it was like a fashion parade. Beaus thronged the choco-
late- and coffeehouses with their red-curtained windows, using their
quizzing glasses to ogle the orange girls and the occasional prostitute
daring enough to walk the streets in this fashionable part of town.

Fops on every corner tried to outdo each other in outrageous fashions wearing bright yellow coats, waistcoats embroidered with flowers
and butterflies, and zebra-striped pantaloons. All wore either lacquer-
hilted swords or carried the newfangled sword sticks, that they juggled
with snuffboxes, fans, and handkerchiefs.

Antonia thought their costumes more suited to the stage than the
street. She experienced a pang of regret that she wouldn't be able to
attend the theater while they were in town. Londoners had an insatiable appetite for social life, and as a result pleasure gardens and new
theaters were opening up in every part of the city.

That night Bernard Lamb sat in the second row at the Olympia,
avidly watching Angela Brown strut about in her suggestive page-boy
costume of tights and full-skirted coat that almost, but not quite, covered the pretty cheeks of her derriere. That was what made Angela so
exciting. She had the face of an innocent child, but her scanty costumes and the saucy things she did with her body let you know she was
a very naughty child indeed. Her voice was sweet as an angel's, and
before her song was finished Bernard went backstage to wait for her.

"Look wot the cat dragged in," she said cheekily, brushing past him.

He took her arm and told her about his prospects.

"Pull the other one, luv, it's got bells on it," she said, refusing to be
gulled.

Bernard pulled out the obituary of the late Lord Lamb that he'd
clipped from the *Gazette* and handed it to her. "My cousin Anthony is
the present Lord Lamb and I'm the heir apparent. He's only seventeen with no heirs of his body, and I can tell you on good authority
he's not expected to live much longer."

"Whose authority?" Angela asked, suddenly becoming very interested.

Bernard smiled cunningly. "My authority, Angel Face." His hand moved down from her arm to cup her exposed buttock.

She saw that he was sporting brand-new clothes, from the latest Petersham neckcloth to the polished Hessians. She wanted to believe him, but was a skeptic by nature.

"My luck has turned. I can't even lose at the card table since I became heir to Lamb Hall. Tell you what," he cajoled, caressing her pretty bum, "let me come home with you tonight, and tomorrow I'll drive you out to see the estate for yourself in my new phaeton."

Angela did have another couple of men on her string, but they weren't as morally bankrupt as Bernie. There was a lurking bastard inside him that quite excited her. She had no scruples and knew instinctively he was the same. Who knew what they could not achieve if they put their brains together, to say nothing of the rest of their throbbing anatomy.

"Well, stup me," she giggled.

"I intend to," he promised.

Angela lived in a single room on the third floor of a building rented out to theatrical people. Until she hooked someone with real money, it was adequate for her needs because it contained two essentials, a big bed and enough space to accommodate her oversized wardrobe.

Bernard took special care to pleasure her tonight. Tomorrow night would be very different. Once she set her avaricious eyes on Lamb Hall and was eaten alive by ambition, Angel Face would be the one who would have to do the pleasuring.

The next step would be to dangle the plum of becoming Lady Lamb before her and she would be willing to cater to his every lustful perversion. His skillful hands caressed her delicious bum as he pressed her onto his swollen sex. Anticipation was half the pleasure.

They had to set out early the next morning for Stoke because Angela had to be back in London for her evening performance. Though he let her believe the phaeton was his, he had only rented it for the day. It was, however, such an improvement over the lumbering public stagecoach, he knew he would never again travel any other way.

Bernard drove her past Lamb Hall at a slowed pace, not daring to turn into the driveway in broad daylight. This would never do for Angela. She hadn't driven out all this way to miss a grand tour.

Without realizing it Angela was being manipulated. She agreed to Bernard's suggestion that they rent a punt upriver in the Medway and she reclined back, enjoying herself as he poled slowly so that they drifted along the bank until they came upon Lamb Hall's boathouse.

From this vantage point they could see the lovely red brick mansion with its carriage house and stables off to one side beneath the stately old elms. The grass was like a thick velvet carpet sloping up to the Hall. Arbors and trellises were covered by wisteria and tea roses. Angel sighed as she pictured herself beneath a frilly parasol, entertaining her theater friends at a garden party.

Bernard caught his breath when he saw the doors to the carriage house standing open and the carriage gone. Thinking to boast a little he hinted at what he had done.

Angela looked at him wide-eyed. "Why on earth would you sabotage their carriage when you could fix their bleeding boat? On the road there's always someone to come to your aid, but out at sea if you get into difficulty there's only a cold, watery grave awaiting you."

Bernard was pleased that Angela was as coldly calculating as himself. Their devious minds were entirely in synchronization. He pulled out a small saw and waved it in the air like a magic wand. "Hey presto!"

He maneuvered the punt alongside the sailboat and they climbed aboard. Neither of them was familiar with the workings of a small yacht, but they were both inventive, imaginative, and very determined.

The saboteurs were long gone before Antonia and Roz arrived home from London.

"I hope Anthony had the presence of mind to get a bill for the new harnesses. He can submit it to Watson and Goldman. I can't wait to give him lessons in how to aggravate and eliminate a guardian."

Chapter 7

Adam Savage was toying with the idea of marriage. He was thirty-two. Most men his age had had at least one wife. In the ruling class marriages were arranged to keep money, land, and titles in the hands of the nobility. Adam Savage had had none of these in the past, but now he intended to return to England and forge a dynasty.

He would need a special kind of wife: one who was at ease in society, who could entertain the highest in the land and at the same time appeal to his senses somewhat. Lady Evelyn Lamb seemed to fit his requirements like a glove. She was coolly beautiful, cultured, and he knew she would make a superb hostess for Edenwood, which would aid him in achieving his political ambitions.

Her cool English beauty appealed to his senses, challenging him to develop her sensually so that they would be able to enjoy a satisfying physical union. Her only drawback as far as he could see was her age. He could not expect her to give him a large family, but he would be content with one son and heir. If he wedded Eve, he would get her with child immediately. Marriage to Eve, of course, would make him legal father to her children rather than just their guardian, and he rather fancied he would make a good, strong father.

Today he was traveling to Colombo with precious cargo for his East Indiaman, the *Red Dragon*. Its holds already contained teak, ebony, and satinwood as well as pepper, nutmeg, and cinnamon. These were cargoes that stored well for long periods of time. When he loaded his latest rubber and tea crops he would have to see exactly how much space was left.

England was luring him home and he had almost decided to sail back on the *Red Dragon*'s next voyage. He would take some of his Indian and Oriental furnishings with him, as well as the fifty tea chests marked with a leopard symbol to distinguish them from the chests that actually contained tea.

One of his smaller vessels from the China run should have made port in Colombo bringing a cargo of incomparable silks that he was importing to England. As soon as the small ship was unloaded he would supervise the loading of Evelyn's cargo that had left days ago for the Colombo warehouse.

Adam had a general idea of what was produced at the small Lamb plantation. It had a cake house for cutting and drying indigo and a large acreage of cocoanut palms, the easiest crop to grow, that produced the greatest number of products. One simply popped the round nuts into sandy holes two feet apart. All they needed to make them grow was a little saltwater every other day and in two years time they produced six crops a year. The nut meat or copra was used for food when mixed with curry, or the oil could be extracted for hair, lamps, and candles. The sap was distilled to make arrack liquor, the shells produced tooth powder or receptacles for gathering latex, while the fiber made rope, baskets, fishnets, cushions, brushes, and mats.

It took two or sometimes three days to make the journey to Colombo. The heavy-laden wagons were pulled by domesticated water buffalo, which were strong but slow. As well as drivers Savage had his own guards, whom he had trained in the use of firearms. Thugs roamed the hills, preying on wagon trains.

All went smoothly. Savage had his own warehouses along the wharf in Colombo, but since the *Red Dragon* stood at anchor, its crew carried the latex rubber and the tea chests aboard from the wagons and stowed them in the cargo hold so that Adam could see immediately how much space he had left.

The captain and crew of the *Red Dragon* were a frightening-looking assortment of cutthroats, whom he had hand-picked. He paid them well for their services both in wages and shares. They were allowed the freedom to do as they pleased when they were off duty and Savage had no doubt they kept many a tavern, gambling den, and whorehouse in business, but when on duty guarding his ships and cargoes, there was not one man who dared to come on watch doped or drunk.

His small ship, the *Jade Dragon,* had only made port that morning. When its cargo of precious silks had been put aboard the East India-man and there was still plenty of cargo space, Adam Savage made the decision he knew had been inevitable. He told his captain he would be sailing to England with him and would likely be ready in two or possibly three weeks at the latest.

For some time now he had been negotiating with the East India Company officials in Madras to sell them Leopard's Leap. When he picked up his mail from the mainland, as they called India, it contained a generous offer from the Company.

Savage boarded the *Jade Dragon,* entered his cabin, and sat down in his captain's chair with his feet propped up on the map table. He threw the letter containing the offer on top of the meticulously drawn charts he'd labored over when he sailed this ship himself on the Canton run. Why wasn't he elated that the East India Company had offered a substantial fortune for Leopard's Leap? His mind traveled back to the early years. He had shed blood, sweat, and tears to make the plantation thrive. He'd sacrificed his youth to the backbreaking labor, to endless hours that had left him bone weary and brain numbed. He'd risked his health and, for the rest of his life, knew he'd suffer from recurring bouts of malaria. He'd risked his sanity, enduring the soul-searing loneliness, until he'd learned to become one with nature, and he had risked his life innumerable times hunting down rogue elephants that trampled his plants, stalking panthers that ate his livestock, putting down insurgence from natives determined to burn him out and rid the land of the white man.

By any reasonable reckoning he should be glad to be free of it all. But Savage was not reasonable, he was unreasonable. Ceylon had insinuated itself into his blood and Leopard's Leap was a part of him. He had built it from nothing with his bare hands. He looked at those hands now. They were brown and strong and scarred. The little finger on his left hand was burned black from when he had been struck by lightning getting in a crop before the monsoon struck.

When he had arrived, he had owned nothing but the clothes on his back. Now he owned this land and it had become precious to him. This was the reason he'd lingered here in indecision long after he'd become a millionaire. He could not bring himself to part with Leopard's Leap.

He took up the letter from the Company and began to write his reply in earnest. He offered to lease his plantation for a two-year period. This would give the East India Company the opportunity to reap the high profits he'd hinted at. If at the end of this time the Company was interested in purchasing the plantation outright, he would renegotiate.

Savage mulled over the proposition he'd just put in writing and knew he couldn't lose. If at the end of the proposed two years he decided he still could not part with Leopard's Leap, he would simply ask a price the Company was unwilling to meet.

He sent back his offer by the return mail boat, knowing they would jump at it. He instructed them to send their plantation manager without delay as he was returning to England in three weeks' time.

Savage sent the wagons back to Leopard's Leap. He would easily catch up to them on horseback the next day. As the light faded from the afternoon the languid indolence was replaced by an air of excitement that always descended upon the city with darkness. High-caste women in veils and shapeless robes disappeared and were replaced by lower-caste women with their silky black hair uncovered.

Music and laughter could be heard as the pace of life picked up. The food vendors' business became brisk and the streets started to fill up with men and women intent on enjoying all the pleasures of the tropical night.

Adam told the crew of the *Jade Dragon* they need not take on cargo until morning. He wanted to supervise the loading of Evelyn's exports for the China run so that he could give her a favorable report when he returned, and morning would be soon enough.

Perhaps this would be his last chance to enjoy Colombo's exotic delights. He had been working eighteen-hour days and felt as tightly coiled as a serpent. A smile touched his lips as it occurred to him where he would go to unwind. He departed the ship and headed into the city of domed mosques. He walked east, away from the port, and at the very end of Kelani Street he stopped before a house known as the Jewel of the East. As Savage stepped through the front portal he removed his wide-brimmed planter's hat and narrowed his eyes until they adjusted to the brilliance within.

The reception room was a myriad of mirrored tile with glittering amethysts set between. He recalled how his mouth had fallen open at such opulence when he had first seen it six years past. Here he had learned of Ratnapura, the City of Gems, where violet amethysts were so plentiful they had no value at all—except when he shipped them to England, of course.

Two darkly beautiful women greeted him warmly. "The Leopard honors the Jewel of the East." The women wore exquisitely embroidered saris in an identical shade of lavender. They looked like sisters, but Adam knew otherwise. They were Pearl and Mother of Pearl, a combination so exciting they could take a man to the edge of madness.

He kissed their hands and exchanged familiar pleasantries with the dusky females before he was graciously asked to make his first choice. The Jewel of the East offered a twofold path, stimulation or relaxation. Previously he had always chosen the former and had never regretted that choice. Tonight, however, he chose relaxation and was ushered through the beaded curtain concealing the archway to the left.

He was seated upon a cushioned divan and given a menu from which he was to make his selections. The menu was not for food alone. He was led to the bathing room, where six dusky handmaidens removed his gun and his garments. Two came into the pool with him while the other four poured in flagons of boiling water until the temperature of the bath was raised to almost scalding and steam filled the small room.

Next they cleansed his body thoroughly with an amazingly efficient tool designed for the purpose, then he was wrapped in a large thirsty towel and led from the steamy room. The dusky handmaidens lined up before him so he could make his choice. Their filmy garments revealed more than they concealed, so Adam had no difficulty selecting his partner for the night. Her name was Delight and long before dawn he would learn that it was most apt.

When they were alone she removed her diaphanous garments and head-veil to display her body, which had been completely denuded of hair. As she stood naked before him her lustrous black hair fell in a waterfall down her back to sweep the floor about her heels. Delight was well curved, her breasts and thighs swelling out from her tiny waist. Her face was sensually attractive with full, pouting lips and enormous black liquid eyes.

She pressed him down upon a hard divan with his head well cushioned, then massaged his naked limbs with oil of almonds. Her hands felt like heaven as she swirled them in long, smooth ovals over every muscle in his body. Adam began to relax and by the time she had finished he felt his very bones were melting.

The food he had ordered was now ready. Delight took the heavy-laden tray from the servant, walked past a table, and set it upon the floor. They reclined naked upon cushions while she lifted the lids from tureens of gold to allow the tantalizing aromas to whet the Leopard's appetite. First she offered him a demitasse containing a sweet blue liquid. Adam let it roll about his tongue, savoring its unusual taste. Everything seemed to slow after that, every movement, every sound, every breath and heartbeat. Then, at a deliciously languorous pace, she fed him with her fingers.

He recalled past visits where each successive dish was spicier and hotter than the last until he had been stimulated to an insatiable lust.

This time nothing was spicy. The foods were comforting, soothing, dipped in smooth syrups that made him lick and suck Delight's delicious fingers.

When he was replete he sighed heavily and allowed her to bathe his hands and face with rosewater. From a shelf Delight took a filigreed casket and sat cross-legged before him upon the table. She opened the casket with its mirrored lid and began to paint herself with henna.

She decorated her palms and the soles of her feet, then she moved on to her breasts, where she painted an intricate pattern of dots and tiny flowers forming circles, spiraling from her nipples. Then she mixed a brighter red pigment into the henna, spread her legs wide, and began to paint her labia with the blood-red maquillage.

Adam had thought himself so relaxed, he could not lift a finger; he was mistaken. His male center stirred, lifted, and hardened as his eyes became mesmerized by what her delicate fingers were doing to her sex. As a female decorates her mouth with red lip salve to attract the male, so Delight decorated the lips between her legs to emphasize the alluring mouth with the erotic pigment.

From the casket she took two bracelets decorated with tiny bells and fastened them around her ankles. Then slowly, sinuously, she raised one foot and lifted it behind her head. She needed the help of her hennaed hands to place her other foot behind her head, then she posed absolutely motionless, knowing the Leopard would arise from the floor, drawn to her almost against his very strong will.

When he stood, his rigid phallus reached to his navel. He moved slowly toward the object of his desire upon the table. Then he allowed his marble-hard lingam to enter the blood-red gates to Paradise. As he thudded into her with strong, slow thrusts, the bells upon her anklets tinkled prettily. When Delight transferred her feet from behind her own head to his, he impaled her deeply enough to tinkle the bell she had placed high within her sheath and Savage smiled with pleasure that he had accomplished such a feat. The rhythmic sound of the bells increased in volume as his strokes quickened violently, then dissolved in a tinkling crescendo as he cried out from his release.

Delight once more invited the Leopard to recline upon the cushions while she rolled him a special cheroot made from Jaffna tobacco leaves mixed with a small amount of ganja from the hemp plant. Adam shook his head at his own folly, knowing he would have a hangover in the morning.

By the time he was finished his relaxing, intoxicating smoke, the languor stole up his limbs and he felt as if he had drifted off into another world where blissful sleep and heavenly dreams would be his reward. Delight came down to the cushions and began to lick his bronzed skin as a test to see if he was yet in the final stage of relaxation. She licked all the way down to his navel, noting with satisfaction how heavy lidded his eyes had become.

She was most surprised when his strong arms came about her and he pulled her beneath his body. He mounted her with powerful thighs, then tortured her with exquisitely slow thrusts that told her in no uncertain terms he was not yet slaked. Delight was awed by the Leopard, for she had let down her love juices twice before he found release. His manhood lay limp along his thigh as she pushed him back down into the cushions. She lay against him and offered the hard bud of her nipple for his mouth's pleasure as he drifted off to sleep.

His tongue toyed with the pretty bauble, his teeth gently bit her, then when he began to suck hard, his shaft started to fill and throb once again. The Leopard was to be commended upon his virility. Quickly she moved down his body and took him into her mouth. It took a full thirty minutes of tender, loving anointing before his seed spurted forth and she drained him of every last drop he possessed. Delight swallowed the copious, pearly fluid, knowing it was the best potion in the world for her complexion. The Leopard slept.

To be more accurate, he overslept. This did nothing to improve Savage's disposition. He graciously paid twice the amount he was asked before he departed the Jewel of the East, but he was annoyed with his own lack of control. The ganja he had smoked last night was an immature indulgence that had left him with throbbing temples.

When he arrived at the wharf where the *Jade Dragon* lay at anchor, her crew was already loading the cargo from his warehouses. He boarded the small merchant vessel and went down into the hold. He stopped speaking in midsentence and stiffened. His dark head went up and his icy blue eyes stared at the seamen in disbelief. His nose told him what to expect when he took a crate from a sailor's hands and tore off its lid.

Opium!

He gazed about at the crates and chests lining the hold, selected another at random, and examined its contents. Lady Lamb was trying to export hundreds of boxes containing millions of poppy heads filled with their oily seeds.

Savage's eyes showed such fury, the seamen stepped back away from him. To his credit he did not unleash his temper upon his crew. He had it under control within a few minutes and banked the embers of his anger so he could vent it upon the author of this abomination. His issued his orders in a curt, clipped voice. "Unload every last crate and stow it aboard my Indiaman. I'll get you another cargo for the China run by afternoon."

True to his word, by noon he had bought a crop of dried red chili peppers and a second crop of tobacco, for the Chinese were great pipe smokers. He filled the remainder of the cargo space with bolts of chintz from his warehouse, knowing the bright, durable cotton would sell because Indian dye techniques were more advanced than those of other nations.

Savage told the factor at his warehouses that though he was sailing to England shortly, he was still in the shipping business, but that his headquarters would now be in London instead of Colombo. He explained that the East India Company was leasing his plantation and instructed the factor to give the Company priority at the warehouses for storage of tea and rubber.

When his banking business was concluded, Savage loaded his pistol, called for his horse, and headed home. If he rode all day and all night without stop he would arrive sometime before noon. His anger at Eve mounted with every mile. If she had been a young girl he could have excused what she had done because of ignorance. But she was a woman grown. A sophisticate, also, who had lived in the East ten years and must know of opium and its deadly properties. If she had asked his permission to export opium on his ships he would have refused immediately. If she had even consulted with him about dealing in opium he would have set her straight in no uncertain terms. The fact that she had kept him in ignorance purposely, damned her. She had also used her feminine wiles on him for permission to use his ship, thus making him an unwitting accomplice.

This was the thing that whipped him to a fury. She had always manipulated the other men in her life, easily wrapping them around her fingers to get her own way. Surely to Christ she recognized that he was different from other men? Lamb Plantation lay straight ahead and he knew he would stop and have it out with her before he carried on to Leopard's Leap!

Chapter 8

Savage had ridden for twenty hours. He was unbathed and unshaven. The sweat and grime of the road were upon him, but he didn't give a goddamn for the niceties. He handed his lathered horse over to a groom and strode into palatial Government House ignoring the sepoys who stood guard outside the entrance and dismissing her majordomo who came forward in the reception hall. His boots left a trail of soil across the white tile floor.

Government House was never without guests. Eve was in the breakfast room with an envoy from the Governor of Madras and a minor prince from the palace of Raja Singha. Both men knew him immediately by his reputation and by the telltale scar on his face. When Savage entered the breakfast room it was without apology. Eve's eyes went wide with shock.

"Lady Lamb and I have important business to discuss. You will excuse her." His deep voice held a note of commanding authority.

Eve arose immediately to avoid a scene before her guests and led him through to her private sitting room. She was wearing an exquisite morning gown. Her lovely blond curls were swept high with her tortoiseshell combs. She whirled to face him, her nostrils pinching with distaste at his disheveled state.

"What is the meaning of this?" she demanded coldly.

She was groomed so impeccably, her demeanor so cool and condescending, he knew an urge to shatter her composure. He took a deep breath to prevent himself from striking her.

"Fucking opium!" he ground out. "Madam, explain yourself."

"Oh, I see." A blush came to her pale cheek. "I—I know it's illegal in some ports. I—I thought you would look the other way, darling."

"I don't give a good goddamn about legal or illegal, as well you know. The stuff is an abomination!"

"I need the money," she explained coolly, as if this would excuse her actions.

He took out his wallet and threw five thousand pounds on the table. "I've bought your opium, madam."

"Adam, I had no idea opium was so—"

"Don't insult my intelligence, Eve," he cut her short. "You've lived in an Eastern society for a decade. You know opium's obscene properties. You know it's addictive, you know it condemns millions to a living death, and you know there is no cure."

"But they are only Chinese peasants," she said faintly.

He took her by the shoulders most ungently, his strong fingers bruising her delicate flesh. "They are human beings! You've heard Russell and I describe opium dens where hundreds lie on wooden pallets in delirium. Millions sacrifice everything to their addiction, their farms, their families, they sell their wives and their children. They run rickshaws all day without food so they can eat opium until they die in excruciating agony. Opium is so odious and corrupting, it carries a curse and befouls any who deal in it." He shook her. "I know! I made my first attainted fortune exporting it to Canton, and I paid the price. I not only carry the scars on my body, I almost destroyed my soul. Now I make just as much money from tea and rubber. I may sometimes work eighteen hours a day, but is is decent, clean work. I can sleep at night."

Eve realized his convictions were so strong, she had made a terrible blunder. She should have waited the few months until he sailed for England before attempting to export her opium.

"It was wrong of me not to discuss it with you," she said softly.

"There are two cargoes my ships will *never* carry to the Orient, opium and ivory. Butchers wound and trap elephants and cut off their tusks while they are still alive. It, too, is abhorrent to me."

Ivory! thought Eve. *Why didn't I think of ivory? Fortunes are paid for Oriental carvings.*

Savage glanced down at her and saw the tortoiseshell combs. He swept his fingers into her immaculate coiffure and pulled out the two combs. "Just like this stuff. Tortoiseshell is taken from the back of a living hawksbill; an inhuman practice!"

He had said all he had come to say and more besides. "Forgive my rude interruption, Lady Lamb." In a voice more cutting than any nobleman possessed he said, "I know no better. I am from peasant stock." He bowed with more than a little irony and arrogance and departed for Leopard's Leap.

Savage called for all his overseers and banyans that same afternoon. John Bull stood at the front door like a sergeant major, ordering them to remove their shoes before they entered the bungalow. They stood respectfully in the master's office, listening to his every word.

"Very soon now, before the next full moon, I shall be returning to England. There will be a new sahib come in a few days. I want you to work as hard for him as you have for me. I am not selling Leopard's Leap. It will still be my plantation, but it is doomed to failure unless you give your loyalty to the new man. This is the only place in all Ceylon where tea and rubber are grown. I brought the seedlings from China and Burma as an experiment almost ten years ago and I have you to thank that Leopard's Leap has flourished. Only now are tea and rubber plantations being cultivated across the water in India. You know what needs to be done in times of drought and in times of flooding. The pruners know the rotation, the cattle keepers know when the manuring must begin. In fact, you will know far better than the new sahib how to keep the plantation running smoothly. My great ship will carry your tea crops to me in London. My nose will tell me if you fail to produce top quality." The harsher planes of his face relaxed and he allowed himself a rare smile.

The Tamils did not smile, however. It was a terrible day for them to learn that the master was departing for his homeland. Leopard's Leap lay in the foothills of Adam's Peak, the holiest mountain in the world. Legend told how Adam had been hurled from the Seventh Heaven of Paradise for his sin with the woman. It had been expiated for one thousand years. He had landed on one foot upon Adam's Peak and had left his footprint there in stone. There was not one worker at Leopard's Leap who did not believe that Adam Savage was the Adam of legend. His size, his strength, and his abilities, to say nothing of his piercing blue eyes, were a gift from the gods. If they shirked their duties he would know all the way from Londontown across the seven seas. They hurried off to spread the word to their workers.

Savage took out the journals that held the tallies and accounts of the plantation to bring them up to the minute, but he was distracted by John Bull's authoritative voice.

"When we are in England, His Excellency will expect you to dress in the English manner. You will shame him by looking like a foreigner. There is no need whatsomehowever to take all your heathen clothes and possessions."

Adam Savage always tried to be diplomatic when he interceded in his servants' altercations. Kirinda was Sinhalese and of a higher caste

than his Tamil manservant. On the other hand John Bull was his majordomo and a man must have dominion over a woman or lose face.

"John Bull, it seldom happens, but this time you are wrong," Savage
said tactfully. "Lotus Blossom is most beautiful in her native dress.
She knows that exotic, brilliant silks suit her best. Please see that she
has as many trunks as she needs for her clothes and personal possessions."

Kirinda gave John Bull a smug little smile from behind the Leopard's back.

"She will, however, need English shoes and slippers. Get her some
immediately so she can practice walking in them. The floors in England are far too cold to go barefoot."

Kirinda's face fell and John Bull smiled at her with condescending
satisfaction.

At dusk Adam was surprised to learn that Lady Lamb had arrived;
yet not surprised. He realized he had been half expecting her. The first
thing he noticed was that she had abandoned her mourning. She wore
a low-cut gown of finest Indian muslin with a rare blue lotus tucked
between her breasts. Her blond hair, without the combs, fell to her
shoulders in waves. The effect softened her beauty. Tonight she did
not look cool at all; in the lamplight she looked quite warm, almost
vulnerable.

When they were alone she came to him and placed her hands upon
his chest. She looked up at him in supplication. "Oh, Adam, please
forgive me?" she murmured softly.

Savage was aware that she had come to seduce him. The irony
wasn't lost on him. Though Eve was sexually frigid she was willing to
play the whore for the sake of his money and jewels. Adam was curious to see how far she would go.

Adam pretended to succumb to Eve's temptation. His head dipped
to capture her lips and he murmured, "I don't want you tainted . . .
by anything other than me."

Eve shuddered. It was an effect he often had on women. She wondered wildly how in the world she would be able to lie naked upon the
divan while John Bull and her own sepoy guard waited in the adjoining room.

Adam's blue eyes crinkled with amusement. "I prefer the *lady* to the
whore," he murmured, then proceeded to render her mindless with his
kisses. The moment he felt her begin to respond, he took his arms

from her. She might loathe his ability to dominate her, but he was determined to leave her wanting more.

Finally she gathered her courage to ask, "What will you do with the opium?"

"Ship it to England," he said tersely.

She raised her head to look into his eyes. "What's the difference between England and China?"

Annoyance nibbled at him. He wasn't in the habit of explaining himself. "In England I can control what happens to it. It will go into laudanum to kill the pain of having a limb removed or the pain of childbirth." He took a deep breath. "Eve, when the *Red Dragon* sails I shall be aboard." He watched her face intently. He saw her eyes widen with shocked surprise. She thought that because she had allowed him a few intimate kisses she would have a say in everything he did, every decision. He was glad he had disabused her immediately.

"So soon?" she asked, but he could not tell if the note of panic he heard was at the thought of losing him. "Have you sold Leopard's Leap?"

"No. I'm only leasing it to the Company."

He caressed her pale shoulder. "Evelyn, why don't you come with me?"

She did not dare to assume he offered anything more than transportation. Silence stretched between them until she finally broke it.

"Adam, Lamb Hall belongs to my son now." Had she been subtle enough? Would he offer her marriage? She wanted his wealth and knew the only way she could get it was by marrying him. Marriage would mean losing her title and she was greedy enough to want it all. Still unsure of him, she continued, "Here I have a palatial home filled with servants."

"Edenwood will be palatial and filled with servants," he said quietly.

Eve felt weak with relief. She had been clever enough after all. "I cannot seriously consider marriage until my period of mourning is over and done with. Go and see your Edenwood. Buy yourself that title we spoke of, then come back for me."

"I don't want you to worry about money while I'm gone. I've arranged for you to draw on my bank in Colombo." He saw her eyes light, then she veiled them with her lashes.

Eve felt compelled to protest. She never wanted him to know how important wealth was to her, and he was a shrewd man. "Adam, you needn't think you have to buy me."

"If my money insults you, I'll give you jewels," he teased, seeing through her as if she were transparent Venetian crystal.

Her hand trailed across his hard chest. "Those jewels we diced for . . . did they come from the fabled City of Gems?"

"Ratnapura, yes," he acknowledged. "I go every year."

"You export diamonds, rubies, and emeralds to England?" she asked breathlessly.

"Yes, but actually I make as much money on the semiprecious stones like beryls, garnets, tourmalines, moonstones, and topaz. They mine every shade of sapphire in the world, blue, indigo, azure, gray, green. A handful of rupees will buy a chest filled with amethysts."

"It's not really that far from here, is it?"

He could hear the excitement in her voice and knew she was becoming aroused at the thought of the jewels. He pulled her gown up to cover her bare shoulder. "As the vulture flies it is not far, but you forget the Sabaragamuwa mountain range lies between. Those mountains are filled with thugs. Have you never heard of the practice of thugee? It is the ritual murder of travelers. Ratnapura is one of the most evil cities on earth. It is inhabited solely by thieves, murderers, and harlots. I forbid you to go there, Eve."

She wondered how he could read her thoughts so easily. He was too wise in the way of women. She had been both attracted and repelled by his overt maleness for years. He drew her to her feet and cupped her face so that he could look into her eyes. "Promise me you won't go and I'll cover you with jewels."

She swallowed hard. How could she resist such an offer? Here was her big chance. She must convince him she wanted him and not the jewels.

"Come to me tomorrow night?" she pleaded prettily, hating him for making her beg.

"I'll try," he said, half promising, half evading her plea.

Evelyn was not the only Lamb who had designs upon Savage's fortune. Antonia checked her appearance in the cheval glass before she left her chamber. Her riding skirt and jacket were black as her period of mourning demanded, but to soften the severity her shirt and stock were snowy white muslin frilled with frothy lace. Tilted over one arched brow a small, saucy hat sat atop a powdered wig with one fat curl falling to her shoulder.

She saluted her elegant image with the tip of her riding crop, clicked the heels of her riding boots together, and set off like a soldier on campaign. Her destination was Edenwood at Gravesend, and since she rode alone and need not pay lip service to convention, she set a bruising pace and covered the dozen miles in record time.

James Wyatt, his shirtsleeves rolled up, recognized her immediately and strode from the portico to help her dismount. "Lady Antonia, I hoped you would pay us another visit."

She smiled up into his intelligent eyes with genuine admiration. "I'm drawn to Edenwood as if it were a lodestone. What you are creating here fascinates me. I've even begun dreaming about it." She dimpled.

She took back her hand and they walked together toward the mansion.

"I am vastly flattered, ma'am. Perhaps you can help me decide upon one or two things. Your dreams might just become realities."

" 'Tis I who am flattered, Mr. Wyatt. I am brimful of ideas."

He was utterly charmed by the rapt attention she gave him. "I would guess you prefer elegance to grandeur."

"I do, sir, but I'd bet his last rupee Mr. Savage prefers grandeur. I believe Edenwood should have both and when you think on it, there is no earthly reason why it should not," she said gaily, planting her seeds.

He showed her the west front portico. The covered colonnade had classical columns that soared elegantly heavenward.

"Oh, it's magnificent, but wouldn't it be absolutely breathtaking if you extended it into a semicircular terrace with a stone balustrade? Dotted about the rail could be urns overflowing with flowers."

"You paint such a vivid picture, I can see it," Wyatt agreed. "I could use Norfolk stone with its soft, variegated earth tones."

Antonia nodded enthusiastically. "Yes, Norfolk stone for the balusters and rail, but the terrace itself must be marble. Since you've designed a Roman portico, the terrace must be imported Italian—that exquisitely veined marble that comes in so many beautiful shades. I suggest a pale biscuit veined with a deep, tawny umber." Though the cost would be almost prohibitive, the picture she painted was irresistible.

Inside the house Antonia continued with her ultraexpensive suggestions. "Italian marble of a different hue could be used in the front hall. Mr. Savage is a nabob and will no doubt wish to display his trophies in the entrance hall—elephant or Bengal tiger perhaps. I would suggest something dramatic. White with black veins or vice versa, perhaps."

"I think you've convinced me," James Wyatt said indulgently. "Come, I want to show you the plasterwork in some of the salons and bedchambers."

Antonia stood gazing up at the exquisite plasterwork that encircled the room just where the walls met the high ceiling. It was on the tip of her tongue to suggest that fourteen-carat gold should be applied, but the pure classical beauty of the white-upon-white would have been ruined, if gilded. She bit her tongue and determined to find somewhere else for the expensive giltwork. Her eyes widened as James Wyatt took her into what would be a bathing room.

"Bathing rooms were one of Mr. Savage's few specific requirements."

This one was next to the master bedchamber on the top floor. Light and sunshine spilled down through what seemed to be a glass ceiling.

"This is called a skylight. It has been designed into larger buildings like museums and palaces, but I don't believe it has been used in a private home before."

There was a sunken bath in the center of the room large enough for swimming, with steps leading down from two sides. Crates of tiles were stacked about the walls in a delicate shade between aqua-blue and seafoam-green.

"Oh! Only think how spectacular this room would be with the new Venetian mirrors across one wall to reflect the light that streams in. And wouldn't it be opulent if some of these tiles were hand painted! There is a wildlife artist in Shepherds Market who does herons and other wading birds. Oh, James, you must commission him to paint some miniatures of waterfowl. Flashing kingfishers, egrets, flamingos, spoonbills, the choice is endless." She was so enthusiastic, he caught her mood.

He now saw the house through a woman's eyes and he knew if he followed her suggestions he could turn the stately home he was building into a spectacular showcase.

"We are so fortunate being close to London. We have the best artisans in the world on our doorstep. Why don't you commission one of the great European artists who now live in London to paint some of the ceilings? And the vast fireplaces you've installed cry out to be carved by Adam."

"There are four Adam brothers; I know Robert and James quite well. They won't just carve a fireplace or the moldings of a room. They have a strict rule that they will only design an entire room right down to the door handles and including all the furnishings. They believe that everything in a room should be in the same genre. The carpet must match the ceiling."

"But, James, what a splendid idea. Commision Adams to do the main salon or the dining room and perhaps the gallery. You have only to please this nabob and the world will beat a path to your door." Antonia blushed prettily. "I'm sorry, Mr. Wyatt, you are already reputed to be the best architect. I am being presumptuous to suggest you need attract clients."

He smiled at her with indulgence. "I have clients aplenty, but they are not always paying clients like Mr. Savage."

Antonia drew her brows together, quite prepared to be presumptuous again. "Whyever would you work for someone who didn't pay you?"

"It is a little difficult to refuse royalty." He smiled.

"Oh, I see," she said, laughing at her own ignorance. "Then now is your chance to make up for your nonpaying clients. My guardian has bottomless coffers." She flashed him an outrageous look from beneath her lashes. "If I get to meet William Kent, I shall persuade him to build elaborate walkways through the gardens with a lake and a stream and a Chinese bridge. Perhaps a tea pagoda or a grotto, or a Temple of the Sun. The possibilities are endless. And a long circuit through the park for riding and driving is an absolute must!" She put her head on one side. "Poor Mr. Wyatt, have I exhausted you?"

You have enchanted me, lady. "You're not leaving?" he asked wistfully.

"You are too polite, James. You should have told me to run along home hours ago."

"Promise you'll come again?"

"Fire, flood, and pestilence couldn't keep me away," she promised him.

At dinner she kept Roz entertained as she recounted her adventure at Edenwood. "I shall go again and again. You must help me think of new and unique ways to spend his wealth. Oh, Roz, it's quite addictive, this squandering money."

Her grandmother was in total agreement. "It beats the hell out of moderation. If you are going to do something, do it with panache, I always say. That applies to everything, from painting your face to making love. Passion in all things. We seldom regret the things we do in life, darling, only the things we don't do."

"I pledge I shall take it for my motto: Passion in all things!" vowed Antonia.

On the other side of the world Adam Savage would have agreed with such a sentiment. The heat of the night enfolded him in the tropical paradise. There was no denying he would miss Leopard's Leap, miss Ceylon and India. He had learned to live life to the full. One could only get out in equal measure what he put in. Only take back as much as he gave. It was a lesson he had had to learn the hard way.

When his father had died from the disease that went hand in hand with poverty, Adam had dedicated himself to making money. His first small, leaky trading vessel had smuggled Indian opium into China. He was soon richer than he had ever dreamed, but at what a price! To succeed in such a venture you eventually became a cutthroat. It all came down to one tenet, kill or be killed . . . destroy or be destroyed.

He would probably have gone on past the point of no return if it hadn't been for the cargo they had offered him in a warehouse in Canton. Fifty prepubescent, delicate girl children for the slave trade. For him the choice had seemed easy. He would not damn his soul peddling child flesh. He agreed to trade the opium for the exquisite females, intending to sail them to freedom. How naive he had been to think they would turn over their priceless cargo. The thugs had sold these virgins a dozen times over and they had not seen the light of day outside the warehouse for over half a year.

Freeing them had almost cost him his life. He had sustained a dozen knife wounds and carried the disfiguring scars on his gut and torso to this day. The Tamil boy he had hired to cook and scrub for his crew nursed him back to life. When Savage had offered him a reward, he had said, "When you go home to England, take me with you."

Savage knew he had been given a second chance at life and this time he vowed he would do it right. He purchased the failing plantation in Ceylon from a Dutchman. He imported rubber plants from Burma and tea seedlings from Souchong. Then he had worked eighteen to twenty hours a day, every day.

He knew it was time to go home, but, oh, how he would miss the heat and sweat, the temple incense and spices, the dirt and the darkness. A rare smile touched his lips as he watched for the last time a leopard come down to drink. Tomorrow he would leave this land of fascination behind. Tomorrow he sailed for England.

Chapter 9

The Southeast coast of England lay sweltering in the unusual heat of summer. Fashionable society left London like a mass migration of lemmings and headed for the sea at Brighton.

At Stoke the Lamb twins took their morning ride an hour early so their mounts would not suffer heat prostration. Anthony was teaching his sister to take the hedges as he did, without hesitation. Her mare often balked at stone walls and Antonia feared too much for the horse's legs to force her, yet Anthony never encountered difficulty.

"Tony, it's not the horse, it's you," he told her. "You are reluctant and you transfer it to your mare. Don't think of a wall or a hedge as a barrier. Think through it. Visualize horse and rider clearing any obstacle to the other side. It's simple; it's a trick of the mind."

"Tony, you mean if I don't think we'll clear it, we won't?"

"Exactly! Once you set your mind to it, you can accomplish it . . . well, to be truthful the horse accomplishes it. You just have to show her you have total faith in her."

It had worked all week. Anthony had set a bruising pace and Antonia had kept up with him and today, for the first time, passed him as she soared over the park hedge into the garden of Lamb Hall. He came thundering after, clods of turf flying into the air. They drew rein, laughing.

Anthony wiped his neck. "God's teeth, I'm sweating like a bull."

"Poor old Neptune has worked up a lather too," Antonia said, pointing to his mount. "Come on, I'll help you rub him down."

As they cantered toward the stables a sudden breeze blew Antonia's long, dark hair about her shoulders, but Anthony's tiewig was plastered damply to his head. "The breeze is picking up, let's go sailing after lunch," he suggested.

"Sounds good to me, Tony. In fact, why don't we get Mr. Burke to pack the picnic basket? I'm going to wear a pair of those wide canvas knee-breeches. It's too hot for skirts."

"It's too damned hot for wigs too. I'm just going to tie my hair back with a thong."

"I'll bring along those yellow oilskins I bought in London. We'll see if they keep us dry like they're supposed to."

"It's too damned hot for oilskins, but bring them along, it's always a lot cooler out on the water."

When they took the horses inside the stable Anthony said, "I'll do this, you see about the picnic lunch."

"I don't mind seeing to my own horse," she protested.

"This is man's work," Tony pointed out, "food is woman's work."

"That's a beastly thing to say, Tony Lamb!"

He looked at her blankly, totally uncomprehending why she should complain.

Antonia sighed. He'd never understand in a million years.

When her grandmother saw Antonia descending the stairs dressed in what looked like a wool-knit undervest and canvas breeches, her eyebrows went up slightly. "I take it we are sailing this afternoon?"

"Yes, Mr. Burke has packed us a picnic lunch. You don't mind, do you?"

"Mind? My prayers have been answered." Roz winked outrageously. "Major Jeremy Blount is paying me an afternoon call."

"Isn't he the member of Parliament for Stoke? Since when did you develop an interest in politics?"

"Since I saw the bulge of the saddle muscles in his thighs, darling."

"We'll be gone hours and hours," Antonia promised, tying back her dark hair with a leather thong.

Anthony joined them wearing identical clothes and Antonia tossed him an oilskin just as Mr. Burke came into the hall with the picnic basket.

Roz said, "Mr. Burke, I don't know how you can look at them and keep a straight face."

" 'Tis the height of fashion to be eccentric," Antonia said lightly, seeing the amusement in Mr. Burke's eyes.

Roz's glance swept over the twins from head to foot. "You go beyond eccentric. I hope Sir Jeremy doesn't see you. He'll think he's having blue devils or double vision from the gin I plied him with last evening."

* * *

In the boathouse the twins climbed aboard the *Seagull* and Antonia covered the picnic basket with the yellow oilskins. They each had specific things to check and certain maneuvers to perform before taking off from the boathouse.

Anthony took the sails from the sailbags while Antonia checked the rigging. A frown creased her brow as she noticed immediately that the lines were tangled. "The lines are fouled!" she exclaimed.

Anthony had total faith in her ability to cope with any hitch and replied, "Get the knots out quickly, I have the jib ready."

Her nimble fingers unknotted the line and she only had time to give the jibstay a cursory check before Tony attached it and they pushed off from shore. She had no time to test the forestay before Anthony hoisted the jib and allowed it to flap while he turned the sloop head-to-wind so he could attach the mainsail.

"Damnation, Tony, why didn't you see that the mainsheet was unfouled when we docked last week?" he asked impatiently.

"You know I always leave everything shipshape. I have no idea how these lines got knotted and tangled." She uncleated the mainsheet and they both worked on the knots so they could hoist the mainsail. As a consequence they paid scant attention to the stays, shrouds, or halyards. The wind was really picking up now and the boat seemed to come alive instantly in the brisk breeze.

As Anthony headed from the mouth of the Medway into the sea, he was grinning from ear to ear. "Jibe-oh," he cried, pushing the tiller away from his body, and in unison they ducked to avoid the boom.

Anthony tacked expertly, changing the *Seagull*'s course by turning into and through the wind. Antonia kept a sharp eye out for other craft, as this was one of the main shipping routes for both navy and merchant vessels. Anthony adjusted the tiller constantly, guiding the *Seagull* over and around the small waves.

The twins positioned themselves close together just aft of amidships so the bow could lift and they headed out to sea on a dead run, sailing with the wind directly behind. The sun blazed down, the breeze played havoc with their tied-back hair, and the seaspray wet their faces with delicious, cool saltwater.

They came about, braced their feet, and leaned their bodies slightly windward for counterbalance, then opened up the picnic basket. Mr. Burke was a treasure. Everything he had packed was finger food. Cold chicken and partridge, thick wedges of cheddar, raw mushrooms and carrots and artichokes sat beside crusty rolls spread with chive butter. Tucked into the corners were russet apples and a slab of butterscotch toffee. Two covered, wide-mouthed jars of cider rounded off the meal. Between them they did a creditable job of emptying the basket. Antonia turned her face up to bask in the sun. There was nothing on earth like being on the sea to make her feel free. Floating between sky and water freed her imagination, her mind, her very soul. Sailing was surely the most exciting, invigorating sport in the whole world. This was perhaps as close to Paradise as she would ever get.

She gazed at the horizon through slitted eyes and watched the shoreline disappear. They were riding at a terrific clip, but she felt no fear. A sailboat was safest at its optimum speed. She wanted to prolong the exhilarating afternoon and knew Anthony felt exactly the same.

They were on a reach, sailing across the wind, when suddenly Anthony turned a weather eye to the west and saw the sky was turning dark. "Get your oilskin on, we're in for a squall."

Before the words were out of his mouth there was a sudden drop in temperature, and as they both reached for the yellow raincapes they heard the roll of the thunder. They shifted to windward to counterbalance the force of the wind.

The *Seagull* was heeling over now, so they leaned out as far as possible. Each felt a small curl of fear as they knew they would have to reduce the wind force to keep from capsizing.

Anthony worked the tiller until they were head-to-wind. He shouted his orders. "Ease the mainsheet, spill some of the wind. Don't cleat it, hold it in your hands so you can ease it quickly."

They both knew they should furl the sails and get them off the deck into sailbags in such a squall. "The sheet's fouled, I can't budge it," she shouted back. Then she saw the spot that was so badly frayed, it would snap any minute. She kept the terrifying information to herself. Perhaps it would hold. She bravely resolved not to panic Tony any more than necessary.

Anthony did the only thing he could, feathering the boat just close enough to the wind to spill some of its driving force. The wind whipped the sea into a foaming froth. The roar became deafening. Antonia heard her own heartbeat inside her eardrums as fear rose up in her. She swallowed hard to keep herself from screaming.

"Find the bailing bucket, we're taking on water!" he shouted.

Antonia's eyes swept about the small sloop. "It isn't here. I'll use a cider jar." But a wave had taken both jars minutes after they'd set them down.

"Christ, it's only a squall, it's not a gale," he denied, trying to reassure both of them and give them heart. Then, as if he were lying in his teeth, Anthony let go of the tiller to tie a long line about Antonia under her armpits, then lashed it to the mast. When he grabbed for the tiller it separated from the rudder where it had been sawn through, and the boat went sideways into the wind.

In the next split second the mainsheet snapped and whipped through the air like a frenzied snake ready to strike anything in its path. With deadly accuracy it found its mark on Antonia's cheek, opening a gash. Her face was numb from the cold and she felt only a sharp sting.

The *Seagull* was totally out of control, but the thing that was really terrifying was the loose mainsail, which swept back and forth with a crashing *whomp, whomp,* forcing them to duck and dodge so they would not be battered or knocked overboard.

Antonia bit her lips so she would not scream, but when the lightning hit the mast and they heard an ominous crack her mouth opened to let out the scream that built in her throat. The sailboat, completely unstable, heeled before the wind and the parallel waves until its rail was awash, then what each of them feared happened. The *Seagull* capsized.

In actuality everything must have happened in split seconds, but somehow Antonia's perception was distorted. To her, everything seemed to be happening in slow motion. She was almost sitting on the rail as it went down into the trough. Her eyes, now wide with panic, saw the mountainous wave rise above them, then come crashing down in a wall of icy water that forced her beneath the surface. She was being sucked down, down, and when she opened her eyes for a moment she learned the meaning of sea-green. Millions of tiny sea-green bubbles surrounded her and she was afraid they would get into her mouth and go up her nose. Then she realized they were coming out of her mouth and her nose and she realized it was her life's breath leaving her body. When the bubbles stopped and her air was gone, her lungs felt as if they were about to burst.

Suddenly, like a cork, she was shooting up through the water. Everything stopped going slowly and accelerated to a dizzying speed. She whipped the wet hair from her eyes with numbed fingers, frantically searching for her brother and the hull of the *Seagull.* She was attached by a safety line, but he was not. She saw him at the exact same moment that he spotted her and they stroked in unison to reach each other.

The twins stoically tried not to communicate their panic. They had turned turtle once in calm seas just to prove they could right the *Seagull* and climb back aboard. Now, like two puppets, they desperately went through the motions necessary to get the sloop upright. They both clung to the keel that stuck up from the water and tried to get a footing on the rail. Mercifully it rolled with their weight, and as the keel went under the water, they held it under with their feet and grasped the rail. Suddenly the keel broke away.

Antonia scrambled aboard to bail while Anthony stayed outside as counterbalance. When the boat began to right itself Anthony climbed aboard to help her bail. What was left of the *Seagull* was totally unstable. There was no time to talk, to pray, to think even, but when they found themselves back aboard they were both laughing and crying at the same time. They were soaked to the skin and cold to the bone. They were also hysterical and nearly mad with fear.

Another wave crashed across the deck. Antonia screamed, "Tony, hang on, where are you?"

Cold terror gripped her heart. "Tony! Tony! Tony!" she screamed over and over. She could see nothing but boiling seas. The visibility was almost nonexistent as gray rain slashed down in torrents. Antonia thought she would be able to spot her brother easily in his yellow oilskin, but she could not. A fear like she had never known in her life engulfed her. She did not fear for her own precarious safety, because her mind was totally focused on Anthony.

Lightning split the heavens with a blinding flash. Antonia smelled sulphur and knew that hell was close at hand. She saw the mast split and come down like a felled tree in the forest. She had forgotten she was tied to it. The next thing she knew she was in the sea, gagging and retching on the saltwater she had swallowed.

She bobbed about like a cork. The water kept closing over her head. She felt the constriction of the line tied beneath her armpits and pulled on it. She realized she was attached to a section of the mast like a floating spar. When it thudded into her side, she wrapped both arms about it and was finally able to keep her head from going under.

Where in the name of God was Tony? She told herself he had likely climbed back aboard and was searching desperately for her. The water was freezing and gradually her entire body numbed. Her mind followed suit. The downpour stopped, the gale-force wind blew the thunder farther out to sea, and Antonia, clinging to the floating wood, went monotonously up and down, up and down, hour after hour, after hour.

Miles away Anthony experienced exactly the same numbing monotony as his sister. He lay across the buoyant picnic basket that acted as a raft, carrying him farther and farther out to sea. His mind drifted in and out of consciousness. In his lucid moments he was thankful that Antonia at least was aboard the *Seagull* and headed in the right direction. Eventually the tide would wash her up along the shore. Anthony knew he was so far out at sea that his only chance lay in rescue. The odds of that were infinitesimal. As dark began to descend, his hopes vanished with the fading light and he slipped into unconsciousness.

A merchant ship had all hands on deck watching a pod of whales that had been driven off course by the storm. In the last rays of light someone spotted the yellow oilskin and a great shout went up. It took a coordinated exercise in courage and ingenuity, rather like a dramatic water ballet, but a gutsy crewman finally hooked the half-drowned, unconscious youth with a gaff and a dozen hands pulled him aboard. Anthony had been rescued by an East Indiaman, called the *Earl of Abergavenny,* outward bound for Bombay.

An air of tension hovered over Lamb Hall from the moment the sky turned dark. The bruise-colored clouds swept in from the west and headed out to sea. When the thunder rolled overhead, Roz apologized to the major. She could not continue the cozy tête-à-tête, sipping her tea and flirting outrageously, when she knew the twins were out sailing.

"I must go upstairs and see how bad this storm is. There's an unimpeded view of the sea from Anthony's balcony."

The major followed her up the staircase and when they arrived they found Mr. Burke before them anxiously watching as the lightning zigzagged from the black clouds as if it would split open the heavens.

"Don't fret, Lady Randolph, Anthony is a good sailor and they are both sensible enough to head home the moment anything looms in the west," Mr. Burke told her.

A torrential downpour at the moment prevented them from going out onto the balcony. "I've never seen a storm blow up this quickly in years," Roz exclaimed.

"It's all that sultry heat that's been hanging about this week. Unnatural here in England," Major Blount pointed out.

The lashing rain was swept away to sea in minutes and Roz said, "My God, it's a gale-force wind. The *Seagull* will be blown to bits."

Mr. Burke tried to calm Roz even though he was extremely worried himself. "I'd be willing to lay a bet they were safely back in the Medway before it hit."

They all three went back downstairs to keep vigil, hoping against hope the twins would arrive any moment. The wind had uprooted a flowering quince outside the dining room window. When they looked beyond the garden they saw quite a number of trees in the park had been flattened.

"Haven't seen a storm come up like that since I was in the Bay of Biscay," declared the major.

Mr. Burke touched his shoulder to warn him not to alarm Rosalind, but she was a woman who didn't get the vapors without good cause. Something had already told her she must brace herself for trouble.

Mr. Burke headed for the door. "I'll go down to the boathouse and see if I can spot them in the Medway."

"I'm coming too," decided Roz. "I can't just sit calmly by and wait."

There was no sign of the *Seagull* at the boathouse, so they walked along the bank of the river that opened up into the sea. The afternoon was no longer hot, but the raging wind had blown out to sea and only a brisk breeze remained on shore. The three walked out onto the shingle beach and scanned the watery horizon. All of them were taut with silence, but all they heard were the waves breaking on the shore and the gulls screaming overhead. Look as they might, they saw no sail, no boat, no swimmer, no wreckage.

The major made a quick decision. "I can do no good here, Roz. Now that the storm has passed and the seas are navigable, I'll take my sloop out. There's still a couple of hours before dark."

"Oh, Jeremy, thank you! Don't venture out alone."

"My neighbor's a good sailor, I'll induce old Kent to search with me. Never fear, if the *Seagull*'s experienced trouble we'll tow her in to safe harbor."

"Lady Randolph, you have no cloak," Mr. Burke admonished. "Go back to the house with Major Blount. I'll walk farther up the beach. The tide is about to change and even if the *Seagull*'s sails have been blown to shreds, the tide will bring her back."

Rosalind decided to return for a cloak, but she fully intended to rejoin Mr. Burke as soon as the major departed. Jeremy Blount gave Roz a reassuring hug before he left and bade her not to worry. She was surprised at the virile strength of his arms and realized how pleasant it was to have a man who would risk danger to aid her.

She took a red cloak from her wardrobe, reasoning the bright color might act as a beacon for the young sailors. As she passed a mirror she was shocked at how haggard she looked. She clenched her fists and took a deep, calming breath, realizing her stomach was tied in knots. She sent up a silent prayer to Jude, the patron saint of hopeless causes, then told herself sternly that the situation was not hopeless. Without hope there was nothing, just a black, frightening void.

Something, not exactly an inner voice, just a feeling in her bones really, told her that all would be well. She clutched her cloak about her trim figure and stepped outside, ready to face whatever was out there.

When she caught up with Mr. Burke on the shingle beach she realized that most of the light had gone out of the afternoon. The sea was a dark shade of pewter, the sky above it was a bit lighter, but still heavy with gray cloud. She clutched his arm for a few moments, taking some of his calm strength into herself, then she let go of him and said, "I'll walk a mile up this way and you go back toward the mouth of the Medway. The tide is really starting to come in now. We may spot them any minute."

They separated and almost an hour later came together again. The light was nearly all gone now and they strained their eyes, still keeping their vigil, still keeping hope alive. Neither of them was willing to give up yet.

"We'll cover the same distance one last time. I just cannot go back to the Hall yet." She knew Mr. Burke had been about to order her to the house. Her words forestalled him.

"All right," he agreed. "Shout if you see anything at all."

Fifteen minutes later it was Mr. Burke who shouted. One minute the rollers were unbroken until they hit the sand, the next moment he saw something black bobbing about between the swells. Without hesitation he plunged into the surf to grab and hold whatever it was. It was not until he had hold of it that he knew it was a person, and not until his face was less than a foot away did he see the yellow oilskin. "Mother of God, are you dead or alive?" he asked the human piece of flotsam. "Roz! Roz!" he bellowed, filling his lungs with air before he attempted to lift the waterlogged youth.

He heard Roz answer him and even at this distance heard the excitement, joy, and relief mingled in her answering shout. As he groped about in the dark seawater he knew something was preventing him lifting the body. He cursed beneath his breath as his seeking fingers came into contact with the line wrapped about the wooden spar and the boy. His nails could not unfasten the knots and finally in desperation he pulled the tangled line off by working it down the legs and over the bare feet.

He knew the body he held still breathed, even though it was not conscious. Roz came running up the beach, breathless. "Oh, my God—"

"It's Anthony," shouted Mr. Burke. "He's still breathing. Christ, he's heavy!"

"Dear God, where's Antonia?" Roz cried.

"No sign of her . . . no sign of the *Seagull.* Anthony was attached to part of the mast."

"Antonia! Antonia!" Roz cried her name desperately into the dark sea. The wind snatched the name from her trembling lips.

"Roz, if we want to save Anthony we have to get him into a warm bed. He's unconscious, near frozen to death. Come Roz, we have to give our full attention to the survivor. Fate has given us one, but not both. If we don't hurry, Anthony, too, may be lost to us."

Like one whose heart was being torn in half, Rosalind knew she must do the practical thing. With one last desperate look out to the insatiable sea, she sobbed, then groaned, then followed Mr. Burke as he carried his dripping, precious burden back to Lamb Hall. Halfway there he sank down to his knees to rest and catch his breath. Roz bent down to brush the sodden black hair back from the boy's brow. When they had him safe and dry and warm, he would tell them where Antonia was.

The servants stood about with eyes like saucers, the maids wrung their hands helplessly as Roz threw out her orders. "Build a fire in Anthony's chamber. He's half drowned and near frozen! Heat some soup quickly! Fetch brandy! Get dry towels from the warming cupboard! Never mind, I'll do it myself!" Then she thought of something else. "Get Bradshaw immediately. Tell him to drive over to Major Blount's with a message that Anthony is safe, but to keep searching for Antonia and the *Seagull.*"

Mr. Burke carried on up the staircase. He would not lay down his burden until he had young Lord Lamb in his own bedchamber. He left a pool of water upon every stair and drenched the carpet along the upper hallway, but they had a lifetime to mop up seawater. He concentrated only upon stripping the heavy, sodden garments from Anthony's frozen body. He tore off the bulky oilskin.

"Oh, Grandma—"

Roz couldn't believe her ears. "My God, it's Antonia!"

Mr. Burke stepped back in surprise and allowed Roz to complete the undressing. Off came the canvas breeches and the knitted shirt, then she wrapped her in a huge warm towel and thrust her beneath the bedcovers.

A maid came in carrying a tureen of soup. "Will Lord Lamb live, ma'am?" the young girl asked in a strangled voice.

Roz stared at her for half a minute. Dear God, the girl was right. Pneumonia was almost a certainty. "Yes, yes, out with you now, my grandchild needs rest around the clock. Keep everyone away from this chamber, there's a good girl. I want Tony to have absolute quiet. I'll do the necessary nursing myself."

When the door closed Mr. Burke and Lady Randolph exchanged worried glances. Mr. Burke laid the fire himself while Rosalind patiently spooned warm soup into Antonia's mouth. Now that she was warmed at last, it was plain to see she was suffering from exhaustion.

Her grandmother tucked the covers snugly about her and soothed, "Sleep now, darling. Tomorrow will be soon enough to tell us what happened."

Antonia's eyes were already closed and as the warmth and safety of home enfolded her, her mouth curved into a sweet smile of gratitude just before Morpheus claimed her.

Chapter 10

Adam Savage paced the deck of the *Red Dragon*. A week of indolence aboardship had made him feel like a caged leopard. He had anticipated the long, lazy days in the hot sun, thinking he'd catch up on his reading, and indeed he'd devoured Homer and Vergil and moved on to Fielding's contemporary novels. Now he realized they had occupied his mind, but his body cried out for action. His unbounded energy screamed for an outlet. In desperation he stripped and shoveled out the hold that held the pair of Arabian horses he was taking to England. Finally he went to his captain and told him to assign him duties as a member of the crew. He also took the midnight watch on a permanent basis. These were the hours when he allowed his mind to roam free. The black velvet sky, hung with a million diamonds, not only gave him the opportunity to study the constellations, but the freedom to wing across the heavens from England to Ceylon or from past to future.

On the midnight-to-dawn watch between sea and sky, between Heaven and Earth, everything fell into perspective. This journey was symbolic. He was closing a door on the past and opening another into the future. He had done this twice before. The first time, when he had left England for the Indies, he hadn't known he was closing a door on his past.

His father had been a cabinetmaker. They lived across the River Thames in Southwark, above the shop. It was no more than a hovel really. They had to store their wood upstairs, for when the Thames overflowed, it ruined whatever lay in its path. His father loved what he did. He was a master craftsman who had been apprenticed to Thomas Chippendale in St. Martin's Lane.

Adam Savage had not inherited his father's artistic hands, so he did the wood buying. When fine wood for furniture became scarce in England, and had to be imported, the cost became prohibitive. Young Savage had seen the mahogany and satinwood being unloaded from the East Indiamen at the wharves and experienced bitter anger because they could not afford it. When he talked to the sailors and learned it could be purchased for pennies in the Indies, he made up his mind to work his passage on a merchant ship and acquire firsthand what his father needed.

Savage quashed the feeling of guilt that arose up in him. How was he to know that his father would die of influenza in the damp hovel while Adam enjoyed the hot sun of Bombay? The thought that he would never be able to provide his father a comfortable living had driven him a little mad. As a result Savage had ruthlessly set about making himself rich. When he came to his senses and realized he was destroying lives for profit, along with his own soul, he again closed a door and opened another.

Savage then channeled his ruthless drive into acquiring untainted wealth and it had paid off a thousandfold. The magnificent house he was going to was another symbol. It was a reward for his hard labor, but it was also where he would bring up his children. They would have the advantages he had never known. He would also give them the benefit of his experience and see they received the finest education available so they would be capable of running their country.

If he married Evelyn Lamb, her children would become his. His mind winged back to Ceylon when he and Eve had said their good-byes. For once Eve had had no guests from the dozens of thriving plantations that stretched all the way to the coast. After dinner she reached across the table to take his hand. "I visited the chaplain to-day. I hadn't been inside the chapel since Russell's funeral. I prayed that you would have a safe voyage."

Savage was a cynic. He wondered what she had really prayed for.

"Stay with me tonight?" It was more than an invitation, it was an appeal, a whispered supplication.

His blue eyes pierced her until she shivered and lowered her lashes.

He knew she was willing to play the whore rather than lose him, but Savage had too much pride to make love to a woman who wasn't mad to have him. Her sexual coldness was a challenge, but he needed time to overcome her frigidity. He decided not to consummate their union on this last night, but to wait until he returned for her. He knew she was beginning to thaw toward him, knew he sometimes aroused her, though she repressed it, but decided to leave her wanting more.

Savage picked her up and carried her to her bedroom. "I won't make love to you in Russell's bed," he said bluntly. He bit her earlobe. "The things I'd want to do would desecrate it," he teased.

An involuntary shudder ran through her body at his outrageously intimate words. She knew he said such provocative things purposely, damn him, damn him.

He laid her on her bed. "You are always so tense." He slipped off her shoes and began to massage her feet. "I want you to relax. I want you to sleep and I want you to dream of me tonight and every night until I come back for my answer."

As he stroked her pale skin, soothing her, his eyes stared into the darkness. Eve hadn't been exactly as he expected. He had initially been attracted because she was older than he with the experience of being a wife and mother. He had expected her to be a voluptuary, a consummate earth mother. Instead, he found her sexually repressed. It would be a challenge to shape her, mold her to fill his needs once she was his wife. And if she did not quite fill all his needs, he would be discreet in his liaisons.

Before he left for what would probably be the best part of a year, he slipped a ring upon her finger. It was a magnificent, blazing, ten-carat diamond. It was not an engagement ring, but a symbol that he would return for an answer.

He stood at the helm of the *Red Dragon,* his ice-blue eyes alert for anything untoward upon the black sea, while his inner mind winged back from Eve and Ceylon. He had deliberately not given her the ring while she was awake. She could not be formally engaged while she was in mourning. He had had no need to see her reaction to the priceless jewel. He had known exactly how her pupils would dilate and how her loins would spasm with excitement to possess such a treasure.

A smile curved his wicked-looking mouth. Eve was an avaricious little bitch, like most women. He thought no less of her for it; after all, she was only human. She would make a superb chatelaine for Edenwood and in return she would give him her children.

A son! A son upon the brink of manhood. He couldn't wait to meet him. He had a wealth of experience to impart to him. A daughter, too, he thought wryly. He was unsure of himself there, all right. He had little he could teach a young girl, but he would give her his protection. The world was filled with untold evil. He would see that it never touched her. But a son . . . Anthony . . . Tony . . . he couldn't wait!

When Antonia opened her eyes she saw that Roz had sat in a chair beside her bed all night. She felt disoriented as she sat up against the pillows, then realized she was in Anthony's bedchamber.

Her grandmother awoke with a start, then heaved an enormous sigh of relief when she saw Antonia seemed unharmed by her ordeal.

"Where's Anthony?"

"Oh, darling, we don't know, but I'm afraid we must brace ourselves for the worst," Roz said gently. "Do you remember what happened?"

A great lump formed in Antonia's throat, so that she could hardly speak. Dear God, surely if she was alive, her twin was also. They were each half of one whole. The fate of one was the fate of the other. How could it be otherwise?

Antonia swallowed hard. "The storm came up out of nowhere. Everything went wrong at once. The mains fouled and we couldn't get the sails off. Tony tied a line around me. We capsized, then somehow we managed to right her, but the *Seagull* was totally unstable. Tony was washed overboard again and I couldn't see him." Her eyes filled with tears and she choked on her words.

Her grandmother's eyes held such anguish, she knew she must keep a tight hold on her emotions and not go to pieces for Roz's sake. "Someone should be out searching for Anthony. I was out there for endless hours before the tide brought me ashore."

"Major Blount and his neighbor are out in his sloop searching the seas. I sent word to him last night that one twin was safely home, but to go out again at first light to look for the other twin or wreckage of the *Seagull.*"

When Antonia tried to throw back the covers and climb from the bed, she fell back with a wince.

"You are hurt!" Roz cried, "You've broken something!"

"No . . . no, I don't think so." Antonia lifted the covers to inspect her body. "Lord, I'm covered with bruises."

"Are you sure that's all it is?" demanded Roz with concern.

"Yes, I'm positive. Help me up, I must help search for Anthony."

"Under no circumstances. Lie still. We have to talk. Mr. Burke is walking the beach, in fact all the servants are out looking for any sign."

Antonia sighed and was grateful to lie back. "Why am I in Tony's room?"

"When Mr. Burke pulled you from the water last night he thought you were Anthony. So did I. . . ." Roz's voice trailed off, but Antonia knew there was more that she wanted to say. "Darling, we must face facts. If Anthony has drowned or is lost at sea, that cousin, that Bernard Lamb, will inherit the title and this house."

An ominous silence filled the chamber as Antonia tried to make sense of her grandmother's words. Then she forcefully rejected them. "No! That is impossible. Tony is just missing. He's not dead. . . . I won't let him be dead!"

"Blessed Virgin, grant that you are right, but if you are not, Antonia, if he does not show up today . . . soon, then indeed he is lost at sea and will be presumed drowned."

Antonia turned her face into her pillow and sobbed brokenheartedly. Anthony was a part of her. She could not pretend strength, even for her grandmother's sake.

Roz reached a hand to her shoulder. "Antonia, Mr. Burke and I talked long into the night. We have a plan . . . it's rather daring in concept, but everything hinges upon you. It's to be your decision entirely."

Antonia struggled up and dried her face with the linen sheet.

Roz licked dry lips, then spoke in a low, confidential tone. "When word of this boating accident leaks out and it becomes known that Anthony is presumed drowned, the new heir will be upon us within a day, claiming everything and turning us out of the Hall. I never told you, darling, but Bernard Lamb came running to Stoke the moment he learned your father was deceased. The ruthless young devil was looking at Lamb Hall with speculative eyes. With Tony the new Lord Lamb, he was well aware of the fact that he was now heir apparent to everything. I gave him short shrift. There was no way I was going to allow the damned upstart to insinuate himself into the family circle. Now that the tables might be turned, he will derive the greatest pleasure from turning us out. He has just been waiting and praying for an accident to occur so he can claim everything."

Antonia was appalled at the picture her grandmother painted. It was her nightmare becoming reality. Perhaps this diabolical Bernard Lamb had been doing more than praying for an accident. Perhaps he had deliberately sabotaged the *Seagull.* Why, that was attempted murder. Perhaps he had rotten-well succeeded too! Antonia groaned and closed her eyes. *No, no,* she told herself, *don't jump to such wicked conclusions. No one could be so evil.* Thinking evil things would only bring terrible punishment down upon their heads. She must think only good thoughts until Tony was returned to them.

"If we pretend you are Anthony, it will buy us time, perhaps as much as a couple of weeks. It will give you time to recover your strength and time to see if Anthony comes home. If indeed he did not survive, it will give us time to pack our things and make other arrangements. We can move to my dower house. It's only a cottage, but it will have to suffice. For the time being we will avoid putting a notice in the *Gazette* about the boating accident."

Her grandmother's words brought home the reality of their predicament. Not only might they lose Anthony, but also Lamb Hall and all the security she had ever known. Antonia suddenly felt very ill.

Roz thought her averse to the idea, so she tried to convince her of its merit. "With your hair slicked back, even Mr. Burke and I mistook you for Anthony. If you temporarily pose as your brother, you will not have to forfeit the title, the town house, or most important of all, Lamb Hall."

Antonia's eyes widened at the sheer audacity of the suggestion.

"Will you even consider impersonating Anthony?"

"Of course I will! I'll play at being Anthony until he returns. Absolutely no one will know," she vowed.

"And if he doesn't return, darling?" pressed Roz.

"If you are going to keep insisting that, I won't have anything to do with it," Antonia cried in anguish. "I'll take Anthony's place to safeguard everything that is his, but only until he returns."

Roz had to be satisfied. One step at a time. Perhaps they'd never get away with the deception, but it was worth a bloody good try. Of that she was totally convinced. Roz took a pair of scissors from her pocket. "The first thing we must do is cut your hair the same length as Anthony's."

Antonia picked up a dark, wavy tress of waist-length hair. "Must we? I can stuff it up under one of Tony's tiewigs."

"You know he didn't wear a tiewig about the house or when he went sailing. He wore his own hair clubbed back unless he was going out and about. I want the servants to think you are Anthony, save Mr. Burke of course. That will be the test. If the household staff believes you are your brother, everyone else will."

Off came the waist-length locks until her hair just fell to her shoulders. Tony closed her eyes in misery, hardly able to bear the thought of losing her lovely, shiny black curls. Suddenly she felt as if she couldn't breathe and her face seemed to be getting very warm.

Roz gathered up the cuttings carefully so she could dispose of them discreetly, then brushed Antonia's hair back and tied it at her nape with a black ribbon. "Put on Anthony's bed robe and stand over by the balcony window while I ring for one of the maids."

Antonia thought this was a waste of time. Their servants had no reason to be disloyal, why go through the rigamorole of trying to fool them? However it would be most interesting to see if she could carry it off.

It was Anna who answered the bell. Roz opened the door when the maid knocked and said, "Anna, ask young James to carry up water for Anthony's bath. You can make the bed with fresh linen while you're here."

Anna dropped Roz a curtsy, then glanced from beneath her lashes toward young Lord Lamb. She blushed to see him in his bed robe, and to cover her confusion the words came tumbling out. "Would ye like me to get ye some breakfast, sor?"

"No, thank you, Anna. I'll breakfast downstairs as usual," Antonia replied, hoping her voice was as husky as Tony's.

"Oh, sor, we were all that worried for ye. Praise heaven yer safe an' sound."

"Thank you, Anna," Antonia said quietly.

The young maid blushed even deeper. It was the first time the young master had remembered her name. She slipped out to find James, and Antonia stepped out onto the balcony in a desperate attempt to fill her lungs with air. For a moment everything swam before her eyes, then all the strength seemed to leave her legs. She leaned against the balcony wall to steady herself. Her eyes went immediately to the boathouse, but there was no one about. Ironically today the water was calm as a millpond.

Antonia forced herself to go back into Tony's room while James poured two buckets of boiling water into the small hip bath that sat in a corner. Before James took up the empty buckets he looked furtively toward Lady Randolph and saw that she was busy laying out the master's clothes. He pressed a guinea into Tony's hand and said low, " 'Ere's your winnings, sir. Paid twenty to one."

Roz followed the servant to the door, then locked it. "So far, so good."

Antonia removed the robe, then stood in front of the mirror to examine her bruises. Her breasts and rib cage had great dark splotches where blood had gathered beneath the skin. One of her hips had a long, tender bruise that spread from front to back. She winced as she touched the scrapes on her shins and elbows. She hoped the water would soothe her skin. That was the last thing she remembered.

Lady Rosalind Randolph had never been so afraid in her life. Her beloved granddaughter had pneumonia. When Antonia lost consciousness and had to be lifted into bed, Roz felt immediately that a fever raged in her body. She bathed her and nursed her continually for six days and nights, holding her hands tightly and talking to her in a soothing voice whenever Antonia rambled wildly or thrashed about the bed.

Mr. Burke stood vigil with her through the long nights, so that if Lady Randolph dozed off, he would be there to tend to Antonia's needs.

Roz prayed as she had never prayed before. "Please, please, God, don't take both of them. Leave me this child and I will ask you for nothing more."

It seemed to Rosalind that God had indeed answered her prayers, for Antonia's fever finally abated, and instead of thrashing about she slept much more peacefully.

Major Blount called every day, but Roz was too burdened down for visitors. She sent him a note thanking him for all he had done and asked him to still carry on the search no matter how hopeless it seemed. Major Blount wrote back saying he was afraid the *Gazette* had gotten wind of the accident, but that he had neither confirmed nor denied their tasteless speculation when they had questioned him.

Rosalind realized that even Jeremy Blount did not yet know it was Antonia who had cheated death, but she would wait until she could explain in person. It didn't do to commit things to paper. Letters had a way of turning up to haunt you.

In the week since the boating accident there had been no further sign of wreckage on the beach. Roz accepted the heartbreaking truth that Anthony would never return. She felt so burdened down, she knew she was defeated. All she could do now was accept the loss with grace and dignity.

With Mr. Burke's help she began to pack her things. She felt blessed relief when Antonia opened her eyes a couple of times and asked for a drink. At last her granddaughter was in her right mind again and her fever was almost gone. Antonia was very weak and there still remained two bright spots high on her cheeks, but Roz knew she was going to recover.

She took the glass from Antonia's hand and placed it beside the bed. When Roz saw her eyes close peacefully, she went downstairs and sat at the elegant secretaire to pen a letter. She had been putting off the inevitable for days, but she felt it was her duty to inform Watson and Goldman that Lord Anthony Lamb was missing at sea and presumed drowned.

It was the hardest letter she had ever had to write. She brushed away a tear and sanded the wet ink. Then she straightened her back and summoned James. She gave him the letter to take to the posting inn in Stoke.

Two hours later, when Antonia awoke and Roz could see how vastly improved she was, she took hold of her hand and told her gently that all hope for Anthony was past.

"How long has it been?" Antonia asked, still quite breathless.

"You've been ill for seven days, darling."

Antonia lay very, very still as she inwardly digested the heartbreaking news about her brother. When she looked at Rosalind she saw how thin and haggard she was and it was brought home to her how much she had endured this last week.

"Thank you, Grandma. You've given me all your love, but you've given me all your strength too. Now it's my turn to be strong for you."

"Dear, I know it will be distressing for you, but it cannot be avoided. I'm going to have Anna go to your room and pack all your lovely things. When you are feeling strong enough, tomorrow or the next day, we will remove to my little dower house."

Antonia stared at her as if she had gone mad. "There is absolutely no need to pack anything. Lamb Hall is our home. I shall never give it up."

"Darling, all our time has run out. All my things are packed and crated and I've notified Watson and Goldman of the accident."

Antonia sat bolt upright. "How? When?" she demanded.

"James took the letter to the posting inn a couple of hours ago."

Antonia threw back the covers and struggled to her feet.

"My God, child, what are you doing? Get back into bed immediately," Roz cried with great alarm.

"I'm going to get the damned letter back. I'm going to be Anthony!"

"Darling, if we carry on this deception any longer, we are going to be in grave trouble when we are discovered. What we've done is against the law. It is a criminal act, to say nothing of being morally wrong."

"There I don't agree with you. Criminal perhaps, but to me it would be morally wrong for Bernard Lamb to step into Anthony's shoes, Anthony's home, or Anthony's title!" She was almost completely out of breath now. Her chest rose and fell painfully as she gasped for air.

When Antonia stood up the room swirled about her. She put out a hand to steady herself. "I'm going to take Anthony's place, not just for now, but indefinitely."

Roz saw her sway and said whatever she thought would appease her or persuade her to get back into bed. "I'll send Mr. Burke to the posting inn to try to recover the letter."

"No," Antonia said firmly, "I'm Lord Lamb; it's my responsibility."

Rosalind feared Antonia was again becoming delirious, but she had expended all her energy and in the face of Antonia's fierce determination she was silenced.

"You lost Anthony, you almost lost me, but you're not going to lose your home!" Antonia was adamant.

She donned Tony's undergarments and decided that they were not all that different from her own underdrawers. She put on his shirt, then searched his night table for studs. She couldn't believe how weak she felt. Before she managed to get the collar attached, she decided it was a fiddling business invented to try the patience of a saint. She pulled on a pair of the straight-legged pantaloons she'd bought Tony in London, fastening the straps under her instep, then walked over to the mirror to appraise her appearance.

"Thank God my breasts are small," she murmured. Then she laughed. "I never thought to hear myself say that!" She imagined the front of the starched shirt was still somewhat raised, so she opened his wardrobe to find a brocaded waistcoat. She stood absolutely still until a wave of dizziness passed. Jehoshaphat, if she felt this exhausted from simply dressing herself, how was she going to ride into Stoke?

The sponge bath she'd been given earlier made tendrils curl about her face, so she again brushed her hair back and tied it with a black ribbon. She stared at her reflection. It was Anthony, yet it was Anthony blended with a smattering of Antonia. Finally she decided it was Tony, the combination of both of them.

She felt strange inside, as if she was waiting for something, and yet it was combined with a sinking feeling that whatever it was would never materialize. Also, a great feeling of melancholy engulfed her. She sighed sadly, trying to accept what had happened. Today must be gotten through . . . and then there would be tomorrow.

Tony gathered her wits together with difficulty. Here she was wasting valuable time envisioning tomorrow when the thing that was so pressing was the letter. She must get it back at any cost. She gripped the oak banister as she descended the stairs, afraid that with each step her knees might buckle under her.

Tony asked Bradshaw to saddle Neptune, because he would be swifter than Venus. Bradshaw led out the horse and was about to ask the young master if he was feeling better, but the flushed look on his face told him Anthony was not fully recovered. Bradshaw helped him into the saddle and stood shaking his head as he watched Lord Lamb take off in his usual breakneck fashion.

Tony was weak with relief when she reached Stoke and the posting inn came into view. Now, if luck was on her side, the mail coach would not yet have departed for London. When she dismounted she had to lean against Neptune for strength. She was saved from having to gather her energy to go inside because at that moment an ostler touched his cap and came to take her reins. "G'day to ye, Lord Lamb."

"Good day, Toby. The mail coach hasn't departed yet, has it?" Tony asked anxiously.

"Oh, aye, sir. Missed it by half an hour at least. Did ye have summat to post?"

"Damn and set fire!" Tony swore, then she was racked by a deep cough that scorched her lungs. At the ostler's words Tony's heart had plummeted to her boots. So near, yet so far. Her resolve hardened. She must get that bloody letter!

"Where does it stop next?" Tony demanded.

He scratched his head. "Let's see now, from here he dips down to Rochester, then Chatham. But if you don't catch him before Chatham, you never will. Once he gets on the London Turnpike, he'll whip up his cattle to breakneck speed. You won't even see his dust!"

Tony waited no longer. She dug in her heels, urging Neptune to a full gallop. Mile after mile she kept her eyes narrowed for the coach, but with each successive mile the chance of catching it grew slimmer. Tony swayed from the saddle, almost falling over sideways. She caught herself in time and shook her head to clear it. She knew she was making herself ill again and fought with her own common sense about pursuing this hopeless mission further.

A voice inside her head told her if she was really replacing Anthony, he would not give up. Her knees urged Neptune to his top speed, and there far ahead on the outskirts of Rochester she saw the dark shape of the mail coach.

The coach driver first thought he was being held up; then, when he saw the young fellow had no weapon save his frenzied voice, he reluctantly slowed and brought the sweating team to a halt.

Tony had the very devil of a time persuading the mail carrier to give back the letter, and only when she asserted her authority did the man give way. "I'm Lord Anthony Lamb, my good sir, and I shall see you are immediately dismissed from your position if you do not return my property to me immediately. I've already dismissed the idiot footman who posted it by mistake. The information in this letter is so damaging, you'll likely see the inside of Fleet Prison if you try to overrule my authority."

The man complied, cursing under his breath, "Wot bloody chance does a bloke 'ave against the bleedin' gentry? Sod the lot of 'em." When he climbed back on the box and whipped up the horses, Antonia knew her good fortune was due to the fact that he thought her a man rather than a woman. She clutched the letter to Watson and Goldman and slid from the saddle. Then, knowing she could go no farther, she sat down on the side of the road and cried her eyes out.

That is precisely where Mr. Burke found her. Lady Randolph had ordered Bradshaw ready the coach so Mr. Burke could go after her to Stoke. When he learned she'd ridden on toward Rochester he couldn't believe it and urged Bradshaw to pull out the lead.

As Mr. Burke lifted her into the carriage, she looked up at him with deepest gratitude. Two pink spots burned feverishly upon her cheeks. "How would I manage without you, Mr. Burke? You are my knight in shining armor!"

A sinking feeling gripped Bernard Lamb as he read the small notice in the *Gazette*. He read it two or three more times, wanting to reject it, yet finally having no choice but to accept it. He had scanned the newspaper for three frustrating weeks. Now finally here in black and white was the first indication there had been a boating mishap. The thing he had hoped for, prayed for, and planned for had come to pass. Yet it counted for naught. Christ Almighty, if what the *Gazette* hinted at was true, the wrong bloody twin had drowned. Filled with uncertainty, Bernard read the item again. "The heavy squall that suddenly blew up last week along the coast damaged many sailing vessels moored in the Medway. We received an unconfirmed report that Lady Antonia Lamb was washed overboard and drowned near her home in Stoke."

Bernard crashed his fist on the tabletop so hard that one of the table legs gave way. He then proceeded to kick it to pieces, needing to destroy something in his frustrated anger. As he thought more about it he began to have very mixed feelings. His murder plot had been successful and he congratulated himself on his cleverness, but a small shiver of paranoia touched him. His cousin, Lord Anthony, probably knew the lines and the rudder had been tampered with and if there was an investigation into the sailboat accident, suspicion must fall upon the one who had most to gain.

Bernard decided he had better keep a safe distance for the present. One twin had been removed. If aught befell the other too quickly, it would hardly be considered coincidental. Bernard would bide his time secure in the knowledge that he was capable of murder whenever the need arose.

A lovely thought came to him as he recalled the details of the visit to Stoke. He hadn't visited Angela in days. He began to whistle as he picked up his swordstick and pulled on his new moleskin gloves.

Angela Brown was still sound asleep as Bernard let himself into her flat with his key. The theater didn't close until midnight and by the time she took off her stage makeup and hung up all her costume changes, it was usually after one in the morning before she got to her flat.

It was a damned good thing Angela hadn't brought anyone home with her, Bernard thought, or he'd carve up her plump white thighs. He flipped back the blanket and poked her with the sheathed swordstick. She murmured a protest, then suddenly sat up as she came awake.

"What the hellfire are you playing at?" she demanded.

"Hellfire . . . an apt punishment for a murderess, don't you think?"

"What the devil are you talking about, Bernie?"

"You may soon have a nodding acquaintance with the devil, Angel Face." He again prodded her. "There's been a serious boating accident. My twin cousin has drowned." He waved the newspaper under her nose, but didn't hand her the notice to read.

Her eyes lit up with disbelief. "Don't tell me you're the new Lord Lamb?" she cried, leaping from the bed to throw her arms about him.

Bernard took hold of her hands and pried them cruelly from his person. He increased the pressure until she fell back upon the bed, then he backhanded her across the face. "No, you stupid bitch. You murdered the wrong twin!"

A look of horror crossed her face. "The girl? It wasn't me, you pig, it was you!" Angela's eyes became riveted upon his swordstick as he slowly drew the long blade from its sheath.

He began to toy with her. He pierced the flimsy fabric of her nightgown, slashing it open, then touched the cold steel to the inside of her knees. "Open for me, Angel." He breathed heavily, feeling his cock turn to marble. Power was so exciting. It was stronger than a drug. Once he exercised power over another, he craved it again and again.

Slowly, with wary eyes, Angela opened her legs for him. The relief she felt made her weak as water as he laid down his weapon to remove his clothing. Angela cried out in terror, however, as he again picked up the swordstick and advanced upon her. His sex stood out like a weapon and she knew it was a sick game he played, making her wonder which one he would bury inside her.

As the sharp point came toward her she closed her eyes and bit her lips to smother the scream that gathered in her throat. With relief she felt the hard smooth shaft go up inside her, but when she opened her eyes she saw that he had reversed the stick and buried its handle inside her.

With startling clarity she saw what he wanted from her was abject fear. Although she was an actress, she did not have to exaggerate the sheer terror she felt at the hands of this handsome young sadist. Angela fed his power by begging and groveling before his authority. When she reduced herself to the status of a slavegirl, Bernard ejaculated and fell limply atop her.

When the Gazette was delivered to Lamb Hall, Tony and Roz were dismayed. They didn't want Watson and Goldman to think Antonia was dead, nor did they want society in general to find out, because then how would she ever be able to take her place in it?

They consulted Mr. Burke and finally the three of them concocted a plausible tale which must go to the Gazette immediately. Tony wrote the notice herself:

Lady Antonia Lamb was safely rescued after being washed overboard from her sailboat. She will be spending the next few weeks in Bath recuperating from her ordeal. The *Gazette* wishes to apologize for any embarrassment to the Lambs, caused by yesterday's erroneous report.

Chapter 11

During the long voyage of the *Red Dragon* John Bull and Kirinda were never seasick at the same time. Though it went against the grain, they provided whatever service the other needed with uncomplaining dignity. John Bull was a far more tolerable sailor than Kirinda, however. She spent most of the time in her berth wishing the master had never saved her from the funeral pyre.

Adam Savage visited her cabin often, keeping an eye on her weight loss. He knew she could have no better nurse than John Bull, because he'd been privileged to be at his mercy once. As they neared the English Channel, however, the choppy seas proved too much for either of them and Savage found himself playing nursemaid.

Kirinda moaned and turned her face to the cabin wall. She was mortified to have the master remove the slop pail of vomit and wash her.

"Kirinda, look at me," Adam ordered sternly.

"Leave me, let me die," she whispered.

"Dying isn't that easy, little one," Adam murmured.

"I am covered with shame," she whimpered.

"No, you are covered with puke, but I'll soon wash away every trace. Only think how often you have bathed me, you silly girl. You have tended me when I hadn't the strength left to lift my eyelids. Sit up now and I'll tell you something that will please you. Tonight you will be on dry land."

She kissed his hands. Adam plopped the strong-smelling carbolic soap back into the bowl and stood up. His dark head almost touched the beams. "I want you to nibble on this dry biscuit and sip this wine slowly. I swear by Vishnu your stomach will not reject it."

She knew she should not drink forbidden wine, yet she must obey his orders. She knew in her heart that her master was a more potent god than any Hindu god or goddess. As he opened the door to leave he said, "I'll tell you something else that will please you. John Bull is much greener than you today."

Kirinda couldn't imagine the immaculate John Bull being brought low by seasickness. She began to perk up immediately.

In his manservant's cabin he performed the same ablutions, but filled John Bull's ears with strengthening words. "This is what you have waited a lifetime for. This is the English Channel. Surely you will be at the rail to embrace your chosen land, John Bull? Kirinda is over her seasickness, I believe. She can't wait to plant her feet on English soil before you do, man."

John Bull moaned softly. "The way I am feeling, you may plant all of me in English soil and good riddance to bad rubbish!"

"Eat this dry biscuit and sip on this wine," Savage instructed, bundling up the soiled linen. Before John Bull could protest about drinking spirits, he said, "Kirinda had the courage and good sense to take some wine and it settled her stomach immediately."

John Bull could not lose face by allowing Kirinda to appear a better sailor than he. If it was the last thing he ever did, he must set foot on English soil unaided.

Dusk had descended before the *Red Dragon* was safely moored at the Indigo Docks in London. A wave of nostalgia swept over Savage as he contemplated setting foot on English soil once more. It was over twelve years since he had disembarked from these docks and all along the water the waterfront looked and smelled much the same. However there were far more merchant vessels anchored here now, and the wharf was crowded with every nationality of seaman from the far-flung reaches of the world.

From the high deck he could see the lamplit taverns that rubbed elbows with the warehouses, and through cynical eyes he noticed how seedy and dirty they looked. The same number of drunken sailors lay about and surely those were the same drabs plying their trade that had been there the night he'd embarked.

When the gangplank was lowered he was the first across. He needed to hire a carriage to carry him and his body servants to a London hotel. The very soles of his feet itched to walk the streets of this familiar old jade of a city, yet he did not give way to temptation. Once he had traveled light with no other possessions than the clothes on his back. Such was no longer the case. Wealth brought with it sobering responsibilities.

Savage hired the least shabby carriage he could find and instructed the driver to wait by the East Indiaman, the *Red Dragon*. Back aboard he unlocked the gun cabinet in his cabin and distributed weapons to the captain and the first and second mates. "I'll rent warehouse space tomorrow. I want an armed guard on my chests in the starboard hold until I personally come for them. These docks swarm with rats, four-legged ones too. You won't be able to keep them off the ship, but keep them away from the tea chests and the spices. Lure some cats aboard."

Savage had packed his own trunk and he picked it up and carried it with him as he rapped sharply upon the cabin doors of his two servants. "John Bull, I have a carriage waiting."

The Tamil servant opened the door slowly and stepped out of the cabin with the gravest dignity. He was dressed in immaculate white with the blood-red turban sporting its great ruby. Across the companionway Kirinda, too, moved slowly, as though she were in a trance. She put one small foot very deliberately in front of the other, afraid she might topple over if she put one foot wrong. She carried Rupee in a wicker cage and a tapestry valise that held her clothes.

John Bull said, "Give me the bird."

Very carefully she placed the valise on the floor, put her hand behind her head with the fingers sticking up in the air like a coxcomb, and squawked at him. Then to Adam Savage's consternation the two servants dissolved into giggles. As he stared in disbelief from one to the other John Bull said, "Exshellency . . . the girl cannot hold her liquor," then hiccuped in what could only be described as a dignified manner.

Christ Almighty, thought Savage, *they are both drunk as deacons.* It was a most curious trio that walked into the Savoy Hotel that night, and though the staff was noted for its impeccable, discreet service, it was beyond their power to keep from staring open mouthed.

It soon dawned on them that this was a nabob and his body servants. Though the powerful-looking man with black hair curling about his shoulders and skin the color of teak signed his name as Savage, they secretly doubted he was a white man. They dubbed him Indian Savage and were left in no doubt of his wealth when he reserved three adjoining suites. When asked how long he would need them, he froze the inquirer with his ice-blue eyes and replied, "For the nonce," which told them nothing and everything they needed to know.

The man in the turban closed his eyes in silent prayer as the exotic bird he carried selected a fine old English word from its vocabulary and screeched, "Sodomite!" at the top of its voice.

The female in the delicate sari and sturdy English walking boots looked as if she had been plucked straight from some heathen temple. Her laughter floated across the Savoy's foyer like tinkling bells.

John Bull opened all the connecting doors to the suites, because the heavy English furniture made the rooms seem small and crowded after the spacious bungalow with its screened verandahs. Adam Savage sat down at a desk to compile a list of information and directions he would need from the concierge. John Bull unpacked his master's clothes and hung them in the wardrobe, shaking his head over the fact that he had only brought one trunk from the dozens aboard the *Red Dragon.*

All went well until the chambermaid arrived. John Bull took it upon himself to deal with the English servant. She had an assortment of large towels folded over one arm and carried three porcelain chamber pots. When she tried to hand them to John Bull, he looked at her as if she was deranged. "These are unbearable," he said firmly.

She looked him up and down, knew instinctively he was going to give her grief, and challenged, "Wot do you mean, unbearable?"

"They are too big. When they are filled they cannot be lifted . . . therefore they are unbearable."

The chambermaid rolled her eyes. "Wot'll hold more will hold less."

"We refuse to drink from such large cups. Bring smaller ones."

"Cups?" the woman hooted. "Yer ignorant devil, that's a chamber pot!"

"Chamber pot?" John Bull repeated blankly.

"Yer know . . . piss pot!"

The mynah pounced on the new word with enthusiasm. "Pisspot! Pisspot!"

John Bull was mortified, not at discussing such matters with a servant, but that his master would be reduced to such an uncivilized practise. "There is no bathing room? No bidet? How primitive!"

" 'Ere, are yer trying to pull my leg? A bloody heathen foreigner telling me we're primitive?"

Savage heard the voices raised in provocation. He came to investigate. The chambermaid in starched gray uniform and mob cap was ready to defend her country against this brown-skinned piece of rubbish.

"Is there a problem?" Savage asked in a cool voice of authority.

The young chambermaid fell back in alarm when she looked up at the tall man's dark, forbidding face. He was accustomed to the revulsion his scarred face sometimes provoked and had schooled himself against showing any reaction. He cursed himself for being sensitive after all these years.

"The woman accused me of touching her leg," John Bull said.

"I never!" the chambermaid denied.

"Yes, Excellency. I informed her the cups were unbearable. Then she taught Rupee to say pisspot, then she accused me of trying to pull off her leg."

Adam Savage took the articles the maid clutched and said, "A small misunderstanding. Good night."

When Savage closed the door, John Bull asked, "Why did you dismiss her? Is she not the punkah wallah?"

"No, John Bull, there are no fans to be pulled. In England we do not need cooling down, we need warming up. I'm expecting the concierge. Just show him in, then take Rupee to another room and help Kirinda get settled for the night. I'll order us some dinner if you will be patient."

"Ah, Excellency, now we are in England I can see I will have to exercise great patience with the lower orders."

"Indeed John Bull, and vice versa."

Antonia, wearing Anthony's clothes and occupying Anthony's chamber, sat with an open book in her lap. The story did not grip her and her mind kept wandering in a melancholy fashion; then she would start to read again simply to occupy her mind and prevent her from grieving. Despite all her prayers and her begging and bargaining with God, Anthony had never shown up.

She felt listless and very lonely without his male presence at Lamb Hall. She was quite determined to take her twin's place, however. She would die rather than see Bernard Lamb snatch the lovely manor from her and Roz.

It was such a pretty day, she longed to be outdoors, but she sighed and focused on her book. Suddenly she flung it across the room. To hell with it. She would have to go out sometime. Fear of being discovered in her deceit had kept her cooped up away from everyone. At last she decided that if she was going to do the thing, she would do it with panache. The key of course was "attitude." With the right attitude, anything in life could be achieved. She was totally convinced of it.

Since she was dressed for riding, that's exactly what she would do. She would ride out to the tenant farms and see if anything was needed. Tony put on a tiewig and a freshly starched neckcloth. She scooped some silver into her vest pocket and picked up Tony's riding crop. In the stables she almost approached Venus, then remembered in time to ask Bradshaw to saddle Neptune.

"He needs exercise m'lord," Bradshaw said approvingly. "Ye can try out the new tack ye got over at Rochester."

The old stable hound came up wagging his tail. She was just about to call him her sweetest boy and other such baby talk when she remembered her attitude. "Hello, you ugly old brute. Still cocking the old leg on everything in sight?" The dog adored the insults seemingly more than the baby talk, so she tucked the information away for future use. Tony cantered through the fields to the first farm, where Harry Simpson and his son were scything hay. Both doffed their caps in deference to Lord Lamb. She took a deep, steadying breath and casually dismounted. Tony thrust one hand deep into her breeches pocket and swished at the tall, dry grass with her whip. "Hello, Harry, looks like a good crop."

The red-faced farmer looked tongue tied, then he forced himself to speak. "Milord, we are all that sorry about yer sister."

Antonia bit her lip and nodded. She swallowed the lump in her throat, knowing this awkward moment must be gotten through. "I rode over to see what was needed."

"Don't bother about us, milord, ye've enough trouble."

Simpson's son, with a defiant look in his eyes said, "T'house roof leaks."

His father's face turned a darker shade of red. "We'll patch it again, once we get t'hay in."

Tony looked toward the farmhouse. "It needs rethatching, Harry. I'll see to it today. You should have told me," she said in reproach. "You get the hay crop in before it rains."

Harry scratched his head at the inconsistencies of the gentry. When he had brought up the subject of the leaky roof before, young Lord Lamb had told him to patch it.

At the next farm Tony found herself being eyed by the farmer's daughters. Though both younger than she, they were quick witted. Her heart sank. She had often spoken to Mary and Lizzie and given them her clothes when she grew out of them. As soon as she opened her mouth Antonia thought she would be discovered. Mary gave her a provocative glance as if the two of them shared a secret. Antonia thought, *She knows!* Then relief swept over her as the girl said, "I'll wait for ye behind the cowshed tonight, if ye've a fancy, m'lord."

Tony was stunned. The girl was inviting her to an assignation. Lizzie was just as informal. "Yer sister won't be needin' her fancy dresses no more. Can we have 'um?"

What an avaricious little beast, thought Antonia. "Where's your father?" she asked in a cool voice.

"In the cowshed . . . told us to keep out until cow's calved."

Tony dismounted. "Watch my horse," she directed, then entered the low door of the cow byre.

"How do?" nodded Joe Bradley. "Can ye give me a hand, m'lord?"

Tony was startled, but knew she could not back off in horror at the sight of a cow calving.

"This un's an owd bitch of a cow. Kicks like a bloody mule. If ye'll just grab 'er hind leg and 'old it away."

Tony stripped off her riding gloves and stuffed them in her pocket, then she took off her coat and approached the rear end of the cow. As she held the milk cow's hind leg she saw with horror that cow manure was smeared across her riding breeches. She soon forgot about it, however as she watched the miracle of birth. The cow lowed, then a huge skin containing a calf was deposited into Joe's hands. He quickly pulled the skin from the baby calf's face and head so that it could breathe, then rubbed down its wet, sticky skin with some hay.

Joe was grinning as he said, "Ye can put 'er leg down now. Sorry ye got covered wi' shit, sir."

Tony glanced down at her breeches, bemused. "Shit's supposed to be lucky isn't it? We could use some, I think."

"Aye, well, sorry fer yer trouble up at t'house."

"I came to ask what was needed, but I can see for myself one of the walls is crumbling. I'll see that it's mended, Joe, and some new partitions put in. When was the last time this place was whitewashed?"

"I've 'ad no whitewash fer two, three years."

"I'll get you some and some long-handled brushes."

"Will ye help put it on t'walls?" Joe laughed.

"By God, I see where Lizzie gets her cheek. Don't push your luck, Joe," Tony said good naturedly.

On the ride back to the Hall she felt her spirits rising. For once she had accomplished something. It amazed her that everyone accepted her as Anthony. A casual attitude and a bit of coarse language, and all assumed she was a male.

On the way upstairs to change her riding breeches she encountered Mr. Burke. "I just helped deliver a calf," she said proudly.

"Good for you, my lord."

"Oh, by the way, do you know what James meant when he handed me a guinea and told me it was my winnings?"

"His father is a turf accountant. Anthony bet on the horses."

"What a shocking waste of money!" Antonia declared.

"Spoken like a female," chastized Mr. Burke.

"Oh! Well, in that case, give this guinea to James and tell him I want another that pays twenty to one."

"That's the ticket." Mr. Burke winked, graciously ignoring the pungent odor she exuded.

As Tony pulled off her boots she wondered what Adam Savage's reaction would be when Watson and Goldman presented him with the bills for the repairs to the farms. Then she shrugged. Worrying about every little thing was decidedly female. She would lose the habit, she decided firmly.

Chapter 12

The very first appointment Adam Savage made was with Watson and Goldman, attorneys at law. His friend Russell Lamb had recommended them to him. When he met both partners he shrewdly assessed their capabilities and decided to become their client.

"The first order of business will be a bank deposit," Savage said. "I've always used Lloyd's for my overseas shipping transactions, but if you can get me a better rate at Barclay's, I'll leave it entirely to your discretion. But you'd better make an appointment after hours for me to deliver the chests of gold."

Watson refrained from looking at Goldman. "Your gold is in sea chests?" he enquired.

"Yes, a dozen to be exact," Savage replied.

"Approximately how much gold does each chest contain?" Watson asked politely.

"Approximately two lakhs."

It took Watson a moment to calculate. It took Goldman less. A lakh was a hundred thousand. Indian Savage was worth two and a half million pounds in gold! The partners could not help looking at each other in awe. They bestowed a reverent moment of silence upon their most valued client before they resumed their business.

"I have a list here. Would you have your clerk provide me with some business addresses? I need a competent secretary, I need some sort of conveyance, and since people have done nothing but stare at me since I arrived, I believe I need a good tailor."

Mr. Goldman took the list and had a private word with his clerk, telling him to include only the finest establishments.

"I've had a house built at Gravesend by William Wyatt. I deposited funds he could draw upon, but I fully expect he'll be overbudget by now. I'll direct all the bills for your scrutiny. My most pressing need is a London town house. I need it today, but I'll give you until tomorrow. In the meantime, gentlemen, I am at the Savoy."

"Mr. Savage, I can see you are a plain-spoken, practical man," Goldman said. "Purchasing a house today is nigh impossible. Perhaps we could rent one if given a few days."

"My friend Russell Lamb assured me you gentlemen were most accommodating," Savage pointed out.

Mr. Watson had been wanting to broach the subject of his guardianship of the Lamb twins and saw his opportunity. "The late Lord Lamb's town house is on Curzon Street. Since you are in charge of the family's affairs, why not take advantage of it? The house is furnished and fully staffed. It will give us the time necessary to purchase a town house for you in a similarly convenient location."

"Your suggestion has merit. It is the expedient solution. I have not yet had the pleasure of my wards' aquaintance."

Mr. Watson spoke in confidence. "They are very young and, having lived in the country all their lives, are quite unsophisticated, unlike the young devils about town. Young men these days are a scandal, I can tell you. Since you were here last, mores and morals have undergone some drastic changes, but Lord Anthony Lamb will give you no problems. He is a likable, amenable young man."

Adam Savage gave him a quizzical look. "Why do I have the feeling there is more to this than meets the eye?"

Mr. Watson cleared his throat. "Well, sir, it is Lady Antonia. She came to see us after her father died, demanding to know how much money she was entitled to. When I assured her that her dowry money was in trust, she wanted to know if she could have it to live on. I informed her you were in control of her finances. She left in a bit of a huff, I'm afraid, and since then she's fallen into the habit of buying whatever she fancies and having the bills sent here for you to deal with."

"Let me see them," Savage directed.

When they were produced he flipped through them, saw most of them were for dresses, petticoats, wrappers, and other feminine knicknacks that all told came to less than a hundred pounds. A couple of the expenses were for the tenant farms at Stoke.

"Settle these out of my account. Anthony receives his allowance quarterly, I believe? It's so small, I don't know how he manages. You had better double it. I'll be visiting Stoke shortly when my most pressing business affairs allow me." Savage stood. "Well, then, gentlemen, I'll bid you good morning. You may reach me at the Curzon Street House." Mr. Goldman handed him the list of addresses and firmly shook hands.

Since Temple Bar wasn't far from the Savoy, he had walked. Now he contemplated taking a chair, but realized his long strides would get him about faster than any sedan chair on the crowded streets.

His thoughts dwelled for a moment on the Lamb twins. The girl sounded decidedly like her mother, and for that matter every other female where money was concerned. The boy, however, sounded uncomplicated and likable. He hoped they could become friends.

As Savage strode along he became aware that he was receiving a great deal of attention, but as he began to notice the people on the London streets he did his own share of staring. By Satan, what had happened to men's fashions? He was the only male on the streets who was not wearing a powdered wig. Most gentlemen seemed to be garbed in satin knee breeches, elaborately embroidered waistcoats, and high-necked shirts with flowing cravats. In Savage's opinion they looked more suited to a ballroom than a London thoroughfare. Whatever had happened to sober broadcloth?

He saw one or two men in red, high-heeled shoes and wondered why on earth they were affecting women's fashions. London had always had its share of queer individuals and eccentrics, but, Christ, every other man he passed looked effeminate and utterly ridiculous. An amazing number of young men painted their faces, wore earrings, and carried fans. Had the world gone mad while he'd been away in the Indies?

Two beaus lounged indolently outside a chocolate shop. One had butterflies embroidered across his waistcoat, while the other was a study in gold lace and full-skirted coat with a nosegay on his breast. Savage looked at him with contempt, while the beau held up his quizzing glass and shuddered at the foreign-looking giant with the long black hair.

Savage eventually dragged his eyes from the men and assessed the women. Earlier there had been only poorer women in striped dimity, but at midday fashionable ladies began to appear in gowns dripping with Valenciennes lace and towering powdered wigs decorated with flowers and birds. Most had a footman or other servant to carry their packages. Women had always effected exaggerated fashions, so Savage didn't raise an eyebrow at the enormous straw leghorns they carried or the black patches that drew attention to a woman's eyes or lips. However, when he saw a lady of high fashion with a black boy in her wake, carrying a chained monkey, he felt a rage within himself that such practices were not forbidden in a supposedly civilized country.

Back at the Savoy, Savage penned a note to Lord Lamb informing him that he was back in England and asking his permission to make use of the Mayfair town house until he could acquire his own. It was merely a polite formality; he would have moved in long before the letter would be delivered to Stoke. He concluded the note by informing his ward that he would visit Lamb Hall the following week.

Fenton, the butler at Curzon Street, welcomed Mr. Savage with stiff formality, unbending a little when he realized he was a friend and neighbor of his mistress and late master from Ceylon. Fenton always asked himself how Mr. Burke would respond to any given circumstance and tried to act accordingly. The town house had a cook-housekeeper by the name of Mrs. Hogg and a young cockney maid called Dora. Both stationed themselves where they could view the odd trio from the Indies.

Dora whispered, "Coo, did ye see their fyces?"

Mrs. Hogg folded her lips in a distinct line of disapproval and muttered, "Heathens! I 'ate 'em!"

Dora, who was not unattractive in a rather cheeky way, stared her envy at the dusky girl in the exotic dress. Fenton showed Mr. Savage to the master bedchamber, but was at a loss regarding the other two. He noted the immaculate white and the turban with the ruby and thought perhaps John Bull was a visiting prince, and the lady his wife or concubine or whatever females were to Hindu princes. To be on the safe side, Fenton assigned them separate chambers and was relieved when Mr. Savage looked pleased and pressed a guinea into his hand.

"There will be trunks and luggage arriving from my ship later today. John Bull will take charge of it." Adam decided to have a word in private with the servants to smooth the way for John Bull and Kirinda, whom he knew would be like fish out of water until they acclimatized. "I'll come down and meet the staff." He picked up Rupee's cage and Fenton led the way downstairs.

Savage decided the best place for the mynah was in the entrance hall where the floor was sensibly tiled and could be easily cleaned up. Then he went into the kitchen and introduced himself.

"My people from Ceylon will no doubt seem strange to you. My man is used to directing a large staff and may come across as high handed. I would ask all of you to do everything in your power to be accommodating, and if any difficulties arise, bring them directly to me without hesitation."

Mrs. Hogg eyed him apprehensively. He looked formidable in the extreme. She knew a dominant man when she saw one, but it went against her grain to be subservient to foreigners.

"Difficulties, sir?" she questioned.

"Perhaps I am courting trouble where there will be none," he said affably. "The only area where I can foresee difficulty will be with the food."

Mrs. Hogg's mouth formed a grim line. None had ever dared find fault with her cooking in the past.

"In Ceylon the food is highly spiced and we eat a lot of fruit and vegetables. When I lived in London years ago, the only vegetable I recall being offered for consumption was turnips, which I loathe. I would consider it a favor if you would take my man shopping for food supplies and allow him leeway in your kitchen to prepare his native dishes."

Mrs. Hogg would have refused, if she had dared.

"I'll be gone on business most of the day. Thank you for your cooperation."

After he left there was an ominous silence, then all three started talking at once. Fenton, feeling rather foolish that the man he had thought a prince was nothing more than a valet, said, "Well, I for one shall leave everything to his own servants."

Mrs. Hogg said, "I'll not tolerate interference in my own kitchen. I 'ate foreigners!"

Dora, her imagination running riot, said, "Ees one 'o them nybobs. I bet she's out of 'is 'arem!"

Mrs. Hogg who had purchased turnips only that morning, spent the next half hour banging about her pots and pans. Suddenly a voice screeched, "Sodom and Gomorrah!" She ran to the hall to see who was uttering blasphemy.

"Wot's that?" she demanded of Dora.

"It's their bird."

"I 'ate birds. Well, it's not stoppin' 'ere with its shameful language. I'll put it in the cellar!"

Dora was filled with curiosity about the new inhabitants. On pretense of dusting she went upstairs to listen at one of the doors and peep through the keyhole. John Bull chose that moment to open it. Seeing the girl upon her knees, he wondered at the custom. "Are you praying?" he asked.

"Prying?" she repeated in broad Cockney.

"I did not accuse you of prying, though I see clearly now that was your intent."

"I wasn't prying!" Dora denied.

"Now you add lying to the offense of prying. Why are you staring at my head?"

Dora sniffed and decided an offense was the best defense. "Why do ye wear that thing round yer 'ead?"

John Bull drew himself up and wondered how to explain to this female who was obviously of the lower orders. "It is my uniform. I wear it for the same reason you wear that rag on your head!"

"Rag?" Dora exclaimed, very much offended. She was wearing next to her best cap. "My caps aren't rags. This one is linen an' I even 'ave lyce."

"Lice?" John Bull looked horrified. "You have lice?" That explained why she covered her hair with the hideous cap!

"I do," asserted Dora proudly.

"Do not come any closer. You are unclean."

"Unclean!" she shrieked.

"You are dismissed. Shoo, shoo."

"You can't dismiss me . . . ye only came 'ere todye!"

"I did not come to England to die, I came here to live!" He went down to the kitchen and encountered the well-rounded cook. "Permit me to introduce myself. I am John Bull."

"If you're John Bull, I'm the Queen o' Sheba," she declared.

"Sheba? Then you are not the pig woman?" he asked, slightly confused.

Dora tittered as Mrs. Hogg turned purple. "Pig woman? Are you making fun of my name?" she demanded.

"No, no, madam. I assure you I am serious."

"I'm Mrs. Hogg to you. I demand respect in my kitchen. I 'ate interference."

"I have no intention of interfering with you, madam, or the female with the lice. I came for a piece of fruit for the master's mynah, as it has not been fed today. Where is the bird?"

"I 'ate it!" Mrs. Hogg asserted.

John Bull went a little pale. "You ate it?" he asked in disbelief. "The master loved that bird."

"Well, I 'ate it. Down it went and down it stays!"

"I am wordless," he said solemnly.

"Brainless, ye mean."

"I could say something nasty, but I recline!" John Bull said, quitting the kitchen with his dignity intact, and retreating upstairs for the remainder of the day.

Before Savage left the house he received a note from Mr. Watson advising him of a house that might suit, but before he went to his solicitors he decided to visit the Saville Row tailor they had recommended. He felt slightly uncomfortable as he stepped into the haute monde establishment. He had never been inside a gentlemen's outfitters before. In his youth his clothes had been secondhand and in the Indies a tailor came to his ship or the plantation.

The men serving in the shop were out-and-out snobs who showed contempt for anything that was not the height of fashion, but when they discerned that money was no object, they fawned upon him. They let it be known that they dressed the Prince of Wales and would transform Adam Savage from a gauche colonial to a nonpareil. It was at this moment they learned Indian Savage had a mind and a will of his own.

He ordered two dozen white shirts and neckcloths of the finest material but plainest design. He was measured for coats in blue, claret, and black superfine and sober waistcoats in slightly contrasting colors. He ordered breeches that fit the leg well, trousers that buttoned at the ankle, and half a dozen pairs of buckskins. They sold him riding gloves and driving gloves, but could not talk him into the new dog-skin gloves that were all the rage. He purchased a beaver hat but were scandalized when he refused every tricorn they showed him as well as the wigs to wear beneath them. They told him he would never be acceptable to society if he insisted upon wearing his own, unpowdered locks. They finally persuaded him to be fitted for black satin for evening wear, but no amount of coercion on their part could talk him into white "inexpressibles." He bought a top hat, a cape, and even silk stockings, but laughed in their faces when their bootmaker suggested high heels.

He was measured for dress boots, Hessians, and top boots to wear with his buckskins, but insisted they all be black. He left them shaking their heads. They had done their best to explain that to be dressed well nowadays was far from being well dressed, and that fashion had become a battle between taste and gaudiness.

When Savage called at his solicitors they told him of a town house that was for sale not far from the Lamb house.

"I prefer a house in the city. It's much more convenient for business. I thought somewhere handy to the banks and the East India Company on Leadenhall Street."

Both Watson and Goldman were aghast. Such an unfashionable address would be a handicap, they assured him. A man of his stature must buy in Mayfair. It was an unfortunate fact of life, but a man was judged by his address.

Savage agreed to view the town house in Half-Moon Street, then hurried off to buy himself a carriage. He selected a coach that would quickly get him from London to Gravesend on the new turnpike and a fine pair of matched bays to pull it. He couldn't resist buying a light perch-phaeton reputed to go thirty miles an hour if you had the right cattle with enough stamina to keep up the pace, so before he left the area he picked out a pair of high-stepping blacks and didn't bat an eye when his bill was tallied at over three thousand pounds.

With unflagging energy he made his way to Leadenhall Street, where the East India Company had its headquarters. As well as the lease he had with them for Leopard's Leap, he owned a substantial number of shares. Inside, the largest chamber with a round skylight and balcony was called the "courtroom." Savage learned there was to be a meeting of shareholders held the following week and he made a mental note to attend.

He turned as a friendly voice spoke behind him. "I can see you are not long back from the Indies. I need advice on my investments and in return perhaps I can give you some about London. It's probably changed a great deal since you were last here."

He offered his hand to a square-faced gentleman about his own age. "Adam Savage, returned this week from Ceylon."

"Now, where have I heard that name?" The man introduced himself as Cavendish, but when the men who passed by nodded and murmured, "Devonshire," Savage realized he was conversing with the Duke of Devonshire. They struck up an immediate acquaintance, each recognizing that they shared similar qualities. Both were no-nonsense mens' men with good heads for business and a knack for garnering more than their fair share of this world's goods.

They touched on many things in the short time they spoke, including politics. "We need men like you in the house," Devonshire declared.

"I have no seat," replied Savage, stating the obvious.

"A bribe of a few paltry pounds can obtain you a seat in the Commons," Devonshire enlightened him.

Savage tucked the information away.

"We're having a dinner party at Devonshire House next week. I'll get Georgiana to put you on the guest list. Do come. Half the people will be friends of my wife and the Prince of Wales, but I assure you I've invited some intelligent people too. James Wyatt, the architect, and Pope, the writer-philosopher fellow. I could invite Warren Hastings, the ex-Governor from India, if you like."

"I already know two of those gentlemen. Wyatt has designed a house for me in Gravesend that I haven't even seen yet."

"That's where I heard your name, of course!" Devonshire said, thoroughly pleased with making his acquaintance.

"It will be my pleasure to come," Adam accepted. "By then I should be in possession of more civilized attire."

Savage did not return to the house in Curzon Street until it was time for dinner. Upstairs, both John Bull and Kirinda met him with woebegone looks. They had laid out fresh linen for him, but felt shame that the master would have to wash with water in a jug and bowl.

"What is amiss?" he asked John Bull.

"I have two terrible things to relate that will greatly disturb you, Excellency. The servant girl has lice. I would not let Kirinda go downstairs for fear of contamination."

"How did you discover this, John Bull?"

"She told me herself. She said that was why she covered her hair with that hideous cap."

Savage assumed he'd again gotten hold of the wrong end of the stick and asked calmly, "And the other thing that will disturb me?"

"The pig woman ate Rupee!" he blurted.

Savage bit his lip to keep from laughing. Though Mrs. Hogg was likely guilty of greed, he doubted the scrawny mynah had whetted her appetite. "I take it you did not integrate well with the staff," he said dryly. He looked at Kirinda. "Have you eaten today?"

She lowered black lashes over liquid eyes and shook her head.

Savage knew there was absolutely no point in castigating John Bull. The stubborn Tamil would have fasted a month before he would have lost face, and poor Kirinda would not even be considered.

"In that case, shall we go down to dinner?"

"Whether we are in Ceylon or England, it is unacceptable for us to dine with you, master."

"Since you insist I am your master, you must obey my orders, and I order that we go down to dinner, John Bull."

"Yes, Excellency," he replied, chastized.

In the dining room Savage said to Fenton, "Would you inform Mrs. Hogg there will be three for dinner?" He held Kirinda's chair and bade John Bull be seated.

Mrs. Hogg bustled out and almost dropped the soup tureen when she saw she would have to serve Savage's servants. The grim line of her mouth showed her resentment.

In a silken drawl Savage said, "Mrs. Hogg, I should like to apologize for leaving my mynah bird in your hall. I had no idea you would take exception. Kindly remove it to my chamber."

"Yes, sir," she replied.

"Also, Mrs. Hogg," he drawled, "I profusely apologize if John Bull addressed you as pig woman. He meant no disrespect, I assure you. It was simply a mixup of language."

"Apology accepted." Mrs. Hogg bridled, casting a scornful look in the servant's direction.

Savage's next words dropped like icicles. "Now it is your turn."

As she looked into his icy blue eyes a shiver ran down her spine. "My turn?" she questioned.

"Yes, your turn. You will apologize for your disgraceful treatment of this man and woman. You left them without food and drink all day, simply because the color of their skin is different from yours."

Mrs. Hogg's face turned motley purple. "I apologize," she muttered, having little choice.

Savage's silky voice returned, but his blue eyes remained glacial. "Mrs. Hogg, if what I smell coming from your kitchen is turnips, I suggest you save them for your own delectation and serve us something a little more appetizing."

Mrs. Hogg thwarted was not a pretty sight. She disappeared into her sanctum and did not return. In a few moments Dora appeared to serve them dinner. Three pairs of eyes converged upon her cap. It was lace. Adam Savage's eyes brimmed with amusement. "Very pretty," he murmured, watching the corners of her mouth turn up with pleasure.

Chapter 13

With the invaluable help of Messrs. Watson and Goldman, Savage's gold was deposited, a male secretary by the name of Sloane was engaged, and an offer made for the town house in Half-Moon Street.

When the post was delivered there was the promised invitation for the dinner party at Devonshire House and also a reply from Stoke. Savage tore it open, then scanned the page of beautiful writing from Lord Lamb.

Dear Mr. Savage:

Thank you for your note informing me of your arrival in England. I extend the hospitality of Curzon Street for as long as you may need it. I regret to inform you that Lamb Hall is in mourning and we are not receiving at the moment. Should the need arise to contact me, you may do so through Watson and Goldman, attorneys at law.
Anthony Lamb.

Savage realized Russell's children would be in mourning because of their father's death, but it was months past and no fit reason for refusing to receive him at Lamb Hall. The curt note told him plainly that his wards wanted him to keep his distance. What were they up to? The note only served to precipitate a visit to Stoke sooner than Savage had planned.

He spoke with John Bull. "I have to leave London immediately for a few days, but that creates a dilemma. I know you have no desire to remain in this house without me, so the only alternative seems to be to take you both to the house at Gravesend. I planned on letting you choose the servants you will need to staff Edenwood, but at the moment there is no time for that."

He explained further. "The house is unfurnished and without servants, but perhaps you can make do for a few days."

John Bull, eager to occupy his own domain, replied, "Once we arrive, Excellency, it will not be without servants. A mat upon the floor will suffice."

Savage knew that John Bull meant exactly what he said. "I don't believe we'll have to resort to such Spartan measures, but thank you." As an afterthought he decided to take along his new secretary. The things he would have to deal with would be unorthodox, but it would be a damned good test to see how he coped.

Savage decided to drive his own carriage and the team of bays. Kirinda sat inside with most of the luggage, while John Bull rode one of the Arabs that Savage had brought from Ceylon. Jeffrey Sloane sat next to his new employer as they bowled along the new turnpike, admiring his skill with the horses. He also made notes as Savage gave him instructions. "I've never seen the house, other than in my mind's eye," Savage told him, "so if the place is not yet habitable, we'll put up at an inn. As I see it, the most pressing things you'll have to acquire are fodder for the horses, food for yourselves, and utensils to cook it in. Then, of course, you'll need beds and linen. Everything else can wait. Let John Bull select whatever he wants. He has an unerring eye for choosing the best. You will be in charge of the purse strings, however. John Bull tends to haggle for everything and I don't wish to offend the merchants of Gravesend before they've even seen me."

As Adam Savage approached Edenwood, he experienced a strange sense of coming home. As the carriage emerged from a stand of oaks, the magnificent house rose up before him in all its splendor. It was the culmination of his every hope and dream. He pulled the horses to a halt outside the stables and strode up the drive that led to the front entranceway. He needed to be alone while he viewed the house for the first time. As he moved from room to room, drinking in as many details as he could, he fell hopelessly in love. He took the circular staircase two steps at once and by the time he had stepped out on his bedchamber balcony atop the west portico he had surrendered up his heart.

Wyatt was a master, a genius. It would be a labor of love to furnish Edenwood. Though it would take time, he vowed to select each and every piece to beautify and enhance this perfect setting. Savage wanted to linger, to look and touch and breathe in every last detail, but duty called him. He knew he must carry on the other twelve miles to Stoke to meet the twins he had begun to think of as his son and daughter. That he had Edenwood to return to was a comforting thought.

Leaving his people to cope, as he knew they could, Savage mounted the Arab that John Bull had ridden and made his way to Stoke. He was struck by the remoteness of Lamb Hall. It was a lovely, warm country hall with a couple of tenant farms, but Stoke itself was just a rustic village. The Hall sat isolated on the edge of the Medway, just before it opened into the sea. It was a lovely place to bring up young children, but rather removed from the world for a youth of Anthony Lamb's age, thought Savage.

Antonia saw the dark, powerful man astride the black horse as she glanced through the front window. She knew without being told who it was. Panic arose in her. "Roz! He's here!" she cried, taking the stairs two at a time in hasty retreat. "Get rid of him!"

She now occupied Anthony's chamber and she flung herself into a chair by the window where she would be able to see the unwanted visitor take his leave. She picked up her book, then set it unread upon her knee as her mercurial thoughts flashed about and her heart beat wildly with trepidation.

"Oh, God, Tony, why did you have to leave me to face him on my own?" she whispered accusingly. It had been almost two months since he had been lost. In her mind she was always careful to think of Tony as "lost" rather than "drowned." She recalled how her brother had resented having a guardian to answer to, while she herself had had an insatiable curiosity about the man in Ceylon and the stately home he was having built.

Good God, what had possessed her to make all those extravagant and extremely costly suggestions to improve Edenwood? She'd done it from rancor. Since she had been deprived of money to spend, she had spent his, and with a lavish hand. Of course that had all happened before the boating accident while she thought their guardian in far-off Ceylon. Now she was masquerading as her twin brother and Adam

Savage was a very real, flesh-and-blood authority figure who must be faced.

One glimpse of the powerful, dark-visaged man told her she had behaved idiotically. Only a fool would deliberately anger the man who had control of her life and finances until she became of age, and he did not look like a man who suffered fools gladly. Her heart sank as she realized she had no choice but to face him, but, oh, please God, not today.

Mr. Burke opened the door and took the man's measure. Savage had no calling card, but in a deep voice he introduced himself to the majordomo and told him he was come to see Lord Anthony Lamb.

Roz came forward to greet him. "Good day, Mr. Savage, I am Rosalind Randolph, Anthony's grandmother. Won't you come in?" She exchanged a surprised look with Mr. Burke that told him Savage was nothing like she had expected. As she led the tall, dark man into the sitting room her heart did an erratic little dance at the impact of his dramatic looks. His face told her he probably had a sinister past and that his reputation with women would be scandalous. He was a man to be reckoned with. A devilishly attractive scoundrel.

Adam Savage's penetrating blue gaze noticed every detail of the attractive older woman. This was where Eve had gotten her elegance, yet he could see Rosalind had been far more beautiful than her daughter. He waited until she sat down then took a seat opposite her. Without preamable he said, "Lady Randolph, I came to bring you words of comfort on my first visit. Your daughter is recovering well from the shock of Lord Russell's death. She is a practical woman and knows it is better this way than having Russell linger for years as an invalid."

"Thank you for news of my daughter, Mr. Savage. Eve has a resilience others would envy."

Savage knew immediately that Rosalind was a shrewd woman. "From the moment I knew I was returning to England, I looked forward to meeting Antonia and Anthony."

Suddenly a wedge of grief choked Rosalind's throat and she had to fight back the tears. The man before her looked as strong as the Rock of Gibraltar and she had an overwhelming urge to tell him of their great loss. "Mr. Savage, we have had another bereavement. I'm afraid you will never be able to meet my granddaughter, Antonia."

Savage was shocked. The note he'd received said they were in mourning, but he'd had no idea there had been another death. Dear

God, when Eve learned she had lost her daughter, she would be distraught. His heart went out to the brave lady before him. "I am saddened by the loss, but when I think of your loss, madam, I am humbled. However did it happen, if you can bring yourself to speak of it?"

The note of compassion in his voice almost undid her, but she recounted the storm and the sailing accident with touching composure.

"You never found her body?" he asked.

Roz shook her head. "It was almost two months ago, so all hope is gone, I'm afraid. I have accepted it; I had no alternative," she said sadly.

"You are very brave. Courage is a quality I supremely admire."

"Thank you, Mr. Savage. Lord Lamb has suffered such a deep loss, however, he is still withdrawn. Twins are bonded closer than other siblings, and it will be a long time before Anthony is back to normal, I'm afraid. He asks not to be disturbed today."

"Lady Randolph, it sounds like he is already disturbed. I am most anxious to meet him, now more than ever."

"Do you think that wise, Mr. Savage?" Roz asked, hoping to keep him from pressing the point. She hoped in vain.

"I do think it wise. He has been without the strong guidance of a father for too many years, in my opinion. It is wrong to leave him alone in his grief. This place is so isolated, he may never shake off the melancholy. Something or someone must fill the void. I believe I can help do that. He should be kept busy, don't you agree?"

How could she honestly argue with such logic? She wanted to protect Antonia, but at the same time she knew instinctively that Adam Savage was a positive force who would not be denied. Moreover, he had a strength that they could all draw upon.

"With your permission I shall go up and have a quiet word with him." It was not a question. His gaze was so direct, it had a mesmerizing effect upon her. He was a man whom Roz found impossible to deny.

When Antonia heard a knock upon the door she assumed it was Mr. Burke come to tell her the coast was clear. "Come in," she called, then her eyes opened wide in disbelief at the swarthy man who entered the chamber. All her preconceived ideas of her guardian were washed away in an instant. In all her life she had never seen a being who looked like this one. First, he was larger than other men, filling the door frame with his powerful body and wide shoulders. His hair was the blue-black color of a raven's wing and he had an abundance of it, clubbed back and falling below his shoulders. His face was tanned a deep mahogany and in startling contrast his eyes were a light, piercing blue.

A scar cut into his face from one nostril down through his top lip, but it did not detract in any way from his appearance. Instead it bestowed upon him a fatal attraction. He looked as if he came from another world, which indeed he had, but he looked more alien than that. He looked like a god who had just stepped down from Olympus.

Adam Savage's preconceived ideas of Anthony Lamb were instantly erased. The tall, slim boy who jumped up in alarm looked so unmanly, so much younger than his near seventeen years, Adam felt deep disappointment.

"Tony? I'm Adam—Adam Savage. I'm so very sorry for your loss." He saw the boy's dreamy eyes fill with tears and knew it was a time for strengthening words. "I know how close you were to your twin, but if your sister could see you now, she would vigorously protest your falling into a decline over her. I am a blunt man, so I shall be plain with you. I have learned that Death is a part of life and must be accepted. In my experience the sooner the better. There are many ways to deal with your situation, some of them healthy, some of them decidedly unhealthy. My advice is to put up a brave front. When you think of your twin, think of the happy times you shared. And from now on be determined to live life to the fullest. It is incumbent upon you now to live for two, don't you think?"

Antonia was furious. How dare he walk in uninvited and issue his orders? It was all so cut and dried to him. Her twin was dead and so she must get on with life. Tears clung to her long, dark lashes, clumping them into spikes as she looked deeply into his ice-blue eyes. She thought him the coldest, most cutting human being she had ever met. Well, if he liked plain speech, she would accommodate him.

"I was prepared to hate you," Tony said bluntly, "but hatred is such an alien emotion to me, I find I cannot do it." Tony stuffed her hands into her trouser pockets. "I shall have to settle for detesting you instead."

"Oh, do try to hate me. It is such a strong, manly emotion, it will give you a little backbone," Savage said cuttingly. *Christ, he's too pretty to piss,* Adam thought angrily. Tony Lamb was a prime example of the unfairness of life. The spoiled youth had not only been born to privilege and a title, but the gods had seen fit to gift him with exceptional beauty. Adam felt a stab of remorse at his unworthy thoughts. Because his own face was ruined didn't give him the right to resent this lad simply because he had perfect features. He sighed. "Let's try to endure each other."

"It will take a considerable effort on my part. I think you totally insensitive to my pain," Tony said.

"You think I'm a stranger to pain?" Savage mocked lightly.

"I don't know what you expect of me," Tony said.

"I expect you to bear it with the strength of a man rather than the grief of a child."

His words made Tony ashamed of her tears, and since she was masquerading as Anthony, she blushed to think she had let this guardian see Lord Lamb weep.

Adam saw the down upon the pretty face and was secretly appalled at how effeminate he was. For the first time he felt anger toward his late friend Russell. Why couldn't he have taken his son with him to the Indies? He had been left with only a grandmother and a sister for companions. He had been totally deprived of male role models. Savage's resolve hardened. By Christ, he would make a man of him!

"Your father was my dear friend, but I fault him for not giving you the opportunity of experiencing the Indies. You'll have to be strong, you know, for your mother's sake. She may go to pieces when she hears about Antonia."

Tony had not written to her mother. She kept hoping Anthony would turn up, and neither she nor Roz wanted to put the deception they had concocted down on paper.

Adam Savage took a chair and stretched his long legs out before him. Tony perched on a corner of the desk and swung a booted foot. She studied the toe of her boot for a moment, then lifted her eyes to his. "I haven't told mother and I don't intend to." Implicit in the words was the message that Tony didn't want Savage to tell her either. "She is half a world away. Why break her heart?"

"That's a very noble sentiment, but you cannot shield her from the truth indefinitely. Eve will find out sooner or later."

"In this case I'd prefer it to be later rather than sooner," Tony said bluntly, needing to impose her will on this point at least.

Savage spread his powerful hands. "The decision is yours. I shall respect it."

"Thank you, Mr. Savage."

"Please, call me Adam." He picked up the book that had fallen to the rug when he came in. "What are you reading?" He saw that it was a novel by Samuel Richardson entitled *Pamela: or Virtue Rewarded.* Tony flushed slightly. "It's the story of a servant girl who resists the improper advances of her mistress's son and so he marries her."

Savage gave a sharp bark of laughter. "Try Henry Fielding's *Adventures of Joseph Andrews.* 'Tis a parody on this very book, about a virtuous footman who resists the improper advances of his mistress. It's a rollicking adventure among the alehouses and chamber pots!"

Tony was not shocked by his frank, easy conversation, though she realized she should be. Moreover, she made a mental note to get the book.

Savage decided if Tony was going to become his son, he was in sore need of an education. There was a world out there that would swallow this innocent whole if he didn't take him under his wing and give him a dose of worldly experience. Christ, he was willing to lay odds that Tony Lamb was still a virgin!

"I told Mr. Watson to double your allowance. I honestly don't know how you've managed on the pittance granted you."

Tony was startled. With a guardian in charge of the purse strings she imagined money would be difficult to obtain. Dear God, if he'd already been in touch with Watson and Goldman they must have presented him with the bills for the gowns and other stuff.

"I spent my last quarterly allowance on new harness for the horses. I'm afraid my money couldn't pay for things my sister and grandmother needed. Now that you've told them to give me more, I'll be able to settle the bills," she said stiffly.

Savage dismissed the idea with a wave of his hand. "Everything has been taken care of, including the farm expenses. I'd like to inspect your tenant farms. If there are any improvements you can make, I think you should get the work done. It's far less expensive in the long run to keep property well maintained than to wait until it's run down and dilapidated."

Antonia hoped that at least they could continue being frank with each other. It was hard enough to deceive him about her identity. It would be a relief if she could be truthful about all else.

"I don't know a great deal about money matters, Mr. Savage . . . Adam, but I do know I shouldn't dip into my principle."

"I'll reinvest your money at a much higher return. Unfortunately your finances haven't been handled as well as they might have been, but I'll change all that."

Tony believed him. It was clear that here was a man capable of changing the world if he put his mind to it. In spite of herself she already grudgingly admired his directness and utter confidence. She knew immediately she could learn more from this man than all the tutors she and Anthony had had over the years.

Savage reached into his pocket and pulled out a cigar case. He took out a long, slim cheroot and then a thought came to him to offer one to his ward. He was well aware that the young man had never smoked before, but here in private was a perfect opportunity for him to experience tobacco without embarrassing himself in public.

Tony, startled, shook her head, "I've never—" Her eyes met his and saw the tolerant amusement. "I've never smoked Indian tobacco, only Turkish."

"There's a first time for everything, Tony," Savage encouraged.

She felt strangely warm inside. His words were intimate and held a wealth of unspoken innuendo. Tony took the finely rolled tobacco leaves and, pretending a confidence she didn't feel, stuck it between her teeth waiting for him to light it for her.

Savage gave his ward no instructions, guessing the lad was shrewd enough to copy whatever he did. Adam lit his own first. He did it slowly, biting off the sealed end, then removing the piece of tobacco leaf with his thumb and forefinger. He struck a match, held it steadily to one end while he slowly drew on the other end with his mouth. Then he puckered his lips to blow out a cloud of fragrant blue smoke.

Tony took a deep breath and tried to hold the cheroot steady until it was lit. It shook only imperceptibly as Tony's lips pursed to draw upon it. Suddenly she felt as if her tongue was burned and stopped drawing immediately. However, when she saw the smoldering tip was in danger of going out, she drew again and got a mouthful of smoke. She almost swallowed it, realized that would be disastrous and blew it out quickly. She did not want to meet Adam Savage's eyes. Suddenly it was extremely important that he admire her. If she saw contempt in his eyes she would be mortified.

She observed his hand, watching his expert fingers handle the cigar. She followed his hand to his lips and watched him inhale. The gesture was almost negligent, yet was palpably sensual. Carefully avoiding his eyes, she again drew in smoke, savored the feel and taste of it in her mouth, then slowly, casually, exhaled, keeping her eyelids half-lowered so the smoke would not sting her eyes.

When she felt fairly competent she glanced into the pale blue eyes.

There was no contempt but neither was there admiration. His face showed that he took it for granted Tony would smoke a cigar well. They smoked in silence, each casually observing the other. Savage butted his cigar in a brass candleholder and Tony did likewise, suddenly feeling a little queasy.

"Show me the farms," Adam suggested decisively, getting to his feet.

Tony resented his takeover attitude. Obviously Savage felt her incapable of meeting the tenants' needs and thought her next to useless, but at the moment she felt worse than useless.

"All right," Tony agreed reluctantly, knowing she had to be private before she totally disgraced herself. "Ask Bradshaw to saddle Neptune for me and I'll meet you at the stables."

As soon as Adam Savage closed the door, Tony leaned against it, closed her eyes, and moaned softly. Devil take the man! It was as if he had been sent deliberately to plague her. There was something about the dominant devil that touched her pride. Not for the crown jewels would she let him know she had never smoked before.

For one awful moment she thought she was going to be extremely ill. She barely had time to open the commode and drag out Anthony's chamberpot before she was indelicately sick. Amazingly, once she had voided the contents of her stomach, the room stopped spinning. She washed her hands and face, picked up her brother's riding crop, and walked downstairs very, very gingerly.

Tony saw the anxiety upon Roz's face as she descended. Mr. Burke stood in the hall by the front door. Concern was also etched upon his features. Tony didn't dare open her mouth. Instead she crossed her fingers and held them up to indicate so far, so good. If the Fates smiled upon her, she would carry it off.

She saw his beautiful Arab mount outside the stable but no sign of Adam Savage or Neptune. She went inside, trying not to breathe in too deeply. Usually the miasma of mingled horseflesh and manure had no effect on her; today, however, she was quite uncertain she could keep her gorge from rising.

She saw Savage and Bradshaw engaged in a lively conversation, but no move had been made to saddle Neptune. As Tony approached them, Savage picked up a saddle, handed it to her, and kept right on talking to Bradshaw. She got the message. Her guardian expected a young man of seventeen to saddle his own horse if he had any self-respect.

She groaned inwardly. Adam Savage was easily the most masculine human being she had ever encountered. He exuded strength and power. It would be the easiest task in the world for him to haul a saddle high upon a horse's back and attach the necessary riding harness. Savage was enough to make a girl feel weak at the knees. As Antonia she would have glanced at his powerful muscles, fluttered her eyelashes, and watched breathlessly as he saddled her mount for her. As Anthony she could only struggle with the damned thing herself. With resentment simmering inside her Tony swung a long leg across the saddle and, without waiting, headed through the park.

Savage caught up with her as she galloped across the fields.

"Did you bring the Arab from Ceylon?"

"Yes. I brought two, but I'm looking for more. Do you know of any decent horses about here for sale?"

Tony shook her head and said shortly, "Not with bloodlines like that." She was irritated. He knew damned well Arabs cost a fortune!

At the first farm they tethered their horses and walked about. Savage paid more attention to the animals and the farm buildings than he did to the small farmhouse. Tony introduced him to Joe Bradley and Savage asked the man a few pertinent questions. "Could you husband more livestock if Lord Lamb acquired them for you?" He listened to what the man had to say and made some suggestions. He saw two girls eyeing Tony with whispered giggles, but was concerned when the young man paid no attention to the females whatsoever. One of them summoned enough courage to say hello to Tony and sent him an unmistakably inviting glance. Tony muttered repressively, "Mary, run along, we're talking business."

Savage raised a brow. From what he remembered of seventeen-year-old youths they were walking erections; so bloody randy, they were ruled by their cocks. This pair, ripe for the plucking, apparently burned for young Lord Lamb in vain. Tony obviously thought a cock was only for pissing!

After they had inspected the second farm and were on their way back to Lamb Hall, Savage said, "If these two tenant farmers cooperated with each other, one concentrating on selective crops, the other on livestock, they could be far more productive and profitable. Harry Simpson has a son who seems ambitious. They could double their production next year. The other farmer, Bradley, has only daughters, but it would pay in the long run to get him a hired hand. You have to spend money to make money."

Tony listened to his suggestions and grudgingly saw their merit, but thinking on a grand scale came naturally to one who had unlimited resources. "Not everyone has your money," she said resentfully.

Savage glanced at Tony astride his beautiful hunter and thought him rather spoiled. Born to privilege, he had no idea what hard work, hunger, or responsibility were all about. Certainly he didn't wish hunger upon anyone, but, by Satan, it wouldn't hurt the lad to have a taste of hard work and responsibility. Savage let go of the reins and held out his calloused brown hands. "Everything I have, I got with these. I was not born to privilege." He did not need to add, *as you were.* The unsaid words were obvious. Yet it was also patently obvious that *privilege* would have been abhorrent to the man.

Tony had an immediate response. "If you had your choice of being born with money or earning it, you would choose the latter."

Savage grinned. "You see right through me."

The impact of his strong white teeth and light blue eyes against his deeply tanned face made Tony's heart skip at least three beats. She blinked a couple of times to make sure she wasn't dreaming. His attraction was magnetic, dangerously so. Already she thought of him as the *"man with everything."* She had tried to avoid meeting him, dreaded spending any time with him, counted the minutes until he would leave, and now, inexplicably, a part of her didn't want him to go. Her feelings about Adam Savage were totally and completely ambivalent.

When they dismounted at the stables, Savage removed his horse's saddle and rubbed him down. Tony followed his lead. They washed their hands in a stable bucket, then strolled together up to the Hall.

"I can't stay this time. I have a great deal of business in London and I haven't spent any time at Edenwood yet."

"Edenwood," Tony breathed reverently, a dreamy look coming into her eyes.

"It's the house I had built in Gravesend."

"Oh, I know! I've been to see it many times. James Wyatt is a master architect."

Adam Savage saw and heard the passion in the young man's voice and thought it unusual for a youth to feel so strongly about building and design. "Would you have liked to be an architect?"

"Oh, yes! I have dozens of books on the subject. It's not just exteriors that interest me, but interior design as well. London absolutely overflows with the greatest artists and craftsmen in the world. Perhaps these names mean nothing to you, having been away from England so long, but we have Thomas Sheraton, George Hepplewhite, Robert Adams, and Thomas Chippendale."

"Well, it seems we have an interest in common. My father was a cabinetmaker. He studied under Chippendale."

"Oh, how marvelous, but you speak of him in the past tense, so he cannot be alive."

Adam Savage looked bleak. "Poverty killed him before his time," he said shortly, then changed the subject. "I'm about to start furnishing Edenwood. How would you like to lend your expertise and assist me?"

Tony longed to jump at such an offer, but she hesitated over the many obvious pitfalls.

Savage saw Tony's reluctance. "Lamb Hall is lovely, but I honestly believe you need a change. You should spend time in London with young men your own age, and young women too," he added pointedly. "There is a whole world out there. Aren't you eager to experience it? When I was your age I was ready to swallow it whole!"

Tony felt Savage's contempt. She feared that he thought Anthony Lamb gutless and lacking in all manly qualities. Suddenly she was filled with an overwhelming desire. By Heaven and Hell she'd show him what sort of a man she could be!

Inside the Hall, Tony rang for Mr. Burke, gave him a most speaking look, and said, "Help me pack a bag, I'm off to London."

Roz fluttered about Adam Savage as if she were a young girl. As Tony and Mr. Burke disappeared up the stairs, Adam took Roz into his confidence.

"Lady Randolph, I think I've succeeded in dispelling Anthony's unhealthy melancholy. He's agreed to come to London to help me pick out furnishings for my new house at Gravesend."

Roz wondered if Savage was forcing Antonia, but dismissed the thought almost immediately, knowing her granddaughter's passion for Edenwood. It was highly improper for her to go off alone with him, but that couldn't be avoided without causing suspicion.

"Surely you'll stay for dinner before you set out," Roz said, playing for time.

"Thank you," he said absently, his mind elsewhere. "Lady Randolph, Anthony seems very unwordly for a young man of seventeen."

Roz bit her lip. "Well, the twins were going to London for the season, but when we got word about Russell, it seemed out of the question."

"Lord Lamb is on the brink of manhood and in my experience it does young bucks a world of good to sow a few wild oats before they settle down to their responsibilities as men. Since Russell made me Anthony's legal guardian, I feel a deep responsibility toward him."

"That's very admirable, Mr. Savage. I'm sure he'll be quite safe in your hands." Roz thought no such thing. Never had she encountered such a worldly man. She trembled for the things he might teach Antonia. Lord, what a coil! "Ah, here is Mr. Burke. Please pour Mr. Savage a drink before dinner. I'll just slip upstairs and give Anthony a message for the servants at the town house."

"Oh, Roz, I hope I can carry this off. He is the most dominant, infuriating man on earth, with an opinion on absolutely everything. He thinks my education has been sadly neglected, but, Roz, he seems quite willing to teach me things, or rather quite willing to teach Lord Lamb. I'm going to soak up everything like a sponge. He began with nothing. Everything he now has he acquired with his own two hands."

"Well," Roz teased, "he certainly has you eating out of them."

"That's not true! I've been absolutely brutal with him. I told him to his face he was cold and indifferent to my pain and that I detested him."

"And what was his reaction?" Roz asked faintly.

"He said we'd have to try to endure each other. Perhaps it would be a good idea if you slipped up to town in a couple of days."

"Oh, darling, that's a splendid idea. It's highly improper for you to be alone with him, you know."

"Oh, Roz, of course it isn't. He thinks I'm a man—well, not a man, a boy, a very green boy to be truthful."

"But you are not a male, you are a female, and Adam Savage the most spectacular man you and I are ever likely to see in this lifetime."

"God, yes, the man with everything. So you are not immune to his magnetism either?"

"I'm an old woman. You, darling, are very vulnerable. Do guard against becoming infatuated and falling under his spell. I can't believe your mother let him get away."

Antonia was shocked at her grandmother's thoughts. She tried to put herself in Roz's shoes, then her mother's, to view Savage through their eyes. The masculine features of his face looked as if they had been hewn with an ax from darkest mahogany. His long blue-black hair had a wild curl to it, making a woman long to release it from its leather thong to run her fingers through it. Tony wanted to dishevel it and learn if its texture was silky or coarsely springy. The planes of his face were broad, the nose and cheekbones prominent, the jaw square, stubborn, and bold.

His body was tall and powerful, the shoulders impossibly wide, his legs like young oaks. His hands were strong, brown, and exceedingly attractive. He had an air of supreme confidence about him that she knew did not come from being rich. It came from deep within the man. One look immediately revealed he was tenacious, resolute, determined, self-willed, unyielding, tough, and hard bitten. On top of everything else he was sinfully good looking. She suspected he was wicked and dangerous to boot. The single most riveting thing about him was his ice-blue eyes, so unexpected in that swarthy face. They could freeze a person to the spot with one glance.

She sighed heavily, realizing that through any woman's eyes, of any age, he was devastatingly, dangerously desirable and she suspected the number of women who had made fools of themselves over the man were legion.

Chapter 14

It was going dusk when the pair of riders arrived at Edenwood. Tony had not viewed the finished house, and it took her breath away. She wondered briefly what Adam Savage's reaction would be when he was presented with the bills for the costly imported marble, hand-painted tiles, and all the other expensive additions she had suggested. Then she shrugged. After all, they had been Antonia's ideas; he could hardly blame Lord Lamb.

The vast stable with the fountain for watering the horses at its center housed a magnificent pair of matched bay carriage horses, leaving dozens of empty stalls to choose from for the horses they were riding. Tony thanked the stars she had learned how to tend her own horse, actually an odd accomplishment for a lady. Savage expected a man to put his mount's needs before his own.

At the front door they were met by an exotic-looking creature in a silk sari of pale orchid. Her arms were filled with tall blue irises from the garden. She smiled shyly and bent her knee. "Welcome home, master. Edenwood is like a palace. The flowers are strange, but just as beautiful."

Savage raised her and drew her small hand to his lips. "This is Kirinda, Tony. Sometimes we call her Lotus Blossom." He watched Tony's reaction to the lovely young woman and saw that he stared with great curiosity. Adam hid a smile. If Tony wasn't aroused by the tempting female, the lad wasn't normal.

The pale marble floor that began outside was carried through the cathedrallike reception hall. The mynah bird raised his small crest at the sight of Adam and screeched, "Savage! Sinner! Hellbait!"

"This is Rupee," Adam told Tony.

"Let me guess," Tony said, laughing, "that's what you paid for him."

Savage nodded. "I was robbed."

Kirinda, holding a long taper, began to light the candles and lamps. She moved about so silently and gracefully, it was pleasurable to watch her. The light illuminated the creamy white marble and picked up its fine golden veins. James Wyatt had chosen well.

"No Bengal tigers," Tony said lightly. "I thought all Englishmen who went to the Indies were great white hunters."

Savage flashed him a cool look from his icy blue eyes. "I hunt from necessity. I do not take trophies."

A native man came forward in immaculate white garments with a ruby-red turban. He carried a silver tray that held two small glasses.

"This man is like my right hand. John Bull, I want you to meet Lord Anthony Lamb."

"Good evening, Excellency, good evening, my lord. I have waited many years to come to your beloved country. It is a great honor for me to meet an English Lord of the Realm." His turban touched his knees.

"Oh, please, John Bull, do not bow to me. I bow to you. You are far more accomplished than I."

"Accomplished?" he asked, astounded.

Savage watched Lord Lamb closely to see if he was being condescending.

Tony was most sincere. "Your first language cannot be English, yet you have mastered it to perfection."

John Bull glowed.

"And your wife is one of the loveliest ladies I've ever seen."

John Bull glowered.

Savage gave a bark of laughter. "Both of your observations are extremely wide of the mark."

John Bull ignored Savage's remark and launched into a reprimand. "We were not expecting you, Excellency. The food I prepared is adequate for you, but unfit for the Lord of the Realm. Moreover, we do not have enough beds."

"Christ, John Bull, you're stiff as a starched shirt. Tony and I don't give a shit about food or beds. We'll sleep on the floor. Tony is to be treated as one of the family. Where is Jeffrey Sloane?"

"Your secretary is very busy with his papers. He is working upstairs in the library. I do not wish to cast my shadow upon his character, Excellency, but I must tell you that he pays whatever price a merchant asks for his goods."

"Thank you for sharing that with me, John Bull. Tony, make yourself at home. I'll just go up and speak with Sloane, then we'll have the grand tour."

"You must forgive the master. He has a great disliking for formality, but I have met your mother and think the memsahib would be outrageous if she knew the Leopard expected you to sleep on the floor."

"I haven't seen my mother for over ten years. What is she like?" Tony asked rather wistfully.

"Ah, very very beautiful. Like an English queen."

Tony smiled. Obviously John Bull hadn't seen the Queen. She realized, however, that her mother's legendary beauty was real.

"Why do you call him the Leopard?"

"It is what his people in Ceylon call him. His plantation is named Leopard's Leap."

"How fascinating! Will you tell me all about it, John?"

"I will try, Lordship, but it is your country which is fascinating."

"We will exchange information. I have some books at Curzon Street you'll enjoy."

John Bull rolled his eyes. "I made a very bad impression at Curzon Street. I called your Mrs. Hogg, pig woman."

Tony laughed delightedly. "Now that you mention it, she does have rather porcine features and manners to match. People do sometimes resemble their names, like Lotus Blossom. I'm sorry that I assumed she was your wife."

"A lotus is a common water lily," he disparaged. "She is the master's body servant."

Tony blushed at her own ignorance. What a cod's head she was. The exotic creature was Adam Savage's concubine! She felt an inexplicable stab of jealousy. Her eyes were drawn up the elegant staircase. Clearly here was another who resembled his name.

As Savage descended she knew why his people called him the Leopard. Suddenly she felt shy. She turned to John Bull instinctively. "For what it's worth, I offer you my friendship."

"Ah, Lordship, that would be worthless to me!"

"He means priceless," Adam said quietly, most grateful that young Lamb was tolerant and unbiased.

Tony laughed outright. "I never realized how ridiculous the English language was. Priceless and worthless ought to be synonyms."

"There's just enough light left to take a look at the grounds. I'll postpone the grand tour of the house until daylight. I don't want to miss a detail."

Savage led the way into the gardens, where paths and flower beds had been carefully laid out. They strolled across daisy-strewn grass that would soon be turned into manicured lawns. They came upon a natural stand of yews that had been thinned to create a yew walk.

"This is splendid," Adam said. "How I have missed the trees."

"But surely a plantation is nothing but trees," Tony said.

"You mistake me. The Indies has magnificent trees. Mahogany, ebony, teak, satinwood, are the things that drew me there in the first place. Then at the plantation we use dadap and eucalypti to shade the delicate tea plants. I meant I missed English trees."

As they emerged through the other side of the yews a small lake stretched before them with a pair of black swans gliding across the surface. Tony caught her breath at the beauty of it. "Is Ceylon as lovely as this?"

"Every bit as lovely in its own exotic, untamed way."

Darkness had begun to fall. Everywhere was deeply shadowed. The navy-blue sky and black trees were reflected in the lake and in the hush that had fallen she could hear the frogs and, farther off beyond the densely wooded park, the flowing of the River Thames. Suddenly the call of a night heron came hauntingly across the water and they lifted their heads in unison to see if they could spot it.

Adam's deep voice stole to her and Antonia thought it sounded like dark velvet. "At Leopard's Leap at dusk I would stand at the edge of the lake to watch the day transform into night. As the sun sinks the buffalo come up out of the cooling water and swarms of monkeys scold and chatter at them from low-hanging tree branches. Clouds of gnats hover over the water and as the fish jump to feed, they in turn are snapped at by the crocodiles. The little monkeys are so damned cheeky, they get as close as they can to the reptiles, daring the crocs to eat them for dinner. Sometimes they do. The moths are more numerous than butterflies, some of them a foot across. The night scents are heady enough to steal away your senses . . . jasmine . . . camphor . . . pomegranate. The air is filled with the music of the night—the flutter of a million bat wings, the banshee cry of the jackal, the low growls of jungle cats. If I was patient enough to wait until the moon rose I often caught a glimpse of a leopard come to drink. They have this trick of appearing out of nowhere, then in the blink of an eye they disappear."

The brilliant picture he painted with his words told Tony that he loved Ceylon.

"You miss it."

"Yes, but not nearly as much as I missed England."

It was a moment filled with magic. He had taken her with him to another time and place. It was as if they were alone in the universe. She wanted him to touch her so badly, it made her weak. He stood slightly behind her and she wanted to lean back against him to feel his strength. She imagined him kissing her, very gently, on the nape of her neck. She shuddered involuntarily.

Something swooped past them. "That was a bat!" Tony exclaimed, emerging from her fantasy. "Are the bats in Ceylon the same as ours?"

Savage laughed softly. "No, they are fruit bats. They gorge themselves on *kong*-tree fruit until they fall down dead drunk. They know no moderation. Perhaps that's the difference between the two worlds. England is moderate. In Ceylon everything is gloriously immoderate."

Back inside the house Savage's words were borne home as Kirinda came forward and asked softly, "Are you ready to be bathed, master?"

"Yes." He turned to Tony. "Will you join us in the bathing pool?"

Tony had never been quite so shocked in her life and the horror showed on her face.

"You are staring at me like I was the bloody whoremaster of Malabar. It is customary in the East to bathe, not simply to wash. It can be extremely pleasant. I'd like you to experience many things from different lands. Surely, Tony, you are not so narrow minded that you are not open to new experiences?"

"Of course not," Tony said faintly. "It's just that I wouldn't dream of spoiling what must be an intimate ritual between you and Lotus Blossom."

Ridiculous as it seemed, Savage had begun to doubt the lad had ever been naked with a female. "Has all the stuff we brought from the ship been unpacked yet?" he asked Kirinda. "Give him one of my robes and show him to another bathing room. John Bull simply won't feed us if we are unclean."

I wouldn't dream of spoiling what must be an intimate ritual between you . . . how in the name of God had she conjured such a phrase? She tried desperately to push away pictures of the "intimate ritual," but didn't quite succeed. Tony honestly had not thought about what he would look like beneath his clothes. Now, however, her mind began to undress him. Frantically she tried to block the pictures from her mind, but they only became clearer and more insistent. What must those wide shoulders look like without his shirt? Undoubtedly he would be thick with muscle. Was his chest as deeply tanned as his face and hands? Her mind refused to form a picture of a pale Adam Savage. Somehow she knew he would be bronzed. He would be covered by a devastating pelt of black hair too. She simply knew it. She had already glimpsed the thick saddle muscles of his thighs clad in skintight breeches, so it took only a little imagination to envision his legs bared.

Antonia had never seen a naked man. Of course she knew the male of the species had a sex thing, vastly different from her own private parts, but her imagination did not try to conjure it. She was truly too innocent to picture him below the belt. Her mind's eye saw him in the bathing pool with the naked Lotus Blossom and her cheeks burned so hotly, she closed her eyes praying for a measure of composure. In the span of one day since she had met Adam Savage she had had more disturbing thoughts regarding men than she had had in her entire life before. What on earth was the matter with her?

It was as if her outwardly male appearance had turned her thoughts and her body ultrafemale. Her breasts and her mons were suddenly sensitive in the extreme. She blushingly admitted to herself that whenever Savage drew close to her, those wicked parts of her body actually tingled. Damn the dark devil to hell and back!

Tony was given a choice of robes by the beautiful young Sinhalese woman. One was black silk embroidered with golden dragons, the other woven from fiber that resembled fine rope in texture and color. Tony chose the latter. It was far too large, but she turned back the wide sleeves until her hands were uncovered. The robe brushed the floor when she walked, but she was quite tall and it didn't trail enough to make her trip over its hem. She bathed alone, taking as little time over it as possible. She deliberately kept her eyes from her own body and slipped the robe over her nakedness as soon as she was dry.

The meal was delicious. John Bull served them curried lamb on a bed of fragrant saffron rice. There were strange vegetables and fruits served upon the same platters and luscious sweetmeats that tasted like almonds, dates, and coconut rolled in honey. The tea was aromatic and tasted of oranges. Tony did not need to ask if it came from Leopard's Leap.

"I can't recall when I've enjoyed food so much," Tony complimented John Bull, who smiled his joy.

"Pour us two brandies," Savage directed. He was wearing the black silk robe with the dragons. It came only to his knees, revealing his heavily muscled calves and tanned bare feet, which were more disturbing than she had pictured.

John Bull handed Tony a glass that she didn't hesitate to take. Whether she would actually drink it or not was another matter. When he served Adam he said, "Now we are in England, it is not fitting that you sleep upon the floor, Excellency."

Savage replied, "You are correct as usual, John Bull, but when I choose my bed a great deal of thought will go into it. A bed must almost be an extension of yourself. Of all the pieces of furniture in a home, a bed is the most personal and intimate. It is for sleeping and for making love. I will share it with my wife. My children will be conceived in it and perhaps even born in it. It must be pleasing to the eye, comfortable to the body, and large enough for sport. When I go to London I promise you that beds will be the first item on the agenda. In the meantime can I trouble you to roll out a couple of Indian rugs for us in the master bedchamber?"

As John Bull bowed low, a small frisson of panic arose inside Tony. He expected her to sleep in his chamber!

Savage led the way out onto the balustrade and sat down upon the stone rail. Tony copied him, setting her brandy glass down beside her. He pulled his gold case from the pocket of the silk robe and offered her a slim cigar.

"The second one won't make you sick," he promised quietly, and she was amazed at his perception. Dear God, she would have to be on her guard with this man. He was too perceptive, too shrewd. It would take only one slip for him to guess that she was a female. She must remember to swagger when she walked, lounge against furniture when she stood, and pepper her sentences with curses. Tony took a large gulp of brandy and by the grace of heaven managed not to choke. Suddenly a blood-red rose blossomed inside her chest and she began to relax to the point where she felt she was floating.

"It would have been helpful if you could have filled me in on the current mores of London, but you are so bloody unworldly, we shall have to learn together."

His voice held no censure, but spoke fact. How could she take offense at the irregular things he said to her? Tony had never met anyone like Adam Savage in her life, and yet, and yet—they sat so companionably, smoking and sipping brandy, it seemed they had always done it.

"I thought liquor was forbidden in the Indies," Tony remarked. She watched the blue smoke spiral into the darkness and his voice came, rich as velvet. "There was never a time when intoxicants were not used in the East. To a sybarite an intoxicant enhances leisure. Indian mystics use drugs to open wide the doors of perception. Hookah pipes are used to inhale scented tobacco mixed with hashish. Intoxicants are thought to heighten sensuality to full-blown sexuality. Eastern poetry and song are filled with parallels between the madness of love and the headiness of inebriation. Ivory boxes painted with poppies are commonplace. They are designed to hold opium."

The topic was so wicked, she should not listen. Yet how was she to learn unless she opened first her ears, then her mind? "Are *you* familiar with drugs?" she asked in fascinated horror.

"Unfortunately I am."

She was shocked, yet she heard the regret in his voice. "Even I know opium is unspeakably evil." She tried not to sound judgmental but couldn't help it.

"I am relieved that you know. However, try to be objective. All things under the sun are both good and bad. Used as a medicinal opiate, it can be a godsend. I wouldn't like to contemplate having my leg cut off without it."

Tony tossed her cheroot over the balustrade. "I wouldn't like to contemplate having my leg cut off at all!" They laughed together and Adam Savage stood and stretched his limbs. They strolled back into the house, deep in their own reflections.

Tony thought him a font of information, like a tutor or a parent, yet the things he told her were not the things a tutor or parent would speak of.

When they entered the spacious bedchamber Tony's thoughts were brought back to the present. How on earth would she sleep on the floor? She knew damn well Savage had proposed it to toughen up pampered little Lord Lamb. She was thankful he lit no candles.

The moonlight shining through the undraped windows showed her a thick-piled Indian rug with a tassled cushion tossed upon it. She sank down to the floor, stretching stiffly out with her arms behind her head as she had seen Anthony do. The brandy had warmed her blood considerably and she needed no blanket.

Tony's eyelids began to droop in spite of the fact that she shared the chamber with a strange man. The moment her eyes closed she curled over, hugged the cushion, and tumbled headlong into a dream.

Antonia was longing for something, she knew not what, but her longing was so intense, it was painful. She was disguised, but it was not as a man, she was disguised as a swan. A black swan. Suddenly from nowhere appeared a leopard. She glided out upon the lake thinking to escape, but the leopard swam after her. Suddenly she was transformed into a female leopard. The powerful male swimming toward her was her mate for whom she had been longing. Before he could reach her, however, the black swans turned into painted tiles, the lake became the bathing pool, and the leopard was transformed into Adam Savage.

He stood waist deep in the water, the bronzed muscles of his wide chest gleaming with iridescent droplets. He held out his hand to her. "Will you not join me?" She resisted. If she removed the robe he would know she was a woman!

His eyes, bluer than the water, compelled her. She longed to go to him. He was everything to her, teacher, father, brother, lover, protector, god. He was an all-encompassing male force she could not resist. The robe slipped to her feet and she stepped into the pool among the floating lotus blossoms.

She longed for him to enfold her in his powerful arms, where she knew nothing again could ever hurt her. Instead he began to bathe her. She cupped her breasts with her hands to shield them from the blue flame of his eyes. Gently, but firmly, he removed her hands. "There is no shame in the naked body." His voice, like rich velvet, compelled her to allow his hands to roam over her. His palm cupped a breast. She caught her breath in a gasp at the feel of his strong brown hand. Rough calluses abrased her silken skin and she found that she liked the roughness. The water was fragrantly scented, she could feel the heat from his body, but her eyes could not see his limbs beneath the surface. He washed her shoulders, her back, her breasts.

"How could you hide these from me?" he demanded.

"I lied to you," she confessed, "I am not Anthony, I am Antonia!"

His laugh was savage. "I, too, lied. I *am* the whoremaster of Malabar. I'd like you to experience many things from different lands. Surely, Tony, you are not so narrow minded that you are not open to new experiences?"

"Of course not," she said faintly.

He carried her to a massive bed in the shape of a swan. It was draped with black silk sheets embroidered with golden dragons. She knew that he, too, was naked, yet still she had not looked upon him below the waist. His powerful arms took her down to the bed with him and he pulled her to lie on top of him. Her soft breasts were crushed against the hard slab of his chest. His thighs beneath hers felt like marble. All of him was too hard, his hands, his body, his mouth.

Suddenly her eyes flew open. She realized it had been an erotic dream. Her cheek was pressed into the deep pile of the red, blue, and gold Indian rug. Her nostrils breathed in its faint scent of incense. Instead of Savage's body, it was the hard floor that crushed her soft breasts. She took a deep breath of relief and let it out on a sigh, but she was left with a strange longing that she could not dispel. Her shameful body ached for the rough touch of a man. This man.

Antonia had a great deal of trouble going back to sleep. She feared another erotic dream, yet even that was preferable to lying beside him awake all night.

Chapter 15

Sunshine streaming in through the long windows of the bare bedchamber almost blinded her the next time she opened her eyes. Someone was shouting her name.

"Tony! Come and take a look at this splendid bathing room in the daylight. Devil take it, I wager you've never seen anything to equal it!"

Tony got to her feet slowly. Every bone in her body ached. Savage, a towel wrapped about his hips, lather covering his prominent jaw, and his hand wielding a wicked-looking razor, appeared in the doorway.

"It's about time you joined the living, it's after six," Savage complained.

"Six? Judas, I thought it was at least noon." Lud, where was Mr. Burke with her chocolate? she thought longingly.

"You haven't a brandy hangover, surely? If you do, I have an infallible cure."

"No, no," Tony replied faintly, "I have a helluva hard head for liquor."

Savage's naked torso wrapped in the towel was stunning in its male beauty. Her imagination hadn't done him justice. For the rest of her life, whenever she pictured a naked man, it would be Adam Savage with a towel skimming his hips. To her horror she found herself fantasizing about what was beneath that towel.

The black pelt she had imagined was very real. Its path ran down beneath the towel in a narrowing line drawing the eyes and the senses to his secret male center. She could not picture it, but it had such a forbidden quality, it filled her imagination with wicked thoughts.

When he turned around she saw clearly that his dark tan line ended at his tapered waist. She actually saw the shallow cleft where his bottom cheeks began and it dawned on her for the first time that a man's posterior was shaped entirely differently from a woman's. His bottom cheeks were small and flat and taut. She was drawn after him like one who had been hypnotized.

The sun streamed in through the glass skylight, sending a myriad of tiny rainbows dancing across every surface. Because of the wall of Venetian mirrors, the room seemed double in size. The water in the bathing pool shimmered with such a sparkling blue-green, Tony had to narrow her eyes against its brilliant reflection.

"Look at these painted miniatures. They're exquisite," Savage enthused.

Blue herons, ibis, snowy egrets, terns, and wood ducks nesting in reeds were placed at random about the walls and inlaid in the floor. Tony saw a black swan and her dream, full blown, came flooding back to her. To cover her embarrassment she said, "The artist is Maximilian Robin in Shepherds Market."

"*Nomen est omen,* the name is the destiny," Adam remarked.

Tony could not help applying those words to him. The name Savage described this man's appearance perfectly. Was it also an indication of his nature? She watched as the ebony-handled razor sliced smoothly down his jaw. His keen eyes were on her as he asked sardonically, "Don't you shave yet?"

"S-sometimes," she lied. "I don't really need to," she added lamely.

"You never will unless you get started."

She could hear a trace of disgust in his voice.

"When I was your age I grew a beard." He opened a tooled-leather case and extracted a pearl-handled razor. "Here's a present for you. Put it to good use."

Tony took it, thinking it would come in handy for slitting Savage's throat. Reluctantly she took up the shaving soap and began to make a lather. He watched her openly until she wanted to scream at him. She had a terrible fear that if she shaved she would sprout whiskers.

She wore men's clothes, she had cut her waist-length hair, she even smoked, but she was damned if she was going to encourage a five-o'clock shadow! She dawdled, playing for time, hoping he would leave so she could rinse the lather from her face. Savage, however, was waiting to see how she handled the steel blade.

Reluctantly she picked it up and pulled the skin of her cheek taut as she had seen him do. The moment the sharp blade touched her skin, she cut herself.

"Shit!" she murmured.

Savage rolled his eyes in disbelief. "When you're finished, wipe your ears . . . you're still wet behind them," he mocked.

When he left, she pulled a hideous face after him. Just once she would like to wipe the contempt from his face when he looked at her.

John Bull had washed and starched Tony's shirt and cravat. Never had she seen linen so finely laundered. She thanked and complimented him.

"Excellency has such high standards. Edenwood needs many servants; a cook, a laundress."

"I doubt if you will find any who can equal your own skills, John Bull."

"Ah, we shall see. Today I must employ many maidens."

"Maids," Tony supplied.

"Maiden, maid, what is the difference, please?"

Savage strolled in. "A maid is a female servant. A maiden is a female with her virginity intact," he explained matter-of-factly.

John Bull held up his hands. "Maids will take me all day to find, maidens would take forever."

Adam Savage smiled at John Bull's attempt at humor and cast Tony a sideways glance.

Damn him to hellfire! She knew he was amused because he suspected Lord Lamb was still a virgin.

Breakfast consisted of fruit and sweet black coffee. While he ate, Savage discussed business with John Bull. "You don't need me along when you hire your staff for Edenwood," Adam directed. "I'll be in London at least a week before I can return."

"The house staff is my domain, but I am preferring you pick the grooms and a carriage driver."

"Done!" Savage agreed, knowing John Bull's advice was sound. "If I purchase that town house on Half-Moon Street, it, too, will need staffing. Do you trust my judgment?" Adam asked his majordomo.

John Bull nodded firmly. "You are far too shrewd to hire night flyers."

Fly-by-nights, Tony thought. Actually John Bull's English made perfectly good sense if you listened closely. She was greatly relieved that Savage was considering his own town house. Living under the same roof at Curzon Street would be most disturbing.

Savage's effect upon her kept her continually off balance. He both lured and repelled her, had her one minute wanting to kiss him, the next wanting to kill him! She told herself sternly that he must never catch her looking at him like a bitch looked at a bone. She knew she must distance herself from him.

Tony said, "You must want to see the house alone, the first time you go through all the rooms. I was here several times while it was being built."

Savage cast Tony a look of gratitude. "Go and have a look at the library. It's a masterpiece," he suggested as he strode from the breakfast room.

Jeffrey Sloane looked up from the desk as Tony entered the library. He had a preoccupied air about him, as if his mind was constantly on letters and figures. He was of middle age, but looked old before his time. His shoulders were slightly stooped and he was pale as if he never went outdoors.

Tony said, "The last time I saw this room it wasn't finished. I imagine this is one of the rooms Adams designed," she added with awed reverence.

It was paneled in a deep, rich mahogany. Two walls had floor-to-ceiling, built-in bookcases, a third wall had a magnificently carved ebony fireplace with a massive brass fender and andirons. The remaining wall had long, floor-to-ceiling windows to let in the light. The chairs were in a bottle-green Cordovan leather, the seven-foot desk had an inlaid leather top and carved claw feet. The floor was covered by a thirty-foot Indian carpet in pale green. Beneath the carpet the floor was deep green malachite stone that also served as the hearth for the ebony fireplace.

Tony drew closer to see what had been carved into the polished ebony. No fruit or flowers as she had expected, but leopards, cobras, and mongooses; elephants, monkeys, and iguanas. Her fingers could not resist tracing the exotic creatures who prowled there; the hunters and the hunted. Her hand came to rest upon an animal she could not name.

"That's a bandicoot," a deep voice informed her.

"Your people call you the Leopard because you have their knack of appearing with no perceptible approach."

"It will sharpen your reflexes and teach you never to be caught off guard," he said bluntly. "What do you think?"

"It's truly a magnificent room," she said, glancing over the brass wall-lamps and framed hunting scenes. She noticed upon closer inspection that among the fox and hare hunts was a jackal hunt. "These are actual paintings, not just prints," she commented.

"I like this one best," Savage said, pointing to a beautiful picture. "It's called *Mares and Foals* by George Stubbs. If you spot more of his paintings in London, be sure to acquire them for me. I don't have many books yet, just the ones I brought from India and Ceylon, but London has so many publishers and bookshops, there may not be enough shelves here to hold everything I want."

"It must be extremely pleasant to have enough money to acquire whatever takes your fancy."

"It is," he said enigmatically. Then he added, "If you're interested, I'll teach you how to make money."

"I am interested," Tony said eagerly, "very!"

A cynical smile touched Savage's lips. "First you have to sow some wild oats, show some spirit. Then when you are brimful of the devil and hellfire, we'll harness it and make a damned fine man of you."

Tony wanted to slap his face. He didn't even have a title, yet he was such a superior swine. She looked him up and down insolently and drawled, "You're a bit of a bastard, Savage."

"So I've been told," Adam said silkily.

Savage left his Arab at Edenwood because he had another in London. Since Tony did not keep a mount there, she saddled Neptune while Savage harnessed the bays to the carriage.

"Fasten him behind the coach, I want you to ride with me," Savage directed.

"Why?" Tony asked warily.

Savage answered the question with another question. "Have you ever handled a pair of carriage horses?"

"No," Tony said faintly.

"Then your first lesson is about to commence."

Tony shrugged. Anthony would have had to learn to handle a team and she considered herself equal to anything her twin could do. She watched Savage for the space of half an hour. When he turned the reins over to her he gave no direction, but decided to see what young Lamb could do on his own.

Her confidence grew with every passing minute. Soon they were bowling along the turnpike at quite a clip. Up ahead she saw that the road curved and she drew back on the reins to slow down the horses. The full-bloodied bays were into their stride and she wondered wildly if she had enough strength to curb them.

Savage casually handed her a pair of leather driving gloves. "Try these."

Tony quickly pulled them on and gripped the reins fiercely, bracing her booted feet and pulling back with her whole body. They slowed only slightly. The carriage leaned precariously. Inside the driving gloves Tony's hands were sweating indelicately. The horses rounded the curve and picked up speed. She was surprised he didn't snatch the reins from her and hurl a curse at her head. She cast him a wary glance and was astonished to see his eyes closed and his head leaned back in repose. She thought him a fool. She could have had them dead in a ditch!

Finally, she began to relax and when she did so, she noticed the bays were far easier to handle. She felt an urge to destroy his composure. It would be almost worth confessing her gender to wipe away his air of complacency.

Then her thoughts took another tack. She wondered if perhaps Adam Savage was man enough to teach a female the things he would teach a male. What an extraordinary thought. What was it about this man that made her think him unique? He was fashioned from a different mold. He was a law unto himself and he absolutely and totally fascinated her. As a matter of fact, she feared she was becoming infatuated. Pray God she find the cure!

Tony didn't see much of Savage the first two days they were in London. He was out attending to business and she spent one full day adding to her male wardrobe. She bought a cane with a curiously clouded amber head and she purchased some high-heeled shoes with tongue and buckle. Though most men's fashions were becoming extremely bright and flamboyant, Tony shunned them, thinking them far too effeminate. She bought half a dozen black silk Steinkirk cravats and asked the haberdasher to show her how to achieve some of the intricate knots.

Tony bought a new tiewig and a supply of powder as well as a tricorn hat. She also bought a coat with brass buttons cut in a military style. Because of all her purchases she took a chair back to Curzon Street, where Fenton helped her unpack and hang them in Anthony's wardrobe.

A lump came into Tony's throat as she saw her brother's London clothes. She touched the satin knee breeches and brocade tailcoats with a loving hand, knowing she felt very close to him whenever she put on his clothes. She asked Fenton to bring her a tray and she finally fell asleep reading Mr. Fielding's scandalous adventures of Tom Jones.

The next day Adam Savage wanted Tony to accompany him into the city. He was visiting a couple of cabinetmakers' shops to select some furniture for Edenwood. The first stop was a house in St. Martin's Lane owned by Thomas Chippendale. There were many pieces displayed in the Chinese design, but Savage's taste did not run along these lines, nor did he care much for the heavily ornamented Rococo style. As well as actual sample pieces there were dozens of design books to choose from.

Savage asked Tony if he preferred "ribbon-backed" or "ladder-backed" chairs for the dining room at Edenwood.

She bit her lip in indecision. The ladder-back was plainer, more masculine, but finally she told the truth. "My preference is ribbon-back. The style is French and exceedingly elegant. The interlocking ribbons are so beautifully curved, I don't think you'll find craftmanship anywhere in the world to compare with this."

Savage took her advice. The dining room would be done by Chippendale. He ordered twenty-four chairs and an oval twenty-foot dining table with matching sideboards and half-round serving tables. Since the dining room itself had curved walls to make the room a unique oval shape, the Chippendale table and ribbon-backed chairs would look like a match made in heaven.

It didn't take long because Savage was a decisive man who knew what he thought beautiful and what he thought hideous. Tony found her taste ran along very similar lines to his. He wanted no elaborately designed commodes or Gothic torchères. He wanted nothing decorated with intricate swags and urns. He passed up all the beds on display and exchanged a grimace with Tony over a pagoda-shaped, lacquered bedstead. Before they departed the shop, Savage bought mirrors, hall console tables, a pair of velvet-covered settees, and a small supper table with a couple of comfortable padded supper chairs.

When they left St. Martin's Lane, Savage asked Tony if he'd like to visit the tea spitters in Mincing Lane, which was in the same area as the East India Company's headquarters. When they got to Eastcheap, however, they had to push through the crowds that were following a cart on its way to Tyburn.

They gaped along with their fellow Londoners at the Yorkshire highwayman who was bandying words with the crowd on his way to be hanged. He stood in the cart beside his coffin, wearing a nosegay and bowing to the crowd of courtiers who offered him a flask of Dutch courage.

Tony stared at the well-dressed ladies and their escorts who were on their way to Tyburn for a bit of excitement. She shuddered.

"How can he make jokes when he is on his way to die?"

Savage shrugged and replied, "He must show game before the crowd." His ice-blue eyes surveyed the pretty court ladies with contempt. "The English are every bit as uncivilized as the so-called primitive cultures." He turned away. "We'll never get to Mincing Lane in this crush. Let's go and have something to eat."

Tony nodded agreement and Adam led the way. They cut down Hanging Sword Alley and stopped at a place called Jack Ketch's Kitchen. Tony viewed the tripe and trotters on display with alarm. Briefly she wondered if this place was on his list for *"making a man"* of his ward. Savage ordered them both pig's feet and as Tony watched him liberally sprinkle them with salt and malt vinegar, she realized that he was enjoying himself.

Savage grinned at the pleasurable surge of nostalgia he experienced. "I used to eat here when I was a stripling. Couldn't seem to fill my belly in those days."

"Where did you live?"

Adam pointed, "Across the river. Come on, we can walk and eat." As they sauntered down Lower Thames Street, Tony gathered her courage and began to nibble on the white, jellied trotter she held. It wasn't nearly as repulsive as she had imagined, and after a few bites she began to chew without fear her stomach would reject it.

At Billingsgate Fish Market, Adam bought them paper cones filled with winkles. The stall supplied them each with a pin and Adam showed Tony how to pick the little blighters from their shells. By the river there was a pirate hanging in chains and a man in the pillory for publishing insulting pamphlets about the mad King.

Savage eyed the youth who strolled beside him. "Is this the first time you've been in this part of London?"

Tony nodded her head. Then she grinned. "It won't be the last." They bought something from every hawker they passed, meat pasties, black peas, roasted chestnuts, and hot cross buns. They were jostled by watermen, horse officers, foreign sailors, and drabs willing to hike their skirts for a penny. The whores would try to wheedle them; then, when they saw the men weren't pigeons to be plucked, they shouted coarse cant after them. "La de dah, sorry wer not good enough fer yer bleedin' Lordships!"

One cheeky-faced slut took hold of Tony's arm. "Come wiv me, luv. I'll suck yer duck till it quacks!"

Savage couldn't help grinning at Tony's discomfort. As another female approached, Tony tried to ward her off with his amber-topped cane.

"Polish yer nob, sir?" She winked.

Finally Tony burst out laughing at their outrageous suggestions.

"That's better," Savage approved, "there's no call to look down your aristocratic nose at the whores of the docks." Savage had an afterthought. "But never fuck one of them. Syphilis is rampant down here."

Sheltered as she was, Tony knew more or less what *fuck* meant, but she was shocked beyond belief that Savage had used the word in a sentence to her. Did men use such language among themselves? She was dying to say the bad word herself and wondered what his reaction would be. "Who shall I fuck?"

Savage measured Tony with a glacial stare, wondering if he was being mocked. Then he realized Lord Lamb hadn't the faintest notion who was fuckable and who wasn't. Splendor of God, he was a milk-faced innocent!

"Most young men wealthy enough to have servants usually gain their first experience by tumbling a serving maid or their tenants' daughters. Yours seemed willing enough. Here in London there are plenty to choose from. The fashionably impure are referred to as Cyprians or you can take your pick of ballet dancers or actresses. There are scores of abbesses who offer young novitiates for the edification of titled young men."

"You mean nuns?" Tony asked with disbelief.

"Christ, of course I don't mean nuns, not real nuns, that's just a slang term for a girl in a high-class brothel." Savage paused. "You do know what a brothel is?" he demanded.

Tony wanted to lie because she couldn't bear Adam Savage to hold Lord Anthony Lamb in such contempt. "I haven't a clue, but since you're my bloody guardian, you'd better educate me."

"This is thirsty work. I'll buy you a pint," Adam said, turning in at the Rainbow Tavern. "They used to have a fellow here who could sew with his toes," he said, apropos of absolutely nothing.

The landlord pulled them two pints and they sat down at a table where they could talk. Savage took a deep draught of ale and wiped the back of his strong hand across his mouth.

"Once a man becomes sexually active, it's almost impossible to abstain, and why should he abstain when there are so many willing partners? Now, I know you are not so naive that you don't know most wealthy men keep a mistress."

"Of course not. Roz says even married men keep a mistress tucked away somewhere."

"The cost of a mistress can be prohibitive, especially to a young man like yourself, so there are houses, commonly known as brothels, where you pay the madam in charge for a female companion for an hour, an evening, or an all-nighter. You pay for her sexual services. In a high-class house the females are usually pretty, extremely inventive in ways to please a man, and most importantly, they should be clean so you don't come down with a dose of the pox. London caters to every taste and pocket."

"I see," Tony said as a couple of things that had always puzzled her clicked into place. Her cheeks were warm but the subject fascinated her.

"Those women who tried to sell themselves were streetwalkers. It's never a good idea to use a common whore."

"I do know what trollops are, Savage. Around Charing Cross they are thick as fleas on a dog's back. I was simply ignorant about houses of sin."

Savage smiled at Tony's prudish term. "The English are such hypocrites about sex."

"As compared with people from the Indies?" Tony inquired.

"Compared with any! In France they are called 'houses of joy.'"

Tony was irritated that Adam Savage was so familiar with such places. "I cannot understand what the attraction is. The girls are common, illiterate, and only want money. There are so many lovely, refined young ladies make their debuts every season."

"The attraction is simple. It's against society's code of honor to fuck a debutante. They hold out for marriage."

"That's because of society's double standard. Women cannot control their own destiny. They have no money, no power, they go from a father's authority to a husband's authority, if they are lucky enough to catch such an elusive creature." She suddenly realized she was speaking as a female and shut her mouth.

Savage remarked dryly, "From what I've observed, husbands don't wield much authority. Once a woman is married she's fair game for fucking."

"That is outrageous! Only a rake would pursue a married lady."

Savage looked at Tony and spoke frankly. "There are a lot of sex-starved wives out there, and it is usually they who do the pursuing. I'm surprised you haven't been seduced by a society matron or the mother of a friend." Adam observed Lord Lamb closely. "Perhaps you go about with blinkers on, blind and deaf to the lures that are cast your way."

Tony finished her ale, wiped her mouth as Savage had done, and said cynically, "Now that you've torn the veil of innocence from my eyes, I expect I'll have a very full social life."

"Let's hope so," Savage remarked lightly. "By the way, we are dining at Devonshire House tomorrow night. Perhaps we'll both get lucky."

Chapter 16

By the time Tony came down to breakfast the next morning, Adam Savage had departed. Midmorning brought a footman with a note informing Lord Lamb that his guardian had moved into his own town house in Half-Moon Street, which was on the other side of Shepherd's Market, closer to Green Park.

As Fenton gave Savage's luggage to the footman, Tony could have kicked herself for not going through his belongings. He was such an enigma, she was wildly curious to learn everything there was to know about him. It was too late now, of course.

No sooner did the footman depart than Roz and Mr. Burke arrived. Tony was overjoyed to see her coconspirators; somehow they lent her confidence. They would both be able to advise her about socializing with the Duke and Duchess of Devonshire. When she contemplated dinner at Devonshire House, for one terrible moment she wanted to make some excuse why she couldn't accompany Savage, but it soon passed. For one thing she couldn't bear his look of contempt for not being courageous enough to attend, and for another here was her chance to make the debut into society she had been denied earlier. Admittedly it was as Anthony rather than Antonia, but wasn't she experiencing everything for both of them?

When she thought about it she realized that impersonating her brother would give her a male perspective to which no other female would ever be privy. It was so risqué, her wicked juices began to bubble and she felt her excitement begin to rise.

After much deliberation it was decided that Tony would wear the midnight-blue satin knee-breeches with white silk stockings and the newly purchased buckled high heels.

"The points on this damned collar are so high, they'll poke my ears off," she complained, while Mr. Burke, impressed by her swearing, patiently fashioned the snowy neckcloth into a waterfall. A powder-blue waistcoat buttoned across her breasts, flattening them, and the new white tiewig covering her own dark locks was fitted on. Then Mr. Burke eased her into the blue-and-gold brocade coat.

Roz observed her critically. "You need a snuffbox, darling."

"No, I prefer cigars to snuff," Tony said matter-of-factly, and Roz almost fell off her stool.

The powder was barely whisked from her shoulders before a footman was knocking upon the door to summon Lord Lamb to Adam Savage's carriage. Her guardian was not one for small talk, so Tony kept a silent tongue on the ride to Devonshire House.

Enclosed in the dark carriage, sitting in such close proximity, Tony allowed her imagination to take flight. Instead of men's knee-breeches and a tiewig she pictured herself in a deliciously feminine crinoline that showed off her tiny waist and upthrusting young breasts. She would be daring enough to paint her face and she would wear more than one provocative black patch. Perhaps she would place one upon a cheekbone to draw attention to her wide green eyes, or one at the corner of her rouged mouth to invite kisses. Even more daring would be one upon the curve of a breast to draw a certain man's eyes inside her bodice. She flushed at her own risqué thoughts.

"I bought you something." The deep masculine voice sent a shiver down her spine. The intimate setting invited exchanging presents for small favors of appreciation such as kisses.

Savage thrust something made of silver into her hands, which immediately transformed her into Anthony.

"A cigar case; how thoughtful," Tony said faintly.

"It's filled with my custom-made brand. If you prefer a milder blend, visit the tobacconist in the Burlington Arcade and order whatever you fancy."

Savage gave both their names to the majordomo, who announced them with great pomp and circumstance. The raised heads and eyebrows were for the man who towered at Lord Lamb's side.

Indian Savage wore his own black hair unpowdered. His linen was immaculate, yet stark in its plainness. He wore black; his only concession to fashion were black satin knee breeches. Even his stockings were black silk, rather than white.

The crowd in the drawing room was gathered about a young man and woman. Tony envied the beautiful girl her pale green gown of tulle. She was extremely animated, a born coquette, flirting outrageously with her fan, while her powdered curls bounced upon her daringly bared shoulders. The man with her was a glittering figure in his own right. He wore white satin knee-breeches, his coat was spattered with blue spangles and gold-braided epaulets. Though he wore a powdered wig, it was obvious that the handsome young man with the fresh complexion was fair and had the bearing of a hussar. As he turned to make a remark to the man beside him, Tony saw the flashing diamond star upon his breast and realized with a jolt that it was the Prince of Wales.

"Obviously this is to be a royal occasion," said an amused voice, and she looked into Savage's sardonic ice-blue eyes.

The next moment the Duke of Devonshire was greeting Savage with friendly familiarity. "I apologize that Georgiana is not beside me to greet our guests, but His Highness tends to monopolize her."

"Your duchess is very lovely," Savage complimented, and Tony felt like scratching out his eyes.

"She's young," Devonshire excused. "We live entirely separate lives. Her friends at Carlton House bore me to tears, I'm afraid."

So, Tony thought, *that's the infamous Georgiana, Duchess of Devonshire. She has the most exciting salon in Court circles, yet she can't possibly be more than a couple of years older than I.*

Savage and Devonshire began talking politics almost immediately and Tony knew she was out of her depth. She watched as the people in the drawing room turned their attention from the Prince of Wales to Adam Savage. Although seemingly unaware, he drew every eye.

It wasn't long before dinner was announced and Tony saw the women elbowing each other aside so that they could sit close to the rich nabob from the East. The Duke placed Savage on his right and Lady Isabella Sefton virtually pushed Lord Lamb aside so that she could lay claim to the chair on the other side of Savage. Tony silently wished them all in hell and moved to the opposite end of the table where the beautiful Georgiana held sway.

She fanned her eyelashes at Tony. "You have me at a disadvantage, sir."

"Lord Anthony Lamb, Your Grace."

She tapped him playfully with her fan. "My friends call me Georgy."

"Mine call me Tony."

"Ah, now I can place you. Your parents lived in Ceylon. You've only just come into your title."

Tony realized how very astute she was in spite of her frivolous reputation. Everyone remained standing about the table and Tony realized the whole room waited for His Royal Highness to take his seat first. George and Georgie, however, cared not a fig for the other guests and kept them waiting with total indifference.

"May I present His Royal Highness, the Prince of Wales? George, this is Tony Lamb."

Antonia bowed with great ceremony and the Prince of Wales bowed back. Then everyone relaxed and began to chatter at once. In quick succession Tony was introduced to the prince's equerry, the Earl of Essex, and to the playwright, Richard Sheridan, affectionately called Sherry.

Finally Prince George decided to sit, and this was the cue for a great scraping of chairs. Tony waited politely, thinking to sit in whatever chair was left vacant, but His Highness took hold of his arm. "Sit by me. Tell me, who the devil is that dark giant who arrived with you?"

For a breathless moment Tony couldn't believe she was holding a conversation with the man who would become the King of England, and then a very curious thing happened. She suddenly saw him as a flesh-and-blood young man totally unsuited to the royal role into which he'd been born. He was playing a part just as she was, and it suited him no better. He was vastly immature; a boy, really, who looked as if he longed to be a dashing hussar when he grew up.

"His name is Adam Savage, Your Highness. He has just returned from Ceylon."

"Is he a friend of yours?"

"Actually, he's my guardian, Your Highness."

"You lucky devil! None ever returned from the Indies without the wealth of a nabob. You can dip into his pockets when your own are empty. Damnation, sorry, Georgy darling, but everyone has someone to frank them save myself. Georgy here has Devonshire to bail her out of debt every day of her life. Do you know when they palmed Carlton House off on me it was in ruins? I've been forced to spend a fortune having Henry Holland rebuild it and just as it's becoming habitable, I'm afraid I shall have to suspend further improvement for lack of blunt. I've commissioned Holland to build me a Marine Pavilion in Brighton. He has already employed a hundred and fifty workmen because I want it finished before next summer. 'Tis a disgrace that I, the Prince of Wales, have to resort to moneylenders." He leaned toward Tony confidentially. "I'm in debt up to here," he said, grasping hold of a powdered curl at his temple, "and no prospect of repaying until the King dies."

"George darling, I'll play some faro with you after dinner. That should lift your spirits."

The prince patted her hand. "Only if you promise to lose, Georgy darling."

"I always lose. I have a reputation to maintain."

Tony couldn't believe the number of courses being served. After the soup three different courses of fish were served, then entrée after entrée followed, each more delicious than the previous one.

"George, I've offered you fifty thousand pounds for your chef, Carême. All you need do to get money is sell something."

"Georgy darling, you are so practical!"

Essex and Sheridan choked on their wine, but the prince continued with deep sincerity. "I wouldn't part with my Parisian chef for a million. He is the only reason people kill to dine at Carlton House. I, too, have a reputation to maintain. I'll have to sell something else."

The Earl of Essex, ever the optimist amid gloom and doom, said, "Perhaps you'll win at Newmarket next week, Your Highness."

George shook his head sadly. "I went into obscene debt for my stud of thoroughbred racehorses. Now I can't even afford to place wagers on them. They eat their blasted heads off, you know." He turned to Tony with a brilliant smile. "Do join us at Newmarket next week, we'll have a ripping time. Sherry is bringing little Amoret and my dearest friend, Charles Fox, is bringing Liz of course, so do fetch your mistress, she'll be quite welcome."

Tony felt her cheeks flush. The prince noticed immediately. "My dear fellow, don't worry about Georgiana here, we can't shock her. She's aware of all our foibles while we know only half of hers." Everyone laughed at his wit.

"Your guardian doesn't keep you on too tight a rein does he?"

"No, Your Highness, as a matter of fact he takes a keen interest in horses. Looking to buy some, I believe. After dinner why don't I introduce him to you?"

"By Jove, that would be sporting of you, old chap. I'm always delighted to make the acquaintance of someone I've not yet borrowed from." All the Whigs laughed.

By the time dinner was over and the ladies stood up to leave the men to their port or brandy, an unbelievable amount of food and drink had been consumed. Tony stood politely with the other men and watched the ladies retire. Now, she thought with a little frisson of anticipation, was the opportunity of a lifetime. She was one of the few women on earth to have the opportunity to learn what men did and said when the opposite sex retired from the dining room. Tony almost fainted from shock. The first order of business was a scramble to open the sideboards and pull out the chamber pots.

Her eyes nearly popped from her head as over a dozen men reached into their satin breeches, pulled out their equipment, and relieved themselves with groans.

"Never had to piss so badly since the last time I sat in Parliament," commented Sheridan.

"That's because you drink too much, Sherry. I never start on the cherry brandy until the ladies leave the table."

Tony lived and learned. Not only did she see that men came in different shapes and sizes, she learned they also came in many shades from mushroom through vermilion. She also knew exactly what the royal penis looked like. It was quite large with a pink head and sprang from a nest of golden curls. Tony blinked as His Royal Highness quite deliberately shook off the last drops before returning it inside his white satin inexpressibles. He then handed his chamber pot to the waiting footman and accepted a hand towel dipped in rosewater.

Tony accepted the brandy offered by a liveried footman and selected a cheroot from her cigar case. She knew her cheeks were flaming and desperately hoped a cloud of blue smoke would cover her embarrassed stupefaction.

The conversation went over her head for the next few minutes as the liquor glasses were filled and emptied in rapid succession. Finally one or two curse words penetrated her brain, and realizing the men's language had coarsened considerably now the ladies were absent, she began to listen more closely.

Lord Sefton approached the Prince, bowed formally, then, with that out of the way, lapsed into informality. "I've found out the name of the lady m'wife invited to the theater two nights ago, Your Highness."

"Sefton, I shall be forever in your debt. You have only to name your price if you will but divulge the lady's name."

"I must warn you she is not a light-skirt, Your Highness, but a respectable widow."

"Sefton, as if she would be in Isabella's box at Covent Garden if she was a Cyprian. One glance told me she wouldn't lift her skirts until all the conventions had been observed."

Sefton nodded, satisfied. "Her name is Maria, Your Highness. Isabella tells me her late husband, Thomas Fitzherbert, left her quite a bit of lolly and a town house in Park Street."

"Maria Fitzherbert." The Prince breathed the name reverently. He turned to Essex, who had acted as the go-between in previous sexual liaisons. "I want to know everything there is to know about the lady. Her beauty dazzled me. She has the most glorious golden hair, which she wore unpowdered."

Sherry, already in his cups, said to Tony, "Hair be damned, it was her magnificent tits that dazzled him. His Highness is a breast man, you know."

Tony, lightheaded herself from cherry brandy said, "Likes breasts, does he?"

"The bigger the better. S'pect he was weaned too early. Queen had fifteen, y'know, popped 'em out like pups. Poor George wasn't as fortunate as a pup. When a pup gets shoved out at least it can suck hind tit."

Tony blinked rapidly. She knew the prince could hear every word Sherry uttered, but instead of taking offense he concurred with his friend's analysis. The prince winked at Tony. "Sherry isn't a breast man. Ask him which part he prefers."

"Pussy," announced Sheridan. "Like 'em small and tight."

Tony wasn't precisely certain he meant what she thought he meant, but Good God Almighty, what other part of a woman's body could be called a pussy?

She looked up as the Duke of Devonshire approached the Prince of Wales. "Your Highness, Georgiana will be mad as fire if we don't soon join the ladies."

"My pleasure, Devonshire."

When Prince George stood up the connecting doors to the large salon were thrown open so that the sexes could once again mingle. Tony scanned the dining room for Adam Savage and saw him in deep conversation with her friend, James Wyatt. Good God, she must be on her guard when they came face to face. If anyone could recognize that she was Antonia, it would be the gifted architect.

She could hear music and wandered out to the ballroom. She stood admiring the painted ceiling, but when she lowered her eyes she saw to her dismay that three young ladies had gathered about her. Speculation or invitation was in every eye and it was patently clear they were all expecting Lord Lamb to partner them in the dancing. Tony rubbed her leg and murmured, "Came a cropper yesterday; jade threw me." She limped away stiff legged and took refuge in the card room.

Tony took a goblet of wine from a proffered silver tray and thought she might learn a few things by watching the card players. Georgiana called to her immediately. "Tony, come and hold the faro bank for us, Sherry's too foxed."

Tony with confidence bolstered by the amount of wine she had imbibed, sat down at a baize-clothed table across from the prince and his equerry and watched the faro box produce one solitary card after another. She noticed that little heed was paid to the game and reasoned that it was no wonder the Duchess of Devonshire lost consistently.

The Prince of Wales looked at Georgiana, wondering if he dared ask her help with Maria Fitzherbert. Georgiana was his closest and most intimate friend. She knew things about him no other living person knew.

When he first set eyes on her he had been smitten badly. She was a tiny creature with the prettiest face in England. She reminded him of a kitten. They met at a low point in his life. His mistresses had all been chosen from the stage and his latest liaison with "Perdita" Robinson had ended in disaster.

He had been a naive young fool, sending her flowery letters of undying devotion, filled with their sexual intimacies. When the affair ended, Perdita threatened to publish the letters and he had been forced to pay a fortune to get them back. The worst part of it was his devotion had been sincere. He wore his heart on his sleeve and the grasping little actress had taken gross advantage of him.

When he saw Georgiana he swore off actresses for life, vowing his next mistress would be a lady. He wooed Georgiana with sincere flattery and undivided attention until he won her. Their rendezvous had been a total disaster. He remembered every painful detail.

They were extremely affectionate toward each other, touching and kissing and calling each other pet names.

"Kitten, you have such exquisite taste in gowns, I am breathless to see what you have beneath."

"Towser, you are a wicked boy. Surely you don't expect me to take off my dress?"

"Of course not, Kitten. I shall do it for you. Come and sit on Daddy's lap."

Georgiana had come eagerly, breathless that a Prince of the Realm was about to bestow the honors of his manhood upon her. He recalled undoing all the tiny buttons and fancy geegaws as she sat upon his knees, hindering him by pressing teasing little kisses all over his face.

His royal scepter inside his satin inexpressibles was almost to the bursting point as she wriggled about in his lap.

When he got her down to her petticoats she playfully began to undress him. He was well endowed and extremely proud of it. He was more than eager to show himself off to his little kitten. Her happy giggles were silenced, however, when he stood before her jutting out a mile. Georgiana had suddenly lost all enthusiasm for her big doggy and he recalled how he had to tease her back to a playful mood.

After what seemed like hours he managed to remove the last of her pretty undergarments one by one. It was now his turn to lose enthusiasm. When he removed her frilled corselet, he also removed her delicious curves along with it. Kitten owed her tempting little figure to padding.

She stood before him, breastless, hipless, and thighless. She had the body of a ten-year-old child. Seven rampant inches of princely erection dwindled to less than an inch in the space of a heartbeat. They climbed beneath the bedcovers glumly yet gamely, determined to salvage what they could in the face of their differences. No amount of kissing, cuddling, rubbing, or stroking could persuade Towser to harden. They tried every trick they had ever heard of to arouse him and coax him from his wrinkled cowl, but all to no avail. They were distraught. They were both on the verge of tears. Then sweetest Georgiana had saved the day.

"Darling Georgy, let's be best friends instead of lovers! We can share each other's secrets and dreams and private thoughts that we would never dare divulge to another soul. Being best friends is the most intimate relationship in the world!" Bless her. She was his dearest darling. He knew he need have no qualms with her whatsoever.

"Georgy darling, I want you to add Maria Fitzherbert's name to your guest list and you may let it be known to London's hostesses that unless Mrs. Fitzherbert is invited, I shall not attend any function." He was well aware that no ball was of any significance without his presence. To be snubbed by the Prince of Wales was social suicide.

From the corner of her eye Tony saw Adam Savage enter the card room trailed by Lady Sefton. He wore a polite mask, but Tony knew he was bored to death by the woman. Savage waited patiently while she stopped to speak with the hostess and the Prince of Wales.

Without mincing words George said, "Isabella, I'm very vexed with you at the moment. Why on earth didn't you bring that charming creature Mrs. Fitzherbert with you tonight?"

Her eyebrows went up. "Maria is only just out of mourning, Your Highness, and very retiring." Lady Sefton, seeing which way the wind was blowing, trimmed her sails accordingly. "As a matter of fact I'm having a musical evening next week in Maria's honor. It would be a privilege if you would grace our gathering, Your Highness."

"The privilege is mine, dear lady."

Tony looked up to see Savage's ice-blue eyes upon her. She tossed off the wine and plunged in with an introduction. "Your Highness, may I present my guardian, Adam Savage? Mr. Savage, the Prince of Wales."

"Do join us at faro, my dear chap. Tony tells us you're just back from Ceylon."

"I prefer baccarat."

Incredibly, Savage had just declined an invitation from the Prince!

Georgina put her pretty head on one side. "What a very poor hostess I am, Mr. Savage. Of course we will play any game you have in mind." It was definitely a double entendre. Adam smiled down into her exquisite face. "I would love to play with you, but you already have three partners."

Tony scowled. Though she was brimful of wine, she caught the biplay. "You may take my chair, Adam. I learn so mush . . . much, just watching you. By the way, we're invited to the races next week. His Highness has some thoroughbeds . . . thoroughbrides . . . some studs he might be willing to sell."

Savage threw her a look she couldn't interpret. She didn't know if it was contempt or admiration. She shrugged. She didn't really give a tinker's damn at the moment. She watched him sit down and she stood behind him.

Whenever a king was turned up, His Highness cursed, "Damn the King!" The card was quite openly nicknamed the *Lunatic.* When Prince George caught Savage's quizzical glance he explained, "M'father's quite mad. That's why they are preparing a Regency Bill for me. I should have been Regent years since, for he's been mad for quite some time. Well, I ask you . . . he issued a proclamation 'for the encouragement of Piety and Virtue, and for preventing and punishing Vice, Profaneness, and Immorality.' "

Savage's lips twitched. "That would tend to take the fun out of life."

Tony's ears began to hum and she heard the voices of the people at the table from a long distance away, as if they were in another room. She heard the tinkle of their glasses, the whisper of their cards, the chink of their guineas, but their laughter and their voices faded away. She tried to make sense of the conversation. It was all about fighting and boxing matches and meeting tomorrow at Gentleman Jim's for a few rounds.

Tony tipped her chair back and balanced it on two legs. What the hell, she'd take them all on. Boxing might be fun!

She didn't remember much of the carriage ride back to Curzon Street, but the quality of his silence told her that she'd finally made an impression upon him. Good or bad didn't really matter. As the carriage halted, Tony emitted a loud hiccup that reverberated off the velvet squabs. She felt a firm hand beneath her elbow as she climbed the steps to the front door.

When Mr. Burke answered the bell, Savage handed Lord Lamb over to him. "He's gloriously dog bitten, I'm afraid."

When Mr. Burke took her inside and closed the door she mumbled through clenched teeth, "Get a bucket."

Chapter 17

How in the name of the devil did she get herself into these situations and what the bloody hellfire was she doing at Gentleman Jim's? Apparently the latest craze of the bucks was boxing, because His Royal Highness the Prince of Wales had taken a fancy to the sport.

The boxing ring in this particular establishment provided the opportunity for the gentry to strip to the waist, put on the gloves, and go a couple of rounds with professional pugilists. Only a few had guts enough to try it; the rest were enthusiastic spectators. Of course it provided yet one more diversion where large amounts of money could be wagered.

Tony sat hunched, nursing a hangover she couldn't believe. The miasma of male sweat made her gorge rise, yet she was the only one present who seemed to even notice it. The place was crowded with the prince's cronies, who seemed to have accepted her as one of them, much to her surprise. She put it down to the fact that she felt so miserable, she had hardly acknowledged their introductions and bored disinterest was all the rage. They'd mistaken Tony's half-closed eyelids and pinched nostrils for languorous ennui and thought him one helluva decent chap.

At Sherry's and Edmund Burke's urging Prince George decided to favor his intimates with a demonstration of his prowess. His gentlemen helped strip him down to his white inexpressibles, and Tony thought with a lack of enthusiasm, *Now I know what the rest of him looks like.*

His Highness was certainly well made, but his wide shoulders remained in his coat when he removed it and his flesh was not hard like Savage's. His muscles were covered by a generous layer of fat and his belly looked soft. In contrast with his florid face his milk-white body skin was almost distasteful to Tony after the sun-bronzed color of Adam Savage. She was willing to bet all the other men present were just as pale as George.

The prince put on a creditable demonstration with his trainer Angelo, who went down on one knee a couple of times from the impact of His Highness's blows. All present, of course, realized the boxing instructor could have half killed him without much effort, but all applauded the royal courage.

Others were urged to go a few rounds, but there were no takers. Savage pushed Tony's feet from the bench where they were propped. "Come on, boy, let's see what you're made of."

Tony couldn't believe her ears. For a moment sheer terror gripped her. There was no way on earth she could strip to the waist, and the last thing she wanted was for some uncouth boxing instructor to plant her a facer. She scowled. "I haven't the energy of a slug this morning."

Savage's ice-blue eyes filled with contempt. "You mean you haven't the guts of a louse."

Tony hated him in that moment. Her anger was so strong, she wanted to fly at him and tear out his mocking eyes, but she knew she must keep her temper under control with so many eyes upon her. In a lazy gesture she used her cane to tip her hat to the back of her head. Then she drawled with studied insolence, "Kiss my aspidistra, Savage. If you're so keen on the bloody sport, let's see what you're made of."

All present were so enthusiastic over this suggestion that His Highness asked him if he would oblige them. Reluctantly Savage stripped down to his breeches. Angelo had no intention of pulling his punches once he saw the breadth of chest rippled with hard muscle. Once he'd felt the numbing jab of Savage's long reach, he had no intention of following the Marquess of Queensbury's rules either.

Tony suddenly began to sit up and take notice. As Savage side-stepped while he aimed a powerful blow, he was somehow able to anticipate the moves Angelo made. When the boxer did manage to land blows, they were brutal and always below the belt. Savage was willing to be a gentleman only up to a certain point. When he felt the searing pain from another kidney punch, his restraint snapped. Through gritted teeth he challenged, "Shall we take off the gloves?"

Barefisted fighting was far more exciting for the spectators and they began to wager wildly as Savage deliberately and methodically set about cutting the trainer's face to ribbons.

Tony shuddered at the blood and brutality, but she didn't close her eyes. They were riveted on the magnificent body of Adam Savage. He was more than a match for the professional fighter; Tony knew without a doubt he'd be more than a match for any who challenged him for whatever reason. Savage had learned all the dirty tricks that could be dished out in the hell holes of the world. A few rounds at Gentleman Jim's was child's play to him.

Surreptitiously, beneath her lashes, she watched him dress. She could not help responding to the sheer male force of him. Only when Savage was safely clothed did she allow her eyes to meet his.

"You really must be able to defend yourself in this world, Tony. If not with your fists, then with sword or pistol. The choice of weapon I leave to you, but I insist you take lessons in self-defense."

Though she realized the wisdom of his words she chafed against him issuing his orders. "Poor devil," she mocked, "you've really got your work cut out for you, making a man of me."

The look he returned her from his piercing blue eyes told her clearly what Savage thought of her manhood or lack of it. In that moment she felt humiliation not only for herself, but for her brother Anthony as well. Her resolve hardened. He'd told her to sow some wild oats; so be it. Hell raising would become her quest! And as for Savage, well he could bloody well reap what she sowed.

Before the Prince departed he remarked, "I shall see you both at Carlton House tonight."

Tony realized that, too, was tantamount to an order. After His

Highness and his entourage left, she said to Savage, "I never expected you of all people to follow orders meekly."

"I'm in the process of fleecing him of his stud of thoroughbreds. Dining at Carlton House is a small price to pay." He changed the subject. "Would you care to come and help me select some French wallpaper for Edenwood?"

Tony made a rude noise. "Choose your own damned wallpaper. I've an assignation this afternoon."

Adam's eyebrows rose slightly and his lip twitched. "In that case, my lord, I'll leave you to your own . . . vices."

The "assignation" was with her grandmother, who was avid to learn the details of the affair at Devonshire House. "Did you see anything of his Royal Highness?"

Remembering, Antonia began to laugh. "I saw more than I bargained for and what I missed last night, I made up for this morning at Gentleman Jim's. What is it that makes a man want to strip down and measure himself against every man in the room?"

Roz and Tony caught each other's eye and went off into peals of laughter. "Oh, darling, I believe you've just answered your own question."

"I've learned enough about men in the last little while to know that I should never really wish to be one, in spite of the privileges they enjoy."

"Oh, darling, we've done this all wrong. We should have found a wealthy husband for you instead of resorting to this deception."

"Roz, please don't feel guilty. I couldn't bear to be sold on the marriage market. I love my newfound freedom." Her eyes twinkled. "And being a man is so diverting. His Highness invited me to bring my mistress when we go to the races."

Roz blinked. Antonia was enjoying the lark, but Roz was beginning to have grave misgivings. She made a mental note to have a word with Mr. Savage.

"His Highness is about to acquire a new mistress, from what I learned last night," Tony said.

"Really?" Roz was hungry for details that she could cast before her dearest friend, Frances Jersey.

"Her name is Maria Fitzherbert."

"But I know her!" Roz seemed skeptical. "Are you sure of the name, darling? She's a respectable widow, distantly related to Isabella

Sefton. Lord, she must be at least six or seven years older than George. She must be approaching thirty."

"Does she wear her hair unpowdered and have spectacular . . . er, a lush figure?"

"That's the one! Yellow hair the color of corn. Most unfashionable. Still, she must have her head screwed on the right way, for she's had two old husbands who left her well lined in the pockets."

"I'm dining at Carlton House tonight, by the way. His Highness and his friends speak most disrespectfully of the King and Queen. The King is openly referred to as the lunatic and Richard Sheridan said the Queen had popped out fifteen offspring like pups."

"And looked as if she was carrying all fifteen at once," Roz remarked dryly.

Antonia laughed and rebuked, "You have caught Lady Jersey's cutting tongue."

"You're too kind to me, darling. *I* give *her* lessons."

"Ugh, lessons! Savage is determined to give me lessons in the manly art of self-defense. As a matter of fact I believe he wants to squash me and remake me in his own image. He makes me so furious, it's constantly on the tip of my tongue to tell him where to go and what to do when he gets there. He angers me so much, I'm in constant danger of letting the cat out of the bag."

"You must learn to bite your tongue, darling. It's so difficult for a lady to constantly be polite in mixed company, but I have an infallible method of letting out my spleen." Rosalind went quickly to her rosewood desk and took out a leather-bound volume. "Here's a brand-new journal for you. Write down all the unspeakable things you'd like to call him. Don't hold anything back, no matter how wickedly evil. 'Tis a delicious purge."

Tony took the journal. "The things I long to say will scorch the pages. Come and help me choose something to wear to Carlton House tonight."

"You must promise to give me every last detail tomorrow. His Highness has reportedly spent hundreds of thousands on the renovations."

When Mr. Burke announced Adam Savage, Rosalind came to greet him. "I'm sorry, but Tony left for Carlton House hours since. A couple of dissolute young devils stopped by for him." She took a deep breath, then plunged in. "Mr. Savage—Adam, if I may—I'm rather worried about Tony. Don't you consider the Carlton House crowd rather wicked?"

Savage's brows drew together slightly. "Wicked? Hardly that, Lady Randolph. Perhaps a trifle wild and rackety, but I firmly believe Tony will benefit from male companionship. Don't worry, I'll keep an eye on him."

Tony, in a reckless mood, was having the time of her life. When she first entered Carlton House it held all her attention. She'd never quite seen anything to compare with what she could only describe as vulgar ostentation. The Prince of Wales had developed a passion for chinoiserie and as a result the drawing room was done in Chinese Chippendale, its walls hung in yellow silk. The dining room however was the focal point of the establishment.

It had been made larger to accommodate the infinite number of intimates in His Highness's circle. Columns of red and yellow granite had been added to lift the ceiling and were reflected in the wall panels of glittering silver-gilt. It opened into the ballroom paneled in crimson silk, which had platforms at both ends for the orchestra.

Tonight there were only gentlemen invited to dine. Though there was to be no dancing, nevertheless the ballroom doors were thrown wide, the lusters and chandeliers lighted, and the orchestra played dinner music.

The Carlton House set, as George's friends were called, soon diverted Tony's attention from the rooms themselves. Apart from Sheridan, Burke, and Essex, whom she'd already met, were other prominent Whigs such as Charles Fox. He was reputed to be the Prince's most intimate friend and the one who constantly tried to get more money for George from Parliament. It was he who was presently pushing for the Regency Bill.

Fox was at least ten years older than the Prince, making Tony wonder what the attraction was. She decided Fox must be a father figure, though a decidedly odd father figure, for at the moment he was expounding the merit of blue hair powder in a decidedly wine-thickened voice.

Whenever she was introduced to a new face, Sherry was at her elbow to fill her in on all the dirt. They were drinking *diaboleños,* the latest craze. Sherry urged Tony to try one. "I do believe you're cold sober. You'll have to swill them down if you ever hope to catch up with the rest of us."

Two other royals were present; Frederick, Duke of York, the

Prince's younger brother, and Henry Frederick, Duke of Cumberland, the Prince's uncle.

"Is that the wicked uncle?" Tony asked, amused.

"Mmm, shocking influence. Can carouse from dusk till dawn. Known in every pleasure haunt in London. First time a prince of the blood ever appeared in divorce court. Lord Grosvenor cited him as correspondent when he found obscene letters to his wife revealing their passionate affair. Cost him ten thousand pounds damages and gave Grosvenor his divorce." Sherry finished his drink and reached for another. "Lucky old swine turned round and wed that pretty piece of pussy, Anne Horton. We love the new Duchess of Cumberland dearly. She's deliciously vulgar and quite liberal with her favors."

The fashions in the room were ludicrous. Every man was draped in satins, laces, and bows with yards and yards of ribbon at elbow and knee. Embroidered waistcoats were worn over underwaistcoats, all topped by white leaded faces and high wigs loaded down with Venetian talc. Charles Fox was the exception. He wore one of Truefitt's nutty-brown wigs reeking with perfumed oil.

Of all the guests present Tony liked Henry Luttrell best. She was already familiar with his satirical poems and Sherry gave her a thumbnail sketch that whetted her appetite. "He's only welcome here because of his wit. He's the son of an Irish peer and his gardener's daughter. Hasn't a pot to piss in or a window to throw it through, but he dines out in style every night." Sherry tapped Luttrell on the shoulder. "Here's an admirer of yours Henry; Tony Lamb. Give us a limerick, old man."

"Well, let's see," Henry drawled, "would you like one about excrement or one that abuses the clergy?"

"Oh, abuse the clergy, by all means," Tony urged.

"There was a fat priest of St. Giles
Who was much too wide for the aisles.
Passing to and from mass,
The pews pinched his ass,
And gave him a bad case of piles."

Tony burst out laughing and Henry was most flattered.

"Lord, man, we're not in mixed company, give us something with a little more zing," Sherry urged.

"There once was a monk of Gibraltar
Who buggered a nun on the altar.
'Good God,' said the nun,
'Now look what you've done:
You've gummed up the leaves of the Psalter.' "

Sherry bent double with mirth and began to cough. Tony had to clap him on the back to stop him from choking.

Suddenly a shot rang out, engaging everyone's attention. "By Satan, we're going to have a little pistol practice. George has one of the finest collections in town." When they arrived at the other end of the room, the betting was heavy and the money piled high.

His Highness bade a footman put up a portrait of the King and they all took turns, wagering obscene amounts of money. When Tony selected one of the pistols it was much heavier than she had anticipated. She admired the workmanship of the weapon with its smoothly polished olivewood handle and long silver barrel.

His Highness said, "Ah, here's a fellow after my own heart. Loves the feel of a gun in his hand. That one has a hair trigger."

Before she could be warned to take proper aim, her finger brushed the trigger and the pistol exploded. The bullet nicked the wire holding up the portrait and it crashed to the dining room floor. For a moment Tony was aghast that she'd put a hole in the plaster, but a cheer went up and they declared Lord Lamb the unconditional winner. She sat down white faced as two hundred guineas was pressed upon her.

The enthusiasts moved into the ballroom for greater scope, but the occasional wild shot soon had the orchestra scattering for cover. They behaved like a gang of unruly schoolboys let loose at a fair, with His Highness egging everyone on to join in the madcap antics. He sobered somewhat when a footman took a bullet in the shoulder. As the servant was carried off His Highness turned to his friend Charles Fox. "We can't continue like this. Good footmen are hard to get these days. After dinner we'll visit your *tir.*"

Tony turned to Sherry. "What's a *tir?*"

"It's a shooting gallery. Haven't you had training in the code duello? Wrote a damned good duel into m'last play, but damned if I can think of the title."

Something made Tony look toward the entrance of the ballroom. The tall dark figure of Savage loomed in the doorway, a look of frozen contempt on his face for the juvenile antics he'd just witnessed. His eyes flicked over Tony, then dismissed him as if he were no more than a spoiled puppy.

As if Savage's arrival was some sort of cue, dinner was announced and the assembly filed back into the dining room. Tony had never seen so much food consumed in her lifetime. Without realizing she was doing so, she began to count. There were four soups, then four fish courses, followed by thirty-six entrées. The menus were printed entirely in French. She had learned a smattering of the language from a tutor and read:

Coq au Vin Quatre grosses piéces pour le contre-flanc.
Les petites croustades de mauviettes au gratin.

Tony didn't have a clue and wondered idly if it was a direct result of the *diaboleños* she'd imbibed. Claret and burgundy were considered too thin; sherry, hock, and port were served instead. As a result long before the meal was over some of the men had drunk themselves speechless and a footman loosened the ridiculously high neckcloths of those who had fallen beneath the table before they asphixiated themselves.

Frederick, the young Duke of York, toppled over dead drunk. His Highness, who was famous for his wit, glanced down at him with mock solemnity. "And there, according to our royal father, lies the hope of our family."

As those who could still walk arose to make up a party to follow Charles James Fox, Tony asked Sherry, "Where is this *tir?*"

"It's somewhere in the bowels beneath Fox's gaming hell."

"He runs a gambling house?" Tony asked surprised.

"By Satan, you're a babe in arms. After we knock off a few rounds belowstairs, we'll gamble till dawn."

Tony felt her winnings inside her pockets. "Hellfire, I thought I'd save my money to wager in Newmarket."

"Oh, we're not going. Hadn't you heard? His Highness sold his horses to that Indian fellow."

Adam Savage observed everything that went on at Carlton House through narrowed eyes. He had cynically assessed and catalogued the lot of them as useless spendthrifts down to the last man. The floridly handsome Prince of Wales might have easy and engaging manners and be a patron of the arts, but he couldn't see that his Whig friends used him. Savage knew the Regency Bill would not be signed, for George gave more time and attention to his tailor and bootmaker than the business of the realm.

Charles Fox was easily the most influential of the prince's friends. He drank heavily and sat for days at a stretch at the gaming tables, usually in his own establishment. Wags said his charm came from his great-great grandfather, Charles II, but Savage knew he was both profligate and dissipated.

Richard Sheridan was dissolute. He and Edmund Burke often abused each other in the House of Commons, but they all pissed in the same pot and believed themselves the masters of England.

Savage was determined in his own small way to effect changes. They wouldn't happen overnight, but with a genious like Pitt now running the government, England stood a better chance than it had in years of doing something to improve the lot of its common citizens. Granted, he would have to use the system of bribes and patronage that had been in place since the early Georgian reign, but if he was relentless enough, insistent enough, determined enough, and forceful enough, he could effect change.

It had been Fox, Sheridan, and Burke who had introduced a bill to deprive the East India Company of its powers and trading privileges. As a result the government fell and Pitt became chief minister. The fools did manage to have poor old Warren Hastings, the Governor of Bengal, impeached. They spoke witheringly of matters about which they knew nothing. Burke in particular was a hypocrite, for his family had made its money by dipping its fingers into the Indian pot of gold.

Suddenly Savage's regard became fixed upon his young ward, Anthony Lamb. A lecherous-looking rake had his arm about the youth's shoulders and a disquieting thought rose full blown in Savage's mind. Instead of thrusting the thought away, he examined it carefully. Anthony was a beautiful youth with his long legs and dreamy green eyes. A succulent plum to be plucked by a profligate seducer.

The muscle in Savage's jaw flexed into a lump of iron. Was this the reason for the lad's disinterest in women? No, Tony was innocent, he'd not yet been tainted, but the sooner he was introduced to the addictive pleasures of female flesh, the better. He made a mental note to see to it himself before the week was out. As he moved down the room toward Tony, the group started to depart.

"Leaving so soon?" Savage asked lightly with a lifted eyebrow.

Tony got the impression she was being checked up on. Savage

hadn't bothered to disclose that he'd bought George's thoroughbreds, so she said almost insolently, "We're off to a *tir,* if you must know. I've chosen my weapons as you suggested. My choice is pistols, hands down."

Savage looked after the bucks thoughtfully. London stretched for ten miles along the Thames from Millbank to Blackwell. There were grog shops by the thousand and every denomination of bawdy house from the bagnios of Covent Garden to the padding cans of London's underworld. Gaming hells were notorious, from respectable clubs like White's and Watier's to the Gamecock's Spurs in the slums. But Savage guessed they would end up in Charles James Fox's very own hell.

He waited until two in the morning before he strolled in and picked up the dice to play hazard. He found Tony, drunk as a lord, his pockets turned inside out. Savage tipped his top hat over his eyes, bade the occupants good-night, and hauled young Lamb to his feet.

When Mr. Burke opened the front door of Curzon Street, the family servant thought it his duty to protest. Savage took the blame without a word. Before Mr. Burke got the door closed, Tony muttered, "Get the bucket."

Chapter 18

Tony lounged in a chair before the fireplace in Half-Moon Street. Her mouth was very sulky as Savage ripped up one side of her and down the other.

"You haven't the brains you were born with. How much did you lose?"

"Two hundred," Tony mumbled.

"Couldn't you see they were out to fleece the lamb?"

Tony inwardly cringed at the pun, but her anger began to rise. "Surely you're not suggesting I was cheated?"

"No, I'm not suggesting, you gullible young fool, I'm telling you flat! His Highness is in debt to his eyebrows, the beauteous Georgiana can't even tally her gambling debts! Tell me, Tony, when you add two and two together are your wits too addled to come up with four?"

Savage took a deck of cards from the drawer of a cherrywood wine table and began to shuffle them. "Christ, that's why I never play faro. You never get to touch the cards and all too often the cards are trimmed or roughened to hold together in the brace box. A crooked box and a clever dealer can impoverish a prince."

Savage rifled the deck. "Pay attention. Anyone with a degree of smoothness in handling cards can be taught a 'blind' shuffle in five minutes. This puts the desired cards at the bottom of the deck. It's all a matter of 'stocking' and 'culling.' The one single artifice that gives you the greatest advantage is bottom dealing. Damn it all, boy, I don't want those men you were with last night corrupting you!"

In light of how he was now urging her to learn how to cheat, Tony saw the dark humor of it. "Obviously you prefer to corrupt me yourself!"

"I am merely educating you. If you learn all the tricks, you will be able to detect cheating. Whether or not you play on the level is a decision you can make for yourself," Savage said coldly.

Tony picked up the deck of cards, determined to master the blind shuffle. "Are you finished reading the riot act?"

"I've only just begun. I don't care a pinch of bat shit that you spew your guts up every night, but I do care that you are drinking to the point where you have no control over your own actions."

"You forbid me to see my friends now, I suppose?" Tony challenged.

"You're missing the point. I want you to be able to handle yourself in any company or any situation from the card room to the bedroom, from the glittering court to a dark alley."

Some of the wind went out of Tony's sails as she recalled the plans that had been made for the evening. She glanced at Savage and said, "How the hell do I get out of going to the Turkish baths in Covent Garden? For six guineas you get to bathe, sup, and sleep with a fashionable harlot."

"I can think of more corrupt ways to spend your time," Savage warned lightly.

"I'll just bet you can," Tony retorted angrily.

Savage shrugged. "Tell them you're going to the theater with me . . . the engagement slipped your mind."

Tony felt vastly relieved. There was something else she had enthusiastically agreed to be part of when she was half sotted, but she didn't dare breath a word of it to Savage. She searched her mind for a safe subject. Demonstrating her finesse with the cards, her long, slim fingers shuffled the deck, cut it, then proceeded to lay out four aces, followed by all the face cards. "I'm a quick study. When are you going to start teaching me how to make money?"

"So you can lose it all in some gaming hell?" Savage asked dryly.

"Don't be daft, from now on I shall win consistently. How about South Sea shares? Everyone and his mistress are buying them."

"That's precisely the reason you will not. They're inflated beyond their value." Savage's eyes were forbidding as Arctic seas. You did not disobey this man's orders.

Tony shrugged. "Well, as I told you, the only unwritten law I know is that I cannot dip into my principle."

His voice came to her like silk as he demanded with exquisite sarcasm, "How in the name of the Father, the Son, and the Holy Ghost can you increase your interest without spending your principle?"

"I—I don't know," Tony stammered.

"Risk is the name of the game. The higher the risk, the higher the return. I'll offer you a deal made in Heaven. Take every copper you have to your name and buy a cargo for the Indies. Then with the fat profits, buy a cargo to fetch back to England. Use one of my ships; just over eight weeks in each direction. In four to five months with the right cargo you can quadruple your money held in trust by Watson and Goldman."

"But the risk—ships go down every day of the year. I'd lose everything."

"I'll even insure you, seeing I'm on intimate terms with the vessel and the crew."

Tony was overwhelmed by his generosity. "That's very noble of you. Why would you do such a thing?"

"Believe it or not, I care about you." Savage hesitated for a moment, then added lightly, "Think of me as a father."

Antonia thought of him often and in many capacities, but the last thing she ever wanted from him was a fatherly relationship.

"We shall continue your lessons this evening," Savage said lightly, dismissing her.

"Are you chucking me out?" she inquired. Their relationship had reached the stage where they could be very plain with one another.

"I am. I have a great deal of business to get through before we go to the theater." He took out a gold watch. "I'm expecting someone."

"Excuse me for cluttering up your life," Tony said with a tinge of amused sarcasm.

Savage shrugged philosophically. "It takes a deal of time and patience before a cub is housebroken."

Tony only pretended amusement. She was piqued that all he wanted to do was read her the riot act, then dismiss her. She walked slowly around the corner and waited a few minutes. She doubted he had a business appointment. She felt better when a well-equipped carriage drew up with a crest upon its black, shiny door. Savage had been telling the truth after all. She felt decidedly worse when a beautiful woman was handed down from the carriage, elegantly attired in cream damask and black ostrich feathers. He had business to attend to, all right. Funny bloody business!

When the Countess of Essex was shown into Savage's office, he had nothing but business in mind. He was determined to loosen her purse strings for a cause that was important to him. She threw out obvious lures to which he responded verbally, but he had more good sense than to seduce the Earl of Essex's wife when he might need the man as a political ally.

Tony sat in the window seat of Anthony's bedchamber with her knees drawn up to hold the journal. She dipped her pen and wrote decisively:

Adam Savage is inhuman. He is part man, part beast. The beast is definitely a leopard. I am not the first to mark the resemblance. He is aware of it himself, for he named his plantation in Ceylon Leopard's Leap. Savage wears a mask, as does everyone in today's society, yet I suspect his mask disguises a personality that is fathomless. If the mask were stripped away I do not yet know if I would find him uncivilized or ultracivilized. I suspect beneath the surface he is wild and untamed.

He is dominant and controlling, yet clever enough not to oppress or bully. He goads me to anger, then mollifies me with his wisdom, his generosity, or his humor. His advice is always sound, and inexplicably this infuriates me. The single thing, however, that shoots my temper to the boiling point is his look of utter contempt. I am determined to wipe it from his arrogant face.

He allows me a great deal of slack and thinks I am unaware he has me on a leash. He is in for a shock, for I intend to slip the line. I do not underestimate him, for I have heard the growl beneath the velvet voice and felt a hint of his claws when he mauled my character this morning. He intends to make a man of me, but I would much rather he make a woman of me.

Tony clutched the pen so intensely, the nib made a large blot of ink. She snapped the journal closed, appalled at where her thoughts were leading. The damned journal lured her secrets from her. She decided to put her time to better use than daydreaming over Savage. She must decide on a cargo to export to the Indies.

That afternoon she browsed about London's shops, but the only things that struck her fancy were furnishings for Edenwood. She purchased a pianoforte on the spot, knowing instinctively Savage would want the latest musical invention, which was a vast improvement over the harpsichord because it could be played loud or soft on the same keyboard. She also bought a dinner service for twenty-four designed by Wedgwood, in a pale shade of lavender with white ornamental relief. The classical design was perfection, the craftsmanship unparalleled. Edenwood should also have a tea service of Sèvres china and probably a breakfast service as well, but knowing Savage she thought perhaps he'd make those purchases on a visit to the Continent rather than pay inflated import prices. By the amount of imported goods in the shops, however, other people must be willing to pay the inflated prices, she realized. Then it struck her: The rarer the object, the higher the price, the greater the demand. Only think what the demand in the far-off Indies must be for scarce Continental and English goods!

The thought of making money made her mouth go dry. She licked her lips and thought of her mother and the other ladies transplanted to the East. They must create an insatiable demand for the latest fashions, especially those that lent themselves to a hot climate, such as parasols, leghorn hats, painted fans, muslin undergarments, tulle evening gowns, satin slippers.

After a woman adorned herself, she adorned her home. Tony's excitement built as she thought of exporting Venetian mirrors and crystal goblets and all the other elegant French and Italian furnishings. She couldn't wait to tell Adam Savage that she had decided upon her cargo.

On the carriage ride to the theater she broached the subject. Adam watched Tony through narrowed eyes as he became animated about women's underpinnings, parasols, and other fal-lols to frippery. Young

Lamb's ideas were not without merit but they were decidedly feminine.

Crushing down the curl of fear inside his gut, Savage was determined to eradicate the youth's effeminate tendencies and allow his masculinity to assert itself. After the theater they would visit a bordello, where he would make certain Tony was initiated. In his wisdom Savage knew that the youth would remain in limbo until he had asserted himself sexually. Once this first hurdle had been taken, nature would do the rest.

Adam had been thinking of attending the opera; now he changed his mind and decided to visit the Olympian, where a broad sex farce was playing.

At first he watched Tony from the corner of his eye as the scantily clad beauties romped about the stage delivering lines ripe with innuendo, but soon he was caught up in the bawdy fun of it all and his laughter rolled out frequently. The entire plot was taken up by men trying by one device or another to get into their ladies' knickers, but it was all done with such clever, sly banter, the audience was almost rolling in the aisles.

Tony laughed, too, but she was glad the lights were low, for her cheeks were suffused with blushes. Before the halftime curtain came down, the principal actress strutted to center stage and sang a song about "The Dew Upon the Lily." She was an outrageously saucy baggage and the men all sat forward, rapt with undivided attention.

The minute the curtain was down and the house gaslights were lit, Savage stood up. "What a delightful little dollymop. Let's go backstage."

Tony was annoyed. "You're easily pleased. I thought the song insipid."

As they made their way backstage, Adam cocked a dark brow. "Don't you know what 'dew on the lily' is?"

"Of course I know . . ." Tony faltered. Obviously there was a more subtle meaning. "I suppose I need a translation," she admitted.

"It means she wants it so badly, she's wet for you . . . dew on the lily." Savage clearly saw Tony still did not fully comprehend. He was beginning to think the lad would make a monk.

Backstage was crowded with performers, dressers, scenery movers, and members of the audience who were seeking assignations. Savage walked a direct path to the actress of his choice and joined the circle of admirers who surrounded her. He introduced himself and the saucy cocotte held out her hand for him to kiss and told him her name was Angela Brown.

"I should like to introduce you to my young friend, Lord Anthony Lamb."

Her eyes went wide and then her smile did the same. A young man who stood beside her said, "Well, stab me, you're my cousin Tony. I'm Bernard Lamb. Small world, isn't it?"

Antonia almost fainted. She stared at Bernard Lamb and hoped the horror she felt inside of her didn't show upon her face. She could almost taste her fear. Here was the greedy cousin who coveted her twin's title, Lamb Hall, and all their worldly goods. Why did bad luck dog her footsteps? Bernard Lamb must learn nothing from her. Very coldly she murmured, "How d'you do," and turned away to strike up a conversation with a petite girl from the chorus.

The girl had overheard that the young buck who spoke to her possessed a title. She hung on to Tony's every word, managing to touch the hand and brush against the thigh of the slim young man all at the same time. She chattered on in animated fashion, but all Tony heard was that her name was Dolly. The only thing she wanted was to escape from Bernard Lamb's presence.

Adam Savage was angry. He shook young Bernard Lamb's hand and told him he was delighted to meet one of Tony's relatives. He covered the best way he could. "I think Tony was going to invite the young lady to supper, but could see you had beat him to the prize."

Bernard laughed. "Angela and I are old friends. We would be delighted to join you some other time."

Savage noted the youth's polished manners and wished to God his bloody ward would exhibit a few manners, polished or otherwise. "When my house in Gravesend is finished, I shall be having a housewarming party. I'll send you an invitation. Please come." Savage's eyes caressed Angela's impudent breasts and saucy mouth.

"Don't mind if I do," she said, winking cheekily. "I must run, the curtain's rising." She looked over her shoulder at the two men and added outrageously, "among other things."

As everyone headed back to their seats, Adam spun Tony around by the shoulder. "You insufferable young snob." Savage's eyes and voice were icy. "Just because he's untitled and she's a common actress, you snubbed them."

Tony looked him straight in the eye. "If you couldn't see he covets my title and everything else I own, then you are blind."

"Horseshit! I saw no such thing!"

"All you saw were tits!" Tony said crudely.

Savage grinned. "I'm a leg man, myself."

A few days ago Tony wouldn't have known what he meant. Now she did. Holy Mary, men had divided up the female anatomy and chosen the parts they found most delectable!

What if women did that? She stared at him, remembering how he'd looked in only a towel. Judas, she'd be hard pressed to choose between his wide shoulders or his darkly furred chest, his strong brown hands or his sensual scarred mouth. She was spoiled for choice and she hadn't even seen all his parts yet!

"What are you staring at?" Savage asked.

"God's gift to women," Tony mocked, lowering her eyes lest he see the physical impact he had upon her.

The bawdy show had definitely made Savage feel randy and in the mood for a woman. He debated where he should take Tony for his first taste of tenderloin and decided he would take him to a place where there would be a bit of fun. No sense intimidating him by visiting a house that catered to sophisticated tastes, lest he take it all too seriously.

Opposite Somerset House on the Thames was a floating bawdy house called the *Folly*. On the first deck a band entertained while water nymphs took supper with the gentlemen, who were referred to as "Tritons."

"Where are we going?" Tony asked, as they walked toward the river.

"Do you see that barge that's all lit up?"

Tony could hear the music and laughter now they were closer. "Are we going out on the river?"

"Yes and no. The *Folly* never actually weighs anchor."

"Ah, is it a floating card palace?" Tony asked, becoming interested.

"No, it's a floating brothel. We'll take supper with some delectable water nymphs on the first deck and then when you grow tired of the world the second deck has small, convenient rooms where you may take a girl to bed."

Tony tripped on the gangplank.

"I knew you'd be eager," Savage mocked. "Take a stroll about while I pay our blunt."

Savage spoke with the proprietress, letting her know it was the boy's first time. "He's a bit shy in these matters, but I want to be absolutely certain he loses his virginity."

"Ah, milord, I've just the little nymph! She's so eager, she'll do all the work. She does it all, front door, back door, French door! All he has to do is lie there and breathe."

Savage took out his billfold. "I don't think so. Do you have a shy nymph who can pass for a virgin? One with a little more class and subtlety, perhaps?"

The madam's painted face lit up. "I have a new girl, quiet little thing. I'm amazed at how many gents ask for her."

"Send her to our table." He glanced up to find three females frankly assessing him. "Ladies, won't you join us for supper?"

Tony wasn't hungry, her appetite had fled along with her courage. Savage must have found the seafood delicious by the number of oysters the laughing nymphs fed him. Tony knew what Savage expected of Lord Lamb and decided bravado was the only thing that would carry her through the evening. She appraised the young girl sitting next to her and was surprised to find that she looked apprehensive. She sat as quietly as if she were in church, not even listening to the sallies of the rowdy nymphs who were lavishing all their attention on Savage.

Tony reached for her cigar case. "Do you mind if I smoke?"

"May I light it for you, my lord?" the girl asked sweetly.

Tony held the cheroot in her lips while the young girl lifted one of the candles from its trident bracket and held it steady. "What's your name?" Tony asked, hoping the smoke would mask the look of rising panic in her eyes.

"Lily, my lord."

Tony almost choked on a mouthful of smoke as she saw Savage lift his eyebrows and waggle them suggestively. She needed to get away—someplace where those piercing blue eyes of his couldn't observe her. She got to her feet. "Come on, Lily, let's find a place where we can be private."

Tony could feel those damned piercing blue eyes on her back, as they climbed all the way to the second deck. Inside the small stateroom there was only a bed and a tiny commode with a mirror and a wooden chair.

Tony sat down on the chair, propped her feet on the bed, and tipped the chair back to balance it on its back legs in a pretense of nonchalance.

Lily fell to her knees before Tony and cried, "Oh, please, my lord, be gentle wi' me!"

What the devil was the girl on about? Tony crushed out the cigar and brought the chair back onto its four legs. Lily's begging increased. "Hush, Lily. I won't even touch you! Are some men rough with you?" Tony asked in outrage.

Lily turned off the wailing as quickly as she had turned it on. "I was only trying to excite you, my lord. Most gents love it when I'm afraid."

"Well, *I* don't love it, and please don't call me *my lord.* My name is Tony."

"Tony, would it excite you if I undressed you?" Lily offered, ready to oblige.

"Good God, no!" Tony said repressively.

"Would it excite you if you undressed me?"

"Nothing you do will excite me, Lily," she stated firmly.

"What would you like to do with me, Tony?" Lily asked blankly.

"Can't we just talk? Look, my guardian dragged me here against my will. Damn it, he's hellbent on making a man of me."

A light of comprehension dawned on Lily's face. "I know your secret," Lily whispered.

Tony stared at her a moment in disbelief, then let out her breath in a huge sigh. "Thank God! What a relief."

"You need a man's arms, not a woman's," Lily said knowingly. "You probably lust only for that handsome devil who brought you here. Am I right?"

Tony blushed and laughed self-consciously. "He certainly does strange things to me."

Lily licked her lips. "Like what?" she asked breathlessly, sitting on the bed and crossing her legs.

"Well, he makes my insides feel like jelly."

"Because of his great size?" Lily asked avidly.

"Partly. He's the biggest man I've ever seen, but he's so dominant. He likes to be obeyed."

"Does he beat you?" Lily asked wistfully.

"No, but sometimes he looks as if he'd like to. When he slashes his damned riding crop against his boots I think he wishes he had me over his knee."

"Riding crop?" Lily repeated with a delicious shudder. "How big is his Willie?"

"Willie?" Tony asked at a loss.

Lily laughed. "I'm Irish, we call it a Willie, but English girls call it a Peter, a Roger, or a Dick."

The last name rang a bell. Tony knew what a dick was. She blushed profusely. "I've never seen it," she confided shyly.

Lily considered for a moment, then acknowledged the lad could be telling the truth, since he'd always enter through the back door. "I can tell you haven't been together long. Are you jealous when he comes to a place like this?"

Tony knew that she was. Secretly she longed to have Adam Savage laugh and tease her, then take her to a private room. To cover her wicked thoughts she changed the subject. "What about you, Lily? Why do you do this?"

"To earn my living. My mam had six kids to feed. She took up with an Irish fighter who shagged me on the floor every time she turned her back, so when I turned thirteen, I left. Might as well get paid for it."

Tony was appalled. She wished she hadn't asked. Her education encompassed such a wide range of subjects these days, she realized how sheltered her life had been until she met Adam Savage.

Lily uncrossed her legs and stood up. "Look, are you sure I can't fellate you or something?"

"I don't think so," Tony said doubtfully.

"Well, would you mind then if I went and served another customer?"

"Of course not, Lily. It's been nice talking with you."

Tony glanced about the decks of the *Folly*. It was crowded with laughing sea nymphs and their Tridents. Savage was conspicuous by his absence and she'd be damned if she'd hang about kicking her heels while he indulged his vices.

When Mr. Burke opened the front door of Curzon Street he had a bucket in his hand. She swept him up and down with a cool glance. "You've a damned cheek, you scurvy devil!"

As she ascended the staircase with affronted dignity, Mr. Burke grinned and shook his head; she had the role of a young lord down pat.

Chapter 19

Whenever she found herself wide awake in the middle of the night, Tony wrote in her journal. She noticed with a little grimace that the pages were filling up and a definite pattern was forming. Each entry started out vilifying Adam Savage, cataloging his faults, listing her suspicions about his past, then spelling out her outraged sensibilities. Then philosophically came a notation whereby she rationalized or excused those faults. After that came grudging praise for either his wisdom or ability, followed by a sentence or two that clearly showed she was becoming infatuated and mooning after the man.

Tony sighed in exasperation at herself. Determined to fill a page that had nothing to do with Savage she put pen to paper.

Men! Since passing myself off as a member of the opposite sex, my eyes have been opened. Men lead two entirely separate lives in two completely different worlds. Whenever ladies are present they pay lip service to being polite, well bred, refined, faithful, and more or less civilized. When ladies are absent, off comes the mask and they are none of the above.

Men have conspired to form a closed circle for the sole purpose of self-indulgence and gratification of the senses. They eat what they fancy, drink anything that intoxicates, go wherever they please, say whatever they wish, place wagers on anything that moves, and throw good money away on bad women.

A double standard exists for society's sons and daughters. Girls are brought up to be obedient, polite, self-effacing, and chaste. Above all else, chaste. Boys on the other hand are taught that "chaste makes waste," and are hustled off to a brothel to prove their manhood about the same time they sprout their first whisker.

The hardest part to swallow is that men make the rules, not only for themselves but for women as well. From what I have observed they are free to break the rules while women are not. *For her own good* a young lady passes from the authority of her father to the authority of her husband. She must be a virgin so that her new lord and master can indulge in some traditional, self-indulgent, hypocritical hymeneal rite.

Men are allowed, nay encouraged, to acquire their knowledge of sex from any and all available sources, while women are only allowed to be taught by their husbands.

What about her? Chances were she would never have a husband! Antonia lifted her pen as her thoughts drifted off. If she were free to choose her teacher, she knew who it would be. She began to scold herself for her wicked thoughts, then she stopped. Damnation, females weren't supposed to indulge even in *thinking* about it. She decided to rebel, even if it was only in thought.

Tony lay back on the bed, crossed her ankles, and folded her arms behind her head. Then she conjured a picture of Adam Savage in a towel. He was easily the most rugged-looking man she had ever seen, and the darkest. His weather-beaten masculinity made her feel weak. 'Twas the fashion for men to be pale, with the soft, smooth hands of a gentleman. Their clothes ornate and colorful, their hair powdered. None of these things appealed to her.

Savage's hands were calloused, scarred, and rough skinned as a laborer's, yet the thought of him touching her with those hands made her want to scream. Savage's skin was swarthy and hirsute, tempting her to learn its texture, to feel, to lift the towel and explore . . . everything, everywhere. Antonia felt warm, not just in her cheeks. Her skin began to tingle, then her bones felt as if they were melting and her insides began to ache with a sort of longing.

She wanted him to look at her as he looked at other females. She wanted him to think her attractive, special. She wanted him to kiss her . . . on the lips. She shivered, covered with gooseflesh, but it wasn't because she was cold. The ache in her belly spread upward into her breasts. She cupped them and they felt full and heavy and swollen. Her nipples hardened into diamonds. She removed her hands from her body and jumped from the bed quickly to dispel the guilt that stole over her.

Adam Savage spent the early hours of the morning with his secretary. Word of his wealth had spread like wildfire even beyond the City of London. Each day's post brought proposals for business ventures that Jeffrey Sloane screened before he took up Savage's valuable time.

Anything with the least possibility of merit he brought to his employer's attention.

Savage stood over a wastepaper basket with a sheaf of letters. The first scheme to hit the basket was a proposal to make saltwater fresh. The second was to extract silver from lead. The third was to transmute mercury into fine metal. Another for trading in human hair would probably prove vastly profitable, but it was distasteful to him. One of the letters concerned a new lottery scheme. Lotteries were extremely popular and the profits were obscene, but the money came from the poor who made up three quarters of the population and again it was distasteful. Savage was more interested in freight and new methods of shipping goods from one place to another. Manufactories abounded in England's industrial towns, but methods of transporting what was produced were archaic. He scanned a proposal for importing jackasses from Spain.

He glanced up at Sloane and drawled, "Hardly necessary when there are already so many in England."

A letter from Abraham Derby, however, who said he had discovered a method of smelting iron from coke, caught his attention, as did a proposal to build a network of canals throughout England. He told Sloane to acknowledge these proposals and set up meetings with the men involved. He especially wanted to meet a civil engineer by the name of Telford who designed tunnels, bridges, and aqueducts.

Another idea Savage knew had great potential was railroads. Stone for the town of Bath had been carried from the Combe Hill quarries by carts on rails. The day was hardly long enough for all the things Savage planned.

He intended to buy a sailing vessel to carry cargo between England and the Continent. Edenwood still needed furnishings, some of which could be purchased abroad. He must also make time for a visit to the head offices of the East India Company and today he was seeing Lord Bathurst at three with the intention of buying his seat in Parliament. Savage was willing to go as high as ten thousand for a seat at Westminster, but shrewdly toyed with the idea of offering him four. At two o'clock he expected a visit from Lady Elizabeth Foster, a looker who was so alluring, it was reported no man could withstand her.

Savage rapidly fired off acceptance or rejection of two dozen social invitations, gave Sloane a list of ladies who were to receive flowers, then finally came to the last item of business. Lord Anthony Lamb. He had put off the inevitable all morning, but he must bite the bullet and confront him. Savage cursed as he heard his manservant answer the door and let someone in. He'd have to leave by the backstairs to avoid the caller.

"Get rid of whoever that is," he directed Sloane.

"Too late," Tony drawled, walking into the office and straddling a wooden chair.

Savage nodded to Sloane. "Leave us."

The moment the door was closed, Savage lashed into her. "I paid out good money last night, why didn't you fuck her?"

Tony was stunned. "How the hell do you know I didn't?"

"Because I paid the girl for information."

"You bastard!" Tony spat, feeling cornered.

His ice-blue eyes froze her with a look of contempt.

"What did she say?"

"She told me you had no interest in females. She told me you only fancied men. She told me you were a bum-boy."

"What is a bum-boy?" Tony asked, only knowing it was something that had put Savage in a black rage.

He didn't speak for a full minute while he grappled with the dilemma before him. If the lad truly did not know, perhaps he shouldn't enlighten him. Surely no one could be that innocent. He had forgotten there could be such untouched innocence in the world. Savage controlled his black anger.

"Have you ever made love with a man?" he asked bluntly.

"No!" Tony replied instantly. Then reminded herself to answer his questions from a male viewpoint.

"Has any man made physical advances to you?"

"No," she replied truthfully, although she was puzzled.

"How would you feel if a man touched your cock and propositioned you?"

Did men do such things to other men? she wondered. "I would feel outraged, disgusted. I would slap his face."

Relief washed over Savage, yet he laughed with contempt. He picked up his swordstick. "Tony my lad, you are going to have to learn how to protect yourself. You don't slap somebody's face. That wouldn't put the fear of God into him. Always remember that *attitude* is everything. Let me demonstrate."

He grabbed her by the coat lapels, held the blade of the swordstick to her gullet, and growled, "I'll slit you from neck to nuts."

Tony swallowed hard. Savage was so menacing, she felt herself start to swoon. She grabbed hold of the chair back and held on.

Savage pressed the swordstick into her hands. "Your turn."

Again she swallowed hard. Then, contorting her face with what she thought was a dangerous look, she waved the blade about wildly and shouted, "I'll drown you in your own blood!"

Savage kept a straight face, but it was difficult to keep his amusement from showing. "I think perhaps a better *attitude* for you would be to deliver your threat in a silky voice. It can be far more effective than shouting, and always remember to threaten his balls. It does the trick every time. Try again."

Tony raised one lazy eyebrow, held the blade absolutely still against Savage's throat, and drawled silkily, "Would you care to lose a testicle?"

"Perfect!" Adam laughed, removing the deadly weapon from Tony's hand.

"Now, you still haven't told me why you didn't get laid."

Tony had never heard the expression before, but she knew he was referring to the sex act. She thrust her hands deep in her pockets and turned away from him to look out the window.

"I've been too embarrassed to confess my ignorance. Other than kissing, I don't really know what a man does to a woman."

It finally dawned on Savage just how much the boy's upbringing had insulated him against the real world. He'd been brought up by his grandmother with only a twin sister for companion. No wonder he seemed effeminate. He had never had the benefit of a father's influence or that of any other male. He'd never had the companionship of brothers who would have boasted who could pee the farthest, or shown him the best way to masturbate, or who had the longest cock.

"You *are* attracted to girls? I don't necessarily mean the soiled doves on the *Folly,* I mean other females?"

"Of course I am," Tony improvised, knowing it was what he wanted to hear and realizing Lord Lamb would have a healthy interest in the opposite sex. "Actually that little actress I met backstage at the Olympian was the prettiest little thing I've seen in ages. Dolly . . . that was her name! I've been trying to think of it all night."

Adam didn't have time right now to sit him down and explain the infinite details of sexuality. The minutiae involved in awakening desire, in arousal and foreplay. The nuances and differences between men and women, their tastes, their likes and dislikes. It would fill hours, if not days.

Savage ran his hand along the volumes in his bookcase. A lot of his books were at Edenwood, but he took out two bound volumes he had acquired in India.

One was the *Kama Sutra,* the other was the story of a concubine named Jemdanee and what went on behind the closed doors of the harem.

"Try to keep an open mind when you read these books. There are likely things in here that will shock you at first." He put a fatherly hand on Tony's shoulder. "If there is anything in here you want to ask me about, anything at all, don't hesitate." He smiled. "I'm quite willing to share any knowledge I've acquired about the mysteries of the opposite sex, and I'm certain Dolly wouldn't reject the advances of a Lord of the Realm, despite your lack of experience."

Savage walked to the door with him. "I don't mean to chuck you out, Tony, but I am expecting someone on business."

Tony tucked the books under her arm and walked down Half-Moon Street. Before she had taken a dozen steps, a black carriage drew up with its noble crest upon the door. Tony felt her stomach knot as the elegant female was handed down from the coach. Then her mouth fell open. It wasn't the lady who had visited him previously. It was another beautiful countess entirely. "Funny business," she muttered, "bloody funny business."

Lady Randolph's face lit up as Tony entered the room. "Ah, you've been to the lending library, I see." She patted the love seat. "Come and sit with me, darling, and we'll both have a quiet read."

Tony said, "Uh . . . is that *The Ladies' Quarterly?*" She firmly pushed the two volumes beneath her buttocks as she sat down. "Read me the funny bits."

"Well, let's see. There's a very strange new wig style called the she-dragon. It's quite hideous. I shall talk Frances Jersey into buying one. And speaking of wigs, did you know that the ladies of Rome have created a rage for red perukes? Would you believe there are several hundred shades to choose from? The French and English, however, still have a passion for white."

Roz turned the page. "The latest fashions in Paris are scandalous. Hoops are said to be going out of style and gowns have begun to follow the lines of the female form."

"Hoops are a damned nuisance anyway," Tony said. "After breeches and trousers I don't think I could ever go back to them."

"Hoops cover a multitude of sins. They disguise some frightfully lumpy figures."

For a moment Antonia felt sorry for herself. Sometimes she absolutely lusted for frills and ribbons. She recalled with envy the fashion plate who had an appointment with Savage. Appointment? Ha! Assignation!

"Good God, listen to this. Here's a recipe for ophthalmic lotion for sore eyes. Mix together white vitriol and bay salt. When the detonation is over, pour on a pint of rosewater. I presume they mean if you are not blinded by the detonation! Mix in refined sugar and apply."

"Doesn't sound too refined to me!" Tony grimaced.

"Ah, darling, when I was a girl, animal excrement figured prominently in most medicine. Cat dung was a particular favorite for removing a low hairline."

"Daubing cat caca on one's face sounds hazardous to me."

"Not nearly so dangerous as painting your face with white lead. Lady Coventry died from it."

Tony stood up, quickly tucked her books under her arm, and started for the door.

"What are you reading?"

"Oh . . . er . . . Eastern philosophy."

"Good for you, darling. It's time you broadened your mind."

In her chamber Tony threw off her coat, neckcloth, and boots and, stretching out on the bed, opened the story of Princess Jemdanee. She quickly became absorbed in the fascinating, exotic word-pictures it painted.

A harem is like an aviary, for we are all caged birds. Still I am happier here with my lord than I was in my father's Court of Kings, which was known as the Orchid House because of its stifling decadence.

The rooms are beautiful, with reflecting lotus ponds and fountains that spray colored water. The ornamental fish have gold rings through their noses. On hot days the fan boys pull cords so that the silken fans hang like sails from the high ceiling to emulate a sea breeze. To sweeten the air, camphor or a different fragrance of incense is burned day and night.

I am become an expert at *shatrant,* a form of Indian chess with jeweled pieces, played on an ivory and ebony board, for sometimes it amuses my lord and keeps him longer at my side. Best of all he likes *chaupar,* a game of chance played on the floor with a cross-shaped board.

The preparation for a visit from my lord is most pleasant. I sweeten my mouth with *paan,* which is a slice of betel nut mixed with lime, wrapped in a leaf and kept close by in a cunning little casket. Then begins my self-adornment. I paint my nipples and spread rouge in the hollow between my breasts to make my body more desirable. With my own hands I prepare my lord an aphrodisiac of crushed rubies, peacock bones, and the testicles of a ram, so that his great phallus will remain like marble throughout the night and into the dawn.

I pull on diaphanous pantaloons knotted at the waist by intricate silken cords and tassels. At first these seem impossible to undo. By the time my lord solves the secret pattern we are both in such a fever of anticipation, he is ready to fall upon me and bury his great weapon deep inside my silken sheath. My lord is sometimes so hot with desire that my maid must fan us with peacock feathers as we perform the dance of life and death over and over again.

Tonight my lord is hunting by moonlight. I can hear the tinkle of the lamb's bell which he uses to bait and draw the wild animals. If my lord kills the leopard before it reaches the bait he will be a great hero to all the ladies of the harem for saving the innocent lamb's life. All will seek to attract him from me. If my lord does not come to me tonight, my maid will have to spread a cooling paste of henna between my thighs to soothe my longing.

Tony closed the book with a snap. Would to God she had some paste of henna to cool her own hot center! She felt flushed and decidedly breathless. She knew exactly how Jemdanee felt, for she had become the princess and naturally her lord was none other than the Leopard.

Tony could take no more of their erotic tale for the present, but she could not resist taking a peek at the *Kama Sutra.* It was a fatal mistake! The pictures and commands blurred before her eyes. They were mesmerizing, wickedly erotic, yet intimately beautiful. The command inscribed upon the first page read: "You must fetter his soul before you bind your body to his in lovemaking."

Tony turned on her back and gazed up at the ceiling. Fetter his soul
. . . fetter his soul . . . bind your body to his . . .

Antonia was lost, lost. The room tilted and everything seemed to
slide away out of her control. She could no longer handle her emotions; she could no longer cope with this lie she was living. She longed
to stop time, then make it all go backward so that everything she had
done could be undone, and everything could be exactly the way it was
before . . . before.

Tony forced herself to breathe slowly, to calm down. She had momentarily let go of the strands and they had slipped through her fingers. Mentally she picked up the threads, one by one, and took a firm
grasp upon them. She would cope. She would face it all squarely.

The first thing she would examine were her feelings toward Adam
Savage. She was attracted, intrigued, but daunted. Nay, she lied. She
was not daunted enough to keep her sinful thoughts from him, and
attraction was far too pale and pallid an emotion for what she felt. Yet
she knew it was not love. She had no sweet thoughts about him. No
soft sighs, no illusions.

He was dangerous, immoral, and most likely wicked and corrupt.
She doubted if his kind of wealth could be accumulated without cheating and stealing. Despite all this, or perhaps because of it, she wanted
to be with him constantly. He drew her like a lunar tide. She swore she
would keep her distance, then against her will she would seek him out,
to look at him, to listen to him, to be with him. Morning, noon, or
night, it mattered not the hour when the longing struck.

She distilled her thoughts and her feelings down to one word. *Hunger.* She hungered for him. She hungered to touch him, have him
touch her. She hungered to kiss him, have him kiss her. She hungered
for him to teach her all his knowledge, all his skills, all his worldly
experience. She hungered to bind her body to his in lovemaking.

God, what a coil she was in. Her situation was impossible, yet she
must accept responsibility for what she had done. She sighed for what
might have been, then turned over and curled up in an effort to ease
her ache.

Chapter 20

Adam Savage looked over the merchant vessels that were for sale and by a process of elimination was left with a clipper that promised speed as well as spacious cargo holds. It had been neglected, run nonstop for profit obviously, and now that the wear and tear was visible, its owner intended squeezing the last half-penny out of it.

The telltale smell of opium still clung belowdecks. For that reason Savage determined to pay only half what was being asked. The thoroughbreds he had bought from the Prince of Wales were to be delivered to Edenwood today, so he decided to kill two birds with one stone. He'd sail the ship to Gravesend to see how it handled before he made an offer.

When Tony received the note from Savage telling her he was going to Edenwood, she heaved a sigh of relief. Wasn't it amazing the way things had of working themselves out? Today was the day she'd agreed to take part in the great race to Richmond.

It had seemed a lark at the time to agree to the phaeton race. After all, the winner stood to gain a small fortune, but she had been three sheets to the wind and the fact that she owned neither a perch phaeton, nor horses to drive it, hadn't deterred her. Her guardian always seemed to possess whatever she lacked and he had encouraged her to drive his carriage.

Tony knew it was unconscionable to race his cattle without his permission, but she reasoned, Savage would admire such initiative and daring. There was no denying it would take guts for her to carry it off, but just the thought of a glint of admiration, rather than contempt, from those ice-pale eyes made her want to risk all. She closed her eyes for a moment and clenched her fists. The need to prove herself knotted her guts.

The race was for couples. Sherry was taking Amoret, Charles Fox's mistress was Lizzie Armistead, and of course Georgiana was partnering the Prince of Wales. She wasn't the prince's mistress. No one filled that position at the moment because it was reserved for Maria Fitzherbert, who had a lovely house on Marble Hill in Richmond. She was playing coy at the moment and had retired from London so George would go running after her. He did, of course. It was rumored he drove out to Richmond every day, which gave the prince a distinct advantage in familiarity with the course, but Tony knew every single man racing was heavier than herself.

She scribbled a note inviting Dolly to spend the afternoon in a fun-filled drive to Richmond, signed it Lord Anthony Lamb, and dispatched it to the Olympian Theater. She felt confident the little actress would jump at the chance to rub elbows with the Carlton House set. This done, she lost no time making her way across Green Park to Stable Yard Road, where Savage kept his horses and carriages.

Tony felt a qualm when she saw the spanking, brand new high-perch phaeton. Its finish was glossy and without a scratch. The hostler took off his cap in reverent admiration as he told Lord Lamb it had been rubbed with eighteen coats of varnish.

The high-steppers Savage had acquired to pull the new rig were a breed apart from the sturdy carriage horses she had tooled along the turnpike, but Tony swallowed her misgivings, telling herself she'd been around horses all her life and that "attitude" was everything. She believed it and she knew Adam Savage held the same conviction.

She wanted to win this race more than anything she'd ever wanted before. Not only did she want to vindicate her brother's manhood, she wanted the prize money for herself. Savage passionately admired the ability to make money. She hungered to show him he was not the only one who could do so.

The hostler harnessed the horses in tandem between the shafts and walked the equipage outside into Stable Yard Road. In the sunlight the dark burgundy of the phaeton glowed deep red and the glossy coats of the blooded horses reflected the same color exactly. The stableman nodded toward the long whip standing erect in its pinch ring.

"These cattle are mettlesome, my lord. Don't touch 'em up until you are out in the country."

Tony knew the reins would be quite enough for her to handle and the whip would remain securely in its holder. She climbed up on the high perch with her heart in her mouth. Maneuvering about London's streets would be the tricky part; she had nothing to worry about once she reached the country road.

Amazingly she encountered no trouble as she guided them down the street. Everyone had enough sense to get out of the way, even the languid macaronis who made a profession of sauntering quickened their pace to give her a wide berth.

Tony managed to turn the first corner smoothly enough and when she turned the second corner into Green Park she saw it was almost clogged with horse-drawn phaetons and a boisterously noisy crowd.

Postilions and post boys swarmed about between the carriages giving aid and advice to all the contestants. Tony felt discouraged when she saw that the Prince of Wales's team consisted of three horses, but then her optimism rose again when she realized that he and Georgiana would take a royal postilion with them.

Crowds of spectators had gathered to vicariously experience the pleasures of the upper class, and a couple of turf accountants were collecting wagers. Colonel Dan Mackinnon was taking care of the private wagers and Lord Onslow was holding the prize money of a thousand guineas.

Southampton and Edward Bouverie, two of the Prince's gentlemen, strolled up to admire Tony's horseflesh. They raised their eyebrows and dashed off to find Dan Mackinnon to change their bets. Savage's high-strung animals were restless, flinging their heads in the air and fighting the feel of the bits beneath their tongues, but fortunately a couple of quick-witted postilions grabbed their harness and tried to soothe them.

Vendors hawked eel pasties, gingerbread, and cheap gin known as "mother's ruin" to the crowd. As well as availing themselves of the spirits being sold in the park, most of the bucks carried flasks of brandy and by the look of Sherry and one or two others, they had been imbibing to a dangerous degree.

The flowerettes of gaudy ribbon with numbers at their center were handed out. When Tony was handed the last one it turned out to be number thirteen! Her resolve hardened. She would make her own luck. It was another hour before some sort of order was restored from chaos, which gave Dolly Dawson plenty of time to make her way through the mirthful crowd to Tony's phaeton.

Tony blinked at the garish outfit the actress had chosen. Her powdered wig was a foot high, decorated by scarlet poppies; her dress and frilled parasol were also scarlet. Unfortunately they were different shades and the colors seemed at war with one another. The girl drew every male eye in the park as well as the eyes of the horses, who shied away as she approached.

Tony cursed beneath her breath, then gallantly reached down to give Dolly a hand up. The postilion winked at Tony and said, "Blimey, ye should 'ave put blinkers on yer cattle!"

Dolly giggled, lifted her skirts to show a liberal amount of petticoat and ankle, and when the postilion gave her a leer, she replied, "Should 'ave put blinkers on you too!"

She gave Tony a brilliant smile. "Coo, this is ever so exciting, my lord. I can feel my blood rushin' about." She put her hand on Tony's thigh. "Ow about you, Lord Lamb?" she asked suggestively.

"Dolly, I suggest you use your hand to hang on to your wig."

A starting pistol was fired and the Prince of Wales, who had been honored with number one, tooled his phaeton like a wagon driver. He was addicted to speed and had no intention of waiting until he was out of London before he whipped up his cattle.

"That's the Duchess of Devonshire!" Dolly cried with awe. "I can't believe I'm 'obnobbing with 'Er bleedin' Grace!"

Her bleeding Grace was in a reckless mood, urging George to leave the others to eat their dust. Tony didn't worry that number thirteen was the last to start. The city streets were no place to vie for position. Caution would be her byword until she reached the countryside. Others who hadn't the sense they were born with were already out of the race. She passed a phaeton that had lost a wheel and another whose driver had toppled drunk from his perch.

When the road widened and the first trees appeared, the horses picked up speed so rapidly, they outpaced half a dozen other teams in the space of minutes. They were bowling along at such a high speed, all Dolly could do was gasp and hang on for dear life.

Tony saw that the road ahead narrowed and reluctantly pulled back on the reins, knowing there would not be enough space for her and the carriage ahead. That was when she learned the horses must have gotten their bits between their teeth. They surged ahead wildly, passing the carriage as if it were standing still—and to Tony's alarm she saw she had just passed His Royal Highness.

Dolly shrieked as her scarlet parasol turned inside out. She let go of its handle to clutch the seat with both hands and the thing took off like a projectile. Tony knew she couldn't control the horses and began to worry about how she would stop them when they arrived at Richmond Park.

She didn't remember passing any of the remaining racing teams, but suddenly up ahead she saw White Lodge, the royal residence. The gates to Richmond Park had been thrown open and a small crowd had gathered outside. As they thundered through, a great cheer went up. Tony heard it only dimly over the roar of her own blood in her ears.

The horses were thrown off their stride by the crowd and slowed slightly as they climbed the first hill. Tony braced her feet to the floorboards and pulled back on the reins with all her strength, shouting, "Whoa, whoa, whoa," over and over until she was hoarse. The team veered from the path onto the grassy slope and Dolly felt as if her teeth would be jarred from her mouth. The team slowed to a canter by the time it circled the park, and Tony managed to bring the horses to a quivering stop, just as two other phaetons arrived, neck and neck.

"Blimey," Dolly whispered, her poppies hanging limply, obscuring her vision, "if this is wot you do for fun, count me out."

Tony jumped down to fasten the reins to a stout tree with shaking hands before the devil horses decided to bolt. Then she dropped to the grass to catch her breath and gather her wits.

It came as a surprise when she realized the shouts were directed at her. "You won! You won!" regaled the crowd, and suddenly she was laughing and a mollified Dolly was dimpling at the men who competed to hand her down from the phaeton.

The next hour was a blur for Tony as she walked about on wobbly legs accepting congratulations. The Prince of Wales, peeved for a moment that he had lost, told all his friends that he would have won easily if it hadn't been for a bright red, unidentifiable object that deliberately spooked his gee-gees.

When Maria Fitzherbert arrived, however, the race was wiped from his mind. Here was a much more urgent prize he intended to capture. A picnic feast had been arranged on the lawns of Richmond Park. Footmen spread snowy cloths over trestle tables and were kept busy replenishing the food and drink consumed by the royal guests.

A marvelous feeling of euphoria enveloped Tony as she walked among the merrymakers, acknowledging their congratulations. All she could think of was Adam's face when he learned she had won the great phaeton race to Richmond. Dolly had removed the wilted poppies, and without the clashing scarlet of her parasol, her red dress looked quite fetching. Tony's euphoria was wiped away as she came face to face with Bernard Lamb.

"Hello, coz."

She stared at him in disbelief. "What the devil are you doing here?" Dolly and Angela Brown were already having an animated conversation.

Bernard drawled, "Racing, same as you, cousin. Why else would I be here?"

That is precisely what worried Tony. She could have sworn she hadn't passed him in the race, but then she hadn't remembered passing Sherry and the others either.

Bernard's lip curled. "I'd congratulate you, but it's quite obvious it was superior horseflesh and not your driving skill that won the race."

"Yes, blood will out," Tony said pointedly, and had the satisfaction of seeing Bernard's nostrils flare at the insult. She walked away, hoping Dolly would remain with her friends, but she trailed after Tony. There was no way she was going to miss being front and center when Lord Lamb was awarded the prize.

The Prince of Wales took the fat purse from his equerry, Lord Onslow, and prevailed upon Mrs. Maria Fitzherbert to make the presentation. As Tony came forward she was dazzled by the lady's beauty. Maria had learned how to dress in France. Her complexion was like cream and roses and her glorious golden-blond hair fell to her shoulders in unpowdered curls. The magnificent swell of her breasts was breathtaking, even concealed beneath her modest neckline.

She pressed the purse upon Tony, who gallantly clicked her heels and raised the lady's soft white hand to her lips. The crowd applauded that it was prettily done and Sherry immediately touched him up for a loan.

"Shove off! Find another pigeon to pluck."

"You did say pluck?" punned Sherry.

Dolly giggled. "His Royal Highness is going to get plucked before the afternoon is out."

"Nay, the fair lady refuses to be any man's mistress," Sherry informed her.

"He ain't any man, he's a prince. She's very clever. She's probably 'olding out for jewels."

"Or something beyond the price of rubies," Sherry remarked to Tony. Then he smiled at Dolly. "What leads you to believe she is clever, my dear?"

"She called 'er 'ouse Marble Hills didn't she? That's like advertising how beautiful her breasts are."

"Like something out of a play, begod!"

Dolly looked at Sheridan with speculative eyes and confided, "I'm an actress."

"Never!" Sherry said with a perfectly straight face, but Amoret slipped a possessive arm through his and steered him away from the ambitious Dolly.

His Royal Highness could not keep his eyes from Maria Fitzherbert's marble hills, and he longed to hold them in the palms of his hands. The thought aroused and hardened him for the umpteenth time. In fact, he'd been up and down so many times this afternoon, it felt like a flagpole.

Prince George had expended every effort to lure Maria inside White Lodge so she could explore the rooms and so he could do a little exploring of his own. He'd driven to Richmond every day for a week. She'd given him tea and cake, comfits and kisses, but she had not put him out of his misery.

At first Maria had thought him just a boy. She was six years older and had been twice married and widowed. When she realized his feelings were of an amorous nature she was flattered. He was a new experience for Maria because both her husbands had been elderly gentlemen and quite easily handled. His Highness had such an impetuous nature, it quite excited her, yet she still felt worldly when she compared herself with her very royal, but very young, admirer.

The Prince captured Maria's hand and squeezed it meaningfully. He drew closer and she could tell he meant to steal a kiss at any cost. She jumped up, at last amenable to his suggestion that they retire indoors. If she allowed him a kiss it would have to be in private.

"Sweet puss, pop your little paw in mine," George pleaded.

Maria again bestowed her hand upon him and wondered if it was within the realm of possibility to bestow her hand upon him in marriage. She would be the Princess of Wales, then later on, Queen of England! It was impossible, of course, because of that wretched Marriage Act that had been passed. Still, if it was written in the stars, all things were possible.

George's good manners prevented him from taking her to a bedchamber, so he led her to a private salon, elegantly furnished with brocaded chairs and settees. He closed the door firmly and drew Maria into his arms. She allowed him a kiss, then tried to draw away, but one kiss did not satisfy His Highness, indeed it barely whetted his appetite for this delectable female. His arms imprisoned her as his mouth descended. This time the kiss was not sweet, but hot.

"Your Highness." She gasped, her breasts rising and falling with a growing excitement.

"Pussycat, don't call me that. I don't want us to be formal, I want us to be intimate."

Maria blushed deeply. She had been intimate occasionally, but only with a faithful, elderly husband.

George kissed her again, but this time his lips forced hers apart slightly and he slipped the tip of his tongue into her mouth. Then he pressed his sex against her soft thighs to show her he was hard for her. "Don't be cruel, Pussykins, don't break my heart, Maria."

A young rampant male was a new experience for her. He was society's darling, extremely spoiled and able to have his own way about everything. Maria suddenly realized her power. She could have the young stallion eating out of her hand. "Prince George, if you do not behave, I shall faint."

"Sweet Pussy, if you do not be kind, I shall die." He rubbed himself against her belly, his hand firmly reaching for a love apple.

Just as firmly she removed his hand. "If you promise to behave, I will let you take me home in your carriage, but we must go back outside now or my reputation will be blackened beyond redemption."

"Ah, Pussy, you are so hard, yet so soft. Let it be known that a prince obeys your commands." He had a little golden locket for her holding a miniature portrait of himself, but he would give it to her in the carriage where she couldn't escape him. He would order a closed carriage to escort her home to Marble Hill.

Tony glanced at the sun and guessed it was about four o'clock. She was anxious to get Savage's team back to London without incident. She made her way to the paddock where the horses were grazing and asked a postilion to help her harness them into the burgundy phaeton. Dolly looked reluctant. "Stay, if you like," Tony urged.

"No, I can't really, I have to get back to the theater." She hesitated. "Could you go a bit slower on the way back?"

"Snail's pace, I promise you," Tony vowed. She checked to make sure the bits were tight beneath the horses' tongues and took a firm grip on the reins the moment she climbed onto the high perch. Miraculously the horses had decided to behave and Tony, lulled by the rhythmic, springy motion of the phaeton, began to daydream about Adam Savage.

She was startled from her reverie by the sound of galloping horses coming up close behind. She turned in alarm to see Bernard Lamb standing up at the reins whipping his team. The moment she slacked on the reins her own team lunged forward, spurred on by the speed of the other horses.

The space between the carriages widened as the blood stock proved their superiority. Tony was frightened. She knew her cousin Bernard wasn't trying to race. He was trying to kill her!

He hadn't a hope in hell of catching up out here in the country, but London was only a mile away and she would have to slow the team down to maneuver safely. It was the other traffic rather than Tony's efforts that curbed the team's speed, but still they seemed to surge along the city streets at a frightening pace. She was thankful that darkness was still hours away, fervently counting on the hope that Bernard Lamb would not attempt murder in broad daylight.

As they started up Constitution Hill, Tony gave a prayer of thanks that their pace slackened enough so that she'd be able to turn the corner. She thought she was home free as she approached Stable Yard Road, but at that moment her cousin's team pulled alongside and careened into her.

If it hadn't been for the horse and cart delivering coal to Lancaster House, Tony would have been able to swerve out of Bernard's path, but as it was, there was nowhere for her to go. The burgundy phaeton overturned, throwing both Tony and Dolly to the pavement. The horses plunged madly, but miraculously, they were not dragged down by the light phaeton.

Bernard Lamb's carriage was unharmed, but the impact had flung both him and Angela from the rig. Tony's long legs saved her from hitting her head on the curb. Dolly sat crying, holding her ankle, while coal littered the entire road as if there had been an explosion at a colliery.

Pandemonium reigned. The coal carter cursed a blue streak. The hostlers from Stable Yard ran out, as did the entire staff of servants from Lancaster House.

Tony was livid. Never before in her life had she experienced such a blinding rage. She picked up the horsewhip and advanced upon the prone figure of her hated cousin. He threw up his arms to protect himself and shouted, "You've busted my bloody rib!"

"You bastard, I'll kill you," screamed Tony.

Suddenly the whip was wrenched from her hand. "What in Christ's name is going on here?" She looked into ice-pale eyes and froze.

Chapter 21

Savage's day had been unbelievably successful. His horses were all snug and tight in their new stables at Edenwood and the clipper had skimmed up the Thames from Gravesend with a minimum of sail. He negotiated his own price and had decided to spruce her up a bit and name her the *Flying Dragon*.

When he stabled his horse he noticed immediately his phaeton and high-steppers were missing.

"Where are my other horses?" he inquired.

"This is the day of the phaeton race to Richmond, sir," the head groom announced.

Savage raised dark brows. "Your point being?"

"Lord Lamb—" He got no further.

"The young son of a bitch wouldn't dare!" Savage thundered. It was at this point that all hell had broken loose.

"The bastard tried to kill me!" Tony informed Savage.

It looked the other way about to Adam. Not only had Tony taken his cattle and smashed his phaeton to pieces, he had been about to horsewhip his cousin to vent his temper.

"Too bad he didn't succeed. It would save me the trouble," Savage said between his teeth.

Adam helped a distraught Angela Brown to her feet, but a twisted knee prevented her from standing. He lifted her onto the seat of Bernard's carriage. Next he picked up Dolly and lifted her up beside Angela. Savage helped the stablemen unharness his thoroughbreds from the wrecked phaeton. He examined them carefully, running his hands over their fetlocks and hocks.

When he saw they suffered from no more than a frothy coat of lather, he went back into the street to deal with the belligerent carter.

"Wot about my bloody coal?" A shower of abusive curses followed.

"I suggest you pick it up from the road before you are charged with causing an accident." The deadly tone of authority made the coal man swallow his curses. Savage swept Tony with an incensed look. "You can help him!" He strode over to where Bernard Lamb was just picking himself up off the ground.

"What happened?" Savage demanded.

Bernard shrugged. "We were racing. The coal wagon got in the way." He held his side.

"Will you be able to drive?" Savage asked.

Bernard grinned. "Take more than a cracked rib to stop me."

"Good man," Savage approved. He turned to the girls whose tears had transformed into looks of speculation. "Are you both all right?" he asked kindly.

"Well, I'll be off the stage with this a week, won't I?" Angela said, showing him her swollen ankle.

Savage reached into his billfold and slipped the girls some folded pound notes, then saw Bernard and the actresses on their way long before Tony and the carter had picked up all the coal. Savage still held his wallet. "Haul this away on your wagon and I'll make it worth your while."

The coal man touched his blackened cap with a blackened hand and reached for the crisp pound notes with blackened fingers. When the pieces of the phaeton were loaded, Savage said curtly to Tony, "When you are done here, present yourself in Half-Moon Street." He strode off without deigning to glance in her direction.

Once Savage had departed, the servants from Lancaster House began to snicker at the young lord who had been ordered to pick up lumps of coal from the front street. "When yer finished, we 'ave a chimney needs sweepin'," a footman taunted.

"Shut your bloody cake hole," Tony spat, taking aim with a shiny cob of anthracite.

Her feet dragged later as she climbed the front steps of the town house, but she was determined to tell him of the danger she'd been in and how Bernard Lamb intended to eliminate Lord Lamb so that he could inherit.

Tony climbed to the library and was thankful that Sloane was nowhere about. Savage sat smoking and sipping a brandy. Tony opened her mouth, "My cousin followed me to Richmond for the sole purpose of—"

"Don't dare offer me excuses, for what you did was inexcusable," Savage stated flatly.

Tony flushed. "I know I shouldn't have taken your horses without permission, but if I'd asked, you would have refused."

"Correct." Silence filled the room.

"I wouldn't have gotten roped into the race if I hadn't had too much to drink."

"Correct." Silence and smoke now filled the room.

Tony should have known the day would be a disaster from the moment she had drawn number thirteen. It had been an omen. She didn't dare offer bad luck as an excuse, however, for Savage was the kind of man who believed you made your own luck. There wasn't much point in accusing her cousin of plotting her murder, either, for he'd treat it with contempt. To hell with Savage; a tyrant couldn't be appeased.

Tony lifted her chin and drew the heavy purse from her pocket. She dropped it on his desk. "You'll think what the hell you like, no matter what I say, but I won the bloody race and that took guts." She sneered at him. "That'll pay for your precious phaeton."

Savage ground out his cigar. "You've missed the point again, unless you are being deliberately obtuse. You put the animals in jeopardy, to say nothing of the girls. Fortunately the horses are unharmed; not so the ladies."

"The *ladies*"—she said the word with heavy sarcasm—"sustained nothing more than sprained ankles. I think they'll live!"

Adam's eyes and voice lost none of their iciness. "Unlike you, they have to earn their living. They won't be walking the boards of the stage for at least a week." His eyes acknowledged the money on the desk. "This should keep them from starving."

Tony's mouth tightened. "They'll still be able to earn money on their backs; it was their bloody ankles they hurt."

Savage said through his teeth, "The thing I most detest about you is your snobbery."

Antonia felt pierced to the heart. She knew Anthony would never cry in front of Savage, yet she felt her throat constrict. To stop the tears from forming she swiped her hand across her nose in a gesture of disrespect, leaving a black streak of coal dust.

Savage shook his head. "Two young bucks trying to outdo each other to impress the ladies. Get the hell out of my sight."

Another young buck was trying to impress a lady at this same hour. His Royal Highness sat in a closed carriage outside Marble Hill. His blue satin leg pressed against Maria Fitzherbert's soft thigh as he brushed back a golden curl. "Darling Pussy, let me stay the night?" he begged.

Pussy pretended outrage. "Prince George, how can you offer me such an insult?"

"Please don't call me Prince George, Pussykins. And I do not offer you insult, I offer you honor. I would honor you with my body," he whispered, pressing close and capturing her hands.

"That is in the marriage ceremony. Pray do not mock marriage, Sire."

"I do not mock marriage, Maria. I would make you my wife if that were possible."

Maria's heart soared. "Alas, Sire, it is not. It grows late, I must go in."

"Don't call me Sire, Pussycat. Have you no pity in your heart? If you will not take me into Marble Hill, at least stay here with me awhile."

"A little while," she conceded. "What would you like me to call you? I cannot simply use your Christian name, it shows no respect."

"Pussy, I don't want your respect, I want your heart," he said fervently, slipping his arm about her waist, allowing his fingers to graze the underside of her tempting breast.

"May I call you Prinny?" Maria suggested.

"Yes, yes, that is perfect. Pussy and Prinny! I have a little gift for you." He pulled out the locket, wishing it were jewels. "Forgive me my sentimental nature, darling Pussy, but you know you hold my heart in your hands. Wear this golden symbol to show me you will treat it kindly."

"You do me more honor than I deserve." She lifted her lovely golden locks so that he might fasten the little heart about her neck and he groaned as his fingers came in contact with her warm flesh. His strong hands could not be stayed. He unbuttoned the front of her gown and buried his face against her swelling globes. Maria knew she could not make a scene. If the carriage driver and the postilions became privy to what she did in the coach, she would be branded a strumpet.

"Prinny, you mustn't!" she whispered.

"Pussy, I must!" he murmured thickly, pressing her back against the squabs as his hands filled with the glory of her and his mouth came down on hers demanding entrance.

Maria came up for air realizing that her body was not immune to his lovemaking. She was becoming aroused and it was a pleasurable novelty for her.

"Darling Pussy, I am in agony, only see what you do to me." He drew her hand to his male center.

Maria was astounded at its hardness. She tried to give it a little squeeze, but it was as solid as marble. Suddenly she withdrew her hand. In another minute he would have her skirts over her head, and this was not in Maria's plans at all. She buttoned the front of her gown and began to cry. "I have allowed you such liberties, the blush will never leave my cheek. I am such a wanton, you will have a disgust of me."

"Sweetest Pussy, don't cry, you will break my heart. There is nothing wanton about you, beloved. 'Tis I who am wicked and lecherous."

She allowed him to brush the tears from her cheeks and to kiss her good-night. And it had been a good night, she decided. A very good night.

In contrast Tony Lamb was having a bad night. She sat in the bathtub washing black coal dust from her hands and face. She bit her lip as she recalled how gently Savage had carried Angela and Dolly. He treated trollops like ladies, yet she was a real lady and he treated her like a lackey. The thing that really rankled was his accusation of snobbery. It was a totally unfair charge, and the cause of it had been that swine Bernard Lamb. He was evil. In her heart she knew he had sabotaged the *Seagull* and caused Anthony to drown.

Tony wiped away tears, managed to get soap in her eyes, and swore a blue streak. She hoped Bernard died tonight of his injuries. The bastard deserved to die. She indulged in a fantasy that removed the threat of the dreaded Bernard Lamb from her life. She could go back to being a lady . . . well, perhaps not exactly a lady, she'd been exposed to too many worldly things to be a lady, but she could be a woman. Wasn't that a thousand times better than being a lady?

Tony blushed, then lifted her chin. If Adam Savage fell at her feet, she'd step over him! Well, she might as well stop dreaming. Her hated cousin wasn't going to expire from a broken rib. If she wanted him dead, she would have to kill him. A duel! That was the answer. She'd challenge him to a duel and shoot him!

She shuddered and climbed from the cooling water. She would avenge her twin! Even the Bible approved an eye for an eye.

Adam Savage pondered what to do about Tony. At least the virginity thing would be taken care of with Dolly on the job. He again shook his head at the sheer crust of the young devil taking his thoroughbreds and racing them to Richmond. And winning, no less!

The lad was right about one thing. It had taken guts. It was definitely time to channel some of those high spirits along more productive lines. Savage decided to take him along on his voyage to the Continent.

Tony could select and buy his cargo for the Indies. It would be a perfect cover for the smuggling operation he himself was about to set up. He could pick up some art treasures for Edenwood, and if he wasn't mistaken the Carnival of Venice would be taking place shortly. It was the epitome of decadence, where masked men and women roamed the streets seeking liaisons. He'd seen it from the deck of a ship once. A week-long spectacle of music, lights, and fantastic costumes never to be forgotten. This time he would take part.

While the *Flying Dragon* was being readied, there would be enough time to hold Edenwood's housewarming. The house would display his wealth to London's nobility and show his neighbors who would control the entire district. He had bought his seat in the House of Commons, but when election time came around later in the year, he would need votes to keep the seat. Savage wasn't worried. He could win a majority by the simple expedient of promising five shillings to everyone who voted for him.

By the time the sun rose the next morning, Savage was on the London docks hiring his crew. He even signed on a couple of lascars who had crewed for him years back on the China runs.

By breakfasttime he was giving Sloane the guest list so he could issue invitations for the weekend at Edenwood. By eleven he was in Curzon Street inviting Lady Randolph to Edenwood and handing Tony a long list of furnishings that were still needed for the guest bedchambers.

Tony was amazed that he harbored no ill feelings for what had taken place yesterday, and flattered he had enough confidence in her taste to give her the responsibility of furnishing his beloved Edenwood.

"Why don't you go down to Gravesend a couple of days early? John Bull would welcome your suggestions for the party. This is his first effort at entertaining the English and the first time I've seen him a bit overwhelmed."

Tony looked at the endless list in her hand, then raised her brows as she wondered if he were serious. "I've only got a week," she said faintly.

"Good God, boy, the universe was created in a week," Adam pointed out.

With the invaluable help of Roz and Mr. Burke to ferret out furniture treasures from St. Martin's Lane to Soho, she went on a buying spree at Ince and Mayhew, Vile and Cobb, and Robert Manwaring's shop. Tony was in her element, deciding that each chamber should represent the craftsmanship of a famous London cabinetmaker.

Thomas Sheraton's designs were greatly influenced by French furnishings in the style of Louis XIV, and Tony bought matching cream and gilt pieces. The chaise longue and bedhangings were a delicate French blue. A second bedchamber would showcase George Hepplewhite's classical designs. She chose a bed with an oval headboard as well as a matching settee and upholstered armchairs whose oval backs were decorated by the Prince of Wales's feathers. Stunning little rosewood drum tables with drawers to hold money or toilet articles were a specialty of Hepplewhite and they complimented the other furnishings.

Robert Adam's designs were the absolute rage at the moment and as a result the pieces were priced outrageously. Tony didn't even ask the cost of the marble-topped commode and bedside tables with their hand-painted panels of lovers in romantic landscapes. She couldn't resist a pair of carved candelabra stands with ram's heads and world-famous hoof feet. The magnificent domed bed was carved into a festoon of vines and flowers.

On impulse, simply for the pleasure of annoying Adam Savage, she decided one chamber would be Chinese. She chose a pair of Chippendale black japanned armchairs, upholstered in jade velvet, and a black lacquer commode with golden pagodas, temples, and trees dripping cherry blossoms. The bed was a thing of great beauty, with a magnificently carved dragon in rampant splendor forming the headboard. She chose jade velvet bedhangings to match the side chairs.

Tony took intense delight in everything she chose, even down to the porcelain powder bowls and the chamber pots. Everything must be delivered to Edenwood no later than Thursday noon so that she could plenish the chambers later that day or Friday morning at the latest, in time for any early guests who might arrive Friday evening.

John Bull welcomed Tony like a prodigal son. They immediately conspired to have every room perfect by the time Savage arrived with those critical ice-blue eyes. Fortunately John Bull had a full staff of servants who earned higher wages at Edenwood than at any other stately home in England. They carried the furniture up the gracefully curving staircase almost cheerfully and patiently stood by to arrange and rearrange as young Lord Lamb directed. It was amazing how well the carpets and the French wallpaper blended with the furnishings Tony had selected. Savage's taste and hers certainly ran along parallel lines.

By nightfall every last detail was in place. When Adam arrived after dark and strolled about his Eden, no fault could be found with the extraordinary efforts that had been expended to turn his house into a palatial showcase.

Flushed with praise, Tony was happy but exhausted. Savage's presence always disturbed her to an alarming degree, so she was glad to retire. She decided to sleep in the blue-and-gold room with its exquisite French wallpaper, but Kirinda glided up to her with a lighted branch of perfumed candles and murmured, "The master instructed me to put you in the Chinese bedchamber, my lord."

Tony bit her lip to keep from laughing. Chinoiserie was a private joke between her and Adam and she took delight in it. In bed she hugged her knees to her chest. She hadn't felt this happy in a long time. Her masquerade had its compensations. Adam Savage had allowed Anthony to become a part of his life, whereas she doubted if he would have allowed Antonia such liberties. She sighed, then yawned, hoping she would dream about him.

As it happened, she did not. She stood in the cold light of dawn in a black mask and a long cloak. Icy fingers clutched her heart as she selected a long, lethal-looking pistol from a leather case. In slow motion she paced off the field as her second counted to ten. Her opponent on the field of honor had none, for he turned and fired his pistol on the count of nine. She felt the bullet enter her chest, searing white hot, then blossoming into blood-red.

Bernard Lamb removed his mask and murmured, "For what I am about to receive, I am truly thankful. Amen."

When morning arrived, Tony groaned and turned over. It felt as if she had taken no rest at all. She climbed wearily from the dragon bed and grimaced because she ached from head to foot. She brightened, however, when Kirinda came in and handed her a note from Savage. She scanned it eagerly and read: *Tony, put on some old breeches and come take a look at the stable of thoroughbreds I stole from HRH.*

Perhaps a ride was just what she needed. John Bull had told her

Adam intended to provide mounts for all his guests if they felt like riding. She'd been too busy the previous day to visit the stables, but hurried into riding breeches now, foregoing the tiewig and brushing her hair back into a queue the way Adam did his.

At least thirty-five of the forty stalls held a prime piece of horseflesh. A dozen grooms and stableboys were employed polishing tack. A deep voice greeted her.

"How the hell can you sleep so late?"

Tony whirled about, mildly annoyed at the taunt, for it couldn't possibly be any later than eight o'clock. Savage stood in old breeches and rolled-up shirtsleeves. He held a shovel in his hands and was obviously cleaning out the stalls.

"Surely you have enough stableboys for that," she pointed out. Tony definitely did not like the zealous light that shone from Savage's eyes. She wanted to retreat with all speed, but her boots felt rooted in the straw.

With an amused grin that he made no effort to conceal, Savage said, "If there is one thing I've discovered that builds muscle along with character, it's shoveling shit." He tossed over a spade. "You could use a bit more of both, Tony."

Her first impulse was to throw a shovelful in his arrogant face, but then, of course, Savage would have an excuse to rub her face in it. As if he read Tony's thoughts, Adam said, "They do say it's good for growing whiskers."

Tony had more pride than to refuse the task and she ground her teeth because Savage knew exactly that, curse him, curse him. She picked up the shovel and nonchalantly began to scoop manure. She even whistled a merry tune between her teeth to take all his joy out of plaguing her. In actual fact he'd already done three parts of the work. "You've only left me nine stalls," she cheerfully called to him as he went outside for some fresh straw.

"Nine!" she said, groaning and gritting her teeth when he disappeared. It felt like hours later when she heard booted feet behind her. She'd actually managed to muck out half a dozen and was just about at the limit of her strength. She straightened her aching back and turned. An amused sneer on the face of Bernard Lamb almost stunned her.

"What the devil are you doing here?" Tony demanded.

"Your exact words at Richmond, I recall, dear coz," Bernard drawled. "You are becoming a damned bore."

Tony suddenly found plenty of strength to scoop up a shovelful of horse shit.

"Tony!" A deep command poised the muck in midair. "Mr. Lamb is an invited guest. I suggest you get cleaned up."

Tony's lip curled. "I doubt if even your exalted bathing room will remove the stench from my nostrils!"

Chapter 22

Tony bathed and changed, but even though guests would be coming and going all day, she wore riding breeches and jacket. There was no way she was going to be bludgeoned into formal attire before the sun went down. Her one concession was a powdered tiewig.

Tony took herself off to the kitchens to avoid her cousin. The amount of food that had been prepared took her breath away. Most of the food dishes were English, but there were silver trays of sweetmeats and other exotic delicacies for those with an adventurous palate. Actually Savage and John Bull had argued over the food. John Bull contended every dish should be English and Savage adamantly insisted his guests would expect Eastern dishes. A compromise had been reached.

Tony sniffed the spicy aromas appreciatively. "It smells sinful in here."

"I told Excellency this stuff would insult his guests," John Bull said with regret. "This is a very suspicious occasion."

"Auspicious," Tony murmured.

"That too," John Bull agreed.

"Can I help?"

"Ah, yes indeed, your lordship. If you would be so kind as to help with the inspection. You will know better than I if the uniforms pass muster in your exalted country." He opened a door to an adjoining room where a dozen men were in various stages of dressing themselves in livery. Tony felt her cheeks warm at the scene before her, but bit her lip and averted her eyes from those who had not yet struggled into their satin breeches.

The livery was a tasteful shade of gray with snowy stockings and black shoes.

John Bull sniffed. "I ordered scarlet with gold braid, but Excellency countermanded me."

Tony would have loved to agree with John Bull, telling him Savage had made the wrong choice, but as usual Savage was right and it was galling. "I think you may trust his judgment."

"Ah, not always," John Bull said, handing out white gloves, then directing the footmen to take the silver trays out among the guests. "Sometimes he keeps very bad company and takes reckless risks. It is high time he gave up smuggling and settled down."

Smuggling? Ohmigod, that explains so much about him! thought Tony. *His ships, his wealth, his scar!*

"If you are finished dissecting my character, I'd like your aid," Adam drawled.

Tony said lightly, "Strange, you are usually so self-sufficient. Don't you agree, John Bull?"

"Ah, yes, he insists on self-serving."

"I'll just bet," Tony said with narrowed eyes.

Savage ignored the insult. "Since husbands and wives detest each other's company, I thought you might entertain the Earl of Oxford, while I—"

"Serve the Countess?" Tony cut in suggestively.

"I wouldn't have put it so crudely, but I would like to be private with her for about half an hour. Be a good chap and show Oxford the horses."

Tony was furious. Savage was proving himself as disreputable as his looks suggested, and the bloody Countess of Oxford already had a shocking reputation. She furiously told herself that she was not in the least jealous, but when the pattern repeated itself with Tony entertaining Lord Grosvenor, the Earl of Huntingdon, and Lord Shelburne successively, she was seething.

It seemed the elegantly gowned ladies developed an insatiable curiosity to be shown the bedchambers while their spouses fairly galloped to the stables. Savage was a lecherous swine with the audacity to put horns on his noble guests right beneath their noses.

Tony was incensed that Savage found so many women attractive. But perhaps that wasn't it at all. Perhaps he was driven by a need to assert his power over men who were titled. Was this just another way of showing contempt?

Tony had no more time to speculate as four carriages arrived together. Rosalind and Lady Jersey had arrived. She also recognized Georgiana Devonshire immediately and swore not to let Savage be alone with London's reigning beauty. However, when she entered the house she saw that he was in deep conversation with half a dozen gentlemen and it was up to her to entertain Georgiana and the other ladies.

Frances Jersey cried, "Anthony darling, I swear you've grown a foot since last we met. Don't tower over me, dear boy." Her voice lowered to a suggestive whisper. "I've come to catch a glimpse of his concubine."

"Kirinda is not a concubine, Lady Jersey," Tony said stiffly, feeling a misery inside her heart.

Frances reached up to pat Tony's cheek. "Such an innocent boy."

Georgiana and Lady Jersey exchanged such amused glances, that Tony concluded Lotus Blossom was indeed Savage's concubine. How bloody naive could she be?

Tony led the way to the elegant dining salon with its gracefully curved walls covered with rose silk. At each end was a carved Adams fireplace set into a wall of mirrors, which reflected the crystal chandelier over and over again. It held three hundred pale pink candles lightly scented with rose.

Georgiana caught her breath. "Oh, I must do a room in rose; it's like living in a flower."

Frances Jersey tapped her with her fan. "You have a very indulgent husband, Georgiana. Not only does he turn a blind eye to your little peccadilloes, he keeps you in the lap of luxury."

"Lud, he doesn't know I'm alive, Frances. Business and politics fill his every waking moment. He monopolizes Mr. Savage to such a degree, our acquaintance is still in the flirtation stage, I vow."

"Not for long, if I know you, you wicked girl." Lady Jersey shuddered delicately and again her voice dropped to a whisper. "Every woman in London fancies taming the beast. He's only been here five minutes and already he has the reputation of a rake."

"Roz, let me show you the conservatory," Tony suggested to change the subject, but Georgiana and Frances still gnawed on both ends of the same bone.

"I heard a rumor that he's interested in politics."

"He must be," drawled Tony, "he's had every Whig society matron in London up to his bedchamber this morning."

Georgiana looked decidedly piqued; Tony knew a moment's joy.

Roz didn't follow Frances and Georgiana into the conservatory. Instead she took Antonia's arm. "Tony, that was blatant innuendo. Whatever were you thinking of?"

"He's an out-and-out womanizer. He entertains titled ladies in Half-Moon Street every day and frequents brothels every night." Her eyes filled with unexpected tears and her grandmother stared in disbelief.

"Oh, darling, you fancy yourself in love with him."

"Don't be ridiculous," Tony said gruffly.

Roz whispered, "You wouldn't be acting this way if you didn't fancy yourself in love."

Tony sniffed. "It's the house . . . Edenwood. I've fallen in love with his house."

"You and a hundred other women," Roz said dryly.

"That's the bloody problem, isn't it?" Tony said, angrily wiping away all trace of the telltale tears on the sleeve of her jacket.

"If you go on this way, he'll discover you're not Anthony."

Tony pulled herself together instantly. She kissed Roz on the temple. "Stop worrying. I admit he drives me mad, but I shan't have hysterics. I'll save it all up for my journal." She grimaced at her grandmother and led her forward into the conservatory.

It was like entering another world. The air was warm and moist and heavily perfumed by the fragrance of exotic blooms. The ceiling was a huge glass dome tinted green and beneath was a small replica of the Ceylon jungle. Everywhere grew flowering vines amid palm, bamboo, and banana. More than thirty varieties of orchid bloomed in exotic profusion, from pale vanilla to the darkly beautiful black, veined with scarlet and gold. Brilliant butterflies flitted from petal to pistil.

Amid the lush greenery Kirinda sat upon the ledge of a fountain where gold and black striped fishes darted beneath water-lily pads. In her seductively soft, musical voice she was explaining the names of the various exotic orchids to Lady Jersey and the Duchess of Devonshire. Tony felt another stab of jealousy pierce her heart as she saw Lotus Blossom's dark loveliness.

A deep voice came from the entrance. "Everything in Ceylon intoxicates the senses." The moment was pure magic. Every female in the conservatory was mesmerized. The spell was suddenly broken by Rupee, who was being allowed to fly free. He swooped onto Savage's shoulder and screeched, "Hellbait! Repent!"

"Oh, how utterly droll," cried Georgiana. "Adam darling, I must have him!"

Tony held her breath as Adam gave her a solemn wink. "This bird cost a king's ransom," he told Georgiana. "I'll never part with Rupee." Suddenly Tony felt better. She didn't know why. He'd just confirmed he was a liar. When she added that to smuggling and whoring the portrait was alarmingly sinister.

Roz said, "Edenwood is magnificent, Mr. Savage. I've never seen its equal."

For once Lady Jersey was in agreement with her friend. "It is evident every detail has been chosen with loving care."

"Lord Lamb deserves most of your praise. It was he who made suggestions to Wyatt when Edenwood was being built and then he chose most of the furnishings. Even this conservatory was his idea."

Tony flushed but was warmed inside by the praise.

Georgiana looked at him with speculative eyes. "I've decided to redo both the house at Bath and the villa at Chiswick. Tony, you will lend me your expert advice, won't you?"

Tony would rather eat mud. Suddenly she looked at Savage and gave him back his wink. "Chinoiserie! I predict Chinese-style furnishings will be the next rage of the ton."

"Well," Georgiana said grudgingly, "His Highness is doing his Brighton Pavilion à l'orientale and everyone knows George has impeccable taste."

Lady Jersey, an archrival of Georgiana, said sweetly, "His Highness didn't accompany you today. A little bird told me he was off to Richmond again."

Georgiana threw Frances a smug little look. "He entrusted me with a message for you, Adam darling. He'll be here tomorrow to see Edenwood and discuss a business matter."

"Please convey that I shall be honored to receive His Highness at any time he chooses," Adam acknowledged.

"Come, then, I haven't explored the gardens or the park yet. I'll let you saddle one of your thoroughbreds for me so I can ride through the grounds."

Adam smiled. "Tony will do the honors for me. I'll go down and round up a party of those wishing to ride."

Tony would rather eat horse manure. When they arrived at the stables, however, the grooms had anticipated the guests and had a dozen horses saddled and ready. Savage arrived at the stables with six gentlemen and four ladies, all eager to tour the hunting park of Edenwood on horseback. He lifted Georgiana into a sidesaddle, allowed his hands to linger at her fashionably tiny waist, and smiled up into her beautiful face.

"Stab me, sweetheart, but two dozen of my neighbors just arrived and we will need their votes to keep me in the House, you know."

Georgiana pouted her pretty lips. "I lose all my men to politics. She's a demanding mistress."

It seemed to Tony that an intimate current ran between the two of them as she watched the byplay. Christ, had he already bedded Georgiana too?

In disgust Tony turned away to help the other ladies mount. One of them was so young, Antonia's gorge rose as she observed the older man at her elbow. With relief she realized that Lord Harvey had brought his daughter. Charlotte couldn't keep her eyes from Tony Lamb. She'd seen his name lately in the scandal sheets and now that she'd seen him in this opulent background had decided to set her cap for him.

Georgiana led the way and the men sped after her. Tony hung back, knowing she was in a surly mood and no fit company today. Charlotte, however, spied her opportunity to be alone with the attractive young lord.

"When the Season begins, my father has promised me a ball. Will you come, Lord Lamb?"

Tony was ready to give the young miss a setdown when she saw how sweet and vulnerable the girl was. "If I am in London, I would be honored, my lady." To discourage her Tony suggested, "Hadn't you better catch up with the others? The river is only about a mile from here."

The girl blushed and lowered her lashes. "I'd much rather ride through the woods, my lord."

Good God, some randy young buck was going to make a meal of this one. Becoming a part of the male world had shown her there was no such thing as a code of honor where females were concerned. All men were profligate, lifting women's skirts as casually and as frequently as they lifted a pinch of snuff. There was actually a conspiracy abroad to keep very young females in total ignorance of all things carnal so they were utterly unprepared when they encountered seduction.

The sanctity of marriage was another great myth. The whole of society made a mockery of fidelity. There was no such thing as a faithful husband. Was it any wonder that older women no longer even paid lip service to chastity? Savage kept a stable of women much the same as he kept his Thoroughbreds and all were eager to be ridden!

Tony was working herself into a fine rage. She hardly paid attention when something went whizzing past her ear. Her mount shied and Charlotte squeaked, "Whatever was that?"

Suddenly Tony went cold as an horrendous suspicion came into her mind. Within a minute the whistling came again and a bullet entered the tree behind her.

"Someone's shooting at us!"

Charlotte gave a squeaky scream as Tony grabbed the girl's reins and dug her heels into her horse to make it gallop. They thundered off in the direction of the river and didn't slow until Georgiana's party came into view. The girl looked as frightened as Tony felt inside. To reassure Charlotte she said, "Probably someone poaching game. Stay close to the others and I'll go and report the bloody fool."

Tony's fear diminished as her anger grew. There was absolutely no doubt in her mind who had been shooting at her. She had to make Adam Savage believe that Bernard Lamb was trying to kill her. How dare he put her at risk by inviting the evil bastard to Edenwood?

Tony clattered into the long stable and turned the horse over to a groom. She was just about to go in search of Savage when she heard a low, deep laugh coming from one of the box stalls. She recognized it immediately. It was followed by a seductive feminine voice and an intimate laugh.

Tony strode to the box stall, almost blinded by a red mist of anger. What she saw over the top of the half-door stopped her dead in her tracks. Savage, his back covered in bits of straw, was offering his hand to Angela Brown, who reclined brazenly in the hay. Savage helped her to her feet and drawled, "I told you we'd be discovered. I suppose we should be thankful it was Tony and not Bernard."

"My cousin was too busy stalking me in the woods!"

Adam did not believe for one minute that Bernard posed any sort of threat to Tony. His ward was a little spoiled because of his money and disliked Bernard simply because he was poor. Tony was almost preoccupied with the notion that his cousin was out to harass him.

"Tony, for God's sake, you're obsessed," Savage said with disgust.

Tony swept the actress with an angry look of contempt. She was wearing the most flamboyant outfit of red and yellow. If anyone else had dressed this way, she would have been carted off to Bedlam. On Angela it looked stunning.

"How's the ankle?" Tony asked sarcastically.

With a straight face Adam replied, "Having just examined it thoroughly, I can assure you it's good as new."

Angela gave him a saucy sidelong glance and dusted the straw from her skirts.

"Good," Tony flung, "she won't have to spend so much time on her back!"

"What the hell's the matter with you?" Savage demanded.

Bernard Lamb strolled toward them with an amused look on his face. "Silver spoon he was born with got lodged in his throat, perhaps."

Adam and Angela laughed at the cruel remark.

Tony was incensed that Adam Savage stood with her enemy against her. She rushed at Bernard Lamb and slashed him across the face with her riding crop. "You son-of-a-bitch, if you want to shoot me, meet me at Battersea Fields and we'll finish it! My seconds will be in touch with you."

Tony turned on her heel and quit the stables.

Bernard Lamb held his neckcloth to his torn cheek, hurling vile curses after his titled cousin.

Adam Savage narrowed his eyes in thought, but he did not interfere. Something deeply disturbing was between these two young men and he would have to discover what it was. At the moment Tony's rancor had boiled over and Savage knew he wouldn't see reason until he'd had a chance to cool down. He was certain of only one thing. There would definitely be no duel!

He said to Bernard, "What's between you is none of my business, but I regret he assaulted you while you were my guest. Come up to the house and have it tended."

"It's nothing . . . just a scratch," Bernard insisted, and Savage couldn't help but be impressed.

Tony went straight back to London with Roz. She sat up on the box with Bradshaw to avoid her grandmother's questions. No hint of this trouble must reach Roz's ears or she would forbid Tony from taking her revenge. She clenched her fists and shoved them deep into her pockets. She was certain of only one thing. There would definitely be a duel!

Chapter 23

Antonia awoke in a deep sweat. It was the third night this had happened and the third night she had had the recurring dream. It took her a moment to realize that the time was nigh.

She threw back the covers and shivered as the cool predawn air touched her fevered skin. An autumn chill was in the air that she welcomed, for she would of necessity wear a long cloak to conceal her identity.

She moved silently in the dark so she would disturb no one. If Mr. Burke heard her, she was lost. Before she retired last night she had laid out her garments with care and even poured her wash water from the jug to guarantee silence.

She removed Anthony's damp nightshirt, then buried her face in it as if she could gather strength from a garment he had once worn. She stood naked and shivering and whispered, "Tony, help me."

A measure of calm resolve descended upon her. She was doing this to avenge her twin and also in sheer self-defense, for she knew with every fiber of her being that Bernard Lamb was going to kill her if she did not take his life first.

With determination she lifted up the sponge to wash away the memory of the vivid dream that still clung about her tenaciously. It was always the same. They were on the dueling field just as dawn broke, counting, counting. Bernard Lamb always turned and fired on the count of nine.

Tony pulled on shirt, breeches, stockings, and boots with such steady hands, she surprised herself. She felt predestined to do this thing. It all had such an air of inevitability about it that she was calm even though she was afraid. She knew with a knowledge as old as time that her fate rested in her own hands. The conclusion was foregone. If she did nothing, she would lose. If she acted, she would win. That was the secret of everything, really. The secret of life and death.

Tony was grateful to Adam Savage. He had shown her that the most precious quality in life was courage. He had set out to make a man of her and he had succeeded. Tony had the guts of a man, the fortitude and the resolution of a man. Though she lacked a man's strength she

made up for it with a woman's quick wits and intuition. Bernard Lamb
didn't stand a chance.

She had taken advantage of the fact that Adam Savage was tied to
Edenwood and his weekend guests. She knew he had an appointment
with the Prince of Wales and could not return to London until His
Royal Highness had been entertained.

Tony had called on young Southampton and Colonel Dan Mackinnon, knowing their addiction to guns and shooting. They had been
involved in many duels and of course Colonel Mackinnon had that
superb collection of firearms. She swore them to secrecy and watched
their excitement grow. Both were avid for risk and danger. Each time
they acted as seconds their reputation grew, and now they were known
as the Hellfire Bucks.

There was a set ritual that must be observed in the code duello. So
far, all was as it should be. The opponent holding the higher rank
must issue the challenge. They would now call upon Lord Lamb's
opponent with the time and the place and allow him choice of weapons. There was little doubt it would be pistols; duels hadn't been
fought with swords in the last fifty years.

Mackinnon tucked a pistol case under Tony's arm and recommended he take a little target practice at Charles Fox's *tir.* Southampton gave him the address of his favorite brothel in Covent Gardens
and told him to ask for Mrs. Cole. Every man should experience Jassy
Cole before he died. Southampton was only having his dark little joke;
it was understood that the opponents would not aim to kill, but merely
try to render each other hors de combat. Tony took the colonel's
advice and ignored Southampton's.

Sleep had been most elusive mainly because she dreaded the
dream, so she had burned her candles late into the night pouring out
her suspicions and her fears onto the pages of her journal. Upon
rereading it she discovered she had catalogued more grievances
against Savage than she had about her hated cousin. The ridiculous
thing was that she admired almost everything about Adam Savage.
The sticking point was his legion of women.

She finally faced it and admitted the truth. She was envious down to
her very bones. She coveted him as she had coveted nothing before.
She wanted him to make love to her. Longed for it; pined for it. Sex
was slyly referred to as the Game and everyone she knew was a player.
Men flaunted their mistresses while married ladies took secret lovers.

Society had an inexhaustible appetite for pleasures of the flesh and indulged in liaisons at any and every hour of the day or night. Every amusement was designed with coupling in mind. Brothels and bawdy houses stretched from Covent Garden to Shoreditch. Pleasure Gardens such as Vauxhall and Marylebone were specifically designed to pander to assignations in their grottoes, groves, and yew walks. Then there was Ranelagh, up the river and up the social scale, but its theater continually staged sexual romps to titillate its audience before they slaked their appetites in private, recessed little supper alcoves.

Fireworks displays, badger baiting, and cock fighting were merely fashionable excuses to gather, pair off, and mate. It seemed to Tony that everyone was a club member but herself. Posing as a male had given her glimpses of what she was missing, but sex was still by and large a dark, mysterious temptation that left her wildly curious and deeply dissatisfied with her lot.

Rereading her journal shocked her into realizing she was obsessed with sex. Each night, she had blown out her candles convinced her dreams would be sensual fantasies; instead, each night she refought the duel.

Tony picked up the long black cloak and folded it over her arm. She would not wrap herself in it until she was on the flagstones of Curzon Street, just in case she tripped upon the stairs.

She crossed the street to avoid the light from the streetlamp on the corner. As she cut through Green Park it was still pitch-black. She heard men's drunken laughter as a group of bucks left White's Club in St. James's, and she quickly crossed Stable Yard Road where Southampton was to pick her up in a hired hackney.

She glanced about but saw no waiting carriage. She pulled the cloak about her dry throat and swallowed her apprehension. Were they late or was she early? She had never been abroad at this hour before. The empty street seemed to have an eerie, echoing quality. Noises from the river carried to her on the damp air and she jumped as a cat slunk around the corner. Perhaps they wouldn't come. Her imagination took flight. Savage had discovered her plans and put a stop to the duel! No, she assured herself, he didn't suspect a thing. He had called upon her the moment he'd returned from Edenwood. His cutting words still echoed in her mind: "I haven't time for your childish theatrics, so I want your word as a gentleman you won't carry this duel nonsense any farther."

She had solemnly given him her word as a gentleman!

A black carriage turned the corner and Tony stepped out to the curb as Dan Mackinnon drew up the horses. Her heart pounded inside her ears as the door was flung open and an arm dragged her inside. One of the colonel's polished pistol cases lay on the black leather seat and next to it sat a case holding flasks and small silver goblets.

"This is Keate, His Highness's surgeon."

Tony gave him a look of alarm. "I begged you to keep it secret."

"Damn it, common sense demands the presence of a surgeon. Could save your life, Tony. Here, have a tiger frightener," Southampton said, pouring whiskey.

Tony shook her head. "My hand is quite steady," she gritted between her teeth.

Southampton shrugged and drained the silver cup himself.

The carriage ride was of such a short duration, Tony thought time had suddenly speeded up. In fact everything had a surrealistic aura about it and she caught herself wondering if she was still dreaming. As the carriage drew up with a sickening lurch she knew this was no dream.

Southampton thrust a black domino mask at her. "Here, put this on before you open the door and make sure you can see through it."

"Why the devil do I have to wear this thing?" Tony demanded.

"Dear boy, it's a necessary precaution. You do realize we could be arrested for what we do today? Though duels are tolerated, they are highly illegal."

As Tony stepped out upon Battersea Field, a feeling of dread washed over her. Patches of mist swirled about in the darkness and the masculine smells of horses and leather made her nostrils pinch with distaste. She closed her eyes and wished . . . nay, she was damned if she would wish that Bernard Lamb mightn't show up. He would come. It was his big chance, his throw of the dice to take everything he wanted in one fell swoop. She would dispatch him to Hell!

In her heart she felt he had murdered her twin in cold blood, and in cold blood she would now murder him. In the open clearing a group of men were milling about and Tony strode toward them without hesitation. With steady fingers she undid the fastenings of the cloak and allowed Southampton to take it from her shoulders.

As in her dream the first fragile hint of dawn was lighting the sky as she waited for her seconds to finish their whispered consultation with the other masked men gathered. Mackinnon came to her and asked if she wished to withdraw. She was momentarily thrown off guard before she remembered it was all part and parcel of the code duello.

There was now sufficient light for the opponents to see each other. Mackinnon opened the gun case and the other second confirmed that they were loaded.

Two figures stepped forward to select a pistol. Two pairs of glittering eyes met through the slits of their masks. Their hatred for each other was palpable. Then they were being turned back to back. The Lamb cousins pointed their pistols skyward and cocked the triggers.

The drill was so familiar to Tony, she saw it all as if she watched herself from afar. She had lived these same few moments so often in her dream, she knew exactly what to expect. She paced off while the seconds were counting, counting. She turned on the count of nine and fired. Her opponent did the same. She smiled grimly as she saw that he faced her and shot at her exactly as she had known he would.

Tony had the deep, dark satisfaction of seeing him fall to the ground. Suddenly out of the dawn a big man was striding up to her. She blinked rapidly as a powerful hand grabbed her by the scruff of her neck and propelled her to a waiting carriage.

A deep, furious voice promised, "I'm going to thrash you within an inch of your life."

She was thrown against the fine calfskin squabs so hard, the wind was knocked out of her. Savage flung himself into the seat opposite and swore, "Your word as a gentleman isn't worth a pinch of bat shit!"

Tony began to tremble uncontrollably and her teeth began to chatter. Reaction from the duel had set in. A filthy oath dropped from Savage's lips as he pulled off his warm cape and flung it across at Tony.

"If you've killed him you'll go to prison or possibly the gallows, you reckless young fool!"

Tony didn't answer him. She hoped with all her heart that she had killed him, and yet prison would unmask her identity and the scandal would sweep London. She fiercely told herself that arrest would be worth it, at least she'd have the satisfaction of knowing Bernard Lamb would never take what rightfully should have been Anthony's.

"You callous young devil," Savage muttered.

Tony's temper flared. "Don't be a hypocrite! I acted exactly as you would act if someone threatened to take everything you owned. Every chance you get, you hammer home to me to be a man. Must I fight you too? Damn you, I will! I'll take on the whole bloody world."

Savage heard the righteous indignation, the determination, and the total conviction in Tony's voice, and realized he was convinced that his actions had been necessary, even justified. Savage at least admitted that facing an enemy upon the field of honor took courage.

"I'm putting you aboard the *Flying Dragon,* then I'll find out if your cousin is dead or just wounded. In either case you'll have to leave the country for a while. I wasn't planning to sail to the Continent until the end of the week, but you give me no option."

The silence stretched out between them. Tony was thankful for Savage's strong presence. She had never felt more like crying in her life. If only she could cry on his shoulder and have him enfold her in his arms and tell her everything would be all right. Her throat ached unbearably with unshed tears. Finally she managed to murmur huskily, "Thanks for standing by me, even though you're not convinced of my motives."

"Your father was my friend. I shall try to take his place."

Tony wanted to scream at him that she didn't want him for her father, but fortunately they were at the docks and the carriage drew to a stop.

When they boarded the clipper, the smell of tar filled their nostrils. The ship had been recaulked but the cabins had not yet been refurbished.

Savage told his crew they would sail for France on the evening tide and bade his storemaster victual the ship. Tony eyed the evil-looking seamen and repressed a shudder. Some she guessed were Lascars, some Genoese, others were English. She also guessed they were villains to a man.

Savage opened the door to a small cabin with a porthole but no bunk. "You may have this all to yourself," he said as if he were bestowing a royal stateroom.

"There's no bed," Tony protested indignantly.

Savage gave him a look of contempt and bent to a locker. "Here's a hammock. Get down on your knees and be thankful I'm not making you string it where the rest of the crew sleeps."

Tony was grateful for the privacy now that the alternative had been pointed out.

"Everyone on my vessels is expected to earn his keep, but I want you to stay below out of sight today."

"Thank you," Tony said with relief.

"We'll sail on the evening tide. Tomorrow will be soon enough for you to swab the deck."

Tony glanced at him to see if he was serious. Savage was deadly serious. "Roz knows nothing of this business. Could you let her know we are going to buy cargo?" Tony asked hopefully, not daring to suggest Savage wait while Mr. Burke packed some bags for her.

Savage nodded. "I'll be hours. I've my own affairs to see to as well as yours." He made no secret of the fact that he was damned displeased at the inconvenience.

When he departed Tony looked forlornly at the heap of woven hemp he'd called a hammock. Antonia had never actually seen one before. She found iron hooks on the cabin wall and finally managed to stretch it across one corner. She sat down upon it and when it stopped swinging, she gingerly lifted her feet from the floor and stretched out her legs. In the dim cabin she felt alone and isolated. She couldn't prevent a tear from rolling down her cheek, but determinedly she licked it off with her tongue.

Savage sought out Dr. Keate. He learned with enormous relief that Tony Lamb had not taken his cousin's life, nor had he wounded him too badly. It amounted to no more than a crease on the shoulder. However, Keate told him that young Anthony Lamb had caused a scandal by turning and firing on the count of nine. It was unheard of and only a coward would stoop to such an act.

Savage said evenly, "I was present. They turned together."

"That is incidental. The one who did the wounding takes full blame. If Tony had been shot, it would be his opponent who would be ostracized."

"Gentleman's bloody code," Savage derided. "Thank God I'm not one." *But you're trying your damndest to obtain a title,* a mocking voice inside his head whispered. *I don't want the bloody thing,* he argued, *it's for Eve.* The voice again mocked him, *That's exactly what the other Adam said: The woman tempted me!*

Savage's face was set in grim lines all the way to his bank. One of his jewel chests was brought from the vault and he took time to carefully select enough diamonds and pale blue sapphires for a necklace. He slipped them into a black velvet bag and asked the bank manager to return the chest to the vault, then went directly to Carlton House.

Savage fully intended to manipulate Prince George. In fact the game had begun yesterday when His Highness had brought up the subject of jewels. He wanted to gift the lovely Maria Fitzherbert with a piece of jewelry that would both dazzle and delight her. He had given jewels to women before of course, expensive baubles to each of the actresses with whom he had indulged in debauchery. But Maria was different. She was a respectable woman and as a consequence he wanted the jewels to be different. It would take something quite fine and rare to make her capitulate.

The problem, however, was money. With the Prince of Wales the problem was always money. He had confided to Savage that he was half a million pounds in debt. Adam knew it was six hundred and fifty thousand pounds. The Prince had heard the rumors that Savage had imported jewels from Ceylon and hoped against hope that he could barter something he owned, as he had done with his stable of race-horses.

Savage half jokingly told George there was really nothing he wanted, except perhaps a title.

His Highness had shaken his head sadly and told him such things were beyond his patrimony. Prince George was bitterly disappointed about the jewels. He had set his mind upon them, just as he had set his mind upon Maria Fitzherbert, and he could not bear to be thwarted.

Savage smiled grimly as he went up the steps of Carlton House. He knew nothing in the entire world was unattainable. Some things merely carried a higher price than others. When George actually saw the gems, touched the diamonds, and pictured how the pale blue sapphires matched Maria's eyes, he would find a way to acquire them.

Savage hid the amusement in his eyes when His Highness revealed he'd consulted his friend, Charles Fox, about the tricky business of being elevated to the peerage. Adam finally managed to extract the precious jewels from George's fingers and place them back in their black velvet bag.

"I shall be out of the country for the next three weeks or so." He shrugged. "Perhaps by the time I return Your Highness will have found the money to purchase the jewels." He swung the bag between his fingers. "I can get at least a quarter of a million for these gems, but I'll let Your Highness have them for a hundred thousand." Savage knew George was in so much debt, he had nowhere to turn for money. A hundred thousand was as impossible as a hundred million, but he was giving him three weeks to find a way to obtain him a title.

When Savage called at Curzon Street he saw for himself that Lady Randolph had no inkling of the duel, so he told her Tony was sailing with him to Europe and they'd be gone about three weeks.

"I'll pack him a trunk. How careless of Tony to run off without his wardrobe."

"He won't need anything fancy. I intend to put him to work to earn his passage. Just have Burke throw a few things into a bag."

Roz eyed Savage with alarm. "Mr. Savage . . . Adam . . . I hope you aren't serious about making Tony do menial work. He's never really had a robust constitution. I'm afraid he's not as strong as he might be."

Adam smiled. "You pamper the lad too much, ma'am. You also underestimate him. When he was at Edenwood he mucked out the stables for me. Menial work builds character as well as muscle."

Roz paled. "Ship's crews are notoriously rough and dangerous. I don't fancy him mingling with such men."

Adam replaced his smile with a serious look to ease her mind. "Don't worry about him, Rosalind. I've taken him under my wing and shall see that no harm comes to him. I think of him as my son, you know."

Roz thought perhaps she should tell him he should think of Tony as his daughter. Instead she asked Mr. Burke to pack Tony a bag and sighed with the worry of it all.

Adam Savage spent the next two hours with his secretary, Sloane, to clear up the paperwork of his various business deals. He would sail the clipper to Gravesend, anchor at Edenwood, and get John Bull to pack what he would need for the sea voyage.

From Half-Moon Street Savage rode into the city to visit the headquarters of the East India Company, then finally to Lloyd's to check the maritime loss book.

Tony found she could not relax. The tension was coiled in her stomach and she noticed that even her hands were clenched into fists and she was gritting her teeth. After swinging endlessly for two hours she climbed from the hammock and began to pace.

Hardly any of her tension had been released by the duel; not knowing its outcome and hiding here like a rat in a hole made her feel trapped. Two more hours were taken up with her pacing and still the day had not even reached the hour of noon. She certainly wasn't hungry, but her mouth was dry and her throat felt parched. Cautiously, she opened the door of the cabin and looked out. Her nose was assailed by the mingling smells of food, tar, and tidewater. There was another smell, too, she couldn't identify that was faintly cloying, strangely exotic, and insidious.

She made her way along the passage and stepped into one of the cargo holds. The odd smell was stronger here, as if whatever it came from lay in wait, hidden away, yet the hold was empty. Tony jumped as she heard a scuttling noise behind her. A small, wiry man with a ferretlike face asked, "Would ye be lookin' for summat, sor?"

"Er . . . just curious. Thought I'd have a look about, if that's all right, Mr. . . . ?"

"McSwine, Paddy McSwine. Sure 'tis none o' my affair, sor, what ye do. I'm only the sea cook. Would ye like some grub?"

"I could use a drink," Tony ventured.

McSwine winked. "Couldn't we all, sor? Couldn't we all! Come along to the galley."

Tony tried to make conversation. "We are going to the Continent to buy cargo to ship to the Indies. This ship looks like it has quite a large hold."

"It has two more, one aft, one for'ard." McSwine held up his hand. "Don't be tellin' me what ye intend to smuggle, sor, I'm deaf and blind."

Tony followed McSwine into the galley and was about to protest they had no intention of smuggling. Then she held her tongue. She had no idea what Savage would do on the voyage. He was a law unto himself.

McSwine handed her a tot of rum. "Have you no water?" Tony asked hopefully.

McSwine was horrified. "Never touch the stuff. Water's fer drownin'." He took a jug and splashed a bit into the mug to dilute it. Tony didn't dare tell him she meant water *instead of* rum, so she sipped it slowly.

Suddenly about ten men arrived in the galley and she stepped aside quickly before they pushed her out of the way. Their eyes mocked the powdered wig and slim trousers that went under the instep. She was about to take her leave when a motley-looking sailor with a Scots brogue said, "What's the matter, Fancydrawers? Too good tae eat wi' the likes o' us?"

"No, no, of course not."

"Then sit yer arse down. Paddy, what poison are ye plannin' tae palm off on us unsuspectin' innocents the day?"

"Pig's dick an' lettuce," McSwine replied cheekily, and was rewarded by a few snickers.

"Och, I was hopin' fer crumpet an' cream."

Everybody guffawed but Tony.

"Yer bleedin' face willna crack if ye laugh, ye know, Fancydrawers."

McSwine jumped to Tony's defense. "The gentry don't call it that, ye daft bugger."

"What do ye call a woman's fidgety-fork?" the hulking Scot demanded.

Tony took a swig of rum. "P-Pussy," she whispered, hoping her cheeks were not flaming red.

Paddy cut great chunks of crusty bread and ladled mouth-watering stew into pewter bowls with handles. Tony dipped her bread in the stew and took a bite. A smack on the back almost lodged the mouthful in her throat. They were determined to make her the butt of their jokes. "McSwine, have ye told the laddie it's his turn in the barrel the nicht?"

Mercifully Tony didn't know what they meant, but she had a damned good idea it was rudely disgusting. She had two choices: she could retreat or she could dig in her heels. This morning she'd looked down the barrel of a gun; she'd be damned if some ignorant sailors would intimidate her. She knew she must join in their vulgarity before they would leave her alone to eat. She recalled one of Luttrell's limericks. "Heard a limerick about a Scot the other day. Just reminds me of you. Would you care to hear it?"

Paddy McSwine nodded with glee and the others were now ready to make the hulking Scot the butt of their humor.

"There was a young man from Dundee
Who buggered a bear in a tree.
The result was most horrid
All arse and no forehead,
Three balls and a purple goatee."

The sailors lifted their mugs to toast Lord Lamb.

Chapter 24

It was late afternoon when Savage arrived back at the docks. Since he intended to captain the *Flying Dragon* himself on this voyage, he had his first mate, Mr. Baines, accompany him while they inspected the ship from stem to stern. When he was satisfied that it was seaworthy, Savage gave the order to weigh anchor and piloted the vessel from its mooring out into the Thames.

From inside her small cabin Tony realized the ship was moving. That meant Savage must be aboard; they wouldn't sail without him. Wasn't it just like the annoying devil to let her stew in her own anxieties. She would go and find him. Nothing he could be doing was as important as giving her news of Bernard Lamb.

Savage was not in his cabin, nor the galley. She concluded he must be on deck. As she came up from belowdecks, the smells and the sounds changed rapidly. Someone was barking orders above the noise of the canvas being sheeted into place, and the herring gulls screamed as they circled above the mast, gliding on the light breeze that carried the salty tang of the sea.

For one moment she felt panic rise inside her as the clipper headed out toward the ocean. She hadn't sailed since that fateful day with Anthony. She mastered her fear, knowing it would return with full force if they ran into a storm.

As Tony made her way along the deck she realized Savage was navigating. Was there nothing the man couldn't do? She saw that he ignored her presence even though he was well aware of it. Damn the man. His expression was inscrutable and told her nothing. As she watched him she had no idea her own face became transparent with admiration. His black hair was loose and streamed back in the wind. He wore only a light shirt with an open throat that contrasted against his dark face. There was pride and confidence in every line of his bearing. He was in control behind the wheel of a ship, as he was wherever he went or whatever he did. He was one with the wind and the sea.

As Tony's gaze ran over his lithe muscles, she longed to be one with him. Her throat ached and she turned from him to lean against the rail. She dragged her mind from him to concentrate upon the ship. Though he hadn't much sail aloft, the tide was taking them at a fair clip. The Thames widened as they passed Woolwich and she realized that she would be able to have a magnificent view of Edenwood from the Thames.

As they neared Gravesend, Savage maneuvered the *Flying Dragon* from midriver toward the right bank and Tony caught her breath as the magnificent Edenwood came into view. Her tall windows were golden from the last rays of the sun, her brick a deep, warm rose. She gazed at it with as much longing as she had for its owner. She knew she had lost her heart irretrievably to Edenwood. The wave of possessiveness was so strong, its intensity shocked her. She knew she had just committed another deadly sin: *Thou shalt not covet.* Her lips parted and a sigh escaped her.

"Lower the anchor, Mr. Baines," Savage thundered, and she heard the chain clang and clatter through the hawsehole. She swung about to look up at him and he jerked his head in the direction of Edenwood in an unmistakable gesture commanding her to follow him.

Savage disappeared over the side and she thanked God for giving her long legs as she swung them over the rail and climbed down to the bobbing rowboat below. Savage took both oars and pitted his strength against the swift current.

As they reached the bank Tony jumped out and tied a line to a small tree. They strode together to the house and Adam told her what she had waited almost ten hours to hear.

"Your bullet only scratched your cousin, but you managed to cause a scandal by firing on the count of nine and branding yourself a coward."

She knew the bitter taste of failure on her tongue. "I'm no coward," she stated emphatically.

"I know that," Savage said quietly. "How did you know he would turn and fire on the count of nine?"

She shot him a glance while her mind searched for a plausible answer. There was none. "A recurring dream." Tony didn't give a damn if he believed her or not.

"Animal instinct." He nodded his approval. "It always pays to listen to your gut."

His approval warmed her and suddenly she was relieved she hadn't committed murder. Bernard Lamb simply wasn't worth it!

Savage fixed her with a pale blue stare. "Don't you care if your friends blacken the name of Anthony Lamb?"

"Not much." She shrugged. "I know the truth and that's all that really matters."

Savage was well pleased with the lad's attitude.

John Bull materialized from nowhere the moment they entered Edenwood.

"Find Tony some of those white pantaloons you wear. We are on our way to the Mediterranean. I'll pack my own bags. We must hurry before the tide turns."

"Why are you always so self-serving, Excellency?"

Tony hid a smile. "I'm going along so I can choose a cargo for the Indies. What do you suggest, John Bull?"

"Ah, young lord, Excellency will advise you. He knows what is best for you." He took Tony to the servants' wing and handed him a pile of snowy garments. "Try these on."

Tony went into a small, mirrored bathing room in the servants' wing. John Bull was a small man and so his cotton pants were not overly large. She would make them do. Her eye was caught by an array of exotic cosmetics that obviously belonged to Kirinda. There were dozens of little pots, vials, and bottles containing all manner of seductive creams, oils, and fragrant pastes. Her fingers itched to paint her face. Respectable young English ladies were not allowed makeup and she had never had a chance to use it, but London was full of women who did paint their faces to attract men, and it certainly seemed to work.

The allure of the kohl, powder, lip rouge, and silvery-hued eye-paint was too great for Tony to resist. She had just decided to put some on, then wash it off quickly, when she heard Savage's deep voice. "Where the hell is the young devil?"

She swept an armful of the tiny pots into the cotton pants and tucked the bundle under her arm. She'd have to wait until she was in the privacy of her cabin aboard the *Flying Dragon.* Suddenly the great adventure she was about to embark upon hit her. Young men toured the Continent; young women did not. There were definite advantages to masquerading as a man.

Savage carried a small chest and John Bull followed with a valise. Tony was immediately suspicious. Savage was smuggling something and her curiosity was devouring her. Her glance stole again and again to the mysterious chest as he rowed back to the ship.

"Curiosity killed the cat," Savage mocked as he watched Tony's eyes.

She put up her chin, vexed that he could always read her thoughts so easily. Savage rowed close to the *Flying Dragon,* then stood up to gain a handhold. "Pass me the chest," he ordered.

Tony bent to lift it, but found it impossible.

"You can't lift it because it's filled with my hard-earned gold to pay for your damned cargo."

Tony's mouth fell open as she watched him easily haul it to one shoulder before he climbed aboard. She watched him stride to the helm. "Anchors aweigh, Mr. Baines. Hoist the mains'l!" His deep voice seemed to go right inside of her as she took her own smuggled goods belowdecks.

The bag that Mr. Burke had packed sat in her cabin, so she hid the cosmetics under Anthony's clothes. She was extremely grateful to have this cabin to herself. She knew she would never have been able to endure the disgusting company of the rough, coarse seamen.

Tony didn't much fancy going among them for the evening meal, but realized she wouldn't be waited on hand and foot. In fact Savage had told her she'd have to work while aboard. In her bones she feared he'd set her some degrading task, damn his eyes.

When a knock came upon her cabin door she expected to find Savage, but was surprised to see McSwine with a tray.

"Capn's orders. Yer to keep outa the way tonight, sor."

"Thanks Paddy. It smells good." He really resembled a ferret when he grinned.

"Cap'n have me cut in collops an' toss'd overboard if I cooked lousy. I've sailed with him before."

Tony pulled off her tiewig and boots and stretched out in the hammock, balancing the tray. There were a dozen delicious great prawns and some new potatoes boiled in their jackets and dripping with melted lemon butter. Scallions, watercress, and spinach leaves were tossed with herbed oil and vinegar. It was plain fare, but quite delicious. To look at McSwine you would have thought he'd produce pig swill.

As Tony enjoyed her supper she wondered how in the world she would be able to spend the entire night slung in a hammock. As it happened, she fell asleep before she had finished eating. Her dreams were anything but restful. She moved about the ship doing one tiring chore after another, while the sailors mocked her "Fancydrawers," which were long lace pantaloons. She had to scrub the entire deck with a small nailbrush, then she had to empty all the chamber pots. She called Indian Savage every foul name she could curl her tongue about.

When morning arrived she staggered from the hammock dreading the menial tasks that lay in wait for her. She brushed her own dark hair back and tied it with a thong. She slipped on her boots and went up on deck.

She was amazed to find they were in a seaport. Savage was just returning to the ship. Her eyes widened as she saw he was dressed in very rough clothes and was unshaven.

"We can't be in France."

"Of course we are. This is a clipper ship. That's Boulogne." He nodded toward the town.

She braced herself, waiting for his orders, but they weren't what she expected.

"Get yourself spruced up, we'll be in Le Havre before noon. If you're still determined to buy Paris fashions, the warehouses of Havre are stocked to the rafters with female geegaws. I suppose I'd better come along to help you select the underpinnings. You've no more notion of what females prefer beneath their skirts than what they prefer beneath the sheets."

"You'd be surprised," Tony said dryly, hating him for his sexual experience. "Where have you been?" Tony demanded.

"Who the hell wants to know?" Savage replied with an icy stare.

"Just curious," Tony muttered.

"I've been reconnoitering. Actually France isn't a healthy place to be these days. The thunder of the storm has begun to roll over the heads of the aristocracy with their extravagant vices. Havre should still be safe, but in Paris the nobility is actually beginning to fear for its life."

"Surely their excesses can't be any worse than those of the London ton?"

"The English are amateurs; careful, dreary, pennypinching pikers when it comes to indulgence. The French are insatiate, decadent, and debauched with a surfeit of food, fashion, sex, and deviation. Their follies are so numerous, there are fortunes to be made by shrewd opportunists such as myself."

"What about me?"

Savage shook his head. The scar on his mouth stood out, giving him that sinister, bestial look that made her shudder.

"Your soul isn't black enough to take advantage of the weak and helpless, Lord Lamb."

Tony did not wish to pursue the subject further, it was too disturbing.

That afternoon at the warehouses was one of the most pleasurable Tony had ever experienced. If only she could have chosen clothes for herself, she would have been in paradise. She was careful not to let Savage see her looks of longing as she viewed and selected her purchases. Her eyes sparkled at the delicately exquisite materials of the gowns and undergarments spread before her in such colorful array. Silks, gauzes, muslins, satins, laces, pongees, poult-de-soies, tulles, and taffetas in every imaginable hue and design took her fancy and she ordered one of each. When Savage told her to order two dozen of each, Tony shook her head and explained to him that women liked to be exclusive in the way they dressed. It was all a simple matter of supply and demand. A unique design would fetch ten times the price of one copied in every size and color.

Before the afternoon was over, Adam Savage admitted Tony had a helluva lot more patience than himself as he paced about waiting for him to buy millinery, parasols, slippers, hosiery, and gloves. When young Lamb moved on to a wholesale shop piled high with wigs, Savage protested that it was too hot in India and Ceylon for wigs and that ladies simply powdered their own locks.

"Oh, these aren't for the Indies, they are for London. You should know silly slaves to fashion like Georgiana and the Countess of Oxford will scratch each other's eyes out for these ridiculous French coiffeurs." She purposely named two of the women with whom he'd had liaisons.

Savage taught Tony how to barter, haggle, and bid down the price. Then he guaranteed they would be put aboard within the hour by refusing to part with the gold until the goods were in the hold.

Tony's purchases filled one entire hold before dusk fell and she asked Savage where they would next make port. He told her that it was never pleasant crossing the Bay of Biscay from France to Spain and it made for a more pleasant voyage to sail along the coast to Bordeaux, where he would buy some fine wines and champagne for his own use at Edenwood.

In her cabin Tony removed her dress coat and hung it in the wardrobe. It seemed oppressively warm belowdecks tonight, so she donned a pair of white cotton pants John Bull had provided and wondered idly who aboard would do her wash. Then she laughed at herself. She'd have to wash her own shirts and undergarments and think herself lucky she didn't have to do everyone's laundry.

She took her water jug up on deck to fill it from a cask. She saw Adam Savage leave the ship. Again he was dressed in the rough garb of a seaman. His size made him look totally menacing. Without a snowy shirt, stock, and coat of superfine he looked like a cutthroat. Whatever he was up to was obviously dangerous, illegal, and probably criminal. Savage had a sinister side and she admitted to herself that he was just as capable of committing a crime as he was of breaking the law, if he saw advantage and opportunity. She chided herself that she, too, was involved in something quite illegal, impersonating her brother, but she knew it wasn't the same.

She was making excuses for Savage because she was infatuated with him. Tony cursed herself for a fool. He would deceive any woman who was witless enough to love him.

A frown creased her brow. Hadn't he said France wasn't safe at the moment? Why was he so fearless, so damned reckless? He loved risk for its own sake! She knew all too well that risk was seductive, luring you on to abandon all caution. It was addictive, and both of them were tainted with the damned disease.

The only way to hold her fear for him at bay was to keep busy. After she did her washing, she took a lantern into the hold to look at some of the garments she had purchased. She opened one box after another, admiring the exquisite fashions. Tony's glance fell upon a gown that was particularly spectacular. It was designed in two pieces, the skirt separate from the tiny bodice. It was made of gold tissue so delicate, she sighed as her fingers caressed it. The skirt was yards and yards of froth; the bodice, embroidered with tiny golden crowns, was also cut in the shape of a crown, whose points were cleverly designed to conceal and reveal the breasts.

Tony couldn't resist it. She took the gown to her cabin and tried it on. Suddenly she was transformed from a slim youth to a curvaceous woman. She took the leather thong from her hair and noticed for the first time just how much it had grown since Roz had sheared it. Tony posed in the mirrored door of the wardrobe, then began to twirl about the cabin.

She closed her eyes and imagined herself being whirled about a ballroom by Adam Savage. What fun it would be to flirt and tease if he had no idea who she was. All her daydreams and fantasies centered about one man, even though she knew they were impossible. She couldn't get enough of looking at herself. It had been so long since she had worn a dress, she had forgotten how delicious and special it was to feel feminine.

She hated being a man. She wanted to be a woman, a real woman. She longed for it with all her heart. With reluctant hands she removed the tissue gown and hung it in the wardrobe. There was no way she would part with it. The moment her fingers touched the exquisite material she had decided it was hers.

As Tony swung in her hammock, pictures filled her mind, then spilled over into her dreams. There was her mother receiving guests, looking absolutely ravishing, more beautiful than she had ever seen her. Everyone lavished compliments upon Eve, then looked at Antonia and shook their heads in pity. She went to her mirror and saw the shorn-off hair, the male attire that camouflaged her femininity. But, like Cinderella, Roz found her a mask and a gold tissue gown and Tony was transformed into a princess with a golden crown.

When she awoke the ship was moving. She had no idea when Savage had returned to weigh anchor. Idly she wondered when the man slept. Like a leopard he seemed to be a nocturnal creature, out hunting all night, yet his boundless energy allowed him to sail the clipper, and spend hours buying cargo. There was something not quite human about a man who needed no sleep.

When she glimpsed herself in the mirror, last night flooded back to her. The gown had transformed her into another person. The kernel of an idea took root at that instant. At first it was just a glimmer, but gradually it took form and shape. They were going to the Carnival of Venice. What better place for Adam to meet Antonia for the first time? What better place for two strangers to indulge in a liaison?

Doubts assailed her. How would she ever be able to pull it off? Then hope would arise again. Somehow, some way, she must arrange an accidental meeting. The Carnival of Venice was only celebrated for one purpose, sheer pleasure. It was a make-believe world of magic where your wildest fantasies could become reality.

Chapter 25

At Bordeaux, Savage bought fine French wines and cases of the very fashionable champagne for his cellars at Edenwood. Tony asked him if she could make a decent profit by buying champagne and selling it in England. Adam told her it was a good idea, since it was the height of snobbery to drink imported wine rather than the good old domestic variety. Civil unrest would bring a temporary halt to the production of French wine if it got any worse, and that, of course, would make the price soar.

Crossing from Bordeaux to Portugal proved most unsettling to Tony. She stayed in her cabin, fighting mal de mer for two days until they arrived at the beautifully sunny port of Lisbon. Tony found it hard to believe it was still winter in England. They took on two hundred crates of rich, dark Madeira, the only wine that kept well in the heat of the tropics.

Tony learned exactly how intense heat could be as they sailed to Cádiz, Spain, where they bought fine Spanish and Morrocan leather boots and Savage purchased a pair of black tooled saddles. The *Flying Dragon* skimmed through the Straits of Gibraltar, stopped briefly to stock the galley with dates, figs, and sweet, juicy oranges, then sailed on to Cartegena to purchase knives and swords made from the finest Toledo steel.

Tony could hardly believe that only a week had gone by. In that week she had visited the port cities of France, Portugal, and Spain and experienced their people, cultures, language, food, and climate, all so very diverse.

Tony made herself useful by helping McSwine prepare the food, but whenever she went up on deck she kept to herself and avoided the rough, dirty-mouthed sailors. She had no desire to be the butt of their cruel humor. She also gave Savage a wide berth. She feared that he might order her up the rigging or issue some other order to complete a task that was too arduous for a female's strength.

Though she kept out of his way, she was still very much aware of him. When he issued an order it was followed immediately. Command came naturally to him, and it was clear to see there was a healthy dose of fear mixed in with the crew's respect. Although she knew the sailors drank grog, she never saw one of them drunk, nor did she see anyone shirk his duty. Savage was a hard taskmaster, demanding a clean ship above all else, and they scrubbed until the decking was bleached white and smelling of nothing more sinister than sea and salt.

Savage's mahogany skin tanned darker with each sunny day. As a consequence his blue eyes seemed as pale as ice and he could freeze a crew member with a contemptuous glance from across the ship.

On Sardinia they went sightseeing. The buildings were a blinding white with red tiled roofs in the Mediterranean style. The hills stretching back from the azure sea abounded with brilliant, exotic wildflowers. They sat smoking companionably, overlooking a breathtaking bay. Tony could feel the hot sun on her shoulders beneath the stiff cambric shirt. It heated her blood and made her think sensuous thoughts.

Whenever she glanced at Adam Savage her mouth went dry with longing for his touch. Yet she knew if he touched her she would scream. What she really would like to do was touch him. She wanted to feel the texture of his swarthy skin, trace a finger along the slant of his jaw where the shadow of his beard made his face even darker. Her fingers itched to undo the buttons of his lawn shirt and peel it from his rippling shoulders. She ached to run her hands over the hard slabs of muscle on his impossibly wide chest. She burned to press her lips to his mouth and kiss him. She blushed at her boldness, for secretly she longed to lick him and taste the salt upon his tempting flesh.

The next time she stole a glance at him he was leering with appreciation at a couple of peasant girls with dark, slumberous eyes. They were barefoot and carried baskets of oysters. He beckoned them over. They came apprehensively at first, afraid of the powerful man with the sinister, scarred face, but he teased and winked and with sign language managed to buy some oysters. Soon they were laughing, flirting, and splashing water at the men in a most playful and inviting manner.

"Fancy a swim?" Savage asked Tony, peeling off his shirt and not even trying to disguise the bulge between his legs.

"No, thanks," Tony said stiffly. "What the hell do you do when a woman is unwilling?" he demanded primly. "Or has that situation never arisen?"

"Many times," Adam admitted. "I simply resort to the fine art of seduction."

"How the hell can you seduce a woman when you don't even speak her language?"

"Sex is a universal language, Tony. Did you ever look at those books I gave you?"

Tony's cheeks flooded with color.

"I can see that you did," Savage said, grinning. "Christ, try not to be so bloody narrow minded and circumspect. Your cock's for more than pissing through, you know. You haven't lived until you've experienced a Mediterranean woman's hot mouth and quick little tongue all over your prick."

Tony's mouth fell open.

"Here, have some oysters, if they don't make you randy, there's no hope for you, boy."

Tony picked up the crustaceans and left Savage to his señoritas. He was a bloody rake, roué, whoremaster, and ravisher of anything in skirts. When she got back to the ship she was going to toss the gold gown into the bloody Tyrrhenian Sea! She didn't, of course.

The sky was cloudless, the sea a smooth aquamarine, as the *Flying Dragon* glided through the Straits of Messina that divided Sicily from Italy. Paddy McSwine had procured lovely soft cheeses and luscious black olives, as well as a supply of spices brought from far-off ports.

Tony helped him prepare bouillabaisse flavored with fennel and he told her which meats tasted better with marjoram and oregano. She recalled the delicious paella he'd made when they were anchored in Spain and he told her the yellow color and unique flavor was saffron, which was reputed to make you mirthful.

Tony picked up a handful of bay leaves. Simply touching them released their piquant fragrance. McSwine told her they were from a tree native to the Mediterranean.

"Cap'ns partial to curry."

"His man from India, John Bull, told me it's addictive. He said the first taste of mild curry leads on to the *vindaloo,* that's the hottest."

"Curry more than any other substance is responsible for increasing the world's population." Paddy winked suggestively. "Take it from me, 'tis the best aphrodisiac in the world. Forget yer 'Wine of Egypt' with its cantharides, curry will make ye stiff as a bloody poker."

Tony decided to retire from the galley.

"If ye feed it to a female, she'll be so hot, she'll beg ye for it."

Tony was beginning to believe men thought of nothing but sex. Then she blushed. An inordinate number of her own thoughts were preoccupied by the subject these days!

Savage brought treasures aboard for Edenwood at every port they made. He bought marble sculptures from Italy and statues of ancient Roman soldiers that were so lifelike, you expected them to blink their eyes and speak. On Corfu he discovered a small Greek temple and had it dismantled. Then he had the graceful, fluted columns carefully wrapped to take back to his garden.

When they returned to the ship, the crew was diving and swimming about in the tropical waters of the Adriatic, all naked as the day they'd been born. Savage agreed to join them, but Tony declined all invitations.

The Scot called, "Ye'll no catcha fish wi' yer shrunken worm."

Tony replied by thumbing her nose. She took one last look before she went below. Corfu, Greece, was an emerald isle on a turquoise sea. It was one of the most beautiful places Tony had ever seen. Flowering shrubs cloaked the rolling landscape while the knotted, gnarled trunks of the olive trees formed wreaths of silver leaves. The peasants rode mules, the women carried bundles of firewood. Surely this was the spot where Ulysses was washed ashore.

Adam couldn't understand how anyone preferred the stifling belly of a clipper ship to the sybaritic lure of a blue lagoon. He knew that Lord Lamb was a bit of a snob and understood that the uncouth seamen with their cruel humor were not easy to tolerate. He concluded Tony was unused to male rough-and-tumble and had likely never taken his clothes off outdoors. He might even be concerned about the size of his genitals, afraid that he might not measure up before other males.

Belowdecks, Tony discovered that the storage room that had been padlocked now stood open. In fact it now held the Greek Temple, carefully packed in crates. She was certain that Savage no longer left the ship in the dead of night and hadn't done so in fact since they'd left France. She wondered if this hold had been emptied in that country where unrest was visible in the street. What had he smuggled into France? The most obvious answer was guns, and ammunition.

She shrank from the idea. It was corrupt, like selling death and destruction. She whirled about at a noise behind her. It was McSwine. He seemed to be forever creeping up on her, slinking about just like a ferret. "I—I thought you were swimming."

"No, sor! I toldt ye before, I never touch water. Water's fer drownin'."

"What was in this locked hold?" she asked outright.

"I'm blind an' deaf. I toldt ye that before too."

"That strange smell that lingered about doesn't seem so noticeable now. What caused it?".

"That would be opium, sor."

"Opium?!" Tony was staggered.

"Once opium's been smuggled on a ship, the stink lingers forever. Ye can't smell it now because we've had lots of hot, sunny days, but let the damp return, let it rain fer a couple o' days, an' the stink returns like that on a corpse."

"A corpse?" Tony repeated, feeling for all the world like Savage's mynah bird.

"Ye've no idea what stink is until ye've sailed on a slaver."

Tony gulped and backed away. "From now on I'm blind and deaf, McSwine. I don't want to hear these things."

As she swung back and forth in her hammock her mind darted about like quicksilver. Adam Savage's words came back to her. "Your soul isn't black enough to take advantage of the weak and helpless, Lord Lamb."

Tony shuddered. Surely he'd not blacken his soul with such unspeakable abominations? Smuggling was not a game of hiding a bit of tobacco or wool to avoid paying revenue tax, it was an abhorrent evil, an obscenity that left its foul taint on whoever stooped to such filth. Her mind refused to explore further. She would not—could not—believe it of him.

The next day she was surprised to find Mr. Baines knocking upon her cabin door. "The captain would like you to join him on the deck."

"Thank you, Mr. Baines," Tony said politely. He was the only member of the crew who seemed civilized. She smoothed back her dark hair and secured it with a thong, then made her way abovedecks.

Savage stood relaxed with his hands on the ship's wheel. The sun bronzed him more each day.

"We'll be in Venice tomorrow. This voyage up the Adriatic between Italy and the Dalmation Islands is one of the loveliest in the world. I didn't want you to miss it."

Suddenly she felt shy of him and averted her eyes to the beautiful shoreline. "The weather's been exceeding good to us; no storms."

Savage frowned. Was Tony still afraid of storms? "We are bound to run into a summer storm or two before our voyage is over, but there won't be any gales. Nothing to be apprehensive about."

Tony sensed he was trying to reassure her. She searched her mind for small talk. "We've made very good time."

He nodded. "The *Flying Dragon* was a sound investment." He changed the subject. "Venice is the sort of city you will love. It will simply take your breath away. It's a city of splendor, steeped in antiquity; over a thousand years of antiquity. Venice is unique, you'll not find its equal anywhere else on earth. It's made up of hundreds of islands, crisscrossed by canals. The architecture is magnificent, all centuries old, some decaying, but each and every building is a gem, encrusted with carvings or mosaics.

"The ancient squares are called piazzas and there are hundreds of bridges, so you can explore the city on foot. The afternoons are long and languid, perfect for strolling down medieval alleyways and the stone courtyards of her Gothic houses and palazzos. Some of the businesses close in the afternoon for a siesta, but the streets endlessly fascinate. They are narrow, winding, and crowded, then suddenly a magnificent spacious square opens up before you with a church or a palazzo designed by Palladio. The fourteenth-century Redentore, derived from the Pantheon, is considered his masterpiece."

"Wasn't it built in gratitude for the end of the black plague?" Tony asked, caught up in the subject. "I've a book at home about some of the art treasures in the museums."

"There's a museum near San Barnaba with sumptuous trompe l'oeil ceilings, depicting gorgeous creatures in acts of love. There are paintings and frescoes of lovers and centaurs and mythological sculptures."

"Are you going to buy paintings for Edenwood?"

"Christ, yes. I lust for a Canaletto or a Correggio."

"I like Titian and Bellini," Tony said dreamily.

"Carnival doesn't start for a couple of days, so we'll visit the glassworks and buy the mirrors you want. You'd do well to invest in some Venetian crystal, too, while you have the opportunity."

"I—I've been thinking. When we get there I don't want to sleep aboard. I'd like to stay in one of those fabulous Byzantine palazzos with marble floors and priceless art treasures."

"Of course," Savage agreed. "We'll take rooms at a palace right in Piazza San Marcos with a view of the Grand Canal and the misty lagoon. If we stay on the south side, we'll be able to see the domes of the Basilica and the Doges' Palace. Its white marble arches look as if they are sculpted from spun sugar."

Tony hesitated a moment. "We don't have to stay at the same pallazzo, do we?"

Savage gave a bark of laughter. "So you think of me as a watchdog who'll curtail your freedom! Stay wherever you wish. I'll leave you to your own vices, providing you promise to indulge those vices when Carnival arrives."

Savage's eyes in the sunlight looked like blue flames. She held them for long moments. "I do so promise," she vowed. Tony felt so warm, she knew she had to put space between herself and the object of her desire before she did something overtly feminine.

She silently promised herself she would abandon all restraint when she became Antonia for a night at the decadent Carnival of Venice. She leaned against the rail and turned her face up to the sun. A delicate shiver ran over her skin in spite of the sun's kiss. Would she really have enough courage to plan and carry out his seduction?

Venice turned out to be all Adam Savage had said it would be, and more. The very air was charged with the romance of centuries. In whatever direction one looked lay artistic and architectural wonders. The first thing one saw was the great Venetian winged lion staring out to sea from his high column. Somewhere a man's deep basso sang an aria that floated across the water. The setting sun touched the gilded Byzantine palaces and church domes.

The *Flying Dragon* docked at the Island of Giudecca. Savage pointed across to the mystical city. "Venice lies there across the Grand Canal. The view from the Island of Giudecca surpasses all others. The Venetian Empire was built on the power of its sea trade. Its admirals, then its bankers, dominated the world hundreds of years ago."

Savage was obviously going into the city tonight. "Don't the soles of your feet itch to explore the hallowed ground?"

Tony smiled. "I think I'll wait until morning."

"Then take this gold. It speaks a universal language. If you need me I shall be at Casa Frolo. Good night, sweet prince, till it be morrow."

Shortly after he departed Tony became aware that the crew was bristling with arms. Every sailor carried a pistol and a belt full of wicked-looking knives. She realized that the cargo they carried was worth a fortune. She knew without a doubt Savage had left orders to kill anyone foolish enough to board the *Flying Dragon*.

As the lights of Venice started to come on, one by one, an air of mystery fell over the city. Tony leaned against the rail, dreaming of all the sights she had seen in the last fortnight. Cleopatra's galleons had sailed the Mediterranean's azure waters, and here Greek heroes had met their destiny. Perhaps she, too, would meet her destiny. These ancient waters carried a legacy of the ages from the dawn of civilization. The names of the romantic ports rolled off the tongue like music. The scent of oranges, lemons, or almonds perfumed the very air. The Mediterranean had surely mesmerized her. Now Italy's floating city lay at her feet and she was ready to explore its wonders and allow it to work its magic for her.

Tony searched about the hold until her eyes found the right size of box. It was made of cardboard, a little bigger than a hatbox, and held wigs. Back in her cabin she carefully removed the wigs and folded the gold tissue gown inside. Then she packed her bag with her freshly laundered male attire and set them at the cabin door ready for a quick getaway at dawn.

Tony undressed, knowing she would be asleep in minutes. It was amazing how a hammock lulled one to sleep, rather like a baby in a cradle. The gentle rocking of the ship at anchor produced a soothing motion that relaxed every muscle in her body.

As the sun climbed from the sea, Tony climbed from her hammock. She only took time to wash her face, pull on her clothes and a tiewig. She would wait until she was safely ashore before she broke her fast. As she left the ship carrying her bag and her precious box, she knew half the crew observed her departure. She felt their curious eyes upon her back, but did not turn around to acknowledge their stares.

Tony didn't have to go far. A long line of gondolas waited at the Giudecca to ferry passengers across the grande dame of lagoons into the heart of Venice. The gondoliers all looked identical, garbed in black with wide-brimmed hats, leaning idly upon their long poles. Tony chose one at random, allowing the gondolier to take her bag but keeping a secure hold upon the box. Then she leaned back against the cheerful red cushions and drank in the early-morning scene as it glided past.

Piazza San Marco was filled with vendors. Tony bought crusty bread, soft cheese, and fruit, then sat upon some stone steps to breakfast, all the while gazing up at the gilded domes and Renaissance mosaics that surrounded the square. She only glanced down to share her roll with the strutting pigeons. Her gaze traveled reverently over St. Mark's

Basilica and the elegant Doges' Palace. As she sat upon the steps, the ornate beauty of Venice unfolded overhead.

From her vantage point she saw what looked like a hotel and decided to look no farther. Outside the sign said CASA DANIELI, inside all wore ornate Italian livery and powdered wigs. The floors were pale pink marble and gilded mirrors stretched up to Tintoretto ceilings. Tony took the golden key, murmuring one of the few Italian words in her vocabulary: *"Grazia."*

From this moment on she would be Antonia! She felt excitement start to bubble up inside her as she gazed about the beautifully appointed chamber. It was high up on the fourth story and the first thing she did was fling back the curtains to let in the sunshine and the magnificent view of Venice.

She discovered a small, wrought-iron balcony and stepped out. All the buildings rose up four and five stories from the narrow canals and she saw many balconies just like her own. Most were decorated with streamers, ribbons, and flowers, both real and paper. People had already begun their preparations for the festivities of Carnival.

Tony reentered the room and gazed about. The furniture was ornate, lacquered white and gold. Above the tall bed, cherubs held sheer blue curtains that fell about the bed in draped splendor. The rich carpet was patterned blue and gold with a thick pile. Graceful torchères with fluted glass candleholders stood on either side of the window. To the left stood an enormous Renaissance wardrobe with a long mirror on each of its three doors, and to the right sat a marble bath upon a pedestal. Water was piped from a cistern and the golden taps were swan's heads. A stand held an array of soaps, oils, and thick blue towels embossed with golden swans.

Tony was torn between staying to bathe or exploring the shops in the piazzas. She finally decided the bath would have to wait, but before she left, she opened the box and shook out the delicate gold tissue gown and hung it carefully in the great wardrobe. Then she took her comb and brush from her bag and reached down to the bottom to retrieve the precious cosmetics she had "borrowed" from Lotus Blossom and set them upon the gilt-wood dressing table. She sighed with the bliss of it all. The chamber was a perfect setting for seduction.

Chapter 26

The women on the streets of Venice were extremely elegant creatures. They had a great sense of style, catered to by hundreds of shops, each specializing in its own unique goods. There was a shop that sold only velvets, one selling only glass beads, and another masks. Lingerie, stockings, gloves, fans, feathered and beaded hair ornaments, each had their own boutique. Perfumeries lured the coins from a lady's purse as easily as the wig shops that carried every shade including lavender, flame, and even green. They also stocked every conceivable hue of hair powder.

Tony knew the moment she saw it in its crystal bowl that she must have the hair powder that resembled gold dust. At a lingerie shop she could not resist a pair of drawers made from the same gold tissue as her gown. They were completely sheer and wicked as sin. She probably would never be bold enough to wear them, but she handed over her coins without a protest.

The shops and squares of Venice were crowded with people buying items to complete their costumes for Carnival. Window displays caught the eye on every side, tempting customers with masks, disguises, dominoes, and fantastic headdresses made to transform you into a devil, a satire, an animal, or a prince.

As the hour advanced to midday, Antonia found her clothing was far too warm and restrictive. She purchased a simple white muslin dress and a leghorn hat, its brim scattered with white roses. When she arrived back at her Casa her arms were filled with feminine treasures, including slippers and finespun shifts and stockings.

Tony filled the marble bathtub almost to overflowing and indulged her body with a rich lather that smelled like fragrant freesia. She hummed all the while she lathered her hair, then, wrapped in a blue-and-gold towel, she sat in the sunshine on the balcony as it dried into a silken mass of dark curls.

She felt deliciously decadent as she donned a finespun shift and slipped on the white muslin dress. They were the first feminine garments she had worn in months and she whirled about, enjoying the feel of the delicate material against her skin. Heavens, she felt as light and free and happy as if she had been released from a cage.

In front of the gilded mirror she experimented with a little lip rouge for the first time in her life, then put her head on one side to gauge the effect. She couldn't believe the transformation. No sign of the slim youth remained. She was a woman! The last time a mirror had reflected Antonia, she had been a girl. The red mouth and black curls made her green eyes appear enormous, and for the sheer pleasure of watching herself she fluttered her lashes to her cheeks, then slowly lifted them above green orbs that glittered like emeralds. Laughter escaped her and floated off through the window and across the lagoon.

Tony picked up her hat and fitted it on so that it partially concealed her features. Antonia knew exactly where she was bound. She was going to Casa Frolo to make certain Adam Savage was indeed staying there. Tomorrow night Carnival began and she must devise a plan for a meeting. The plan must be infallible. If the two did not connect it would be disastrous. She could wait no longer for a glimpse of him; she was starving!

Tony was surprised to find that the piazza was no longer crowded, then she recalled that it was siesta time. Most of the businesses closed for an interval in the warm languor of the afternoon. All she could do was window-shop, but she realized it was a most pleasant way to pass the time. She stopped to admire the exquisitely wrought flowers, birds, and butterflies of a paper shop. Tony crossed a picturesque bridge, then went down the water steps to speak to a gondolier.

"Casa Frolo?" Antonia inquired.

He nodded. *"Si, donna."* He pointed across the wide lagoon. "Giudecca."

She was pleased that the Grand Canal separated her and Savage. Her secret would be secure. Even in daylight the gondola ride was romantic. The gondolier sang snatches from an opera as he poled rhythmically, while overhead the sound of the churchbells floated in the warm air.

The gondola stopped at Fondamente delle Zitelle, only a few steps away from Casa Frolo. Antonia knew immediately that Savage had chosen this palazzo because of its magnificent view of Venice, which seemed to float and shimmer upon the misty lagoon.

Tony strolled past an antique shop, all the while keeping her eyes open for any sign of Savage. When she did not see him out on the *fondamente* that bordered the canal, she entered the palazzo and let her gaze run over every person in the magnificently appointed lobby. There were only one or two men on their own. Most people were coupled. Most looked like lovers, absorbed in each other. Most seemed to be slowly drifting upstairs. Antonia idly browsed, seemingly admiring the velvet-covered antique furniture and the ornately framed paintings. Time passed, yet still there was no sign of him.

Tony grew self-conscious, thinking perhaps her presence might cause curiosity with the staff of the palazzo if she lingered hour after hour. On the second-floor galleria she saw a restaurant with small tables where the patrons could look down upon the vast foyer to observe the comings and goings of everyone at Casa Frolo. Slowly she trailed up the marble staircase to the galleria and sat down at a table. When the white-gloved waiter approached she murmured the only word she knew that would be appropriate. *"Vino?"*

"Si, signora. Chianti?"

She nodded uncertainly, but when he brought her a goblet of red wine, it was not what she had expected. She tasted it and it was as sour as vinegar. Lord, it was about time she learned the names of the wines she liked. Tony made a pretense of sipping from her goblet while she watched the lovers rendezvous below her.

Suddenly she was struck by a ghastly thought. Savage was no doubt making full use of his bed during these hours of siesta. While she sat here like a naive little fool, waiting for one glimpse of him, he was likely whiling away the lazy afternoon in bed play with a dark-eyed signora.

She began to panic. If she saw him come downstairs with an elegant Venetian lady she would be devastated. He was nothing but a rake, an experienced roué, expert at giving a woman a slip on the shoulder. Antonia sat in misery, her graphic imagination running riot, expecting the worst. She knew she must leave before she saw him with one more woman. She had few illusions left about him. She knew he was unscrupulous, probably even a criminal, but her heart had stubbornly refused to abandon its infatuation. Whatever had given her the ridiculous idea that she could attract a man of his vast experience? She must be mad! Far better for her to revert to her trousers and be thankful for his companionship. A quiet, friendly smoke with him was the best she could ever hope for and was better than nothing at all.

No! It was not better than nothing. It was worse than nothing. Far worse! She had come to Venice looking for romance. Lord, she was such a baby. So unsophisticated, so unworldly, in spite of the knowledge of men she had so recently acquired.

Savage hadn't come to Venice to seek romance. From his own lips she had heard his reasons. Carnival was where the nobility roamed the streets of Venice looking for sexual liaisons. If she saw him with a female she would be shattered. She must get away. She pushed back her chair, then she became aware of male eyes assessing her.

She glanced about to see that no fewer than three men were giving her their undivided attention. The first man nodded. She averted her eyes to another table, where the second man smiled. Antonia broke eye contact immediately by glancing in the direction of the third man. He raised an eyebrow.

How dare they be so blatant? She could clearly see each had been ready to arise when she did, perhaps to openly approach her, or at least to follow her. She was horrified. She did not wish to attract men; she wished to attract one man. Savage. Adam Savage. There was no other man in the world!

She decided it would be a mistake to rise and leave. She would simply outwait them. The waiter approached her with a note. She shook her head vigorously and refused to accept it. In a few minutes one of the gentlemen sighed and left. In a short while another arose and did likewise. Antonia closed her eyes in relief, knowing the enervating heat had gone out of the afternoon and siesta time had drawn to a close. Couples started to descend. When they reached the ground floor of the palazzo they separated, the men going one way, the women another.

When Antonia opened her eyes she saw him. One glimpse was all she needed to stop her breath, to stop her very pulse. He strode into Casa Frolo from the *fondemente* and he was alone. Antonia's heart soared. He was alone! No afternoon siesta for Savage when Venice lay at his feet to be explored.

She observed him from a distance beneath the concealing brim of her leghorn. He climbed to the galleria level, then disappeared down a corridor where she assumed his room must be. All she could do tomorrow evening was arrive early and keep watch on the galleria. Naturally he would wear a disguise, but Antonia felt she would know that powerful, incomparable physique anywhere.

Her heart was singing all the way back across the lagoon. She looked so young and pretty and happy that people turned to watch her as her light, carefree steps took her past the exotic mask shop. She paused at the window display, wondering what sort of a mask she should wear tomorrow night. Some masks were unbelievably elaborate, encrusted with beads, feathers and ornamental mirrored glass. Others covered the whole head and face to completely disguise the identity of the reveler.

Antonia frowned with indecision. She did not want something clumsy or unwieldy and difficult to handle. Her glance fell on a mannequin whose mask had been painted on. With the clever use of painted stripes and a handful of sequins a mask had been created that did not have to come off. She went into the busy shop that was doing a brisk business. She bought a package of sequins and some patch glue. With the aid of her exotic cosmetics she would create her own eye mask!

Antonia bought breadsticks, seafood salad, and ravioli in a pomodori sauce of basil and parsley. She would dine upon her balcony and observe the city below her as would an empress from her throne.

As dusk descended, the lights and torches of the city began to flicker. Gondolas glided about across the lagoons, beneath bridges, and along narrow canals. Some people couldn't wait for Carnival and had already donned their costumes.

Musicians in medieval and Renaissance garb strolled about, plucking their stringed instruments, and even the gondoliers wore small black eye-dominoes beneath their straw boaters. All of Venice was being transformed into a city of mystery and magic.

It was late when Antonia went inside to bed, because she knew she was too excited to sleep. When she finally did drowse, she began to dream, but her dreams were dark and disturbing. She found herself heavily masked in some sort of brothel. All the clientele were rich and titled. Barons, earls, dukes, and princes from far and wide were gathered in this opulent, decadent, glittering salon.

The other women were voluptuous in varied stages of deshabille, their laughter as brittle as Venetian crystal. The heavily perfumed air was so cloying, she could hardly breathe. The men, all masked, assessed her with contemptuous, glittering eyes, which gleamed through the slits in their masks.

Three different men selected her as their partner and she knew she must go through the dark, sensual labyrinth of chambers, pandering to whatever coupling techniques pleasured them. She had no idea what they expected of her, not the slightest inclination, except that it would be wicked and sordid and humiliating.

Antonia froze with horror outside the first door, the brass knob burning a hole in her palm. But she knew she had no choice. Her fate had been set long ago when she took the first tentative steps down the road to ruin. She squared her shoulders and turned the knob. She looked into ice-blue eyes that froze her soul.

Antonia screamed. The scream awakened her.

She sat in bed hugging her knees. It was dark outside her window, morning was hours away. She pushed back her heavy mass of silken hair and shivered uncontrollably. She did not need to have her dark dreams explained to her. It was her conscience crying out that what she planned was wrong!

It was totally indecent for a young, unmarried lady to give herself to a man for a night of illicit love. Ha! It was not love, it was fornication. It was pure and simple sex and sensuality. She had planned to make Adam Savage seduce her. Antonia wanted him and him alone to introduce her to the dark mysteries of sexuality. She was a truly wicked girl. She should be thoroughly ashamed of her prurient interest in carnal matters. Did she really want to beg him to let her play whore to him?

Oh, yes, please!

Antonia snuggled down in bed and spun herself a delicious fantasy. When she awoke, she was sprawled across the covers and the sun was high in the sky. It was the most beautiful morning she ever remembered. She rolled over and hugged herself. This was the day she had been waiting for all her life!

She splashed and sang the afternoon away in the great marble bathtub, and then breathlessly she pulled on her stockings, then the sinfully sheer drawers, and topped them with the crown-shaped bodice. She strutted about before her mirror and reveled in being shockingly outrageous. First she powdered her luxuriant curls with regular powder to cover the darkness of her hair, then she repowdered it with the gold. She lit the torchères so that her face was well illuminated before she began her makeup, and a thousand brilliant motes of gold dust sparkled and glittered from her upswept hair.

She was transformed into a fairy princess from some mythic tale. She stared at her face long minutes, picturing the sort of design that would be both disguising and alluring. She chose to be a butterfly. Her large green eyes would be the "eyes" on the butterfly wings. Carefully she outlined her lashes both above and below with black kohl; then, using iridescent green maquillage, alternating with gold, she painted stripes slanting up to her temples, then down across her cheekbones to create swallowtails. With the kohl stick she drew delicate antennae on her forehead and stuck sequins to the tips. The effect was dramatic. Her costume was perfect. All she had to do now was step onto the stage of Venice and play her part.

The sea had not yet swallowed the sun when Antonia joined the throng. Everywhere was gaiety, music, and laughter. When the barriers of the masks had gone up, all others had come down. Strangers spoke with each other as easily as cast members of a troupe of players delivering their clever lines and reacting to the responses with a smile, a touch, or an overt caress.

The mood of the early revelers was gay and giddy. When dusk veiled Venice, the mood would become one of abandon. The costumes and disguises were spectacular. Some were clever, others unbelievably daring. Seminudity was commonplace. Male and female gender in many cases was blurred to the point where it was undetectable. Some were gaudy, some were bawdy. Many were rude; a few downright crude. All were on display, all were intoxicated, either by the night or by what they had already imbibed.

The mood was infectious, the laughter spreading with abandon from one group to another, linking them in the relentless pursuit of pleasure. Antonia was filled with apprehension. She held herself aloof from hands that reached out to her, and leering mouths that shouted, *"Donna! Bella! Grazioso! Per favore!"*

A crowd jostled each other good naturedly in front of the gondolas as they waited to be taken across the lagoon. A few vestiges of civilization still clung, but Antonia could see it would only take a small spark to ignite a mood-swing to ugliness. It was apparent she would not have a gondola to herself, so she climbed into one that carried other females. She pulled away, shocked, when another woman touched her intimately. As she looked about, it seemed to Antonia that tonight everyone in Venice had the painted face of a harlot. She blushed delicately. She was no different from the others.

Antonia retraced her steps of yesterday along the crowded *fondamente,* smiling in acknowledgment whenever a gentleman touched his fingers to his lips in a gesture of appreciation. She had learned that Italian men were physically demonstrative whenever they saw an attractive female, regardless of Carnival.

The lobby of Casa Frolo was lit brilliantly. Musicians played up on the galleria, their music floating down upon the dancers below along with streamers and clouds of confetti. Antonia examined every face as she searched the crowd for one man. She did not see him, so again she pushed her way through the noisy revelers, realizing how easy it would be to miss him in the sea of masked faces. At last she was certain that he was not yet in the lobby of the palazzo. She decided to go up to the galleria, because she was convinced his chambers were on that level.

She started up the marble stairs and there coming down toward her was a magnificent figure. He wore a crimson turban ornamented with a peacock feather. An Eastern tunic stretched across his wide shoulders. As she gazed up at the raja her heart leapt when she saw his gaze was riveted upon her. The distance between them closed. Breathlessly she realized when he was a few steps above her he had an unimpeded view of her breasts, deliciously displayed by the golden bodice.

Her hand reached out to him. "Signore," she breathed softly, invitingly.

"Voi siete bella" (You are beautiful), *"tesoro."* (darling) *"Baciami!"* (Kiss me) The man reached for her with greedy hands.

Antonia knew his voice was not Savage's voice. Her eyes widened in alarm as she gazed into obsidian eyes.

"No, no," she cried, pushing his hands away. Her reluctance spurred him on and she felt his arm pull her against his body, then he bent his mouth to hers.

She struggled wildly, screaming, "No, no, no, signore, no!"

A bronzed hand descended upon the raja's shoulder. "I believe *no* means the same in Italian as it does in English."

Antonia almost fainted with relief. Savage's dangerous voice was unmistakable. Though cloaked in velvet at the moment, its threat was palpable.

"Per dio!" (By God!) The raja went down to his knees as Savage increased the painful pressure upon his shoulder, then Adam took Antonia's hand and led her safely back down the marble steps to the main floor. She felt the warmth of his hand radiate upward into her arm. He was dressed in black. A black leopard, half-mask stopped just at his lips, concealing the scar. A black cloak swirled about his powerful torso. She knew he represented far more danger than the raja.

"How may I thank you, my lord?" Antonia asked breathlessly.

"I'll think of something, little butterfly. You are English." He sounded intrigued.

Her mouth curved deliciously. Her black lashes swept down to her cheeks, then lifted over dreamy pale-green eyes. "Do you offer your protection, my lord?"

"Against all but myself, *chérie.*"

Though she was tall for a woman, they stood so close, she had to put her head back to gaze up at him. He lifted her hand to his lips. Antonia felt the jolt all the way to her shoulder as his hot mouth touched her skin.

"You, too, are English," she whispered.

"Perhaps by birth, but not by nature."

"A leopard by nature?" She wet her lower lip with the tip of her tongue.

Adam's pale blue eyes darkened with lust. He was going to lick that luscious full lower lip with the tip of his own tongue before he kissed her.

She shivered—and burned.

They were still handclasped. He was intrigued by her beauty, her youth, and her nationality.

"I have a proposition for you, my lord. Are you interested?"

How droll. Wasn't he supposed to proposition the lady? "I shall be enchanted to while away an hour or two, *chérie.* Do you have a name?"

She shook her head and the corners of her mouth went up in a teasing smile.

He would kiss the corners of her mouth after he'd ravaged her sensual lower lip. He wanted to pick her up and carry her upstairs to his bed without wasting further time, since that was where they would end the night. Savage fought the need for haste. He must at least buy her a glass of champagne first. She was very young. He must not frighten her quite yet.

With a protective hand at the small of her back, he led her along the *fondamente,* then drew her into one of his haunts. It was a bar with tables by arched windows overlooking the lagoon. The sky was a deep purple, the candlelight flickered and reflected a million lights in her golden-dusted hair. He ordered them champagne.

Savage picked up the fine Venetian goblet. "I toast your beauty and your mystery, Queen Mab."

Her fingers toyed with the stem of her glass. He, too, thought she looked like a fairy queen.

"Now, what's this proposition you have in mind?" he murmured indulgently.

"I have escaped my guardian for one night. I seek a lover."

Even in the shadowed room he saw her blushes. He covered her hand. She did not see the amusement in his eyes. "Let me guess. You are being forced into a loveless marriage and you long to be introduced to erotic pleasures of the flesh before you dry up and blow away."

She laughed as he had meant her to. "I can never marry. Circumstances forbid it."

His quick mind assessed the possibilities. A convent? Possible. An invalid parent? More probable. "Never is a long time. Circumstances change. If I agree to become your lover for a night, you may deeply regret me someday."

"Never!" Antonia vowed.

"How much experience have you had?" he asked, bemused.

"None," she said faintly.

Savage stood up to leave. "Forgive me, *chérie*, it is impossible."

"Please don't leave me! I am a virgin who is sick and tired of that everlasting state. Is it so shameful of me to want a night of pleasure?"

"There is no shame in it at all, *chérie*. It is simply that our time together would be too short for me to give you the kind of pleasure you crave."

"Then simply unveil the mysteries of sex for me."

"When a man breaks a young girl's barrier, there is blood and pain. There is a certain amount of pleasure for the male, but very little for the female, I assure you."

Her eyes widened. He thought he might drown in the deep green pools.

"Love me tonight," she tempted, wetting her full bottom lip.

Heat built in his groin. He mocked himself for a fool. He had imagined a night of decadence with a practiced voluptuary, perhaps three or four to slake his unquenchable sexual energy, yet here was an innocent English lady begging for the services of his manhood.

"How old are you?" Savage demanded.

"Sev—eighteen," she whispered. It was a terrible lie.

Blood throbbed into his shaft with alarming force, making him full and turgid and thick with need. Christ, if he turned her down she would seek another. A mocking voice said, *Don't pretend you're doing it to protect her.* He'd give her one last chance to withdraw.

"I feel it only fair to warn you, I am scarred on face and body. I will repel you."

"Never that," she vowed fervently, her hand stealing to his.

"Then drink up, Queen Mab, and fly away with me. I am about to

discover if it really is more blessed to give than receive." Tonight he
must truly be the Prince of Fools. He vowed it was the last time he
would ever come to the rescue of a damsel in distress.

Chapter 27

The Leopard drew her down the water steps to a waiting
gondola and gave instructions in the man's own tongue.

"You will always remember that romance first stole to you in a
gondola in Venice." He stepped into the narrow boat, reached strong
hands to her slim waist, and lifted her down to him. It was an intimate
gesture. They stood close, excitement racing their pulses.

Her breath caught in her throat as he drew her to the cushioned
seat in the rear. "Come." His voice was rich, dark velvet, inviting,
luring, compelling. She hesitated as she looked down at his magnifi-
cence sprawled before her, hers for the taking.

He undid the clasp of his black silk cape and draped one side across
the cushions. Her knees turned to water and she sank beside him into
the dark, silken cocoon he offered.

"Where will you take me?" Her voice was soft as a sigh.

"To the end of time . . . to the scented gardens of Elysium . . .
to the edge of the earth." His words were fantasy, magic, whimsy, and
yet they were rich with promise.

He reclined, opened his thighs, and drew her back against him.

To Antonia he felt like a solid wall of muscle. The heat from his
body leapt into hers, shocking, scalding, shiver-inducing. Her heart
raced, hammered, in her breast, thundered and roared in her head.
His lips whispered and lightly grazed her ear and her pulse went so
faint she thought her heart had stopped beating.

"*Tesoro.*" It meant "darling." She melted back against him, taking
the heat of his body into her own. Her blood felt as if it had been set
afire and blue flames ran along every sensitive vein.

They glided from the misty lagoon into a narrow enchanted canal,
away from the noise, away from the revelers, to a place that was
secluded, secret almost, silent. It felt mystical, as if they floated above

the surface of the ancient waters. The richly ornate, gilded Renaissance buildings towered above them in opulent splendor, isolating them, enfolding them in the dream world that was Venice.

"This was once the center of civilization. It sent grain to the East and brought the riches of the East to Europe. Too much wealth and gold, of course, brought decadence."

"Doges, condottieri, Medicis," Antonia murmured dreamily.

"This is the way Venice should be savored, exploring her secret charms." His hand gently cupped beneath her breast, lifting it so that its pale curve swelled up from her low-cut bodice. In the shadows the crown looked deep vermilion against silken gold. He dipped his head a fraction and blew a warm breath upon it. The moment he stopped, the cool air ruched it to a sharp little point.

"Cupid's arrow," he teased.

Her breath caught in her throat. The quick intake told him her body was giving her pleasure. Told him desire had begun to build in all her lovely, scented, secret alcoves.

Antonia felt the hard ridge of muscle rise against her back. His powerful thighs hardened and what rose between them was like a marble pillar. She had glimpsed men's parts when they passed around the thunderpots, but she had no idea a man's appendage could increase to such enormous proportions, nor become as hard as an iron bar. She gasped at the shock of discovery, stiffened slightly, and would have pulled away. If he had allowed her to pull away. But he did not. His arm encircled her waist like a band of steel, imprisoning her, locking her against his magnificent male weapon.

Antonia did not struggle. It was his maleness she craved. His mysterious man-thing. She stilled, feeling it burn into her back. It was so engorged with blood, it throbbed wildly and she felt it pulse in rhythm with his heartbeat that echoed through the wide chest she reclined against.

"*Amore mio.* Little butterfly." The tip of his tongue traced the pulse beneath her earlobe and little tremors ran down her throat, down her back, and she imagined them running along his shaft. Desire leapt between them. Each knew a need to meld with the other, to share the same breath, the same blood, the same body, the same soul.

They pressed together, straining, merging in a primal hunger to be joined into one. It was unendurable that the thirst of their surging blood could not be quenched. They were becoming intoxicated and fevered.

Savage was on the point of ravishing her. To gain control he eased her slightly away from his groin and sat up. Her delicious murmur of protest shot through him like lightning. He warned himself to give her no pain. That way he knew he could make her wildly, sensually uninhibited. He began to whisper again in an effort to cool and prolong their ardor.

"Each year the Doge was rowed out on his magnificent barge into the lagoon to symbolically marry and join the City of Venice to the sea, by throwing a gold ring into the water." He took off one of his own gold rings and tossed it into the lagoon.

Antonia looked up at him and gasped. It was such a romantic gesture, linking them forever to this place.

His gaze fastened on her lips. She held her breath as the Leopard lowered his head to give him access to her hungry mouth. His tongue came out to lick and taste her full underlip. The Leopard's tongue was rough. She shuddered, then gasped as he sucked in the red ripe succulent bottom lip as if he were taking a cherry into his mouth.

She tasted like sweet, heady wine. She tasted like woman. He reclined again and took her with him. She yielded all her softness against him and was rewarded by his rising, burning arousal. One possessive hand slipped into her bodice to capture her bare breast. His calloused palm and fingers sent a jolt of sensation swirling around the silken skin, then spiraled lower into her belly.

His other hand had other fields to conquer. His fingers searched until they found their way beneath her skirt band. The heat of his palm scalded her as his hand inched lower across her naked belly. The friction of heated rough skin against heated silken skin was like bliss. His long, strong fingers splayed downward until the pads of his fingertips rested just above her pubic bone. Just exactly where the tiniest ringlets sprang covering her mons.

The pressure of his strong fingers felt delicious as sin. She sighed from the very depths of her soul. The Leopard was purring in her ear again.

"We are beneath the Bridge of Sighs."

She gazed up past his darkly shadowed face. "What a perfectly beautiful name."

"Not really, *cara*. Beyond this bridge are the prisons. All who pass beneath this bridge heave a sigh as they glimpse their last of freedom through that dense stone latticework."

Antonia sighed again.

"No sadness, *chérie.* Tonight is only for pleasure." His deep command carried to the gondolier. "Casa Frolo."

At his words threads of golden sensations ran from her breasts to her belly. Surely his splayed fingers could feel the deep tremors that shot to her woman's center between her legs. She half turned so that she lay facing him. She sprawled between his thighs, mingling her woman's heat with his.

She filled his arms with loveliness and he made the mistake of picturing them both naked in this position. His shaft bucked against her belly and her mouth formed a delicious O of surprise. He took swift possession of that soft mouth, sliding his tongue deep, then drinking her nectar.

"Shall I take you home to bed?" His voice had a raw edge that sent a frisson down her spine.

"Oh, yes, please." Antonia's voice was husky and velvety with anticipation.

She had always been aware of his body's strength and power, but now that he was expending it to protect her from the disorderly crowd, she felt weak with gratitude. She'd always imagined how it would feel, but the reality of his possessive protection enfolded her, gloved her in dark velvet, so that she was absolutely inviolate to any but Savage.

Her steps felt as if they were floating as they whispered across the marbled floors and stairs of his palazzo. The madding crowd fell away as they ascended. Fancifully she thought even a goddess being taken up to Olympus to receive sacred rites could not feel more radiantly alive or more desired.

So much about Adam Savage was unknown to her, his dark face ever unreadable as if he wore a permanent mask. She felt as if she were on the brink of a revelation, perhaps more than one, and yet she suspected she would never know him completely. Which was just as well. A slight shiver touched her fevered skin.

When he opened the door she saw that his chambers were palatial. Two rooms were joined by an archway of white, sugar-spun marble. From a wrought-iron balcony flowers tumbled in abandon to the waters of the canal below.

He locked the door from the inside with an ornate golden key and allowed his glance to lick over her. All of her. He stepped toward her and opened his palm, where the key lay.

She laughed that he should offer it to her. "Is that to keep you from escaping me?"

He was completely serious. "Take it. When you see my scars, you may not wish to remain. You must feel free to leave at any time."

A tiny frisson went through her, running deep. She knew she would never be free. To show she was ready to obey him in all things, she lifted the key from his palm and laid it upon a marble pedestal that stood beside the door.

He took her hand and led her into the spacious bedchamber. He removed his black silk cape and then he lifted off the Leopard's mask.

Antonia knew his face as well as she knew her own, and yet its impact made her knees so weak and watery, she sank down upon the bed's edge. Since first she'd seen him she had wanted to let her gaze roam at leisure over his dark, intense features. Now he invited her to look her fill.

His brows were black raven's wings, his nose a straight wedge with slightly flared nostrils. The structure of cheekbone and jaw was strongly sculpted, as if his Creator had used a chisel. His lips had a sensual mold. Then, as if the same chisel had been used, a deep gash slashed from the left nostril, straight down through the top lip. His skin was as swarthy as if it had been stained by walnut, then shadowed even darker over the area he kept clean shaven. In startling contrast his eyes were a piercing light blue. She had seen just such a shade in the waters of the Mediterranean.

"Your eyes are as blue as the Bay of Biscay."

She saw the well-remembered self-mockery. "You are a fanciful, romantic child." His hands knifed through his long black hair, once, twice. They were powerful, calloused, capable. Capable of gentleness? Possibly. Capable of cruelty? Assuredly. Capable of arousal and satisfaction? Equally!

She reached out to take his hands into her own. The contrast was marked. Hers were pale, his tanned; hers were long and slender, his strong and square; hers were soft, his roughened and calloused. As her finger traced the workworn skin the corners of her mouth went up with the sheer pleasure of touching him. Her green eyes dared to tease him. "You haven't the hands or the face of a gentleman."

"No," he confirmed. "Unfortunately, though, I suspect I am dealing with a titled lady."

She drew in her breath at his perception.

"Don't look so dismayed." A teasing light now appeared in his eyes. "I shan't put you out on your noble bottom." He brushed the backs of his fingers across her cheek. "You intrigue me. What's your name?"

His touch stole her senses. "An—" Her eyes widened in disbelief. She had almost blurted out her name.

"Ann." His voice sounded like velvet as his tongue caressed the name.

Whatever was the matter with her? She'd be calling him Adam any moment. "Do you have a name, my lord?"

"It is not *my lord* unless that is part of your fantasy, my lady."

She laughed up into his face. "Of course it isn't. How absurd."

"You'd be surprised how important titles are to most women." He lifted a brow. "Will Adam suffice?"

"Splendidly." The sigh reached her toes. His name was so perfect, it would have spoiled her fantasy to call him anything else.

"So then, Ann and Adam it shall be." He spoke as if everything had been settled between them. And in a way it had. He lifted her hand to his mouth and allowed his lips to brush across the back of her fingers. He whispered the question against her skin. "Are you ready to play the game of love?"

Antonia nodded wordlessly, unable to take a deep breath.

He pulled her up into his arms so that all her golden softness was enfolded in his powerful embrace. His arms tightened, imprisoning her against the hard length of him. Breast to chest, ribs to ribs, thigh to thigh, belly to belly, hard male muscle to soft mons. She yielded up her body to his and he rubbed her against his hardness.

The surface of her skin began to tingle as if it were showered by molten gold dust, then the heat penetrated the surface of her silken skin to plunge deeper, to enter her bloodstream exactly like rivers of molten gold. Crushed against him she felt his body's heat leap into hers, scalding her wherever they touched.

His eyes held hers intensely, needing to see her experience each and every tiny flicker of this arousal. Then suddenly he held her slightly away from him while his gaze dropped inside the golden crown of her bodice.

She knew he could see her breasts as if they were naked and the thrill made them quiver and begin to harden. Her nipples thrust out toward him like tiny wanton spikes, then he lifted his gaze to hers so they could share the knowledge that even his slightest glance could bring her shuddering pleasure. He was all hard male dominance, she, soft willing woman.

This was the way it was, then, between a man and a woman. The male gained strength and power, the female grew weak with love.

Domination and submission by touch alone. Every sense was beginning to heighten. The harder and stronger he grew, the softer and weaker she became. She was totally aware that it was his strength that held her upright. If he withdrew it, she would fall, tumbling to lie supine beneath him. Master and slave.

The kiss was a long time in coming. It was replete with its own foreplay. He began the kiss with his eyes, allowing his smoldering glance to fix upon her mouth, allowing her to see the desire, the intent, the hunger, and the raw need he felt to taste her, possess her, devour her. To draw out the anticipation further, he traced her top lip with a fingertip, then caressed the ripe flesh of her full bottom lip, then going further to pinch it between thumb and forefinger like a succulent fruit. Only then did his head dip and he sucked the ripeness into his mouth and softly bit upon it. Then he licked and sucked and tasted the dew-drenched berry until it was love swollen.

Antonia's black-fringed lashes swept to her cheeks and she moaned with her first sexual stirring. And then he kissed her. His lips were firm, slanting across her mouth, caressing, molding, coaxing, generously giving and selfishly taking all at the same time. They lured her lips to imitate his play. With a helpless little murmur of pleasure her arms slipped up his wide back, her hands playing over his rippling muscles as her lips opened softly to a lover's demands.

With the tip of his tongue he teased and played, learning the texture and taste of the honey-drenched alcove. Her own tongue fluttered, then tentatively toyed with his in a titillating game that taught her the beginning of boldness. He allowed her the freedom to explore his mouth before he asserted total male dominance and mastered her.

To Savage she was exquisitely tempting. It was palpably obvious she was both over-young and over-innocent, and yet she was totally unself-conscious with him, reacting to his lovemaking with a lovely, natural sensuality. He had a vague sensation of déjà-vu, as if tonight was the culmination of a long wooing they had both anticipated for—what? months, years, a lifetime?

He crushed down an urge to ravish her. It was a wild need to mark her indelibly as *his.* He eased her backwards to the bed before he withdrew his arms. Then with deliberate fingers he undid the tiny buttons at her waist. "I think we should dispense with this voluminous skirt, delicious though it is. I'll pour us some champagne."

She stepped from the yards of golden tulle just as Adam turned with a glass in each hand.

A little spilled over the rims. "Sweet Jesu!" he growled.

Antonia's face flamed. "Oh, I know these drawers are outrageous."

He shook his head. "Nay, sweetheart, I've seen diaphanous under-clothes before. It's your legs!"

"My legs?" she whispered.

"Your legs are spectacular." His gaze licked over her delicate an-kles, long slim calves, and long silken thighs that seemed to go on forever. "I've never seen such deliciously long legs on a female in my life." He swiftly closed the distance between them, set down the champagne glasses, and swept her into the air. "They were made for wrap-ping about a man," he said huskily.

If that is what he desired, it was her supreme pleasure to grant his wish. She wrapped her long legs about his waist, crossed her ankles behind his back, and squeezed him. As he groaned with sheer plea-sure, her arms went about his neck and she kissed him, as moments before he had kissed her. The thought of his hard mouth beneath hers, with its wicked scar, sent shivers of delight shooting through her. She felt as if her very bones might melt and gripped him tightly with her long, silken thighs.

Jesu, why hadn't he had the presence of mind to remove his clothes? Supporting her lovely round bottom cheeks with his palms, he walked slowly to the bed, swept off the covers, and lowered her onto the black satin sheets.

Her golden hair, gold crown bodice, and sheer golden pantelets against the black satin were an arousing contrast. "You look abso-lutely decadent, *chérie,*" he murmured.

She looked up at him, watching the color of his eyes darken with desire. "You make me feel absolutely decadent."

She watched intently as his calloused hands removed his high black stock and then his shirt. She had seen him naked to the waist when they'd shared a chamber at Edenwood, but now she was free to allow her eyes to take in the full splendor of his musculature covered by the crisp mat of curly black hair. She felt a hunger to see more of him. Then her hunger turned to greed. Not only did she long to *see* more of him, she wanted to *touch* him, to *smell* him, to *taste* him, to *devour* him.

Her green gaze followed his fingers to his belt, then widened as he stripped off his pants. Adam Savage's loins bore knife scars. The one on the right side of his belly looked as if he'd had his guts ripped out. But it was not the scars that made her wildly curious. It was his male center upon which she was riveted. Here at last was the mysterious male sex. His phallus jutted proud and thick from a black bramble-bush of hair, while beneath his shaft nestled two large oval spheres. His thighs looked as solid as young oak trees, yet his hips were amazingly narrow.

Adam's heart leapt when she hardly glanced at his scars, but centered all her female curiosity upon his jutting masculinity. She gazed at it so long in fascination, turning her head on a different angle the better to view it, that amusement filled his eyes. He spread his arms wide as if he were on display, then said, "Here I come, ready or not."

"I'm ready, Adam," she said quite seriously.

With a great whoop of laughter he dived upon the bed and scooped her beneath him. He straddled her with his knees and laughed down into her butterfly eyes.

"Your golden hair is lovely against the black satin, but I would wager a thousand guineas your natural black tresses are far more beautiful."

Her lovely green eyes showed surprise. "How do you know I'm a brunette?"

He shook his head at her sheer artlessness. "Because you have black silk ringlets between your legs."

"Oh!" she gasped, pink tinging her cheeks, then she threw back her head and let her laughter roll out over both of them. "How ridiculous I must seem to you."

"You are an alluring, irresistible golden treasure."

"Mmm, plunder me," she begged.

"What a scandalous waste that would be. I shall savor you."

She watched his deft fingers unfasten her bodice, then she watched his face as he freed her breasts. She watched him lick his lips as they suddenly went dry, and she longed for him to bring the tip of his tongue down to her own mouth again.

As if he discerned her secret thoughts and desires, he bent forward to take her mouth, but not before he cupped her delicious round breasts upon his roughened palms. She cried out from the thrill of his touch and he took her cry into the hot, dark cave of his mouth.

Antonia had never before realized how sensitive were her woman's breasts. She had hidden them for so long that now she took pleasure in simply acknowledging their existence. Once she had thought them small, but in Adam's palms they felt perfect. As he caressed them they felt as if they were growing, swelling, hardening. They became so deliciously sensitive against his roughened skin, she wanted to scream from pleasure.

"Your body is becoming awakened fully for the first time in your life. I'm going to give you a rubdown with champagne. It will make you feel more incredibly alive than ever before."

Antonia thought she must be dreaming. Was she really lying on a bed, imprisoned between Adam Savage's marble thighs while he taught her about sensuality? If it was a dream, she never wanted to awaken.

He went up on his knees as he reached across her for a crystal goblet of champagne. She lifted her arms above her head, closed her eyes, and stretched luxuriously in anticipation of the pleasure of his powerful hands upon her body. When she opened her eyes he was slipping the sheer golden undergarment down her lovely long legs. Her body arched of its own volition and Adam couldn't resist dropping a kiss upon her mons.

She was a delight to him. Already she was experiencing deep pleasure and he hadn't yet begun to even play with her. He turned her facedown on the bed and splashed some bubbling wine upon her back. Initially it felt cool, but as his hands made contact with her soft skin, palms down, it became warm. His strong hands made long, firm sweeps across her shoulders and down her back until she began to tingle and then to glow.

His hands then moved to her ankles so he could massage her legs with long, upward strokes. She easily had the longest, prettiest legs he'd ever had the pleasure of touching. They seemed to go on forever, culminating in the most temptingly round derriere. He made circles around her bottom cheeks, first going one way and then the other.

Antonia alternately cried out and moaned. His knowledgeable hands relaxed and aroused her at the same time. The sensation was completely new and exciting. The excitement built as Adam brought his lips to her silken skin and he began to lick and taste her. Just as the feel of his hands was rough, so, too, was the Leopard's tongue.

It swirled over her, exciting them both until his teeth thrilled her with small erotic love bites. Her body tantalized him.

"I love the way your skin tastes of champagne." Even his voice had a rough, husky undertone, and his warm breath feathering over her skin made it vibrate. His fingers and lips slid all the way down her spine until his mouth came into contact with her delicious bottom. His tongue teased and licked her until she thought she would go mad.

She arched her bum into the air, grabbing fistfuls of the black satin sheet. He stroked her with his tongue until she went up on her knees crying his name over and over.

With possessive hands he turned her onto her back. "I've saved the best until last," he purred, trickling champagne between her breasts. She had thought them sensitive when his hands had cupped and weighed them, brushing his rough thumbs across her aureoles. But when he tongued, then bit, then sucked with his demanding lips and tongue, the sensations heightened a hundredfold. Her breasts ruched, crested, and peaked into impudent spikes, thrusting to fill his mouth with their unique taste and texture.

Her lovely young beauty aroused him, yet he knew it was the fact she was untouched by any other man that sent his sexual hunger soaring out of control. He was the first and he had to crush down a ridiculous longing to be the last. This was a romance for one night. She would vanish with the dawn, as would he, and all that would be left was a haunting, lingering memory. It was preordained.

Chapter 28

It was a most erotic experience performing foreplay on this golden goddess, for instead of closing her eyes and drifting off to a place apart, she watched him intently, watched his eyes, his lips, his mouth, and his tongue in their deliberate provocation of her first experience with passion. Her reaction was intense and very vocal.

As his mouth left her breasts to trail a molten path across her belly, she clasped her long, silken legs about him to draw his flesh to hers. She wanted him. She wanted all of him.

When Antonia felt his rampant male shaft between her thighs she lost a measure of control and came up off the bed to bite the corded muscles across his wide chest. He looked down at the row of tiny, crescent teethmarks and grinned with delight. If he was a Leopard, then she indeed was a Leopardess! Her need built until she was ready to claw him. Christ, what would she do when he entered her with his tongue?

He unwound her legs from his waist and spread them wide, then very gently he combed his fingers through her black triangle of curls. She lay back on the satin sheets, arching her mons into his hand, her eyelids so heavy with sensuality they were half closed, yet he could see the green fire burning intensely in her eyes.

He slipped a finger into her cleft, but did not go deep inside her. Instead he sought the tiny rosebud high in her cleft and stroked and toyed with it until she became erectile. At first she was fever dry, but as he played, a drop of moisture formed against his fingertip and then another, until she was wet for him.

"Does that feel good?"

"Mmm, you know . . . it feels . . . wondrous."

The tension inside her swollen bud built to a crescendo, and then the bud bloomed, opening its petals in a burst of unfurling. It took her breath away. "Oh"—she gasped—"what a lovely thing to do to me!"

Adam smiled knowingly. Then, carefully, slowly, he slipped his finger deeper inside her. He had no intention of destroying her jewel. He would leave intact the blood-red ruby of her maidenhead as a gift to her future husband. Tonight there would be no pain, no blood, only delirious, intoxicating pleasure.

Antonia's sheath was so tight, his strong finger made her feel very full and engorged to bursting. He held absolutely still while she got used to the feeling of being impaled and he was rewarded by tiny fluttering spasms as her sheath grabbed him and pulsated. She drew up her knees, then let them fall open so he could watch everything he did to her, then she propped herself up on her elbows so she, too, could watch.

Slowly, he withdrew his finger all the way, then slid it back up inside her until it touched her hymen. He repeated the tantalizing gesture with slow, rhythmic strokes, creating a hot, pulsating friction that made her sheath cling to his finger possessively. It took a heart-stopping length of time before she built to her first full climax, but a scream built in her throat until it was released at the exact same moment she contracted convulsively, bathing his finger with her love milk. She was primed now and Adam knew not to let her miss a beat. He pulled her legs so she fell back across the black satin sheets, then lifted them onto his shoulders.

She crossed her legs behind his neck, drawing his head closer to her woman's center. She saw his nostrils flare as he breathed her spicy woman's scent, then the tip of his tongue traced her lips, which were now love slick and swollen with need.

She cried out, "Nooo . . . yesss . . . please, more . . . ah, more." She arched wildly upon his thrusting tongue, knowing this was the closest to Paradise she would ever get. Suddenly the scent of violets filled the room. Inexplicably Adam knew the fragrance came from their bed play. She tasted and smelled of dew-drenched wild violets. Her cries of passion pierced his heart. Never had he seen a woman so beautiful in her passion.

Antonia spun away, thinking she would faint, but he had only momentarily drained her like a chalice. Then suddenly she became filled to the brim with energy and renewed life. Suddenly she had sexual energy to burn. She came up from the bed and flung herself upon him, forcing him back to the sheets while she hung above him, deciding how to enjoy him first.

Adam allowed her to take control, to revel in her newfound power.

"Lust is sometimes a virtue," he teased huskily.

She went down against the full, splendid length of him, her legs stretched out on top of his, his manroot rigid along her cleft. Then she touched her lips to his in half a dozen quick little kisses.

"Your mouth is divine. It makes me feel beautiful."

"Sweetheart, you are beautiful. Breathtakingly, heart-stoppingly beautiful."

"You're not so bad yourself." She laughed, drinking in his dark symmetry. "I'm wildly curious about your body."

"Explore me. Satisfy your curiosity," he invited.

She lifted herself from his body and sat cross-legged beside him. Then she felt bold enough to stroke the long slabs of muscle in his chest and tangle her fingers in the crisp black hair that covered him like an animal pelt. Damnation, no wonder women were drawn to him like bitches in heat. He was a magnificent male animal, making every other man pale by comparison.

It would be the easiest thing in the world to fall in love with him. Antonia knew she was infatuated and had been for months, but she refused to admit she loved him, fearing that was the road to heartbreak. Her eyes dipped to his belly. It was hard and flat, yet marred by a crisscross of silver scars. She could not allow her hands to hesitate lest he think the scars repelled her. And in truth they did not. They were a part of him, a part of his past to be sure, but they had played a significant role in forming his present personality.

Gently her fingertips traced the jagged slashes. When her eyes sought his, she found them watching her intently. "Do they hurt?"

After a moment he shook his head. "Only the memory. Which is as it should be to keep me from making the same mistakes."

The self-mockery was back. She put pressure upon the scars, smoothing the edges into his unscarred flesh, then feeling them spring back into ridges beneath her fingers. In a way they prevented him from being physically perfect and that was no bad thing. He was dangerously close to perfection.

At last her eyes sought the object of her wild curiosity. She looked at it a long time, not yet quite bold enough to touch it.

"Well?" he prompted, trying to conceal his amusement.

"It is not quite as I expected."

"In what way?"

"Well, it's much larger, of course. And its shape is curious. It's slightly curved, like a scimitar, and this part"—her fingertip almost touched him.

"The head?" he prompted.

"The . . . head . . . is not the same above as below. It is smoothly curved above, then split into a heartshape beneath."

"It is large because at the moment it is engorged with blood. That happened because your beauty and closeness physically arouse me. The ridge beneath the head is fashioned to create friction inside a female's body."

Antonia felt hot metallic threads inside her sheath pull taut. He heard her swift intake of breath.

"It is slightly curved to follow the curve inside a woman's body."

Adam watched her lick her lips, knowing her mouth had gone dry.

"It is not always this exaggerated size, of course. In an unaroused state the shaft becomes flaccid, the head becomes hooded by the foreskin, and it shrinks to less than half this size."

He took hold of her hand to encourage her and guided it to his phallus. Suddenly her fingers were eager to touch, to feel, to learn everything. "It is so hard and rigid, it's almost impossible to imagine it becoming soft."

"After ejaculation it becomes soft," he assured her.

"Ejaculation?" she questioned, her eyes serious in their quest for knowledge.

"When I manipulated the bud of your sex, you built until you experienced a climax. It is the same with me." His fingers closed about hers so that they clasped his thick shaft. Then he worked her hand up and down a few times. "The friction of coitus ends in climax when my seed is ejaculated."

Her green eyes widened as if a great mystery had been solved for her. She knew what coitus was. The *Kama Sutra* had been titillatingly explicit. She knew they had not yet performed coitus.

"Does it hurt?" Her long fingers tightened about his upthrust sex until she could feel it pulsing with his heartbeat.

"Yes, it does ache and become painful if I am kept in a state of arousal without ejaculating."

As they looked into each other's eyes, each saw a flame leap high at the erotic state of their arousal. The words came and hung in the air; she could not call them back. "I want the curve of your scimiter to follow the curve inside my body."

His arms reached out to enfold her and draw her down to him. "Sweet Ann, I want it more than I've ever wanted anything, but it would be a totally selfish act on my part. Only I would receive pleasure."

"But you gave me pleasure with your fingers and your mouth, and I suspect the pleasure of a rampant male weapon would be ten times as pleasurable."

"A hundred times, love, but before that pleasure comes pain while your sheath is stretched to almost breaking point. We simply don't have time for you to become accustomed to the pain and move beyond it. The hymenal rite is a mystical thing. I intend to leave you intact so that you can experience it in your future."

"But I can never marry," she protested.

Adam smiled. "Never is a long, long time. And even if you never have a husband, you will assuredly have a lover."

"How can you be sure?" she cried.

"After tonight your body will crave a lover's touch. It won't be long before you seek and find someone to love."

"But I sought and found you."

"We are playing at fantasy. In less than two hours dawn will bring reality."

"Adam, I want you to ejaculate."

"Not by coitus, love. What if my seed left you with child?"

"Ah, God, why is there always the devil to pay?"

He shrugged. "Risk makes the game sweeter, I suppose."

"I'm ready to risk all!" she cried recklessly.

"I know that and it makes you utterly desirable, but you are extremely young and I have made myself responsible for you this night."

"You promised to love me!"

"I promised only to unveil the mysteries of sex for you."

She sighed. He was being honorable, damn him to hellfire, and yet how secure she felt, knowing he would protect her at all costs. "Show me how to give you pleasure."

He reached out for her hands, placed one in the crisp dark fur over his heart, and filled the other with his upthrust maleness. "Simply play with me."

Antonia caressed him, stroked him, fondled him, and rolled him, watching in fascination as he became more swollen and engorged. He jumped and bucked in her hand and then Adam began to moan low in his throat at the pleasure she brought him. Suddenly it wasn't enough for Antonia. She wanted to kiss him, to taste him, to take him inside her body. She wanted to give him more pleasure than he had ever known with another woman.

She cupped him with both hands and lifted him to her lips like a precious object she would worship. She dropped a kiss upon the velvet smooth head, then another and another. With the tip of her tongue she delicately traced beneath the ridge, all the way around, then dipped the pointed tip into the tiny opening in the center. Now it was his turn to be vocal and she reveled in her woman's power over him. She slid her lips down to fasten over the ridge, imprisoning the whole head inside her hot mouth, then with her tongue she licked and sucked until he was pulsating wildly.

"Stop love, I'll spend." He gasped.

She gave him a bewitching look from beneath her dark lashes, telling him clearly she had no intention of stopping.

Adam controlled his climax for long minutes, enjoying to the full the intoxicating, addictive sensations as he built and built to explosion. He knew he could not bear much more of her exquisite loving, then finally as he felt himself start, he pulled his swollen shaft from her lips.

His seed arced, then cascaded across her breast and across the black satin sheets, the drops as beautiful as liquid pearls. Antonia touched one with her fingertip, then rubbed his essence between her finger and thumb, marveling at its slippery, silken texture. She lifted her fingers to her nostrils to smell him, then finally her tongue came out to taste him. It was a potent male mixture of salt, sandalwood, and smoke.

"Are you always so impulsive?" he demanded in a raw growl.

"I have learned to seize the moment," she murmured huskily.

With a great whoop he lifted her from the bed and set her upon his wide shoulders. Then he galloped around the room, playful as a boy. He came to a stop before the mirror so they could see how carefree and uninhibited they both looked. He caressed her long, silken legs, loving the feel of them draped over his shoulders, loving the feel of her scalding mons against the back of his neck.

Antonia knew she was already becoming aroused again. Then her eyes dilated as she watched his cock swell and grow until it stood rigid, almost to his navel.

"How could you fill so quickly?"

"I'm fully erect, but all men have a refractory period after ejaculation before they can spend again."

"How long is the interval?" she asked curiously.

"It varies from man to man. A few seconds for a boy . . . perhaps hours for an older man."

"How long is your refractory period?" she asked, rubbing herself against his neck.

"Perhaps five minutes. About the same time it took you to become aroused again."

"You devil! Do you know all my secrets?" she laughed.

Adam went down on his knees so she could dismount. She was about to dance out of his reach, but he was far too quick for her. He slipped to the rug and pulled her down into his lap, then he proceeded to kiss her very, very thoroughly. He didn't leave off the kisses until her mouth was swollen, beestung, and completely slaked, then his mouth moved much lower to render her other lips swollen, beestung, and completely slaked.

She must have slept, for when she awoke they were entwined in the bed, her mouth against the strong column of his throat, his arms holding her a prisoner against his loins.

Adam had lain motionless, his mind in turmoil while she slumbered. He knew he desired this lovely young creature much more than the repressed woman who waited for him in Ceylon. He toyed with the idea of waking her and forcing her to tell him her name and circumstances. Surely his money could erase her difficulties and make it possible for them to be together.

Savage knew he wasn't being fair. She was too young for him, too innocent. His sinister past would taint her. Best leave things as they were. A brief liaison that neither would soon forget was infinitely preferrable to ruining a young life. He sighed deeply for what might have been.

Antonia stirred and opened her eyes. Dawn had already painted the sky a blush-pink. His lips moved against her hair. "Don't leave yet. Stay with me awhile."

Her lips moved against his throat with a silent word. "Forever."

When he sat up and swung his legs to the floor, she was the one to murmur a protest at the separation. She watched with possessive eyes as he stretched his lithe body and knifed his powerful hand through his hair. Then, naked, he walked out onto the balcony to greet the dawn. He looked down and waved to someone below. *"Paisano! Amico!"* Adam's Italian was limited to a few indispensable words.

Antonia heard a burst of speech from below and was amazed that he stood conversing stark naked.

"Veniva?"

She realized he was asking for food!

He grabbed a basket, unfastened the curtain tassel, and lowered them over the balcony railing. Then he came back in for money and tossed down the coins. Whoever was below began to question him and he gave laughing answers. She understood the word *donna* meant woman. They knew he had a woman in his chamber!

Laughter drifted up to her. *"Quell' animale."* They were calling him a wild animal. Their voices were filled with approval.

Suddenly Adam came back into the room. "He won't let go of the food until he has seen you."

Antonia gasped. Then she capitulated. It was far too late to become all prudish now. She slipped her arms through Adam's shirtsleeves and ran out to his waiting arms. He kissed her good morning before his appreciative audience and Antonia quickly tucked the shirttail between her legs, knowing the man below could see her bare bum. He was a good sport.

"Bene! Bellissimo! Vai siete bella."

"He says you are very beautiful," Adam whispered, "and very naked."

"Oh, you devil." As she ran back to the bed all Adam could see were the glorious long legs. She sat cross-legged waiting for him. "What did you get?"

"Fruit, fresh-baked bread, and spicy Italian sausage."

"Mmm. Ambrosia! Food for the gods! You may feed me."

He cocked a dark eyebrow at her. "This food is mine. I paid for it."

"I have no money. What will you take?"

"The shirt off your back will suffice."

She slipped her arms from his sleeves and held the shirt out to him. He was delighted that she had no inhibiting false modesty. He set the basket between them. "Help yourself, my darling."

She pretended to ponder her choice, then reached clear beneath the basket to possess his manhood. "I choose spicy Italian sausage." The contents of the basket spilled across the bed as he grabbed for her.

His pretended ferocity was almost frightening. With a little cry she scrambled away from him, but he caught her ankles and slowly dragged her across the black satin sheets toward him. The slippery material against her nipples felt so sensuous, she realized she was becoming aroused again. In Adam Savage's bed it happened in the space of a heartbeat. She knew he would satisfy her body's cravings, but briefly she wondered what would happen when she was back to being a boy, back to being Tony. She would have to keep her distance from him else he would have her in a continual state of arousal.

She pushed the thoughts from her mind, as a growling Adam pinned her between his thighs, then came down upon her with his full weight, teasing and tantalizing her sensitive skin with his crisp pelt. His beard scratched her face and she found it so thrillingly masculine, she went weak.

"Let me teach you to purr," he murmured against her lips, then he took complete possession of her, mastering her tongue, blotting out everything but the feel and the taste of him.

Afterward he gathered her into his lap so they could feed each other bits of sausage and bread, and the luscious fruit of sunny Italy. Suddenly even eating became a sensual experience, as he licked and sucked her fingers when she fed him. Each knew the time was running out and they tried to prolong their fantasy. She touched and massaged every part of his powerful body, committing it to memory. She ached because she could not have him deep within her to satisfy him as a real woman would, but he was adamant and would not be disobeyed.

He was caressing her lovely round breasts while she rode his marble thigh, and he taught her how to pleasure herself if her need became great enough. Suddenly he pierced her with his ice-blue gaze and said, "Why don't I order us a bath? You can wash the golden powder from your hair and scrub that butterfly mask from your beautiful face so I can see what you really look like."

A look of panic crossed her face. "No! No bath. Sadly, I must be going."

"Sweet, are you certain about the bath? You reek of my male scent," he said huskily.

She shook her head. "It must be noon. I should have left at dawn. Help me to dress."

He fastened her into the little gold bodice, but she could not find the gold drawers. Finally she gave up and stepped into the golden tulle skirt. Her steps dragged reluctantly as she walked to the door. She saw that the little golden key was missing and looked at him with liquid eyes that were ready to spill over.

"I cannot give you the key until you tell me your last name."

"Lam . . . beth," she whispered, knowing half a lie was better than none. She knew she would never be the same again. He loomed over her, dark and brooding. She put her hands against his black pelt and went up on tiptoe to kiss him good-bye. "Thank you, Adam, for the gift of knowledge. It is priceless."

When their lips parted, he pressed the key into her hand.

Chapter 29

Back in her room at Casa Danieli she ordered a bath. It took her half an hour before she stepped into the water. She wanted to keep his masculine scent upon her body, his kisses on her half-bruised mouth. God only knew if she'd ever share in them again.

She washed the golden powder from her hair, marveling at how much it had grown since the night Roz had cut it. She brushed it back severely and clubbed it into a queue with a black leather thong. She dressed in her male clothing, refusing to allow herself to mourn her feminine attire.

Antonia packed her bag, carefully hiding her makeup at the bottom, and then at the last minute she folded the small golden bodice, shaped like a crown, to take with her. The golden tissue skirt was left hanging in the wardrobe, a discarded ghost of her fantasy to be relegated to the past and forgotten.

Before she closed the door upon the make-believe, she reflected upon her feelings. She hadn't the slightest regret for what she had done. She had set out to seduce him, but it had been his mouth that had accomplished the seduction. She felt wonderful. More alive than she'd ever felt in her life.

On the way back to the ship she stopped to order a great quantity of Venetian talc to be sold in England, not only as hair powder, but face powder, for it was infinitely preferred over the dangerous white lead.

Tony was relieved that she boarded the *Flying Dragon* before Savage returned to the ship. She kept to her cabin until the talc was delivered. She was watching it being stowed in the hold when Savage came aboard. He didn't even question her about what she had bought, but went quietly about his business with a closed look upon his face. He seemed as if his thoughts were engaged elsewhere, and yet he was aware of every inch of the clipper ship and every man jack aboard her. After he checked her from stem to stern he lost no time getting her under sail. Savage was England bound and seemingly couldn't get away from Venice fast enough.

For the rest of that day and all of the next he stood alone at the wheel. His demeanor was unapproachable, daunting even, and for once Antonia was thankful for it. It was best to keep a very wide and very safe distance between them.

As Savage sailed the ship through the Adriatic, back down to the Mediterranean, he noted with sardonic amusement that quite a change had come over young Lord Lamb. There he was with a scarf tied about his head like the rest of the crew, scrambling up and down the rigging like a damned monkey. The sun was turning him brown, and he had a new carefree attitude that came with a healthy abundance of self-confidence. Something had obviously happened to him in Venice that had made him grow up. Savage often heard him whistling and singing, and even a stormy crossing of the Bay of Biscay did not destroy his newfound high spirits and laughing temperament.

Savage wished he felt the same. He did not. He searched for words to describe the mood he had fallen into. It was not exactly brooding, but it was decidedly reflective. He had gone to Venice to be dissipated and dissolute, to act the libertine. Instead he had found romance.

Romance was the last thing in the world he sought, and yet he wouldn't have traded his Venetian romance for all the tea at Leopard's Leap. Sailing up the coast of France he became downright introspective. He had laid his plans for the future so carefully for when he returned to England from the Indies. He had built Edenwood and chosen a chatelaine to grace the stately home, who would be the perfect political hostess. His future was settled. Meeting the golden goddess in Venice who was little more than half his damned age had suddenly made him dissatisfied with his life. He swore a filthy curse and purged her from his thoughts. It had been blissful while it lasted, but he was determined never to think of her again!

They made port in Le Havre for the night with the intention of taking on fresh water. Savage issued an order that no crew member must be ashore after dusk, and all seemed inclined to obey. Savage turned a blind eye when McSwine and the Scotsman invited a couple of whores who worked the French docks aboard.

Tony did not stay belowdecks, but she kept to herself as she strolled the deck, listening to the music and laughter of the crew and that of other ships docked close by. Only the Channel separated her from England. Had the scandal of the duel blown over in the month she'd been away, or did she have it all to face down once she arrived back in London? And Bernard Lamb—would he be waiting for her, waiting to avenge himself, waiting to eliminate her at his first opportunity?

Tony was lost in deepest thought when suddenly a shadowy figure glided silently past her, close enough for her to reach out and touch. She remained motionless, not even breathing, then all of a sudden it came to her that it was Adam Savage leaving the ship. His scent came to her first. Never, ever could she mistake it for another. The second thing that told her it was him was his size and the fact that he moved with the stealth and grace of a leopard. He was garbed in dark, rough garments, almost rags. She let him go without a word. She refused to allow her infatuation for him to blind her to the fact that he was dangerous, sinister, and likely up to his damned icy blue eyes in some illicit smuggling operation. She did not know what it could be. She did not want to know.

Suddenly she lost her desire to be up on deck. She knew she would feel much more secure in her own small cabin. She washed her hands and face, then reclined in her hammock, swinging back and forth, thinking of all the ports they had visited this past month. The hammock soon lulled her to sleep, where she had a pleasant dream about her brother Anthony.

About three o'clock in the morning someone was shaking her

awake. She felt a hand upon her shoulder and almost jumped out of her skin.

"Tony, don't be alarmed. It's only me," Savage murmured.

It was pitch-black in the cabin. She swung her legs to the floor to keep the hammock from swaying. "What the devil do you want?" she demanded.

"I need your help with something in my cabin. I don't want to disturb the crew. Will you come?"

"I suppose so," she said stiffly, thinking he'd smuggled something aboard. They moved slowly and silently down the companionway to Savage's cabin and he fumbled with the oil lamp until he got it lit.

Tony turned to watch him shrug out of a tattered black coat, bracing herself for what was to come. The last thing in the world she expected was his next words.

"I've a ball in my shoulder and I want you to take it out for me."

"Ohmigod, why didn't you say something immediately?" She was upset. "This is what happens when you go crawling about the underworld in the dead of night!"

"Save me the lecture, lad," Savage said quietly. His shirt was black and didn't show the blood, but once the shirt was stripped off, blood was everywhere and she saw that he'd lost a copious amount.

There was a low tap on the cabin door. Savage nodded his head, so she answered it. It was Mr. Baines with a kettle of boiling water.

"Thank you, Mr. Baines," she said with relief.

"Can you cope, lad?" he questioned.

"We'll manage," Savage said crisply. "I want you on watch for the law."

Mr. Baines touched his forelock in a silent salute and withdrew. When she turned back to Savage he was holding his knife blade in the flame of the lamp. Tony kept her eyes lowered as she washed the blood from his chest. As her fingers touched the well-remembered muscles she thought grimly, *I didn't think I'd have at him again this soon.* Tony examined the wound closely.

"I know it hasn't shattered my shoulder blade—it's just imbedded in the muscle."

Without a word she took hold of the knife handle. She hesitated for a minute or two as she gathered her courage. Her own common sense told her she must be quick and she must go deep enough to rid him of the ball with one decisive thrust. She must not probe and prick at it incessantly and ineffectually. She took a deep breath, bit down upon her lip, and plunged in the sharp point of the knife.

Red blood welled up and trickled down his chest immediately, but she let out her breath with a *whoosh* as the ball dropped into the metal washbowl. Her glance went to his liquor cabinet. There was wine and there was rum. Quickly she took up the rum and brought it back to the table. Again she hesitated, but Savage said calmly, "I can separate my mind from the pain."

Quickly she flooded the wound with the raw rum and watched him stiffen. She felt a small measure of satisfaction that indeed he had felt the pain. It served him bloody well right for whatever criminal act he had committed.

He directed her to a box of dressings and bandages and she had to apply pressure to the wound to staunch the blood before she could bandage it. They heard footsteps overhead on deck.

Savage said, "Get rid of this lot. Put it all inside the wardrobe and fetch me my dressing gown."

Tony threw the bloodied shirt and towels on the floor of the wardrobe, then she put in the bandage box and even the bowl of bloodied water. She helped him into a claret-colored brocade dressing gown and before he tied the sash another knock came upon the cabin door.

"Quick, get into the bunk," he ordered.

Without thinking she obeyed him. Savage's gaze swept the cabin before he moved across it to open the door. Mr. Baines's square face was unreadable. "Sorry to disturb you, sir, but the gendarme here insists he was following a criminal who boarded the *Flying Dragon.*"

Savage fixed Mr. Baines, then the French official, with an icy blue stare. Then he drawled, "Since you have disturbed us, I suggest you come in and take a good look about. My young companion and I have been secluded in this cabin all night."

The Frenchman directed a penetrating look at the boy in the bed. He could not keep a look of distaste from his face for what had apparently been going on. He looked back at the man in the dressing gown. "I'd like to search the vessel," he said in heavily accented, but understandable, English.

"By all means," drawled Savage. "I'll give you thirty minutes."

When the door closed, Tony jumped from the berth, white faced with anger. "You bastard," she hissed, "how could you use me in such a degrading manner?"

"Easy, Tony, I didn't actually bugger you," he mocked.

Her cheeks flamed. She wanted to smash him in the face. Her fists doubled and she took a threatening step toward him, when to her amazement, Savage staggered on his feet.

"Peste!" she cursed, then helped him to the bunk and brought the decanter of rum. "Have a good swig," she ordered gruffly. Tony held it to his mouth while he took a few swallows.

The mocking light faded from Savage's eyes. "Thanks," he said sincerely.

Tony sat down, and only after she knew he had fallen asleep did she make her way to her own cabin. She lay down, but after a length of time acknowledged the truth to herself. She'd never rest while he lay wounded, doors away. She got up, unhooked the hammock, and managed to drag it along to his cabin. She hooked it across the corner and, leaving the lamp lit, lay down, listening to his even breathing.

Tony must have dozed, but Savage was becoming so restless, he had kicked the wall and roused her. She was across the cabin in an instant, a hand pressed to his brow. He was definitely feverish. His bowl was still full of blood, so she took his fresh-water jug and sponged his face and neck over and over in an attempt to cool him down. Savage began to mutter. She paid little heed to his murmurings until he began to call for someone.

"Ann . . . Ann . . . are you there?"

The color came and went in her cheeks as she realized he was calling for her. He repeated the name over and over, becoming more restless with each minute. Finally in desperation she slipped her hand into his and murmured, "Yes, Adam. I'm here."

"Ann?" he demanded.

"Yes, yes. I'll stay. Try to rest."

He did seem to settle more peacefully after that, but she could feel the heat of his fever through his hand. She wondered wildly what she would do if he was still delirious by morning and the authorities returned. She leaned against the bunk, all her thoughts in disarray. She was elated that he had called for her in his delirium. If only . . . she had never begun the deception of taking her brother's place. If only Adam Savage were not involved in sinister, illegal activities . . . if only he were not a shameless womanizer, having affairs with half of London's society hostesses . . . if only . . .

She slipped her hand from his and returned to her bunk. In less than two hours a knock came upon the cabin door. Tony was roused from sleep when she heard Savage call, "Come in, Mr. Baines."

The first mate opened the door, took in the scene with calm eyes, and said, "First tide, sir. Do we sail on her?"

Savage swung his feet to the cabin floor. "Yes, Mr. Baines. Take us home."

"I'm glad you're recovered," Tony said stiffly, and took her departure along with Mr. Baines.

Tony didn't see him again until they had docked in London. Savage told her he would send word as soon as the *Red Dragon* returned from its voyage to the Indies so that he could supervise the loading of the cargo he'd purchased. Though she subjected him to a close scrutiny, he looked completely recovered and back in total command of himself and everyone about him. Someday she'd like to shatter that arrogant composure to smithereens!

"I expect that business of the duel has blown over by now. In London there is nothing quite so boring as stale gossip. However, I'd appreciate it if you'd manage to keep yourself out of any more scrapes. I have neither the time nor the inclination to keep coming to your rescue."

Adam hoped that by downplaying the danger of the duel, Tony would take heed. He knew if he lectured him too harshly, it might push him headlong into more recklessly dangerous behaviour. Adam now accepted that the cousins hated each other, but it was ridiculous for Tony to think Bernard was out to murder him.

Tony felt like tearing a strip off him, but kept her tongue between her teeth and seethed silently. If he considered attempted murder and a duel to the death as simply a scrape, she would be wasting her breath to enter into a shouting match with him. The trouble was Adam Savage didn't take Bernard Lamb's threat to Anthony seriously. She wished she could feel the same complacency. But she knew it was serious. Deadly serious. And it would never be finished until one of them was dead.

In the salon at Curzon Street, Antonia was able to dispense with male waistcoat, cravat, and jacket while she was with her grandmother. She rolled up her shirtsleeves as she listened to the latest news of the ton.

"Darling, you've been gone so long, all your clothes have gone out of style. It's your birthday next week. Do you fancy something pretty?"

Tony didn't want to celebrate her seventeenth birthday without Anthony.

"You forget I gave up petticoats for lent," Tony said dryly.

Roz made no comment, but continued as if she hadn't spoken. "Side panniers are now dead as a dodo. In fact nothing at all is to be wired. Every lady in town this winter is wearing a loose Dutch jacket with wide sleeves, edged in fur. They say the latest fashion for spring will be muslin."

Tony shivered. The English climate, especially at the moment, was not conducive to wearing muslin. "Why can't women be more practical?" she asked, just exactly as if she were a man. "I'd think woolen shawls and flannel petticoats would be more suitable."

"Oh, speaking of shawls, cashmere ones from India are the very last word in elegance. Brightly patterned calico is also making a fashion statement along with Indian-red taffety."

"Really?" Tony said thoughtfully, with an idea for importing goods on the return voyage of the *Red Dragon*.

"And hairstyles are enough to drive you to drink. The fashion lasts not five minutes! One day you puff your hair at the sides and find yourself in the true sanctum of the mode. The next day you puff your hair at the sides and you are forever utterly cast out!"

"I hope society's concentration upon trivia is not really serious. I hope it's a humorous attempt to shock or amuse."

"Lady Holland, who absolutely dominates Whig society these days, used to have her hair braided across her forehead in the summer, but now she has a great cluster of curls about her face. Such a multitude of ringlets gives her all the charm of a French poodle with distemper."

Though her grandmother was being quite witty, Antonia wasn't amused. She remembered the elegant Lady Holland visiting Half-Moon Street too damned often.

Mr. Burke brought them tea and sandwiches, but within minutes Tony poured all three of them a glass of sherry.

"I have a confession to make. I'm surprised you haven't heard all about the scandal by now." Suddenly Antonia had their undivided attention. "Do you recall the day we visited Edenwood? Bernard Lamb was there large as life, and while I was riding in the woods that day someone was shooting at me. I was positive it was my cousin and I decided then and there to rid myself of him."

"What the devil did you do?" asked Roz, her hand at her throat.

"I challenged him to a duel. I knew he wouldn't play fair, so I turned and shot him on the count of nine. Unfortunately I didn't kill him, I only winged him."

Roz's eyes were like saucers and Mr. Burke's mouth gaped open. "Adam Savage came to stop the whole thing, but he was too late. However, he was in time to see that Bernard Lamb also turned and fired on the count of nine. He thought I might be arrested for what I'd done and so he hustled me out of the country, hoping things would blow over."

"Oh, darling, you can't go on with this dangerous deception any longer. You don't know when that insane creature will strike again. I think we should inform the law; have him arrested."

"I'm the one they'd arrest. I broke the law by challenging him to a duel, and he's so damned devious, he'd likely swear he fired in the air and I deliberately shot him and tried to kill him."

Mr. Burke made a suggestion. "I'm sure that Adam Savage could put the fear of the devil into Bernard Lamb. He has a very powerful physique and looks totally dangerous and intimidating."

"Adam Savage doesn't believe me when I tell him Bernard Lamb sabotaged our boat and killed Anthony and that he's still determined to become the next Lord Lamb. He was outraged over the duel and tells me he hasn't the time or the inclination to get me out of any more scrapes."

"From now on I think I'd better accompany you when you go wandering about London," Mr. Burke said decisively.

"God Almighty, you'll have me in leading strings," she protested.

Roz put her head on one side. "Antonia, I can't put my finger on it exactly, but you've changed since you've been on this voyage. They do say that travel broadens the mind, but it's more than that. You're more assertive, more sure of yourself. It's as if you've suddenly become self-possessed and aware of your own power."

Antonia's lips went up at the corners. "I'll never be the same again, thank God. I learned more about life and about myself in the last month than I learned in seventeen years."

"Good Heavens, a girl usually doesn't change that drastically until she marries and becomes a woman," Roz mused.

Antonia clicked her heels together, gave them both a formal little bow from the waist, and said enigmatically, "Say no more."

Chapter 30

Adam Savage did a very strange thing for a man who had purged a woman from his thoughts. His first act upon returning to London was to pay a visit to Watson and Goldman and ask them to find a young lady by the name of Ann Lambeth. He told them what little he knew of her and advised them to hire a man to trace her. He would pay whatever fees they asked and promised a generous bonus if they were successful in locating the lady.

Tony went about London cautiously. She stopped to gaze in the window of London's most fashionable shoe shop at the St. James's end of Pall Mall. She sighed over the green lace slippers with blue heels, then strolled on. As she passed White's Club, she saw Colonel Dan Mackinnon and Sherry sitting in the bow window. They both hailed her as if she were their savior. Tony wasn't a member of White's, so her two friends came out to join her.

"Has the gossip over the duel blown over?" Tony asked bluntly.

"Silly old thing! As if we'd be hailing you from White's window if you were still beyond the pale," Sherry said, shoving a stack of papers beneath his arm. "I'm writing a new play. Perhaps you can help me out with names for my characters; that's always the tricky part."

"Let's go and eat. I hear the Norris Street Coffee House in the Haymarket serves a curry fit for the gods," Mackinnon suggested.

"Curry becoming popular, is it?" Tony asked, mentally adding it to the list of cargo she'd import.

"By the by, heard that Indian Savage fellow speak in the House yesterday. Usually the members lounge about sucking oranges and cracking nuts during the debates, but there was perfect silence when he spoke."

Though Tony knew Savage had bought himself a seat in parliament, she was surprised he was making speeches. "What did he speak about?"

"Don't recall. Actually I was a trifle foxed yesterday. It's this infernal play that's driving me to drink. Say, you wouldn't mind if I called my main character Anthony, would you?" Sherry asked.

"Absolutely not," Tony assured him.

"Anthony Absolute!" Sherry cried, as if he'd had an inspiration from his muse.

"By Satan," Mackinnon said, dropping his fork and taking a large draft of ale, "I know curry is either mild or hot, but this stuff is Cauldron of Death!"

"Is Prince George still enamored of Maria Fitz?"

"Oh, God yes. They're inseparable, joined at the hip," Sherry mocked.

"Careful or you'll end up in the pillories." Mackinnon tittered.

"No bloody room. A chap was put in the stocks for referring to her as the Vice-Queen when rumors of their marriage circulated."

Tony thought Vice-Queen was rather witty. Sherry shuffled about among his papers and handed a couple to Tony. "Read the latest lampoons."

The first read:

Most gracious Queen we do implore
To go away and sin no more;
Or if that effort be too great,
To go away at any rate.

Tony chuckled, then perused the next pamphlet.

Give the devil his due, she's a prime bit of stuff
And for flesh she has got in all conscience enough.
He'll never need pillows to keep up his head
Whilst old Q and himself sleep and snore in one bed.

'Tis pleasant at seasons to see how they sit,
First cracking their nuts, and then cracking their wit;
Then quaffing their claret—then mingling their lips,
Or tickling the fat about each other's hips.

"Oh, that's absolutely brilliant," Tony said, laughing. "Are you sure you didn't write this, Sherry?"

Sherry winked. "No, by God, but I wouldn't be surprised if our limerick friend didn't earn a few bob, knocking these off."

Dan Mackinnon said, "Maria does have big dumplings. I think that's the attraction."

"Dumplings?" Sherry protested. "They're more like hot-air balloons."

As Tony looked about the coffeehouse, she saw that every man present wore an elaborate powdered wig. She suddenly remembered she'd brought a vast supply of wigs and Venetian talc for sale in London, but for all she knew they were still in the hold of the *Flying Dragon.* She had no choice but to pay Adam Savage a visit.

"Well, I'm off," Tony said, pushing her chair back from the table.

"Wouldn't be our friend if you weren't," punned Sherry.

"Will we see you at the fight tomorrow night at Marybone public gardens near the Oxford Road?" Mackinnon asked.

"Perhaps," Tony replied. "Boxing matches aren't really up my alley."

"Oh, this one's different. Mrs. Stokes, a female fighter, is attracting enormous crowds."

Sherry shook his head sadly. "What the hell is wrong with females today that makes them want to imitate males?"

"It's beyond me, Sherry," Tony replied, but she knew her cheeks were flying red flags.

When Tony ran up the front steps of Half-Moon Street to ring the bell, the door was opened by a very smart butler. "Oh, hello, I'm Tony Lamb. I'll show myself up."

"Indeed you will not, young sir. The master is busy with his secretary at the moment. Perhaps another time would be more convenient."

Tony bristled and was about to push her way past the servant when a daunting thought came to her. Perhaps Savage had a woman with him and the butler was being discreet. She certainly wouldn't want to find him in flagrante delicto, but it would be her very great pleasure to interrupt him.

"Mr. Savage is my guardian as well as my business partner in a shipping venture. I'm sure if you announce me, he'll immediately cease whatever he's doing to attend to me."

"Very well, sir. Kindly wait in the receiving room."

In a few minutes the butler returned. "Mr. Savage will see you in his office, Lord Lamb."

Tony found him with Jeffrey Sloane and it was patently obvious they were up to their elbows in paperwork. "Sorry to interrupt you," Tony muttered, "but it just occurred to me I bought cargo from the Continent to sell in London."

Savage waved a negligent hand. "Already resold the champagne at two hundred percent profit. If you want an exact tally, Sloane will provide it."

"No, no. I'm not worried about profits."

"Then you should be," Savage said shortly.

"Well, then I am. I was just trying to be polite," Tony countered.

"You have a decision to make about the wigs. You can dispose of the entire shipment to a hair wholesaler or you can set up a wig lottery in Rosemary Lane. The masses who can't afford them are always willing to wager a bob or two, which is one of the reasons they can't afford them in the first place. Profits are enormous, but it's a time-consuming business."

"Well, you're the expert at this import-export thing. Might as well sell them to the wholesaler."

"Good decision. We'll make a businessman of you yet."

The butler reappeared. "There is a young woman below to see you, Mr. Savage. I tried to discourage her, but she insists it's a matter of grave import."

"Christ, what next? Well, show her up. The more the merrier!"

Jeffrey Sloane excused himself, as he had obviously been trained to do when a female came calling.

To Adam and Tony's surprise the visitor was Dolly from the Olympian Theater. Her mouth was set in a grim little line, although her eyes suddenly widened when she saw Lord Lamb. She hesitated only a moment, then straightened her shoulders and plunged in. "I'm in the family way, an' Lord Lamb is the father!"

"Why, you lying little bitch!" Tony cried, slapping her in the face.

In a flash Adam Savage backhanded Tony across the mouth, knocking her into a chair and sending it flying across the office. In a biting voice he said, "Never strike a woman again in my presence, you arrogant young swine!"

Tony's eyes were liquid with tears and she pressed the back of her hand against her swollen mouth.

Dolly's eyes were glittering with avarice. Savage had immediately jumped to her defense and that must mean he believed her tale.

"Sit down, both of you," Savage commanded.

Antonia was pierced to the heart that Adam had actually struck her.

"I told you to stay out of scrapes, but I suppose that's asking too much of a blue-blooded young rakehell such as yourself!" He dismissed Tony with a searing look of contempt and turned his attention to Dolly.

"Has your condition been confirmed by a doctor?"

"Yes, sir," Dolly said firmly, her chin in the air.

"Well, since you know marriage is out of the question, I presume you came for money."

Dolly bit her lip. It would have been really something to be wed to a lord and called Lady Lamb, but she'd known all along she couldn't intimidate a man like Indian Savage. He'd hit the nail right on the head. She'd come for money.

"I shan't pay you a goddamn penny!" Tony asserted. "Why the hell didn't you come to me? I'll tell you why . . . because the whole thing is a barefaced lie. You came running to my guardian because you're after money and you know he controls the purse strings."

"I came to Mr. Savage because I believed he'd do what was right!"

"And just how much do you think would be right, Dolly?" Savage asked quietly.

She took a deep breath. "Five thousand."

Savage laughed. It wasn't a pretty sound. He scribbled a note payable on his bank and handed it to her. "Two thousand sounds about right to me, Dolly; give or take a thousand."

She tucked it into her reticule and dried her eyes. She'd only hoped for a thousand and would have settled for half. As she stood to leave, Adam Savage fixed her with his glacial, ice-blue eyes.

"It is understood this is the last we shall hear of the matter."

She sketched him a curtsy and hurried out.

"So that's how you handle females you get up the stick," Tony said with a sneer.

"No it is not, you young lout. If that had been an innocent young girl you'd gotten into trouble, I would have made you pay and pay dearly. But Dolly is another kettle of fish. She's far too wise to get pregnant in the first place unless she intended to set a matrimonial trap. When girls like that do happen to get caught, they know how to get shut of it in half an hour. Now, for Christ's sake Tony, can you keep your nose clean or do you need a wet nurse?"

"If you've finished knocking me down, I'll take my leave." Her mouth was so sore, it hurt her to speak.

"Don't expect me to apologize for hitting you. You had it coming."

"Someday you *will* apologize for hitting me. I guarantee it," she said quietly.

* * *

Tony managed to slip into the house without being noticed. She bathed her face and called Savage every shocking name she could curl her tongue about. She'd have a damn great bruise and when Roz saw it, she'd insist on Mr. Burke accompanying her everywhere. Perhaps she should go home to Lamb Hall. It was within riding distance of Edenwood, the house she'd fallen hopelessly in love with. She'd love to see it now spring was coming. Tony couldn't really understand how Adam Savage could stay away from it. It was his dream home and yet he'd hardly spent five minutes there. What he needed was a wife. Someone who would cherish Edenwood and fill it with children. She reprimanded herself sternly. She must be out of her mind longing to marry a man who had just struck her in the face.

Another lady in another part of London also fancied becoming a wife. Her aspirations seemed just as hopeless. Maria Fitzherbert was taking late supper with the Prince of Wales in his private suite at Carlton House. She had no doubts that George was totally besotted with her. He had made her the toast of London. Every hostess knew her success or failure depended upon whether her guest list was headed by the new favorite. They were thankful for small mercies. At least Mrs. Fitzherbert was a respectable widow, a very different class of woman from the Prince's usual choice of gold-digging actress.

Maria was walking a fine line. She had taken supper in George's private suite once before, at which time she had learned just exactly what England's Prince expected of her. She had only escaped by protesting outraged virtue and by allowing kisses and cuddles to take the place of capitulation and congress.

Since then, however, they had been alone umpteen times in the enclosed royal carriage, where she had learned that a young man in his prime was after larger game than the two plump partridges she used to pacify him. It had come as a bit of a surprise to Maria just how frisky a man in his twenties could be when she measured him against her two elderly husbands. Not altogether an unpleasant surprise, however.

Now, once more her virtue was in jeopardy. She was not naive enough to think she would escape altogether unscathed, but everything had its price and she was determined to make her Prince pay and pay dearly.

"Ah, Puss, it does me good to see how much you enjoy precisely the same food I love."

"Your Highness's chef has no equal," Maria said with a nervous little laugh.

"I beg you not to 'Highness' me. Please let's be Prinny and Pussy, my love?"

"Of course, Prinny. You know I would do anything in my power to make you happy." The minute it was off her tongue, she knew she shouldn't have said it. He had taken her off balance tonight by wearing a brocade dressing gown, which made her downright nervous. As a consequence she had consumed one dish after another as a stalling tactic, but delicious as it was, if she took one more mouthful of trifle she would burst the seams of her Parma-violet satin.

"It is within your power to make me more than happy. You would make me jubilant if you were kind to me, Pussy."

"Prinny, I have been more than kind to you. I have allowed you privileges I would allow no other man on earth."

George came around the table to her, the food at last forgotten. "Give me your little paw," he commanded.

Maria obeyed and he covered it with kisses. Then he drew her from her chair and led her to a substantial couch. Now that he had her captive beside him, his lips touched the rapid pulse in her wrist and trailed up her pleasingly plump arm to her shoulder.

"Pussy, you excite me beyond my endurance. Beneath my princely robes, Puss, I am but a man," he said meaningfully.

"A prince is greater than other men, Prinny."

"That is true, Pussykins. Therefore does it not follow that a prince's needs are also greater? My lovely, it is painful for me to be continually in this condition without hope of release. Surely you do not wish to give me pain, Maria?"

"Your Highness, I cannot give myself to any but a lawful husband," she said primly.

"We are back to 'Highness,' I see."

Maria could hear the great hurt in his voice.

"Your arrows have pierced me to the heart, cruel, cruel huntress. Have you no balm for my wound?"

"Prinny, I love you!" she cried. "Do not bring dishonor to me!"

"Pussy, Pussy, with my body I thee honor, not dishonor!"

"Ah, now you mock me with lines from the marriage ceremony."

"Never that, my lovely. In my heart you are my true wife. I would give anything to be a true husband to you." He could wait no longer to fondle her breasts.

She allowed him to unfasten her gown and let her crowning glories spring free. Maria knew the power of persuasion that her pair of advocates possessed. The moment he took her breasts into his hands, George began to swell. Ah, God, what could he not achieve with this woman? He began to kiss her, but her lips did not deter him long from his real goal. His demanding mouth slid down her throat inch by inch until it finally closed hotly over a large fuchsia nipple. He could feel himself throbbing now and he could deny himself no longer. He began to suck, gently at first, then stronger and stronger.

Maria felt as if there were invisible threads of liquid fire connecting her breasts to her belly, and her belly to a much lower, much more intimate, place. "Oh, Georgie, don't!" she begged. She groped toward him, intending to push him away, but somehow her lover's robe had fallen open and her hands came in contact with his engorged phallus.

"Ooh, Georgie." She gasped.

If her gown had not fallen about her waist, impeding him, he would have thrust home, dissolving her protests like snow in summer. As it was, there was only one fragrantly soft cleft luring him on where he could bury himself. His mouth came up to hers, taking her cries of half protest, half delight, into himself as he pressed her back upon the silk-covered couch.

His large shaft slid into the deep cleft between her breasts and the heat from her body almost scalded him. The Prince began to moan and thrust in earnest. There was no stopping him now.

Maria clasped him to her bosom, delighted with his youthful, manly vigor. He had succeeded in arousing her own sleeping sensuality. This combined with the overwhelming sense of power she felt over the highest Prince in the Realm was enticingly irresistible. After this intimacy there was only one step left. She must not allow him to take that step until he had asked her to marry him.

He felt his seed start and sprawled upon her in a state of exhausted ecstasy. The moment had arrived when both must make their move and push for the thing they wanted most.

"Pussy, Pussy, I adore you. Let me spend the rest of my life making you as happy as you make me!"

"Your Highness, you have ruined my gown," Maria said softly.

"My dearest, I will buy you a thousand gowns. Let me get a towel

. . . let daddy make it all better." He hurried to his bathroom and brought a crested Turkish towel. When he returned, Maria was crying softly.

"There, there, Pussykins, don't cry." Gently and with great reverence he wiped the lovely globes of her breasts and the valley between. He put his hand beneath her chin and raised it so that he could look into her eyes. "You have made me the happiest man in the world, Maria. Why are you crying?"

She raised tear-drenched eyes to his. "I am covered with shame. How could I have indulged in this forbidden tryst? I can never see you again."

"Puss, Puss, I shall die without you. I want you to come and live with me. If I cannot have you with me day and night my life is utterly meaningless!"

"George, don't, please, I beg you! Do not coerce me into a life of degradation."

"Pussy, I love you! How can you say life with England's Prince would be degrading?" he demanded.

Maria pulled up her Parma-violet satin with great dignity. "Even if you were a king it would be degrading without marriage."

They were at an impasse. The Prince of Wales decided in that moment to acquire the magnificent jewels from Indian Savage. They would show Maria how much he valued her.

Maria decided in that moment it would be all or nothing. "I think you had better take me home, Your Highness."

Chapter 31

When Tony returned from the wig wholesalers Rosalind was entertaining Frances Jersey. Tony tried to slip upstairs, but no one ever had succeeded in eluding the elegant Lady Jersey.

"Anthony darling, you weren't trying to avoid me, were you?"

"Ah, Lady Jersey, how lovely to see you again. I swear you must be a witch. You seem to get younger with each visit."

Frances simpered up at Tony from her diminutive four foot eleven. "You flatter me vastly!"

"Lady Jersey, I am prodigiously truthful."

"Anthony, you are one of the nicest boys I know. That is why you won't say no when I ask that you attend Almack's tonight. We have so many young ladies, but not nearly enough dancing partners for them."

"Ugh," grimaced Tony, "I don't mind the young ladies, it's their mothers, aunts, and grandmothers I have an aversion to. You can't get away from them. They have evolved a speech pattern that doesn't require your participation, but it keeps you anchored to the spot for hours while you must politely listen."

"As a special favor to me, dear boy. Roz has promised to attend as a chaperone, so you may escort her."

Tony looked at her grandmother. "You're really going to Almack's?"

"I'm not quite ready for the chimney corner and a shawl yet, you know, I'm only in my forties."

"How old?" Frances Jersey asked with disbelief.

"My *late* forties," Roz amended.

"Mmm, *very* late forties," Frances murmured cattily.

Tony shot her a dirty look. "Have you not told Lady Jersey about your virile major?" she asked as a parting shot, before she escaped upstairs.

Frances turned to Roz with raised eyebrows. "Virile? Major?" she repeated all agog.

The corners of Roz's mouth lifted mischievously. "He's very dashing, in a militant way. At first I wasn't too attracted because he's bald, but, Frances, I swear to you, without his clothes he is the most *naked* man I've ever seen. It's extremely stimulating."

Frances was speechless. Rosalind was satisfied that she had paid her back for the earlier insult.

Tony escorted her grandmother to Almack's and stayed as long as she could bear it. The thing that appalled her was the innocence of the young girls her own age. Actually *innocence* was a misnomer. The young women had been kept downright ignorant of the reality of the opposite sex and the ways of the world. When she could stomach it no longer, she made her excuses to Roz and decided to walk back to Curzon Street.

Tony hadn't walked a block when she felt a creepy feeling as if she was being followed. She glanced back, saw nothing, but nonetheless quickened her pace. She chided herself that she was allowing her imagination to run riot. Her ears were pricked for any furtive footfall, but all she heard was her own labored breathing.

She forced herself to calmness and once more glanced behind her. She saw something that looked like the shadow of a man. Though she had been keeping all thoughts of Bernard Lamb at bay, he now sprang full blown into her imagination. She quickly crossed the street, because the other side was better lit. She tried to reason with herself. There was no possible way Bernard could know she had attended Almack's tonight. Unless of course he'd been following her since her return to London.

She sighed with relief as she saw a group of young bucks ahead of her. As she got closer, however, she saw that they wore the striped pantaloons of the Zebras from Eton. They were drunk and rowdy and actually attempting to smash the gas lamps along the street. To avoid them she cut down Clarges Street, which led into Curzon. As she turned the corner, a wedge of fear filled her throat as a tall figure raised what looked like a swordstick. The scream lodged in her throat as she lurched away from him. Relief washed over her as the gentleman merely touched his hat with his stick in polite greeting and passed on.

Tony picked up her feet and ran the last few hundred yards to the front door of the town house. She didn't bother finding her key, but hammered loudly upon the door until Mr. Burke opened it. He took one glance at Antonia's white face. "Shall I fetch the bucket?"

Tony fell into his arms. "No, no, Mr. Burke, but I could use a brandy!"

Before she went to bed Antonia jotted down in her journal how she had allowed her imagination to take control of her. It acted as a purge and she climbed into bed, laughing at her own foolishness!

Two evenings later was the gala entertainment everyone, but everyone, had been looking forward to. It was a rout al fresco to be held at Vauxhall Gardens. It was to have everything—musical entertainment, a banquet, a dance, and a new play at the Vauxhall Theater, where the Prince of Wales's private box was shaped like a huge, glittering crown. The pièce de résistance was to be a fireworks display, telling the story of the descent of Orpheus into Hades.

By dusk the crowds had begun to cross the Thames to get to Vauxhall, which was across from Westminster Abbey. A mist had begun to float in from the river, which only added to the danger of the public gardens. The ton found Vauxhall an adventurous and glamorous place of amusement because it was frequented by pimps and prostitutes.

Between the highest and lowest denizens of society were vast crowds who simply found the place an irresistible gaze. Tony met some of her acquaintances lining up for wherries to get across the river. She attached herself to their party for the sheer security of numbers. Philip Frances, one of Prince George's younger friends, was probably closest to her own age and they struck up a conversation. It seemed, however, that all he wanted to talk about was dueling and Colonel Dan Mackinnon's gun collection. Tony repressed a shudder and, when they arrived at the gardens, attached herself to Amoret and Sheridan.

The gossip was all about Prince George and Mrs. Fitzherbert. Amoret confided that George had been asking all his friends if they thought he could defy the King and marry without his consent. Most were dubious that it was possible because of the obnoxious Marriage Act that proclaimed a member of royalty could not wed without the King's consent before his or her twenty-fifth birthday.

"Why don't they simply live together for a few short years until he's twenty-five?" Tony asked Amoret.

"Mrs. Fitzherbert prefers death to dishonor. Respectability is her god. But between you and me, she won't let him fuck her until she's the flaming Princess of Wales!"

"Haven't they made love yet?" Tony asked in disbelief. "No wonder the Prince is filled with lust."

"There's only one cure for lust," Sherry quipped. "Embalming fluid!"

"Blimey, this place invites lechery," Amoret laughed, pointing down the walks bounded by high hedges and trees that led to secluded groves and grottoes.

Tony noticed that the mist was turning into fog and it gave the gardens an eerie atmosphere. The hundreds of lamps usually illuminated the whole twelve acres, but tonight the lamplight was dimmed by the patches of fog that floated over the trees and clung low to the gravel paths.

Tony caught a glimpse of a tall dark man with a flamboyantly dressed woman. It might not have been Adam Savage and Angela Brown, but it might just as well have been for the devastating effect it had on her. "It's damp out here. Let's cut through the pavilions and rotundas to get to the theater," Tony suggested.

Some of the buildings were adorned with statues and paintings, while others were decorated by replicas of the sun, the stars, and all the constellations. The number in their party dwindled as many stopped at wine booths and others followed a marching band.

"Don't you think we should dine before we go into the theater?" Amoret suggested.

Tony shrugged. "There's such a crowd here, we'll never get seats."

"That's true," Amoret agreed. "Everyone will want a seat where they can observe the royal box as well as the stage."

"All George wants is a private box at mons Venus," Sherry quipped.

It took Tony a few moments before she understood the sexual innuendo. When she did, she delicately blushed.

"Sherry, my belly thinks my throat's been cut," Amoret complained.

"Oh, all right. I suppose I'm a bit peckish myself. If you're not in the market for food, Tony, why don't you go and save us some theater seats?"

Tony would have preferred they stick together, then chided herself for being ridiculous. Outside the fog was now thicker and the crowd had thinned out, or at least it seemed so because the heavy mist isolated people from each other.

Tony walked along the path, rounded a temple, and went through a portico covered by vines. As she left the portico she became aware of a crunching on the gravel path behind her. She stopped and turned about, but all she saw was pale lamplight through the swirling fog. She hurried her steps in the direction of the theater, but everything looked strangely different in the fog and she began to think she had taken a wrong turn. The music and the noise of the crowds seemed to be growing fainter with every step she took.

Her heart began to hammer because she could still hear footsteps behind her. She kept glancing over her shoulder, probably to reassure herself, because there were no shadowy figures to be seen, no matter how hard she stared along the pathways and into the bushes.

She was breathless now and disoriented and she began to run. Within a few minutes she realized it was the worst possible thing she could have done because she found herself in a remote part of the gardens where there were only lawns and cascading trees.

She knew she must stop running and gather her wits. If there was one thing Tony despised, it was cowardice. Her lungs felt as if they were on fire from running and breathing in the fog. Taking her courage in both hands she stepped onto the lawn and shouted, "Bernard

Lamb, come out in the open where I can see you, you sniveling coward!" Silence.

"Come and fight me like a man, you son of a bitch!"

Dead silence.

Tony fingered the knife in her pocket. "I'll drown you in your own blood!"

Absolute and perfect silence.

Her pulse slowed. She regained her breath. If there was no one following her, how utterly foolish she must sound issuing vile threats into the night. She was going home. Vauxhall Gardens held no more pleasure for her, this night or ever.

Tony began to walk with carefully measured steps, neither too quick nor too slow. Her eyes were keen, her ears were pricked, and every sense was alert for danger as she searched out the right way to the exit.

Tony heaved a great sigh of relief once she had passed through the gates. The road leading to the Thames was busy tonight with people and traffic. Among people once again, her fears dissolved and she felt perfectly safe. Then it happened!

She felt a great, deliberate shove from behind and she let out a terrified scream as she went down before an oncoming carriage. From the road she looked up in horror to see the deadly hooves of two carriage horses hurtling down upon her.

Antonia blacked out momentarily as the horses danced about in their harness to avoid the object that had shot between their legs. She opened her eyes just in time to realize that the coach was passing over her. She knew she would be killed. There wasn't even time for a prayer. Tony heard a woman screaming. For a moment she thought it was herself, then miraculously she knew it was someone else. Men were shouting and helping her to her feet. She was badly bruised at thigh and shoulder where she had hit the pavement, but she hardly noticed. Her powdered tie-wig was gone and her blue satin breeches were slush from knee to crotch, but she was alive. With help she limped to the sidewalk and leaned against a lamppost. Suddenly she sank to her knees, put her head down, and began to sob.

The crowd stood back to gape. She shook so badly, her teeth chattered. People in the crowd were now drawing their own conclusions. Likely the young lord was reeling drunk when he stepped into the path of the oncoming carriage. They began to disperse before they were called upon to bear witness.

Tony cried her eyes out. At first it was from the trauma of the terrifying experience; then it was from sheer helplessness. Bernard Lamb would never give up. He would hound her to her death. There wouldn't be a day or night she would be safe from him. She sat slumped there a very long time. Finally she arose and made her way to the river, wondering if he was still stalking her.

The moment she stepped from the wherry, she hailed a carriage to take her right to her door in Curzon Street. She was thankful Roz was not at home. Likely enjoying the spectacle at Vauxhall. Although Tony had let herself in with her own key, the keen eye of Mr. Burke had noted her condition. She was extremely grateful to him that he made no comment.

Tony bathed, grimaced at the dreadful bruises, then pulled up the covers to plan what she should do next. She made up her mind to go home to Lamb Hall, but her imagination made her change her mind. In the isolation of the country her hated cousin would have far more opportunities to dispose of her without witnesses. Perhaps she was safer in London after all. Apprehension made her indecisive. Nothing seemed to solve her dilemma. Dear God, whatever was she going to do? Inexplicably she felt most aggrieved at Adam Savage. Why didn't he protect her? Why did he look at her with contempt whenever she brought up Bernard Lamb's perfidy? Why did he whore about with actresses?

As it happened, it was not Adam Savage Tony had seen at Vauxhall. Tonight he was running the Channel under cover of dark. It was the third night this week he'd sailed to France. For Savage there were parallels with the years he'd spent smuggling for a living. Now he had other motives in addition to profit; nevertheless, carrying illicit cargo still gave that curl of excitement to the gut because of the danger involved. It was a seductive, addictive pleasure, which he hoped he had almost outgrown and could live without.

His thoughts were suddenly filled with the girl he had encountered in Venice. Why was she proving so elusive? No trace of Ann Lambeth had been found and he realized she must have given him a false name. She came to him again and again, sometimes at the most inappropriate moments. Her elusiveness only added to his obsession. She was like a drug; one taste and he craved her in his blood, wanting more, needing more. He cursed his own folly. His jaw set implacably. He needed no one. There were other females in the world with green eyes and long legs. In any case, he had an understanding with Eve and he intended to stick with his plan for practical reasons. He was past thirty and a little long in the tooth for romantic flights of fancy, and if he had gauged the Prince of Wales correctly, he was fairly close to the title Eve coveted.

At the moment His Highness was leading Maria Fitzherbert from the glittering, crown-shaped theater box at Vauxhall. The blanketing fog had spoiled the plans for the pyrotechnical display, but George was not in the least disappointed for it meant he would be alone with his lady sooner than anticipated.

Once they were enclosed in the opulent carriage, he touched her thigh with his and slid his arm about his beloved.

"Pussy, come home with me tonight?"

"Prinny, you know I cannot. I am a widow who must not besmirch her reputation. If I spent one night under your roof, people would say we were living together in sin. For your sake as well as mine, I must go home to Park Street."

"Then let me lease you a house in St. James's Square where you may entertain me and our friends and the gossips could not say we were living together."

"A house in St. James's Square would cost the earth and you are already in so much debt, Prinny my love."

He removed his arm from her, hurt at her words. "So, Mr. Fitzherbert was allowed to give you a house, but not I."

"Mr. Fitzherbert was my husband," Maria said gravely.

"Pussycat, I think of you as my wife, but, alas, you do not consider me your husband," he said with great bathos.

"Prinny, darling, it is the King and Parliament who do not consider you my husband. Your father would never acknowledge me as the Princess of Wales and Parliament would never allow me to wear the crown jewels."

Sadly, George knew she spoke the truth. He was determined, however, in that moment to provide her with jewels fit for a princess.

Maria chose her next words very carefully. She placed her hand upon his knee and said softly, "If we had a wedding ceremony, I would most assuredly consider you my husband."

"Give me your little paw, Pussykins. Fido is lonely without your touch. See if you can persuade him to lift his head and come out of his little kennel."

Maria patted and stroked Fido and indeed he did lift his head and creep from hiding. George put his lips to Maria's ear. "If you offer him a treat, I believe you could persuade him to perform a little trick, like sitting up."

Maria giggled and offered up the treat her prince slavered for. As his hot mouth closed about her succulent nipple, Fido not only sat up, he began to wag his tail.

Chapter 32

Adam Savage smiled cynically when he read the note from His Royal Highness, the Prince of Wales. Every man had his price, most especially royalty. He regretted that he could not summon George to Half-Moon Street but must attend him at Carlton House. It would mean that he would have to send a note to Countess Cowper postponing their meeting and he would also be late for the House.

He took the diamonds and sapphires from their locked drawer for what he hoped was the last time and walked the short distance to Carlton House. Savage's shrewd blue eyes discerned that the Prince looked anxious.

"My dearest Savage, I hope you brought the jewels."

"I did, Sire," Savage replied, touching his breast pocket, but not yet producing them.

"It is no easy task to locate a vacant marquessate nor get a gentleman approved in that title, but apparently you have considerable influence in the House at the moment and with me as your patron I have every reason to believe the title can be conferred upon you shortly." Prince George paused, allowing Savage time to deliver up the jewels. Savage did not.

His Highness ran a finger about the inside of his towering neckcloth in hope of loosening it a fraction. The leeches that had been applied this morning to make his complexion pale had been an utter waste of time, for he was exceedingly florid at the moment.

He cleared his throat and stepped to a great globe of the world beside his desk. "Actually, my dear fellow, it will have to be the Irish peerage." When Savage did not protest, George brightened. "You have a choice. The Marquessate of Blackwater in County Waterford, or—let's see, what was the other? Ah, yes, the Marquessate of Kinsale on the coast of Cork."

Savage's light blue eyes followed the Prince's finger as it touched Ireland. "How very accommodating you are, Your Grace." He produced the black velvet bag and displayed the dazzling jewels like a conjurer producing a rabbit from a hat.

George's face beamed. He could not resist picking them up to hold their fire and ice in his hands. "They are magnificent. They will show the lady just how much I wish to honor her."

"If I may be so presumptuous as to make a suggestion, Sire? A crown of precious jewels would make a lady feel like a princess and all who beheld her would honor her as a princess."

George's face lit as if he had just been given divine inspiration. "Do you possess such a crown of jewels?"

Savage's scarred mouth stretched into a rare smile. "I do, Sire."

George closed his eyes, not daring to contemplate what Indian Savage's price would be for such a prize, but he knew he would meet that price, however high it proved to be. In his heart he knew Maria would never receive a royal crown, so it would be up to him to provide her with a coronet of her own. He was brought out of his reverie when Savage spoke.

"Though I am exceedingly busy, I shall endeavor to visit both these properties as soon as may be and let Your Highness know my preference."

"Very good. They are both ancient castles, you know. It will take deep pockets for their upkeep," George warned.

Savage bowed and took his leave. He had nothing if not deep pockets, and he didn't give a good goddamn that old money was revered, while new money was thought sordid.

The Prince of Wales decided that tonight was *the* night, and though he had enjoyed the anticipation, he reasoned that he had waited long enough.

"George, I cannot come into your bedchamber, it is most improper."

"Give me your little paw, Pussycat." The Prince of Wales clasped Maria's hand and began to pull her. "I am about to pop a very intimate question, Pussy. The privacy of my bedchamber is the only sanctuary where our secrets are safe, my dearest one."

Maria allowed herself to be persuaded, albeit coyly.

Prince George sat her down upon a thronelike gilt chair covered in Chinese silk and went down before her on bended knee. "Unworthy as I am my dearest angel, it would make me the happiest man on earth if you would consent to be my wife. I shall cherish you forever and a day and hereby pledge you all my love and devotion."

"Oh, George darling, your words make me weep with happiness. My answer would be yes, yes, a thousand times yes, if only it were possible."

He shifted to the other knee. "I have arranged everything with the help of some devoted friends. We shall have the ceremony on Friday evening at your little house on Park Street. Your two uncles shall be witnesses and my dear aide Orlando Bridgeman, who, being from Shropshire, is acquainted with your family will stand guard outside to make sure that the Prime Minister does not try to stop the ceremony."

"But, dearest, what about the Marriage Act?" asked a practical Maria.

"Our marriage, though a secret one, will be legal in the eyes of the Church. The moment I am King I shall get the Act repealed and marry you again so that it will also be legal in the eyes of the Crown. Reverend Robert Burt has agreed to perform the ceremony." He did not add that he had been bribed with five hundred pounds and the promise of preferment.

Maria saw the diamond rings on the Prince's fingers and the great Star upon his breast and told herself that she was not dreaming. This really was the Prince of Wales who was proposing marriage to her. A slightly irregular marriage, perhaps, but a marriage nonetheless.

"Oh, George, my dearest love, I can deny you no longer."

George got up off his knees, flushed with victory. He fumbled in his breast pocket and brought forth a velvet pouch that he placed in Maria's little paw. "You are the fairest jewel in the Kingdom, outshining all others, but I want you to have this necklace as a token of my deep respect for you, Maria."

She gasped at the diamonds and sapphires. "I do not want jewels, George, I want only you, but if it makes you happy, then I shall be honored to accept your gift as a love token."

He swept her into his arms. "Pussy, you have made me the happiest man in the world. Until this moment I have never known what happiness is." He kissed her deeply, overcome with emotion. A tear rolled down his florid cheek. "Ah, Pussykins, we will have such fun together. Do you know that when I was a boy my tutors whipped me whenever they caught me trying to have a little fun? Once, I remember, they caught me jumping on the bed and gave me a cruel thrashing."

"Oh, Prinny my love, I shall try to make up for all that you suffered at their hands."

"Pussy, will you jump on the bed with me?" he asked with childlike sincerity.

"Now?" she asked faintly.

"Yes, now, my lovely little playmate. Let me take your slippers!"

They both removed their shoes and George climbed upon the vast bed and aided Maria to climb up beside him. They held hands and bounced together. The second jump resulted in a fall and they tumbled together, laughing like children.

The Prince was now in an amorously playful mood as they scrambled from the big bed. "Let's play a game, Pussykins. You know how to make all my cares fall from my shoulders."

"What shall we play, Prinny my love?"

"Forfeits. I'll get the cards." The sly devil cheated of course, first taking her fan, then a stocking and then her gown. He let Maria win, too, so that he could forfeit his stock, waistcoat, and monogrammed shirt.

Whey they were in a state of deshabille, Maria blushing and giggling, George laughing and hardening, the cards were forgotten in favor of a little foreplay. Maria Fitzherbert excited the Prince more than any woman he had ever known. She had a lovely face and a complexion like roses and cream. Her hair was so pretty, she never wore it powdered, allowing the pale golden-yellow tresses to fall artlessly about her plump shoulders. But it was her breasts that excited His Highness the most. They were extremely large and soft, giving her a voluptuous yet maternal body for which George lusted and hungered.

With a boyishly mischievous look in his eyes George produced a pink silk bag. It was a newly invented toy called a balloon.

"Whatever is that, Georgie?"

"It's a clever little toy modeled on the hot-air balloon. Warm air makes it float about. Let's play one last game, Pussy." As he inflated the silk bag with his warm breath their dalliance began in earnest.

George bounced the balloon off Maria's breasts and then her buttocks. Soon he was boldly trying to bat it with his long erection, watching Maria's blushes turn her titties as pink as the balloon. The warm air in the room floated it higher and higher and as Maria jumped for it, her beautiful breasts bounced up and down until he was in a frenzy of desire. He enfolded her in his arms and they sprawled breathlessly across the great bed.

Lying upon her back, looking up at the ceiling, Maria saw their naked bodies reflected in the mirrors. It was extremely erotic. She watched in fascination as he mounted her. She had never enjoyed anything so thrilling before. Both her previous husbands had been elderly. George was an extremely large man in the prime of his youth. Maria's body turned him into a vigorous lover.

She was soon wet and slippery with the friction of his great sword of state. She bit her lips as wave after wave of pure pleasure washed over her, but finally she could keep silent no longer. She became so vocal in her excitement that it spurred George to new depths.

Holding a magnificent breast in each hand he plunged to the hilt one last time, then they both cried out their fulfillment. Later as she cradled him in her arms and felt his hot mouth suckle her nipple until he fell asleep, she lay staring up into the mirrors thinking how strange life could be. She had been no more than a nurse to her elderly husbands; now, at the opposite end of the scale, she was a playmate for a boy who would be King.

When Tony awoke it took only a few seconds for her to remember the horrors of the previous night. Her spirits sank immediately and a sick feeling settled in the pit of her stomach. She could not keep what had happened to herself, yet she did not want to frighten her grandmother.

Tony decided to talk to Mr. Burke, and since Roz never came downstairs before the civilized hour of ten, there was no time like the present. At breakfast she signaled to Mr. Burke that she wished to see him privately, and the trusted servant, who had been worried about his young mistress for some time, hoped Antonia would take him into her confidence.

Tony left the table and made her way to a salon that was usually only used for entertaining callers. Mr. Burke followed in a few minutes and deliberately closed the salon doors against the inquisitive maids.

Tony was longing for a smoke, but curbed her desire in front of Mr.

Burke. "Something dreadful happened last night. My cousin must have stalked me to Vauxhall Gardens. I took the precaution of joining a group of acquaintances knowing there was safety in numbers, but somehow, in the fog, I found myself alone and knew I was being followed. I panicked. I lost my way and ran. I felt so trapped, Mr. Burke, like a rabbit being run to ground." A wedge of fear formed in her throat as she relived being hunted down.

Mr. Burke saw her hands tremble and for one terrible moment feared she had been ravished. "Go on, my dear. You can tell me anything," he said gently.

"I knew I must get out of Vauxhall Gardens immediately. Danger lurked down every pathway, beneath every tree. I finally found the entrance gates and heaved a great sigh of relief to find myself out on the busy thoroughfare. My relief was short lived. I was pushed from behind and went down into the road beneath the hooves and wheels of an oncoming carriage. That I escaped death this time was nothing short of a miracle. Somehow the horses sidestepped my body and the carriage went over me without crushing me with its wheels."

"My God, you were injured last night when you arrived home and I did nothing."

Tony shook her head. "I was only shaken up and bruised, but I sustained more than bruises. It has left me frightened. Really frightened, Mr. Burke. I'm not afraid to face Bernard Lamb. I met him on the dueling field without too much trepidation, but now he's stalking me. I have no idea when he will strike me down and I am suddenly vulnerable and frightened to death."

Mr. Burke's lips formed a hard line and his fists clenched impotently. "The filthy coward. His mind is twisted and evil. Your guardian must be informed, my lady. It is his duty to protect you. From now on I shall accompany you wherever you go and I shall not be unarmed!" Mr. Burke had thought for a long time that the burden of saving Lamb Hall was too heavy for the frail shoulders of a girl. The masquerade had seemed plausible in the beginning, but he should never have sanctioned such a shocking, shameful scheme. He should have realized Antonia would be in peril after Bernard Lamb had caused Anthony's death.

Tony's shoulders slumped. "The very thought of having to tell Adam Savage and risking his contempt is abhorrent to me. However, I suppose I have no choice. I have nowhere else to turn. Will you come with me to Half-Moon Street?"

Mr. Burke suggested he follow Antonia rather than walking with her. That way he would be able to observe anyone who was watching for young Lord Lamb and would also be able to keep her back safe.

Tony arrived at the Mayfair town house without incident and waited for Mr. Burke to catch up in the reception hall.

Adam Savage was just descending the stairs, on his way out.

"Tony, just the man I wanted to see. I'm late for the House as usual, but a few more minutes won't make any difference. I want you to do me an enormous favor, but it entails going to Ireland."

"Ireland?" Tony seized upon his words as a means of escape from London and Bernard Lamb.

"Yes, believe it or not I'm about to join the hallowed ranks of the nobility," he said in a mocking tone, "albeit the Irish nobility. His Royal Highness has been bribed into offering me my choice of castles. Not only am I pressed for time, I don't have much knowledge of castles. However, I assume you do. . . ."

Tony's spirits immediately soared at the splendid news. "Well, I did rather misspend my boyhood studying ancient architecture."

"Now is your chance to put your knowledge to the test. I'd like you to visit Blackwater in County Waterford and assess the place. Perhaps next week I'll find time to visit the other property in Cork. Then I could meet you in Blackwater and we'll travel back together."

Just then Mr. Burke arrived. "Good morning, Burke. Perhaps you could arrange to travel with Tony to Ireland. Come upstairs, I'll have Sloane write down how to get there and provide you with funds. Your best route is to sail from Bristol."

Mr. Burke could see that Antonia had not confided last night's events to Savage. At the moment she believed the proposed trip to Ireland was a lifesaver. Mr. Burke knew it only postponed the inevitable confession of her gender to her guardian. He knew his place, however, and did not dream of disclosing her secret. That was her decision entirely.

Tony's steps were much lighter on her return to Curzon Street. "I want to thank you, Mr. Burke, for not forcing me to confess. I will feel so much safer out of the country. You don't mind going with me, do you?"

"It is only proper that I escort you, but I'm quite looking forward to visiting my native land."

Tony glanced nervously over her shoulder. "We must be absolutely certain that my cousin doesn't follow us. If he did so, Ireland would be far less safe than London."

By the time they got back, Roz was in the breakfast room. "Well, you were up and about early, or are you just getting home?"

"Of course not. I was summoned to Half-Moon Street and dutifully asked Mr. Burke to accompany me." It was only a small lie. "Adam Savage is to become a member of the Irish peerage and he wants me to go and assess a castle in Waterford. He quite trusts my opinion since he saw what I did at Edenwood. Of course Mr. Burke shall travel with me," she added quickly before Roz could protest.

Lady Randolph and Mr. Burke exchanged meaningful glances. "Antonia, I didn't want to upset you so I kept quiet, but yesterday I believe I saw Bernard Lamb at the corner of Curzon Street. I want you to be absolutely certain that he does not follow you."

Tony's pleasure in the trip to Ireland was suddenly diminished as apprehension filled her, threatening to expand into full-blown fear.

"I have a suggestion," Mr. Burke confided. "Why don't you put your own clothes on and dress as a lady?"

"What a splendid idea!" Roz agreed. "I'll come with you to the Central Coach Office in Lud Lane to see you off and you can purchase tickets to Bath rather than Bristol. Then you can buy a ticket for the rest of the way when you get to Bath. Anyone who is watching or questioning will think you are Antonia returning to the fashionable watering hole like hundreds of other ladies of fashion."

When Tony thought it through, she agreed that there was merit to their suggestions. She opened her trunk to pack Anthony's clothes and found the golden bodice she had worn in Venice. As her fingers touched it it evoked such private memories that she didn't want Roz to see it. She quickly covered it with Anthony's clothes, then packed an overnight bag with her own clothes for the journey.

Antonia chose a pale green gown with a jade green, velvet pelisse for travelling. She wore her own hair powdered with one long curl falling over her left shoulder, beneath a bonnet of tulle, ribbon and ostrich feathers. It felt strange to be wearing corset and petticoat once again and oddly inhibiting too. In trousers she could stride or lounge about; in skirts she moved more decorously.

Roz packed only two extra dresses for the journey because Tony insisted that would be more than enough. The moment they set foot in Ireland she would once again wear male attire.

The Port of Bristol was a hundred and twenty miles from London and necessitated an overnight stay at a coaching inn. Tony was glad of Mr. Burke's company. He had an Irish wit that certainly helped pass the long, weary hours of the coach ride. She found her clothing very constricting and uncomfortable, and she would far rather have ridden on the box with the coachman, but she had to admit that she was treated with impeccable manners and gallantry by the opposite sex when she was dressed as a female. The gentleman and young lady traveling so companionably together raised no comment whatsoever, for they were taken as father and daughter from the outset.

When the coach stopped at Reading she realized she could not swagger into the taproom for an ale and a smoke, and it was brought home to her once more that it was a man's world.

With every mile they traveled from London, her fear and apprehension about Bernard Lamb diminished. By the time they arrived in Bath her cousin had been banished from her thoughts, and she vowed not to think of him again until she returned to London. His dark shadow had fallen across too many of her days and she was determined to enjoy the respite.

Bristol was a busy seaport, teaming with sailors and ships from foreign lands. Vessels of the British Navy were anchored beside Spanish galleons and India merchantmen, while smaller fishing trawlers vied for space along the docks to unload their catches.

At a dockside inn Antonia changed into Anthony's clothes and, traveling as two men, she and Mr. Burke had no trouble booking their passage to Dungarvan, a large harbor on the coast of County Waterford. Although spring was definitely in the air, the Celtic Sea was unbelievably choppy. It didn't affect Tony, but when Mr. Burke started to look green about the gills, she was able to repay his previous solicitude of her. She firmly held the bucket and gently sponged his brow while he spewed up his heart. Tony didn't return to her own cabin until Mr. Burke had fallen into an exhausted sleep.

When they came out on deck the next morning they were just sailing into Dungarvan Harbor. The sun was shining its welcome and Tony could see that in contrast with the English port of Bristol, this small Irish sea town was inhabited only by locals. On shore with their luggage piled beside them, they drew every eye.

When they made inquiries about Blackwater Castle they were told it overlooked the Blackwater Valley less than a dozen miles inland. They could not rent horses, so in the end they hired a pony cart. Mr. Burke looked most apprehensive, but Tony laughed and assured him she would do the driving. He looked at her askance when she related the story of the phaeton race to Richmond that she had won. When she recalled how Bernard Lamb had deliberately run her off the road, she seethed inside with impotent fury. Then as she remembered the look on Adam Savage's face when he saw his brand-new phaeton, the corners of her mouth lifted wryly and she understood why he doubted it was her cousin's fault rather than hers.

The valley was greener than anything they had ever seen in England. The teasel trees and thornbushes were alive with songbirds. The air was filled with the fragrance of spring flowers mixed with mint and musk and mallow as the path snaked along between open meadows and the River Blackwater. In the distance they saw the battlemented parapets and thrusting turrets of a castle above the treetops, then as they drove closer they saw the castle itself rising from a tree-covered cliff above the river.

Tony drove the pony cart beneath a Celtic arch, past ivy-covered walls to a twin-towered gatehouse, then through the medieval gate into the courtyard. The caretakers gathered slowly, curiously. A stableman, a gardener, and a housekeeper, all with friendly-enough faces, came forward to see who was visiting their ancient castellum.

Tony handed the reins of the pony cart to the stableman. "Good afternoon, I'm Lord Lamb. I'm come to look over the castle for the new Marquess of Blackwater." The words came without much conscious thought, because she knew in her heart there was no question of choosing between this castle and anywhere else on earth.

Her words had a magical effect upon the caretakers. The housekeeper curtsied and the men touched their caps in deference.

"This is Mr. Burke, my butler of many years." The Irish name produced smiles of relief. The doorway of the main entrance was arched with solid plank doors that had scrolled iron strap hinges. Mr. Burke took up the trunk and Tony picked up one of the bags while the housekeeper took the other. They entered a baronial front hall with a log fire crackling in the hearth.

Then the housekeeper, who said her name was Mrs. Kenny, led them through to what she called the banqueting hall, where another fireplace stood with a carved mantel reading CEAD MILLE FAILTE, a hundred thousand welcomes. All the furniture was medieval oak.

"Sure an' ye'll be wantin' to see yer chambers now," Mrs. Kenny divined. "In this wing there's seven double bedrooms an' of course the tower room."

"Oh, I'll take the tower room," Tony said quickly, and Mrs. Kenny led the way up two sweeping flights of stairs, then down a long corridor. Tony smiled sympathetically as Mr. Burke tried to keep up with her trunk on his shoulder.

When they arrived Mrs. Kenny rolled her eyes at Mr. Burke as if to say, "Isn't that just like the gentry to pick the farthest and most inconvenient chamber without a thought to the poor sod who has to lug and carry!"

"When would ye like to dine, my lord?"

"Whatever hour is convenient to the cook, Mrs. Kenny," Tony assured her.

"Well, since I'm the cook, ye can dine at six, an it please ye."

"That will please me very well, thank you."

The moment Mrs. Kenny departed, Tony ran to the window. "The view is breathtaking. I can see straight down into the valley and across the water meadows on the far side of the river. From up here the water is black-green, and, look, Mr. Burke, straight across are mountains!"

"Those will be the Knockmealdown Mountains."

When Antonia turned from the window, Mr. Burke thought she had never looked so radiant. "Blackwater is utterly perfect," she said with reverence.

During the next few days Tony explored every nook of the castle and its gardens. There was a morning room, a sitting room, even a billiard room, as well as a small library and a chapel in sad disrepair. Outside there was an upper and lower garden as well as an orchard of pear, crab-apple, and fig trees. Tony took great delight in using a secret staircase that led from the twin-towered gatehouse down to the flowered walks of the Jacobean garden, overhung with creeper and early rose.

In a small, walled garden outside the morning room Tony discovered a treasure. It was a hammock slung between two shade trees, but the tiny spring leaves allowed the sunshine to filter through and warm the enclosure as if it were midsummer.

After lunch one day she took some papers pertaining to the castle's history that she had found in the library and stretched out in the hammock to read them. Blackwater's history was fascinating. She began to daydream, then slowly drifted off to sleep as the hammock swung gently to and fro.

* * *

At the end of the week Adam Savage sailed for Cork. He'd made two voyages to France already that week and it seemed he was forever walking the deck of a ship. When he arrived at Kinsale he was impressed with the vast acreage that went with its castle. The coast was wild and rugged and he stood on the picturesque headlands with the spring breezes ruffling his black hair. It was most pleasant, but he realized in winter it would be bleak and storm tossed. Before he left he knew he could be quite satisfied with this castle and its holdings.

He tested the title on his tongue. Marquess of Kinsale. It had a certain ring to it. He purchased a horse and decided to ride to Blackwater in the next county, which was forty miles distance, give or take a mile.

As Savage rode inland he noticed that the climate was softer than on the coast. Spring had already arrived and wildflowers filled every hedgerow and early wild roses climbed every stone wall.

Savage traveled the same path to Blackwater that the pony cart had taken. He saw the battlemented parapets and thrusting turrets rise from a tree-covered cliff above the river. He rode beneath the Celtic arch, past the medieval gatehouse, into the courtyard.

A stableman came immediately to take his horse, knowing by the man's powerful figure and air of authority that here was the new Marquess himself. As Savage entered the baronial hall he felt as if he had come home. Mrs. Kenny bustled forward to curtsy, but Savage raised her immediately and told her he would like to look about the place on his own. He liked what he saw. Kinsale faded from his memory.

He spied Tony in a hammock from the leaded casement windows of the morning room and stepped into the small walled garden. As he looked at the sleeping figure, a trick of the light made him blink his eyes. Dark lashes lay upon pink cheeks in delicate crescents. One slender hand lay curled upon his chest. Savage frowned at the youth's feminine features.

At that moment Tony opened her eyes and scowled, annoyed that Adam had found her sleeping. She jumped up, thrust one hand into her trouser pocket, and picked up the scattered pages. "Welcome to Blackwater. You need look no farther. This place is absolutely perfect. It was originally an abbey and it was King John who erected the original castle. Think of it . . . King John! Come and look at the banqueting hall," she urged enthusiastically.

Adam Savage stared hard, thinking Tony could easily pass for a female. His eyelashes curled and his lips were full, almost sensual. As Tony led the way to the banqueting hall, Adam's eyes swept down the tall figure in front of him. Tony's clubbed-back hair was growing very long and the posterior before him was quite well rounded. Was it possible that Tony was a female? No, the thought was preposterous! He dismissed it immediately.

Savage glanced about the beautiful old hall, but his eyes kept returning to Tony. He wished he could see through the cambric shirt. Perhaps it was his imagination, but he thought he had glimpsed the outline of a breast.

"Look at this," Tony urged.

Savage's glances suddenly became furtive. He watched Tony's hand as it lovingly caressed the carved mantel. *He touches things the way a woman would,* thought Savage, unable to dismiss the suspicion that had stolen into his mind. His hand itched to pull the leather thong from the long dark hair and quickly searched his mind for a plausible reason to do so. "There's not enough light in here to read what is carved." He took the thong from his own hair to tie back one side of the drapes. "Give me your thong."

Tony hesitated. She lifted her hand to her hair, then dropped it, not wanting him to see her with her hair about her shoulders. Then decisively she pulled off the thong and handed it to him.

Savage clearly saw the blush that tinged Tony's cheeks as their fingers touched. With his hair falling about his shoulders, the lad was positively beautiful. If he was a lad! Savage told himself his suspicions were ridiculous as his mind went back over the months they'd known each other.

"There's even a billiard room. Come and see," Tony urged. She had never known a more magnetic man in her life. His black hair curled about his neck and she remembered threading her fingers through its crispness. Blackwater's romantic atmosphere was playing hell with her emotions. She longed for Adam to take her in his arms, ached for his mouth to swoop down and capture hers. If she could have only one wish it would be for this man to make love to her, here in his baronial castle.

"No, I want to go down to the river first." Savage knew he must confirm or dispel the notion that Tony was a female and there was only one way to do it. He'd have to get him out of his clothes.

Tony followed Adam, chattering all the way. "The river's full of salmon. If you had a long enough line you could fish from the drawing-room window!"

As they stood on the bank, looking into the black-green water, Savage said, "I'm hot and dusty from the ride, let's have a swim."

Tony took a few steps back. "No, you go ahead. The water's probably cold even though the sun's out."

"Don't be a coward, cold water never hurt a man." Savage took a purposeful step toward her and too late she discerned his intent. He took Tony's wrists in a firm grip and pulled her toward the water.

Tony pulled back with all her strength, but it was useless to resist against one as powerfully built as Savage. All her instincts cried out to her that Adam was about to undress her. When his hands took hold of her shirt, she struggled wildly, then she felt a strong palm cup her breast.

Savage was stunned. His hand was holding one of the firmest globes it had ever encountered. Before he was totally convinced, he knew his eye would have to confirm what his senses and his fingers told him was true. He took hold of her shirt to pull it from her. It tore as she in turn yanked the fabric from his hands.

Savage found himself holding a half-naked female. With the cloud of black, disheveled hair, the fiery green eyes, and the sulky mouth that looked ready to bite him, she looked like an exotic wildcat from the jungle.

Tony's heart beat rapidly as she realized his penetrating gaze had finally uncovered her secret. Her breasts were revealed to his icy stare.

"Who the hell are you?" Savage demanded.

"Antonia Lamb, who the hell do you think I am?" she said on a sob, and fled up the hill, back to the castle.

Chapter 33

Antonia was trembling by the time she reached her tower room. A storm had been brewing between them since that first day when Adam Savage had looked at Lord Anthony Lamb with open contempt. They had weathered a few squalls when the clash of their personalities had dangerously disturbed the atmosphere, but Antonia knew the cataclysm that was about to be unleashed would be more than thunderous. She had seen his face. There was no other word for it, it was *savage*. He was daunting and intimidating at the best of times but when his temper was about to lash into fury, he was terrifying!

She tore off the ripped shirt and reached for a dress. Her hair had come undone and cascaded about her shoulders in wild disarray. The door crashed open. Savage strode in. She whirled about, clutching the green gown to her nakedness, and took a step back from the black rage that blazed from his dark face. He was the devil incarnate. She felt the fire and smelled the brimstone!

Savage checked his stride and tried to leash his fury as he dimly realized he was no longer at liberty to burst into her bedchamber.

"Downstairs, mistress, when you have removed those scandalous trousers." He spun on his heel and again crashed the door, making the candle brackets dance on the walls.

Antonia slumped back against the wardrobe door, her eyes awash with tears. She took a great gulp of air in an effort to compose herself. She would have to make herself feminine and appealing before she went down. When she explained her impossible predicament to him, he would understand everything. How remorseful he would be for his savage temper. It was just as well he had found out the truth. Now he would protect her from the danger of her evil cousin.

Antonia put on a shift and drawers, then sat down on the edge of the bed to pull on her stockings with shaky hands. She slipped on the pale green gown and fastened the ribbons on the sleeves. As she brushed out the tangled mass of black silk curls she assessed the damage of her face. The tears had made her lashes spiky, but her lips were bloodlessly pale. She took out pink lip rouge and applied it to her mouth, emphasizing its feminine fullness. She wondered if she should thread a ribbon through her curls. God, better not overdo it! Her high-heeled slippers made her taller and gave her the confidence she needed to go downstairs to him. By now his temper would have cooled.

Savage stood before the massive mantel in the large banqueting hall. Transversing the entire length of the room took a great deal of courage. Savage's powerful frame almost blocked out the fireplace as she came slowly forward. His face looked as if it had been carved from black oak. The scar that marred his mouth stood out in livid relief.

"What game are you playing?" His voice cracked like a whip.

She caught her lip between her teeth, then plunged in breathlessly. "It's very simple. It was Anthony, not Antonia, who was lost at sea in that terrible storm. I took my twin's place so that I wouldn't lose Lamb Hall."

A look of incredulous horror came into his face. "You devious bitch!"

Her eyes widened in disbelief. "You don't understand. The title and the property go to Bernard Lamb on the death of Anthony."

"I understand only too well. You are a scheming little bitch. Mercenary beyond belief!"

Anger almost choked her. She slapped him in the face.

He towered above her black with rage. Too late she realized what she had done. Fear made her reckless. "Go on, knock me down as you did when you believed I'd made Dolly pregnant! I thought hitting a female was against your rigid code of honor!"

Her scathing words exacerbated the self-disgust he felt toward himself, mainly for having been duped, especially by a woman.

"How the hellfire could I have ever thought you a male?"

"Shall I tell you? You never really looked at me. You took one contemptuous glance at Tony with those glacial eyes of yours and dismissed him as useless. You acted like an arrogant swine and treated him with utter contempt because he'd never measure up to your idea of a man."

"Be silent," he roared. "Your language and your behavior are scandalous, outrageous!"

"You set me such an exemplary standard. You're the one who taught me to curse and drink and dragged me around every brothel in London!"

"Good God Almighty!" Savage muttered, recalling how he'd tutored young Tony Lamb.

"The measure of a man to you is having a whore beneath him every night. Well, the measure of a man to me is courage. I found the courage to challenge my murdering cousin to a duel and, by heaven and hell, I'll challenge you to one if you've the guts!"

Adam Savage clenched his fists to prevent himself from striking her. He had never, ever in his entire existence been so enraged. He spun on his heel and put a safe distance between them before he killed her.

Savage went straight down to Blackwater River, threw off his clothes, and plunged in to cool his fury. She was his ward. Eve's child whom he'd once thought of as becoming his daughter. But she wasn't a bloody child, she was a woman grown. A real raven-haired beauty with the manners and behavior of a wild schoolboy. She needed a damned good thrashing!

She had made a bloody fool of him. He'd lit her cigars and poured her brandy. She'd rattled about with that dissolute Carlton House set, racing phaetons, making wild wagers, and, Judas Iscariot, she'd even been present around the chamberpots to piss!

She was an outrageous female who had violated every propriety. Her behavior was offensive, disgusting, scandalous. Savage's mouth became more grim by the minute. She'd capped it all off by challenging a man to a duel. Outrageous behavior for a young lord, let alone a young lady. He'd had to smuggle her out of the country. His face paled as he thought of the scurvy crew who'd been her companions aboard the *Flying Dragon*. McSwine, for Christ's sake!

Savage pulled himself from the cold river and shook himself as an animal shakes water from its pelt. He slicked his long black hair back from his face and pulled on his shirt and pants. He was in control of his temper now. He would go and lay down the rules for Lady Antonia Lamb. He was her legal guardian, in charge of her money and her morals, for Christ's sake. If a breath of this shocking scandal got out, her reputation would be blackened beyond repair. She would be shunned by all respectable women, and propositioned by the men. No gentleman would ever offer her marriage. She was on the brink of ruin. He had never known a female who needed a firmer hand.

He strode purposefully into the banqueting hall. He saw with a small measure of satisfaction that she was exactly where he had left her. "Antonia." His voice was deep, firm, and brooked no nonsense.

She turned from the mantel in a swirl of rustling green silk. He stared at her in shocked disbelief. She was smoking a cheroot! His calm demeanor flew up the chimney. He took one stride toward her and knocked the cigar from her hand into the fire.

"How dare you?" he raged. "You are supposed to be a lady, not a common slut."

"You have a taste for common sluts," she said insolently.

"Silence!" he roared. "I am your guardian. One more word of insolence and I shall thrash you."

Antonia bit back the words *You wouldn't dare*. She knew Adam Savage damn well would dare. He'd pull down her drawers and tan her arse so thoroughly, she wouldn't be able to sit for a week. Her eyes glittered like green flames, but she held her tongue.

"Now then, Lady Lamb, I shall lay down the rules that you will follow implicitly. This charade is over today. Never again by word or look will you be insolent to me. Never again are you to go out without a chaperone. Never again are you to swear, smoke, or drink. In other words, mistress, you will be a lady in every sense of the word."

"Never again!"

"What did you say?" His voice was dangerous.

She backed away quickly, holding off his threatened attack with outstretched hands. "You haven't the faintest idea how loathsome it is to be a lady! As Anthony I could go where I pleased, say whatever I wished. Choose my own friends. Make a wager. Eat or drink whatever I fancied. I could be sober as a judge or drink myself into oblivion. I could quote Shakespeare or get a laugh with a lewd limerick. I could shoot grouse or shoot out the chandeliers at Carlton House. In other words as Anthony I was *free*. *Free* to choose! As Antonia I must be prim, proper, and polite. I must be a lady. To be a lady is to be prisoner. Never, ever *free* to choose!"

"Enough!" he ordered. "You were born a lady and, by God, a lady you will be so long as I am your guardian. I cannot fathom how Lady Randolph could have countenanced this shameful scheme." His icy blue eyes were filled with contempt for her.

"Then you're a bloody fool! Bernard Lamb tampered with our sailboat so that the rudder broke away when we were in the storm. He murdered my twin and has tried repeatedly to murder me. The night before I left for Ireland he pushed me underneath an oncoming carriage!" She lifted her skirts and tore down her stocking to reveal the massive bruise to her thigh.

Savage stared in disbelief at her immodesty. Christ, her legs were so long, they went on forever.

He licked dry lips. "Seek your room, mistress."

She whirled away from him, crushed that he didn't believe her.

Savage lost no time seeking out Mr. Burke. He found him in the kitchen tailing two fresh salmon that had obviously come from their own waters. Mr. Burke's face had such a passive look upon it, Savage guessed he knew most of what was going on.

"Burke, you obviously know of the deception that has been perpetrated against me. Can you give me an explanation for the deliberate lies, or is Lamb Hall simply a madhouse and its inhabitants lunatics?"

Mr. Burke washed his hands. "May I sit down, my lord?"

"For God's sake, don't start 'milording' me. Surely we can talk man to man."

They both sat down at the massive oak kitchen table.

"I suppose, inadvertently, I was the one who started it all. The twins both wore yellow oilskins when they went sailing. When they didn't return after the storm, Lady Randolph and I nearly went mad searching and waiting. Finally one of them was washed up onshore half dead. I thought it was Anthony. The sea-soaked garments made him heavy to carry and the slicked-back hair made me positive we had found the boy. Roz, too, thought it was Anthony.

When we stripped off the clothes and she regained consciousness, to our surprise we found out Anthony was actually Antonia. This was the third accident that had happened in rapid succession, right after Bernard Lamb paid a visit to offer his condolences for the loss of the twin's father, which left Bernard heir to the title, Lamb Hall, the London town house, everything! We suspected the accidents were more than coincidence.

"Lady Randolph knew what it was to lose her home. Because she had no son when Lord Randolph died, everything went to his *male* heir and Roz came to live at Lamb Hall. If Anthony was presumed drowned, his male heir, Bernard Lamb, would inherit everything.

"The plan was audacious in concept, but Antonia insisted she was simply safeguarding what belonged to Anthony until he returned. It was a long time before she accepted that he would not return."

Savage stabbed his fingers through his black hair. His eyes were no less glacial, his jaw still jutted with outrage. "You actually believe Bernard Lamb had a hand in this?"

"I do, sir. Antonia has been stalked for days. She was pushed beneath a carriage when she left Vauxhall last week. She was terrified to leave the house. When we came to Half-Moon Street it was to seek your protection. When you offered her Ireland she clutched at it as an escape, a way out."

"The whole thing is preposterous. Like one of Sheridan's ridiculous plays!"

"I mean no disrespect, sir, but I'm not laughing. Lady Antonia is the pluckiest female I've ever known."

"Damn it, man, that is beside the point. She should never have been allowed to impersonate her twin brother. The license allowed a young lord in Georgian England is so permissive, he has carte blanche to indulge in debauchery. Antonia is probably ruined!"

"Oh, I realized long ago it was a horrendous mistake. Not only is it highly improper, it is deadly dangerous."

"Well, at least we agree on one point. You may rest assured the folly is finished. It is over, Mr. Burke."

"God be praised for that, my lord."

"Would you be good enough to tell Lady Lamb that I wish to speak with her again? Perhaps the Jacobean Garden would be less confrontational."

Antonia stood gazing at the distant mountains from the tower room of Blackwater Castle. Why had he looked at her with such contempt? When she had told him what her hated cousin had done to her and shown him the bruise, why hadn't he enfolded her in his strong arms and told her he would keep her safe? She closed her eyes against the pain in her heart, but it did not prevent her tears from seeping beneath her lashes. She had made such a wretched botch of everything. The thought of her rattling about in male attire disgusted him. He would never look at Antonia the way he had looked at Ann. She would never be able to attract him in a million years!

Each and every night she relived the intimacy they had shared in Venice. She could still taste his kisses, still feel his demanding mouth molding her lips, parting them so his tongue could explore the intimate warmth of her mouth. She shuddered at the memory of his rough tongue sliding deeply inside her mouth, and deeply inside other intimate places. The Leopard's tongue.

She jumped at the sound of the low knock upon the chamber door. Mr. Burke came in and said quietly, "We have talked. I told him what happened the night Anthony was lost. He would like to speak with you again in the garden. I don't think he will be fierce with you, Antonia."

"Thank you, Mr. Burke. I could never manage without you."

Tony dried her eyes after he left and toyed with the idea of keeping Savage waiting. Better not. Mr. Burke said he wouldn't be fierce, so he must have vented his temper. If she left him to cool his heels it could easily flare up again.

When she entered the garden her steps slowed as she saw his face was still grim. The fragrance of the lovely flower borders stole to her. It was such a poignantly beautiful spot, made for lovers. Her eyes again became liquid with unshed tears for what might have been.

"I have spoken with Mr. Burke and realize that you genuinely believe Bernard Lamb was responsible for your twin's accident."

When Antonia weighed his words, an instant spark was ignited.

"You, however, don't believe any such thing!"

"I shall investigate the matter. I hope you realize there would be no need to fear your cousin if you had not passed yourself off as your twin brother." Savage's temper had ignited again. It was plain they could not even converse without sparks flying.

"I had no choice. If you think I'd hand everything Anthony owned over to his murderer, you must have the brains of a pissant!"

"Be silent! I will not tolerate your insolence." The scar on his mouth made him look sinister and cruel. His glacial stare was merciless.

She heard his words but heeded them not. She was in a recklessly dangerous mood. "Because I'm a woman, you even deny me freedom of speech. I wish to God I were a man!"

"You lying little vixen, you wish nothing of the sort. You are all woman down to your very bones. You revel in being a female with all their devious weapons, but like all women you are greedy and want all the privileges of a man as well. It was just a bloody game to you, swaggering around in breeches, saying and doing every conceivably outrageous thing that came into that she-devil's brain of yours. Making a total fool of every man of your acquaintance."

Antonia tossed her head, making her raven hair sweep about her shoulders in wild disarray. Her angry eyes glittered like emeralds. "I don't need to make fools of men when they manage all by themselves!"

Savage was no longer angry. He was simply taunting her for the sheer pleasure of watching her. When she was angry she was the most breath-stopping creature he'd ever seen.

"You have no scruples whatsoever," he taunted.

"*I* have no scruples? *I* have no scruples! You whoreson!" She flew at him with clenched fists and pounded them against his broad chest. "*You* are the one without scruples. You'd do anything for money because money is power. You flaunt the law. You smuggle anything and everything that's illegal. You bed every influential hostess in London in your afternoons, and spend every night in some brothel. And speaking of *scruples,* you've just *bought* yourself a title, Lord Bloody Blackwater!"

Savage was blazing angry again. She had an incendiary effect upon him. He took hold of her hands and forced them to her sides. He held them in a vice grip while addressing her in a dangerous, silky tone.

"This ridiculous farce of yours was totally unnecessary, as well you know, Lady Bitch. All you needed to say to keep your precious Hall when your brother disappeared was that he had gone to Ceylon to console your mother."

Antonia stared at him in stunned silence. How simple. Why in the name of heaven had she not thought of it?

"I shall remove my unscrupulous presence. London's hostesses are awaiting the return of my insatiable manhood." The silver scar twisting down through his lip mocked her. He waved an all-powerful hand. "Please feel free to enjoy the hospitality of Blackwater Castle as long as the whim suits you. I have a spot of French smuggling to attend to," he told her quite truthfully.

Chapter 34

Adam Savage rode into Dungarvan at dusk and paid his passage on a ship bound for England. Though he tried to put Lady Antonia Lamb and her antics from his mind, he could not. He relived every thought, every word, from the moment he saw her asleep in the hammock and the full realisation came to him that Tony Lamb was not an effeminate youth but a real female.

The discovery had amazed him, and yet at the back of his mind something nagged at him. He couldn't quite put his finger on it. Whenever he thought he was close to what was bothering him, it eluded him.

While crossing the Irish Sea his mind went back over all the time he'd spent with Tony Lamb determined to make a man of him. He groaned over the time he'd taken her home dead drunk and handed her over to Mr. Burke. He recalled vividly handing her a shovel in the stables at Edenwood and watching while she shoveled shit. Suddenly he burst out laughing. She was a plucky female, for by God, she had mucked out at least half a dozen stalls.

He flushed as he recalled telling Tony to climb into his bunk, then deliberately allowing the French authority to believe they were homosexual lovers. Tony's anger after the man left told him clearly she understood the disgusting implication, but she'd stayed and nursed him through a bad night.

Christ, no wonder she had such good taste in furnishing a home, and no wonder she had chosen to import-export ladies gowns and wigs —she had intimate knowledge of such things. How in the name of Mary and Joseph had he never realized Tony was female? A very beautiful and desirable female at that.

He instantly put a stop to such dangerous thoughts. He was her guardian, she was his ward, and the most maddening, exasperating creature he had ever encountered. What was it about her that seemed to stir some other recollection? His senses stirred. What was it, what was it he almost remembered?

He would get to the bottom of the bloody Bernard Lamb thing. If he was a danger to Antonia, he'd soon rid her of him. Savage took a turn about the deck, avoiding both crew and passengers, then propped himself at the prow where the wind could blow the cobwebs from his brain. He was certainly wrong about one thing. Men would clamor to offer her marriage. A beautiful woman with her fire and passion was a rarity. Her mother, Eve, paled into insignificance beside her. Those dreamy green eyes that turned to flashing emeralds in seconds, those long, slim legs. Something clicked in his brain. Green eyes, long legs . . . no, it couldn't be. Ann! Ann Lambeth! No trace could be found because Ann Lambeth was Antonia Lamb!

The thought was repugnant to him. He was suddenly blazing angry. Far more angry than he'd been at discovering Tony was a woman. The devious little bitch! It offended every sensibility! Christ Almighty, he was engaged to her mother! He was Antonia's guardian. She was probably going to be his daughter. It was tantamount to incest! A guardian sleeping with his ward breeched every code of honor. It was morally contemptible. His fury knew no bounds. He was in a blind rage. He strode up to the captain at the ship's wheel.

"I want to return to Ireland immediately!"

The captain stared at him as if he were dealing with a lunatic. "I cannot turn the ship around in the middle of the Irish Sea!"

"Why not?" Savage demanded.

"This is a scheduled run. It's the middle of the night. There are other passengers. They would demand their money back."

"I'll pay you whatever it takes to make it worth your while to take this ship back to Dungarvan Harbor."

The captain looked at him with speculation and they reached a satisfactory agreement within minutes.

Dawn was reaching pink fingers up the sky when Savage again rode the twelve miles to Blackwater. "Red sky at morning, sailor's warning," he murmured, knowing full well of the coming storm-burst.

Blackwater had just begun to stir. The cocks crowed, the cattle lowed. The dew upon the lush green grass sparkled like diamonds and every spiderweb was hung with jewels.

The moment he stepped into the baronial hall the delicious smell of ham and freshly baked bread stole to him. He climbed a staircase, entered a large double bedchamber, and set his bag down. He was drawn to the window, where he quickly drew in his breath as he realized he had chosen the wing that projected out over the cliff. The chamber suited him completely. The oak four-poster was massive, the fireplace hewn from local boulders. The chamber was suspended between earth and sky and the view from the windows was definitely intimidating.

Savage caught a glimpse of himself in the mirror and realized that at the moment his unshaven, unkempt appearance was more than intimidating. *Good,* he thought, *she will not dare defy me today. She has no idea I'm back. It will be a surprise attack,* he thought with grim satisfaction. In the end his pride would not allow his golden goddess to see him looking so disheveled. Savage shaved and changed his clothes before he went downstairs.

In spite of himself Mr. Burke's eyebrows rose when he saw Adam Savage. He had heard Antonia weeping last night after Savage had quit the castle in anger, and thought to fix her a breakfast tray to comfort her this morning. Now he realized that was out. Obviously Savage was waiting for her to come downstairs. He had returned for round two.

Savage had banked the fires of his temper, but the embers glowed fiercely just beneath the surface and threatened to flame up with each passing tick of the clock.

When Antonia came downstairs she was wearing a cream muslin gown with cream-colored roses entwined in her silky black curls. She looked the picture of innocence, vulnerability, and sweetness. His heart skipped a beat. Then his temper overruled his heart. He advanced upon her in a threatening manner. "I must be the most obtuse man on earth not to have recognized your cat's eyes."

"Self-awareness is a priceless gift," she said softly. Her words mocked him, though the tone of her voice did not.

"Have you any notion of the magnitude of your indiscretion?" His voice cut the air like a whip. "I am your guardian. Do you not realize any intimacy between us is unconscionable?"

"Unconscionable," she agreed softly.

His temper escalated to fury. "What you did was scandalous!" he thundered.

"Scandalous," she agreed softly.

"I am in charge of your morals," he roared. "What you lured me to do was forbidden!"

"Forbidden," she whispered longingly.

"Stop it. You are behaving like a promiscuous courtesan!"

"The pictures you showed me in the *Kama Sutra* taught me so much." She smiled seductively.

"Sweet Christ, have you no shame?"

"You taught me that when a man and woman share a bed, there is no room for shame."

"You are seventeen years old!" he shouted.

"That made no difference in Venice."

"Of course it made a bloody difference. Why the hell do you think I didn't ravish you? Take your virginity?"

"You said it was a gift for my lover," she whispered seductively.

He seized her by the shoulders and tried to shake some sense into her. His hands were ungentle, his face dark with rage. He shook her roughly, enough to make her teeth rattle, but when he was done, she moved against him sensually and looked deeply into his silver-blue eyes. "There is unfinished business between us, Adam."

Now, of course, he did not just feel anger, he felt lust, a potent combination. He flung away. She was actually trying to seduce him when he was almost to the point where he needed to throw her to the floor, spread her thighs on the silken carpet, and impale her until he drowned in her.

Adam Savage rode deep into Blackwater Valley in an effort to rid himself of anger and lust. His anger was soon melted away by the beauty of his surroundings. Wherever his glance fell he saw an almost alarming beauty in the high turreted castle, the black-green water, the verdant valley. It was almost as if this niche of Ireland that he could now claim as his was under a magic spell. Or was he under the spell, he asked himself fancifully, and had Blackwater claimed him? He had breathed in its ancient beauty and it had found its way into his heart. The image of Antonia was with him strongly. Though the anger had melted, the lust remained. It seemed only fitting that he had found his golden goddess here, for she was an enchantress. She had cast her spell upon him in Venice. In that eternal city they had found romance. Her vibrant image was before him each time he closed his eyes. With every breath he took he could smell her fragrance of wild violets. Her body had felt like hot silk beneath his calloused fingers. Just remembering her taste and her lingering scent aroused his body. Yet Adam Savage knew it wasn't the green eyes or the lovely long legs that held him in thrall. It was her rich, generous response to him. She found him extremely attractive and she made no secret of it. His scars did not repel her, they excited her.

However, he forced himself to face facts. It was against society's mores to make a young ward your mistress. He was an ambitious man. He needed the approbation of his peers and all those who wielded influence if he was to have a voice in ruling England. He indulged in enough clandestine activities that must be kept absolutely secret, he could not afford a liaison that would condemn him in the eyes of the ton.

In any case Antonia deserved better. She needed a splendid marriage. One that would keep her secure from the Bernard Lambs of this world. She had a passion for stately homes, magnificent furnishings, and informal gardens. She needed a husband wealthy enough to indulge her passions. There would be no more confrontations between them. They would be friends. When she had posed as Anthony, there was nothing that they couldn't discuss. And so it would be now. They would talk it all out and make plans for her future. As he rode back to the castle, the Marquess of Blackwater felt almost noble.

Antonia was nowhere about the whole afternoon and it gave Savage the opportunity to explore his castle, gardens, and thirty-five hundred acres. He spoke with all his tenants, learned their names, found out who planted crops and who kept livestock. When he asked them how much rent they paid to the Crown, he frowned with annoyance, knowing it was a hardship to scrape together so much. He cut the rents in half and gave up a prayer of thanks that he was wealthy enough to make such a goodwill gesture. He learned that nearby Tallow was a market town that held horse fairs, and decided to pay it a visit one day before he left.

Mr. Burke told him dinner would be at eight, but that the salmon, caught and smoked locally, would be worth the wait. Adam Savage shaved carefully and changed from riding breeches and boots. He donned a fresh linen shirt, but didn't bother with a stock or neckcloth.

When he entered the banqueting hall the firelight at the far end flickered up the walls as it must have done centuries ago. He saw immediately that Antonia had arrived before him, seated at the candle-lit oak refectory table. As he took a seat across from her, his eyes widened at what she was wearing. It was the golden crown-shaped bodice she had worn in Venice. His pulse quickened, his balls tightened, so he quickly clamped down his desire with an iron will.

When he had gained control of himself he smiled wryly. He knew exactly what game she was up to. She was trying to seduce him. In Venice she had succeeded, but tonight would be decidedly different.

He spoke first, as was his right. His voice was deep and firm. "Antonia, tonight will mark a new beginning for us. We know each other too well to be formal, so I hope we can deal comfortably together."

There was no way Antonia was going to provoke an argument between them tonight. She gave him her rapt attention without saying a word, hoping that the romantic atmosphere and the alluring bodice promising its glimpse of breasts would entice him to dalliance.

"I beg your pardon for all the demands I placed upon you when I thought you young Lord Anthony Lamb."

He waited politely for a reply, but she simply dipped her spoon into her soup and gazed at him with those dreamy green eyes.

She wanted to say that she accepted his apology, but she knew the words would be incendiary. Adam Savage was doubtless a man who seldom apologized.

He finished his soup. "From this moment on we must fiercely guard your reputation. I have already explained to Mrs. Kenny that you traveled here in male attire to dispel gossip, because you had no female chaperone. She was bursting with curiosity at your unconventional antics."

Mr. Burke brought in the smoked salmon with its parsley and dill sauce. He also served tiny new potatoes, asparagus tips, baby carrots, and parsnips. A salad of scallions, fresh mushrooms, watercress, and fiddlehead ferns completed the course. Plumb partridges and rabbit pie were being taken from the oven as they tasted their salmon.

It was Antonia's turn to smile to herself. First she'd been a male, then a female. She wondered what Mrs. Kenny would make of her tonight.

As Adam watched the play of light and shadow over Tony's lovely face and bared shoulders he wondered what her secret thoughts were. She looked as if she knew something he did not. He made the mistake of looking at her mouth, and its effect upon him was immediate and pronounced. Her mouth was made for making love.

She dipped her finger in the sauce and licked it. He was hard and throbbing. He shifted imperceptibly to ease the fabric stretched tautly across his swollen groin. He tried to tamp down his desire, but it blazed merrily out of control as he remembered taking her sensual lower lip into his mouth. He felt a jolt all the way to the tip of his phallus as she reached for her goblet and her breast almost spilled from her bodice. He was no longer hungry for food as another hunger gnawed at his belly.

When Mr. Burke brought in the next course, he shook his head and told him that would be all. Savage's voice became husky when he tried to speak. He cleared his throat. "When we return to London you will make your debut into society as Lady Antonia Lamb. You will say you have been visiting friends in the country. I shall let it be known that Lord Anthony Lamb has departed for Ceylon."

Antonia gazed at him, not really listening, as he put her world in order. He had an unstudied arrogance sitting here in the banqueting hall of his own castle. With his long black hair and scarred face he could have been a warrior from another century. She shivered delicately as she thought of his bronzed body conquering her and forcing her to yield to him. A fantasy she would give her soul to play out.

Adam Savage threw his napkin on the table and pushed back his chair, waiting for her to arise. He looked so self-composed and in total control that more than anything on earth she wanted to shatter that composure into a million shards. As she arose from the table Adam stood up, but what he saw momentarily rooted him to the spot. With the exquisitely feminine gold tulle bodice she was wearing tight trousers and high-heeled slippers. The boys' pants emphasized her long, slim legs and molded her deliciously round bottom. He remembered her legs wrapped about his naked body and he was lost.

All thoughts of marrying her to someone else vanished into thin air. She was his. He would keep her forever.

He strode to her and swept her up into his powerful arms. His voice was as smoothly sensual as black velvet. "There is unfinished business between us."

Chapter 35

Antonia's arms entwined about the thick column of his neck and she shuddered as her fingers tangled in his long black hair. Her cheek rested against his wide shoulder and she could hear the deep, steady beat of his heart as he strode toward the staircase. The linen of his shirt felt rough beneath her soft cheek and she suddenly went weak all over, as she knew without a doubt his naked chest with its furred pelt would be far rougher than linen. She closed her eyes as his man-scent stole to her, making her dizzy with desire.

As he swept up the stairs, his arms tightened about her body and she felt the brush of his marblelike thighs against her bottom cheeks and knew an overwhelming rush of power that she had the ability to do this to his magnificent body. He carried her with such ease, she rejoiced in his great sexual energy, knowing he would expend it all on her.

Suddenly she became shy and apprehensive. What if she wasn't woman enough for Savage? She stole a look at his face as he carried her into his bedchamber. Silver-blue eyes gazed into hers with such intensity, it was like fire and ice. His mouth was set and hard and looked unbelievably cruel. She drew in a quick breath. She had never seen his face look like this before. He looked like a satyr, nay, he had the ferocity of a wild animal, primal, untamed. He looked like a leopard.

Heat leapt from his body, almost scalding her. His intense masculinity overwhelmed her. Was she mad to let him carry her to his bed? He was too frighteningly dark. He was too big for her, he was too old for her! He was an experienced libertine, immoral, well versed in debauchery, corruption, and sin.

As Adam Savage carried the prize to his bed, he felt a surging wave of lust that threatened to drown him in need. The very blood slowed in his veins and he felt a throbbing in his chest, his loins, even in the soles of his feet. His sex was so engorged, he had difficulty climbing the stairs, and when his phallus brushed against her bottom cheeks, it was exquisite torture.

Her black hair, just the color of his own, spilled over his arm like a waterfall. Her green eyes were wide, bottomless pools. Before he was done with her he would watch them darken with desire, turn smoky with sensuality, blaze with a flaming lust he would ignite, then turn pale and dreamy with delicious languor.

Her fragrance was an intoxicating mixture of violets and woman-scent. He wanted to taste her but did not trust himself not to bite and crush the soft mouth that tempted him to madness. As he swung her into his bedchamber his gaze ran along the length of her long, slim legs encased in the trousers. He had never knowingly seen a woman in pants before and the effect was unbelievably erotic. Tony had known the effect it would have on him. She had deliberately worn them with the ultrafeminine bodice and high-heeled slippers to provoke his man-hood and steal his senses.

Her clinging to him, as if her need was as great as his own, spurred him on to ferocity. As he put her down upon the wide bed he caught a look of panic on her face and suddenly realized she was afraid. A curl of tenderness spiraled inside his chest. He sat down on the bed, gazing down at her as she lay absolutely still. He took her hands into his. "Sweetheart, are you afraid of the act or are you afraid of me?"

"I—I don't know," she said faintly.

"A little of both, I suspect," he murmured.

"You . . . suddenly seem dangerous."

He cocked an eyebrow. "You wouldn't play with fire unless you wanted to get scorched."

She remembered him telling her in Venice that he would not break her hymen because they did not have time for her to become accus-tomed to the pain and move beyond it. Tonight they did have time.

"Adam, the last time we were together was the most wonderful night of my life. Can you make it like that again?"

"I can try," he whispered, brushing the back of his fingers across her cheek. "Last time, because I refused you, you wanted it so badly you thought you would die. Now because you know I am going to com-plete coitus, you are not so sure you want it at all. It's perverse human nature, and you are the most perverse female I've ever encountered."

The corners of her mouth went up as a delicious thrill ran through her. The way he looked at her, as if he would devour her, made her feel beautiful and desirable above and beyond all other women. The countless pennies she had dropped down the wishing well as a child must have miraculously worked their magic.

Adam knew he would have to bank the fires of his desire while he rekindled hers to such an intensity that it consumed every last shred of fear and apprehension. He braced himself on his arms and leaned over her. He bent down until his mouth almost touched hers, then he began to tease her. "I dimly recall forbidding you to wear male attire ever again. Then you flaunt those long, beautiful legs at me in pants to deliberately arouse my anger and my lust." He brushed her lips with his.

"Did I succeed?" she whispered breathlessly.

"I'm aroused, all right," he said huskily, this time brushing her lips with the tip of his tongue. "I'm going to take off your pants, but I don't know whether to tan your bottom or kiss it."

Antonia's heart fluttered at his words and at his very nearness. She opened her mouth to answer his taunt and he invaded it instantly, mastering her and taking complete possession. The kiss was deep, branding her as his woman. It had such an arousing effect upon her, she wanted to be his slave and do his bidding, no matter how depraved his demands were.

He stood up but his eyes never left her face. He wanted to watch every small flicker of emotion she was feeling. Her eyes followed his hands as he removed his linen shirt and stripped off his breeches. Her green eyes dilated with pleasurable delight as the splendor of his full nakedness was exposed. Surely he was the most magnificent male nature had ever created.

He displayed his dark virility before her and she was awed at such a superb specimen of manhood. She longed to be naked with him, longed for the clinging of bare bodies, the hot slide of skin against skin, the fusing of mouths, the sharing of body heat until they were both mindless with need. The need for just what was still a deep, dark mystery, forbidden until this moment.

He removed her high-heeled slippers, then held his breath in anticipation as he pulled the boys' pants from her long, slim legs. She wore nothing beneath them and he was rewarded by a glimpse of rose pink beneath the black silk curls between her legs. When he removed her bodice his eyes never left her face but his calloused thumbs brushed against the soft peaks of her breasts for the thrill of feeling them thrust up into hard little spears. He saw her eyes darken with desire, never realizing that his own eyes had changed their shade.

"Your eyes are as blue as the Bay of Biscay," she murmured. She would always say these words to him. It would be part of their ritual. They would always be an invitation for him to make love to her. Tiny tremors touched her breasts and belly and thighs and he missed not one quiver.

He came full length against her on the bed and she groaned as his body seemed to touch every naked inch of hers. She buried her face in the hollow of his throat, smelling, tasting, kissing the well-remembered bronzed flesh she had craved since Venice.

He threaded his fingers through the wild tangle of her hair, then cupped her face and brought it up to his. He kissed her softly, lingeringly, and between kisses he whispered love words, telling her how lovely she looked and felt to him.

Her hands were free to explore the hard muscles of his shoulders and the crisp pelt of his chest. She felt his phallus rise up between their bodies, then press into her soft belly, hard as marble. She reached down to caress him and gasped at his great size. She pulled slightly from his arms to gaze down at the mysterious man-root. It jutted proudly from a nest of wiry black curls. It was extremely thick and curved beautifully toward his navel. The head was satin smooth and shaded vermilion from his throbbing blood. She remembered he had told her it was curved to follow the curve inside a woman's body. Her body! She shuddered.

She could not believe anything so thick and long could fit up inside her body. She recalled vividly being unable to resist taking the smooth head into her mouth. She had wanted to feel him inside her body and her lips had no trouble accommodating his great size. She moved down his body now, needing to taste him, to feel him swell and throb against her tongue.

Before she reached her goal, Adam brought her face back up to his. "No, sweetheart, not tonight."

Her eyes were smoky now with a sensuality she needed to express in a physical union. His hot mouth blazed a trail down her throat, then he weighed her breasts with his calloused palms and lifted them to his mouth so that each could receive his tribute. First he kissed the proud little crest, then licked it, then he curled his tongue about it and sucked it whole into his mouth as if he were plucking a succulent cherry from its stem. He had to stop himself from biting her, she was so delicious.

Antonia was in a fever of need, wanting it more than she'd ever wanted anything before, yet simultaneously wanting it less than she'd ever wanted anything. She felt as if he were driving her to the edge of madness. "Please, please," she begged him. "Please don't hurt me too much."

"Sweetheart, let your fear melt away. I will be patient and gentle with you. . . ." His voice trailed away, then he added firmly, "Once."

"Not always?" she breathed.

He shook his head. "Only this first time. When I make love I am feral, savage, even cruel. My lovemaking will be stormy as a tempest, white hot, with driving ferocity to bury myself inside you, and bury myself hard. My darling, you are so splendidly uninhibited, I doubt you will need me to be gentle more than once."

Her eyes flamed with the lust his provocative words ignited. He spread her lovely long legs apart and combed his fingers through the silky tendrils, seeking her pink center. When she began to arch her mons into his hand with incoherent little cries, he slipped the pads of his fingers inside her cleft to tease her until she became wet for him. Then he knelt between her thighs, placed his thumbs on either side of her cleft, and spread her pink lips apart.

He lowered himself until the swollen head of his shaft was firmly pressed against her protruding bud, then he took away his thumbs and her tight sheath sucked the tip of his phallus inside and tightened upon him with tiny strong muscles.

Adam did not thrust inside her, but took her mouth with his and centered his lovemaking there, showing her with his tongue exactly what he was going to do with his male weapon. Drugged by his kisses, she felt no pain as the love-slick walls of her sheath drew him deeper. When he was halfway home, she felt only a fullness and a wonder that he was at last joining his splendid body with hers.

He thrust his tongue into the honeyed cave of her mouth and she was suddenly hungry for him, craving for him, *all* of him. Her nails dug fiercely into the flesh of his shoulders and her legs wrapped high about his back as she arched up to him, demanding the full honors of his manhood.

He was filled with a wild joy that he had needed no patience to coax her into a giving mood. He caressed her sensual lower lip with his own, while he contemplated how he would go about breaking her barrier. He had aroused her sexuality to such a pitch, she bit him, and suddenly he, too, could hold back no longer.

When he plunged into her, she screamed and her nails tore his flesh bloody. He held rigidly still, waiting for her pain to subside. She felt so full of him, she feared she might burst from the fullness of him. Then—as he held still while her sheath stretched to fit him like a kid glove—she realized she could bear it, and she began to like the feel of him inside her. It gave her an incredible power over him. Gradually she became aware of his words in her ear. He was telling her how hot and tight it felt to be buried deep within her. His words were intimate, erotic, seducing her to match his passion and express her woman's sexuality to the full.

They scalded each other. Finally, when neither of them could bear the burning torment longer, he began to move. Her green eyes widened in surprise as they locked intensely with his ice-blue gaze. The sleek heat became a wet slide with the friction of his strokes. He was anchored deep, making the sensations for both of them exquisite, silken torture as he molded her to his stunning body.

Though he had shaved, his beard scratched her soft cheek and she reveled in his maleness. His male-scented body acted as an aphrodisiac upon her. Everything about his mating with her was rough and elemental and she knew what had happened to her was cataclysmic and she would never be the same again. Not her mind, not her soul, not her body.

Their mingled breaths were husky, their lovemaking so sultry, they felt as if they would go up in smoke. Tendrils of long black hair entwined about their throats and shoulders, no longer belonging to him or her, but to both in a wild tangle. Then the night exploded. Antonia screamed again, this time from pure sensual bliss.

Adam cried out harshly as he spilled inside her like a firestorm. He gripped her fiercely, as if he could never get close enough or deep enough, and she felt every pulsebeat of his hot, shuddering release. He gathered her close and they collapsed together. Her eyes became pale and dreamy, then finally closed as she drifted between Heaven and earth.

Savage silently contemplated what he had done. There was no turning back now. What was done was done. Shamelessly, he had no regrets. She was extremely young, but age had nothing to do with it. They were two of a kind. Though society would be scandalized that a guardian should be intimate with his ward, he doubted that they would be ostracized. He was too damned rich and she too wellborn to be seriously censured. In any case he didn't give a damn about the so-called ton, except for Antonia's sake. He felt extremely protective of her, yet she was so outrageous, he doubted she gave a good goddamn either. Now that he had known Antonia, he was horrified to think he might have married Eve.

He wished he had never become romantically involved with both mother and daughter, but he could not undo the past, and long ago he had learned to live with the fact that he was a dishonorable bastard.

Antonia floated back to him. He brushed his lips across the tendrils of hair at her temples before he allowed her to uncurl her body from his. Her face was alive with her newfound knowledge, her eyes sparkling like emeralds at having performed the long-forbidden act. Together they saw the blood smeared across her thigh. He reached out a strong hand to wipe the blood away before it upset her, but she quickly grabbed his fingers and brought them to her breast to smear the blood upon her naked flesh as if he had left his brand on her. A brand she was proud of.

Her gaze trailed down his body, and by the time it fell upon his phallus he was semihard again. She reached out a finger to the blood-covered head, then daubed his chest above the heart. "I dub thee noble Savage."

He grabbed her then and they rolled about the bed laughing and nipping and biting each other in a rough play of love. She had almost as much energy as he. Almost. Before the night was spent they had exhausted each other, falling into the deep sleep that inevitably claims the totally sated.

Antonia awakened at dawn but kept her eyes closed in apprehension. My God, what had she done? Everything, she told herself as a blush covered her from her cheekbones to the tips of her breasts. When he looked at her with his ice-blue eyes she would die if she saw one flicker of contempt.

Adam's acknowledgment began with a caress. She opened her eyes and found him above her. His kiss remembered last night's passion and spoke of tonight's possibilities. She realized she needed this recognition that she not only lingered in his consciousness, but filled it! Thus began the epilogue that made the cycle of lovemaking complete.

When he had loved her he didn't allow her to drift off to Paradise, but lifted her from the bed and carried her to her own tower room. "I want you in your own bed when Mrs. Kenny brings your bathwater. I don't wish to scandalize the servants. I don't think she's quite sure yet if you are male or female."

Her hands raked through his long black hair, pulling it fiercely. "You are, though," she said with the confidence of a woman who was beginning to realize her power.

His mouth captured hers and she went weak, as he left her in no doubt who was the master.

Adam was surprised when Antonia joined him for breakfast. She was wearing a morning gown embroidered with forget-me-nots. Her wild black curls had been tamed with a simple blue ribbon. Though the table separated them, they made love with their eyes. It was difficult to believe the innocent beauty across from him was familiar with cardsharping and the inside of a brothel. Tony was game for any madcap suggestion, and he realized this was a big part of her attraction.

Suddenly he was smiling at her, and her heart turned over in her breast. It was rare that Adam Savage's face lost its dark, forbidding look. It was infectious and Antonia, too, began to smile. Next thing they were laughing together, recalling every outrageous thing she'd done while masquerading as her twin.

They explored the castle together, then, handfast, they sought out the secret staircase in the towered gatehouse that led to the garden. The flowers were releasing their seed-power, turning the air they breathed to perfumed mist. They wandered through the orchards, where the fruit trees were just budding into blossom and the bumblebees were coated with pollen.

Tony leaned against his shoulder and his arm stole about her. "Let's pledge to return in autumn so we can pluck the fruit."

He hugged her to him. He had already plucked the fruit. At midday they eagerly accepted Mr. Burke's suggestion of a picnic lunch and took it up on the cliff where they could enjoy the view. They saw more rainbows in one day than they would have seen in a year in London.

In the early afternoon they made their way down to the river, where a wooden punt was anchored beneath the trees. Adam picked up a fishing rod. "Let's try our hand at catching salmon."

"To hell with fishing!" she said, sitting on a rock to remove her shoes and stockings. "I don't have to do those damned male things anymore!"

"I'll fish, you can simply look beautiful." He stretched out, his back against the bole of a tree, his eyes narrowed against the dazzle of the

sun on the water's surface. It was a warm, lazy afternoon. The drone
of the insects added to the drowsy atmosphere.

Antonia pulled up her skirts so she could dabble her toes in the
water, then she hiked them further as she let the water cover her
ankles.

"If you expose any more of your tempting long legs, you'll find
yourself on your back in the grass," Adam teased.

"Are you fishing or leering?"

"Both," he said, grinning.

"You told me to look beautiful," she said, removing her feet from
the water, but still holding her skirts high.

"Come here."

It was a command she had no wish to disobey. His hand caressed
her slim calf, then moved up her thigh. "You hussy, you aren't wearing
any drawers."

"I knew it wouldn't take you long to discover my secret," she teased.

He pulled her down into his lap, the fishing forgotten, as his hand
slipped up her skirt to explore her silken curves and hot moist crev-
ices. She was close enough to see the heavy pulsebeat in his throat and
she put her lips against it as his fingers toyed and teased among the
curls.

He stripped quickly, but the arousing that followed was long and
slow and deliberately drawn out, tantalizing her almost beyond endurance. For almost an hour he held himself back from driving into her;
his desire for her was too strong to let him take her before she was
fully ready for his explosion of passion.

She lay in the long grass in a wanton sprawl as waves of pleasure
built and receded over and over. What he was doing to her made him
so hot and hungry, he was ready to devour her before his entrance.
Again their lovemaking was almost violent in its intensity. A leopard
in the grass with his mate. Yet afterward he was so tender with her, it
made her throat ache with unshed tears. He was endlessly capable of
gentleness both before and after, but not during, and Antonia didn't
want him any other way.

Chapter 36

They spent every moment of each day together. They went for endless walks and rambles through the deep valleys and high hills. Adam had boundless, inexhaustible energy, so when Antonia's flagged he carried her on his shoulders, teasing, "I don't do this for you, I do it for myself. When you pull up your skirt and dangle those legs over my shoulders, I think I've died and gone to Heaven."

"You Devil, you'll never even get close to Heaven."

"Don't crow. I've tainted you and now you, too, are damned."

She lifted her dark hair with both hands and let it fall sensuously about her shoulders. "I consider the world well lost."

"I wonder," he said seriously. "I wonder if you will always feel so?"

Antonia shivered as if a shadowy finger had reached out to touch her. She shook off the dark feeling. She refused to even think about tomorrow while they still had today . . . and tonight.

They went for rides in the pony cart, they visited the surrounding market towns, and one day he took her to the horse fair in Tallow and bought her a lovely white mare with a silken mane and tail.

"I'll take her back to Edenwood for you," he said absently.

"Edenwood." She whispered the name lovingly, wistfully. Obviously he expected her to come to Edenwood often enough to ride, but he hadn't invited her to live there. He hadn't asked her to marry him. She pushed the thought away. She would not spoil their time here together by wishing for things. In Venice she had found romance, but in Ireland she had found love. She was mad in love with him.

He watched her quizzically. "Edenwood! So that's it. I wondered why a beautiful young titled lady would give her favors to an ugly brute like me, but Edenwood is the attraction."

She protested loudly. "That is untrue! It's not only Edenwood, it's all your chests of gold, your East Indiamen, *and* Blackwater Castle that attract me."

"Little bitch," he swore. But he was glad she cared passionately for Edenwood, for it was his lifetime dream come true. He knew exactly how it felt to be possessive over property. He hadn't been able to sell Leopard's Leap because of all the toil and sweat that had gone into the plantation. Once a thing became a part of a person, he couldn't lose it without paying a tremendous price. He could survive, but he couldn't happily thrive, and life was for thriving, not just surviving.

Savage knew that Antonia was becoming a part of him. She was unique. He knew he had never been in love before, never even wanted to be in love. He cursed. Why the hell did it have to be so complicated? Why did she have to be Eve's daughter? He shrugged. The heart wanted what the heart wanted. There was naught he could do about it!

Every time he thought of Bernard Lamb his gut knotted. She had been in mortal danger for months and he'd scoffed with contempt each time she'd tried to tell him. He blanched as he recalled showing her how to deal with an enemy. He had grabbed her coat lapels, pressed a swordstick to her gullet, and growled, "I'll slit you from neck to nuts!" And plucky wench that she was, she had defended herself amazingly well, especially in the haunts she had frequented. He felt a chill run up the back of his neck and vowed she'd never have the need to protect herself again. Bernard the Bastard would be his first priority when he returned to London, and return he must.

They were up on the battlements of Blackwater watching the sunset. The sky turned from violet to vermilion, then became flame riven with red and gold.

Adam drew Antonia against his side, and her head fell back against his shoulder. "Blackwater is displaying its beauty to us because it's our last night here."

"We're leaving tomorrow?" she asked wistfully.

"I'm leaving tomorrow. I have urgent business I've neglected for a week. I want you to stay on a couple of days." He turned her to face him and his finger traced the mauve shadows beneath her eyes. "Get some rest. Mr. Burke will bring you back safely. I'll take your milk-white steed to Edenwood."

"Mr. Burke knows we are lovers; we haven't fooled him for a moment."

"The whole bloody castle knows, we've been so besotted." Though Mr. Burke had never said a word, Savage knew he disapproved of his scandalous deflowering of Antonia. Burke also expected him to do the honorable thing. And so he would. But unfortunately the honorable thing was not marrying the daughter before he had honorably broken off with the mother.

Even in sleep Adam sensed they were no longer joined in body or spirit. He opened his eyes to darkness. He did not need to grope in the bed to know she was gone. As his eyes became accustomed to the predawn shadows he saw her by the window.

His lithe body slipped from the bed soundlessly, then his arms captured her and he turned her face up to his with a puzzled frown. There was enough light for him to see the silver tears that lay upon her cheeks. He brushed them away with his lips. "Tony, don't shed one tear over me, sweetheart, I'm not worth it."

She swallowed hard. He would be gone in an hour, perhaps two, and he had said no word of love. She could have borne the fact that he had not proposed marriage. A man like Savage could not be bludgeoned, shackled, and forced to play the role of dutiful husband. But love. She needed his love to go on breathing. When she loved him so deeply, so shamelessly, so inordinately, how could he *not* love?

He pressed her to the length of him and his hot sex felt like a candle flame being held to her belly and thighs. She pulled away, burned.

"Yield to me," he demanded.

She searched his face. She did not see love written there, she saw hunger. "I have yielded . . . everything."

He swooped his arm beneath her knees and lifted her against his heart. "Let me show you that you have not."

The kissing was fierce, passionate, savage. They did not release each other's mouths until they were swollen and throbbing and her lips were too tender to bear the brush of his lips in one more kiss.

That's when his mouth moved to her throat to ravish and worship its curve. This was only a prelude to how his mouth first plundered, then ravished, her breasts. His hot breath stirred her nipples, which had ruched at his first lick. His husky whispers showed her just how sensitive he had rendered them. "Tell me you *want* this. Tell me you *love* this!"

"I do want it, I do love it," she cried.

He moved down her belly. His mouth, his tongue, and his teeth made her throb with a hundred pulse points she hadn't known she had. "Tell me you *want* this, tell me you *love* this," he demanded again.

She cried out in a fever of need as her thighs fell apart and she arched up to him shamelessly. "You know what I *want,* you know what I *love.*"

Then he ravished her with his tongue. She shuddered uncontrollably as she realized her fantasy was now reality. He was conquering her with his bronzed body until she was forced to yield to him. She was going to explode upon his rough tongue and she didn't care, didn't care, didn't care. She came hot, wet, and slippery into his mouth. She *wanted* it, she *loved* it! The Leopard licked the cream.

Savage slid up her violet-drenched body, hung above her for what seemed like eternity, then plunged to her depths to drown in her, not caring if he ever surfaced again. The animal cry torn from his throat merged with her own moaning cries as she met his thrusts, then matched them, submitting to every last demand his powerful body made upon hers. She built again so quickly, it stole her senses and hurtled her to the edge of the precipice. The stroke that brought them to climax carried so much force, she thought he had pierced her heart. Together they spun over the edge, then soared to the peaks before they plunged down to the deep depths of darkest sensuality.

He growled, *"Now* you have yielded everything."

She was too languorous to utter one word. His lips brushed her ear. "Now it is my turn. I yield you my heart. I *want* you, I *love* you."

She sighed with contentment. She had managed to achieve the impossible. Indian Savage, the magnificent Leopard, had pledged her his love. She closed her eyes in pure happiness. When they again fluttered open, she realized he was fully dressed and about to take his leave.

He moved to the bed and she stood upon it, naked, and clung to him. Her fingers threaded through his long black hair.

"Darling, come to me at Edenwood. I'll try to be there by the end of the week, but if I am not, wait for me."

Her fingers traced the scar upon his mouth. That same mouth that never begged, just ordered and commanded. "I'll wait," she whispered. It felt so deliciously female to yield to his demands.

Two nights later, Adam Savage sat in the darkened theater, laughing as Angela Brown strutted about the stage in corset, stockings, garters, and little else, singing the saucy words to "Come Tickle My Fancy." Before the final curtain rang down, Savage entered her dressing room backstage and pretended surprise when he encountered Bernard Lamb. "What a pleasant coincidence. You're the very man I wanted to see."

"Savage! I haven't seen you in ages. Have you been out of the country?" Bernard asked pleasantly.

"Several times," Savage admitted.

"Was my cousin Anthony with you?" Bernard asked casually.

"No, he's been to The Hague on business. His ship docks at Wapping later tonight."

Bernard smiled. "You said you wanted to see me?"

"Yes, you seem to have a proprietary interest in Angela and I thought perhaps I could make it worth your while to look the other way while I . . . borrow her once in a while."

Bernard's smile widened. "Why not tonight?"

"Well, I should meet Tony. I suppose I could take Angela to supper at the Prospect of Whitby, an inn that's been in Wapping since 1509."

"I have a better idea. Why don't I meet my cousin and you can take Angela somewhere that will tickle her fancy? In fact why don't I disappear before she comes offstage?"

"It's very civilized of you to bow out for the night," Adam said silkily.

"What are friends for?" Bernard asked generously. "What's the name of Tony's ship?"

"The *Red Dragon*," Adam replied softly.

When Angela entered the dressing room and found Savage instead of the dreaded Bernard she threw her arms about his neck in delight. "Adam! How lovely to see you."

He pulled her arms from about his neck and, with her hands still captured in his, fixed her with his pale blue gaze. "I am about to make you richer by five thousand pounds if you will give me what I desire."

She licked her lips in anticipation. Christ, she'd be willing to commit any perversion he'd like for free. "Whatever you desire," she said breathlessly.

"I desire information, my angel."

She blinked in surprise, and felt his powerful hands tighten about hers.

"Why do you give your favors to Bernard Lamb when he is penniless and up to his eyes in debt?"

She licked her lips again, afraid now. She knew Savage would settle for nothing but the truth. "He is heir to a title and an estate, you know that."

"Being heir to someone younger than himself doesn't give him very good prospects," Savage pointed out.

Angela bit her lip. Bernard was a cruel bastard and she owed him nothing, yet she would be willing to bet the dangerous man who stood before her with the icy eyes and scarred face could be infinitely more cruel than Bernard had ever dreamed of being.

"Accidents happen all the time," she whispered hoarsely.

"Are you hinting, guessing, or insinuating?" His black eyebrows rose questioningly above those cold, piercing eyes.

"No," Angela said, experiencing a vengeful relief in the telling. "Bernard intends to eliminate his cousin. He's already planned accidents that have failed. Next time he said he'd use a knife. He's very good with knives." She shuddered uncontrollably as she remembered the threat of his blade between her legs.

Adam Savage dropped her hands and reached for his money belt. He had felt her ragged pulse and knew her fear.

"If he knows I peached on 'im, he'll do me too," she cried, lapsing into cockney.

Savage placed a calloused hand beneath her chin. "Didn't I tell you? Bernard said good-bye. He's leaving the country tonight for a very long time."

After Indian Savage had departed, Angela stared at the incredible pile of money. If Bernard was leaving the country, it was not by his own choice.

The tall, dark shadow moved silently down the water stairs, then loomed motionless against Wapping Wall. The shadow seemingly had infinite patience. Farther down the dock half a dozen tall ships lay at anchor. The lights and the voices from the decks merged in friendly banter and the crew of an East Indiaman loaded the last of the cargo that had been piled on the quayside.

Bernard Lamb's footsteps quickened as he caught sight of the ships and hoped his quarry had not yet disembarked. His eyes were already raised to read the names of the ships that rocked at anchor. The shadow allowed him to pass, then loomed up tall and terrible at his back and brought a heavy cudgel down upon his head. It took every ounce of willpower Savage possessed not to smash his skull into red ruin.

A bare-chested Lascar loped down a gangplank and along the darkened dock. Without a word he bent and lifted the unconscious body over his shoulder, then retraced his steps aboard the East Indiaman. After a necessary measure of time had elapsed Adam Savage boarded his *Red Dragon.* By midnight he had inspected the cargo in all the holds, save the one that was locked and barred. He instructed his crew to drop Bernard Lamb on the island of Madagascar, thousands of miles away.

All the lovely things Antonia had selected on their voyage to the continent were carefully stowed in the dry holds of the *Red Dragon*, which had made port in London over a week ago while he had dallied in Ireland. He was glad that the Indiaman sailed on the morning tide before Tony returned, for if she were here he knew she would insist upon looking into every box to assure herself that her exports would arrive undamaged.

He chuckled to himself and shook his head at his own folly. She had been one helluva lot less trouble as a male than she would ever be as a female. He thanked God she had obeyed him for once and stayed put in Ireland for a few days until he'd taken care of the pressing problem of Bernard Lamb.

In Ireland, Tony felt almost abandoned. The rains came to Darkwater and it was as if the sun had gone out of her life when Adam Savage departed. Now that her whole attention was not riveted upon the object of her desire, she noticed that Mrs. Kenny and the rest of the staff looked at her askance, with disapproval written all over their faces. Perhaps it was her imagination, but even Mr. Burke seemed to have figuratively taken a step back from her so that a cool, polite distance was between them.

The rains were so persistent, she could neither go for a walk nor ride in the pony cart. She tried to amuse herself by wandering about the empty chambers of the ancient castle. The endless shadows took their toll on her thoughts. Why had he left her alone? Why couldn't they have traveled back together? What business in London was so urgent and important that it took precedence over her? Damned funny business if she knew aught of his affairs. Affairs! There was an apt choice of words, she told herself mockingly. Why hadn't she questioned him about his pressing business? Because she had been too bloody besotted with him to even think coherently in his presence. Why was it even necessary to question him? If he had nothing to hide, why hadn't he told her why he must return?

Oh, ye of little faith, Antonia chided herself. Hadn't he given her his heart? Hadn't he told her he loved her? When she stepped across the threshold into his bedchamber a wedge of emotion stuck in her throat. His dominant presence was tangible in the very air. She licked her lips, still tasting him there, still feeling the crush of his mouth that made her heart beat so wildly, she almost fainted from its touch.

She reached out a hand to the bedcovers, then snatched it back quickly, afraid that if she caressed the sheets where they had mated, she would be undone. She wrapped her arms tightly about her breasts to still the ache and moved to the window that jutted out over the cliff. Suspended between the earth and the sky was exactly where he had left her!

Antonia went in search of Mr. Burke. "I'm going to pack. I want to leave today."

"Yes, my lady."

"I'm not running after him!" she flared.

"I should hope not, my lady."

By using her formal title it seemed to Antonia that the very proper Mr. Burke was emphasizing her scandalous indescretion. "You won't look at me with such disdain when I am Lady Blackwater!"

A look of surprise flickered across his face. "When is the wedding to be, my lady?" he asked politely.

His question pinned her to the wall like a helpless butterfly.

"None of your bloody business!" she flared.

Tony packed away her boy's clothes and swore never to wear them again. They were far more comfortable and unrestrictive than dresses and all the underpinnings that went with them, but as Antonia she would not be in danger. There was also another reason for her decision. The competition for Adam Savage among the women of London was fierce. Now that he was the Marquess of Blackwater he would be even more openly sought after. She knew she would have to compete for his affection. Affection? What a ridiculous, pallid word to describe what was between them. Surely he had never made love to anyone the way he had made love to her?

She tried to push that thought away, but others flooded in to take its place. He was more than twelve years older than she, a mature man. Very mature! He had lived for years in the East, where erotic sexual practices were the norm. A picture of Lotus Blossom flashed into her thoughts. A handmaiden in a bathing pool.

Tony slammed the trunk lid closed and fastened the leather straps. He hadn't even hinted at marriage. Perhaps she was just another conquest. No! No! Hadn't he told her he loved her? Hope was not yet dead. If he married her and took her to live at Edenwood, she would live happily and securely ever after.

A dreaded thought crept in. The moment Bernard Lamb learned that it was Antonia who had survived the boating accident, he would claim Lamb Hall. Adam Savage must marry her and take her to Edenwood, there was no alternative!

On the sea voyage home and on the coach ride from the coast to London, Tony made herself totally miserable. To insulate her heart against Savage's rejection she catalogued all the reasons why she should not marry him. She had no trouble counting the reasons. He was a dangerous man. He had a sinister side that she chose to ignore. His past was murky with unsavory acts of corruption. Aye, and not just his past, if she faced the truth. He was an immoral devil who dabbled in smuggling and God knew what other villainous activities to keep his coffers filled.

She was far better off sharing a passionate liaison with him than shackling herself with the bonds of matrimony. He had told her he loved her and she believed that he did. But she had been privileged to discover that men's ideas of love differed greatly from women's. To a woman love and marriage went hand in hand. To a man love and lust were synonymous. A wife was someone who took second place to a mistress, or even a whore, if that whore satisfied him in bed.

By the time she arrived in Curzon Street, she had convinced herself that she wouldn't marry Adam Savage if he were the last man on earth.

Chapter 37

 "Antonia, thank Heaven you are returned!" Roz said dramatically.

Tony's heart sank to even lower depths. Whatever else could go wrong? She had thought things couldn't possibly get blacker.

"We have a letter from Anthony!" Roz cried.

"Anthony?" Tony murmured blankly.

"Oh, darling, he didn't drown as we all assumed. He's alive! What a wretched boy to make us wait so long to tell us."

"How . . . where?"

"Here, read it for yourself, darling!"

Antonia's hand shook like a leaf in the wind as she unfolded the pages to breathlessly scan her brother's unmistakable scrawl. "My God, he's with mother in Ceylon!" Her knees went weak with relief and she sank down upon a brocaded settee to read the amazing story of his being rescued at sea by an East Indiaman on its way to Madras, India.

The words jumped from the page. "They made me work my passage and it almost killed me at first. It was soon brought home to me what a sheltered, pampered life I had led. All in all it's been the best thing that ever happened to me. By the time I reached India, it had made a man of me, which was a damn good thing because it was no easy matter making my way to Ceylon without a penny in my pocket. Almost half a year has elapsed since I was washed from the deck of the *Seagull* and it will take this letter two or perhaps even three more months to reach you in Curzon Street. I hope you haven't been too worried about me. Ceylon is fascinating. Wish you were here. Love, Tony."

She jumped up, laughing and crying at the same time. Rosalind and Antonia embraced joyfully. "He hopes we haven't been too worried about him!" She went from Roz's arms into Mr. Burke's, the coolness between them now evaporated. "When I get my hands on him, I'm going to throttle him. He ought to have been smothered at birth!"

Mr. Burke poured three glasses of sherry to celebrate the joyous tidings and Roz actually kissed him. "It not only means we shall have Anthony back, but Antonia as well. Do please burn those hideous trousers you've been parading about in for months."

Tony smiled to herself. Not everyone found her trousers hideous. "I can't wait to tell Adam! Oh, I was right not to tell Mother Anthony had drowned. Think of all the anguish I've saved her."

Roz set her empty glass down firmly. "Darling, you can't simply drop in on a gentleman as Tony did. Half-Moon Street is a bachelor's establishment. You'll need a calling card and a chaperone."

"Women come and go at Half-Moon Street as if it were a public convenience. Half the countesses and duchesses in London frequent the place."

"But they are married ladies, Antonia. They are not bound by the strict moral code that applies to an innocent, unmarried young lady."

"I may be unmarried, Roz, but I am not innocent. Mr. Burke will no doubt testify to that as soon as he gets you alone. There's not much point in locking the stable door after the horse has bolted, and if you think I am going to be hidebound by society's ridiculous strictures after enjoying total freedom, you are deluding yourself."

Tony swept up the stairs to bathe and change before she rushed to the arms of her lover. She took special pains with her appearance and selected one of the chic outfits that had been made for her debut. It was a jonquil yellow walking dress with a matching pelisse with bishop sleeves. In Ireland she had neither powdered her hair nor worn a wig, and Adam had taken a sensual pleasure in the black cloud that cascaded about her shoulders. She would put it up, of course, for the sheer pleasure of having him take it down, but she would not cover it with white powder.

The yellow gown made her vivid and exotic. Tony painted her lips scarlet and selected a beauty patch to emphasize her right cheekbone. Then she swirled about and laughed into her mirror, thinking how absolutely delicious life was after all.

As soon as Tony had run upstairs, Roz fixed Mr. Burke with a steely gaze. "Whatever does she mean, she's no longer innocent?"

Mr. Burke was a model of discretion. "She means, of course, that she saw far too much of the way young men behave when she masqueraded as one. I think we will have to allow her a little more freedom than other young ladies."

"If you say so, Mr. Burke. I suppose we can rely on her good judgment."

Mr. Burke managed not to choke on his sherry.

"All the same, I think I'll have a discreet word with Mr. Savage and explain that Antonia is actually a woman."

"Mr. Savage discovered that for himself, my lady."

"Thank Heaven! As her guardian he will see the need to protect her virginity, even if she does not."

This time Mr. Burked choked.

Antonia's heart was singing as the carriage made its laborious progress to Half-Moon Street. She couldn't wait for the driver to tether the horses and open the door for her, but grasped the handle firmly to open it herself. At that moment the front door of Savage's town house opened to reveal the beauteous Georgiana Devonshire. She was wearing an outfit that must have cost the earth. It was palest blue satin, whose matching jacket was trimmed with ermine tails at shoulder and hip.

Georgiana's powdered coiffeur, held in place by blue ostrich feathers and ermine tails, was in the prettiest disorder, and no matter how deftly her fingers tucked up the curls, they fell down again about her shoulders.

Antonia sat back quickly so that Georgiana would not see her. Her heart was no longer singing, it was bleeding. Bleeding as if Savage had plunged a knife into it. A red mist obscured her vision as anger replaced anguish. She flung open the carriage door, ran up the steps, and hammered the brass knocker. The door was opened by a liveried servant almost immediately. Without saying a word she jabbed her closed parasol onto his foot so that he stepped back in surprised pain. When he did so, she swept past him, straight through the reception hall, and up the stairs.

Adam Savage was in his office and looked up with annoyance at the intrusion. The annoyance didn't leave his face when he saw who it was. She had flaunted his orders to stay in Ireland until the end of the week, barely giving him time to dispose of Bernard Lamb.

"Tony, this is a surprise—though it shouldn't be, knowing you as I do."

"I'll bet it's a bloody surprise! You are nothing but a lecherous swine."

He arose from the desk and came toward her. "Why are you angry with me? It should be the other way about, sweetheart."

"Don't sweetheart me!" She spied a scrap of blue feather on the carpet and pointed her parasol dramatically. "That's why I'm angry! You left me at the back of beyond because you had pressing business in London. Pressing Georgiana Merrylegs to the mattress!"

His eyes were filled with amusement. "Darling, you're jealous. Georgiana was here because she owes so much money, she's in queer street."

"I'm not jealous, I'm angry!" she spat.

His strong brown hands closed about her arms. "You've never made love while you're angry. You have a revelation in store." His voice was deep, persuading.

"Just because I let you make love to me in Ireland, you think I came running after you and here I stand with my little bowl held out, asking for more."

Her fragrance filled his senses. "Mmm, let me give you more." His hands closed on her bottom and he rubbed her against his loins as he hardened to marble.

"Take your hands off me. I can only imagine where they've just been," she snapped angrily.

"Your imagination is so inventive, darling, it's one of the things I adore about you." He swept the papers from his desk and lifted her to sit upon it.

"Stop this, you whoremonger!"

"All in my past, I swear." He dipped his dark head to take her scarlet mouth, but she leaned back away from him, her eyes flashing fire. The next moment her back was on the polished desk and he was looming over her like a predator about to devour its prey. She was seething with anger. His gaze licked over her like a blue candle flame. "I've never seen you in yellow before. It's your color, my beauty. This moment you are so vivid and exotic, you stop my breath."

She drew up her knees to jab him in the solar plexus. "I'll stop your bloody lying breath!" She panted.

"I want you while you're angry. I want you spitting and clawing at me." His voice was low, intense, seductive as black velvet. He swept her into his arms and carried her toward his bedroom.

"Put me down!" she demanded. His nearness, his male-scented skin, stirred her desire so that her body began to tingle with anticipation despite her blazing anger. This only fueled her fury. Now she was angry at herself as well as him.

His lips were on her throat. "You are hotter and tighter when you are angry," he murmured. "When you scream a curse at me, your sheath will tighten further on my shaft until it bucks and rears like a stallion being broken to the saddle. Hold on to your anger, darling, and I'll give you the wildest ride of your life." He laid her on the bed and she began to struggle madly. Her struggles succeeded in arousing her further, while he reveled in them.

"I don't want to tear this lovely yellow outfit, so just hold still until I have you naked, then you can continue to writhe and seethe." His teasing voice was so seductive, clearly telling her how exciting he found her, that she began to doubt that he had made love to Georgiana, Duchess of Devonshire. To her own chagrin she found herself lying still while he stripped her. Suddenly she remembered his answer when she'd asked him how he handled an unwilling woman. "I simply resort to the fine art of seduction." She went weak with longing. She was about to be seduced by him and she suddenly knew she wanted to experience the Leopard's hypnotic seduction. She would continue to spit fire at him, while he persuaded, enticed, lured, and blandished her to give him exactly what he desired.

He spread her dusky curls across the pillows. "You've never looked as beautiful as you do at this moment," he began.

All sex was a fine art to Adam Savage. "Flattery won't get you anywhere," she hissed.

"Flattery will get me exactly where I wish to be. Here." He showed her by cupping her mons and thrusting a finger up inside her.

"You bastard!" she cried.

"Mmm, you contract so tightly on my finger when you shout, I can't wait to feel what you do to my erection."

Neither could she. She bit her lips to keep herself from screaming with excitement. "Surely you're far too busy for this," she said scathingly.

"I can't think of a more productive way to spend an afternoon than making love to you."

"I prefer making love at night, when it's dark."

"Liar," he said, removing his shirt and trousers, "you like to see me naked in broad daylight." He sat down on the edge of the bed to remove his shoes and said over his shoulder, "Anyway, I'm busy tonight."

He felt the impact immediately as she flew at his back to rake his flesh with her nails. "Sheath your claws, you little wildcat, before I maul you." He sprang at her, forcing her facedown on the bed, while he straddled her. Then he lifted her long silken tresses aside so he could nip and bite the back of her neck.

For a moment she thought he was growling, but as her ears became accustomed to the strange noise, it actually sounded as if the Leopard were purring. A shock ran down the entire length of her back and she arched up beneath him. He arched his body over hers, going up on his hands and knees. He knew she would do the same. The moment she did, every part of her was vulnerable to him. His long, thick man-root unerringly sought the hot, dark cave, where he entered boldly. She closed her sheath over the swollen head, far too tight for him to gain full penetration from this angle. Then his palms cupped her breasts and his calloused thumbs stroked their hardening peaks until her sheath produced a pearl of moisture.

His lips began to nibble her ear and his love words became blatantly erotic, telling her just exactly how her sugared sheath felt upon the marble head and thickly ridged shaft as he inched inside her. The pearl drops were forming rapidly now, making her slippery enough to anchor deeply.

When she was love slick, his firm hands grasped her slim waist so that when he thrust forward he could pull her backward at the same time. The impact as he thudded into her was indescribable. His strong hands thrust her forward each time he withdrew and she was so tightly sheathed about him, his foreskin was drawn up the ridged shaft in hot friction.

Her cries mingled with his low, raw moans as he drove hard into her fully aroused body. Their passion was hot, wild, and swift. She clawed and tore the bedcover to shreds as they climaxed together hard and strong. He collapsed on top of her as their liquid tremors went on and on and on. When the last faint, delicious spasm was spent, he rolled with her until they were on their sides. His large body curved tenderly around hers.

"God, Tony, I love you so much, how could you even think I'd look at another? You are my woman."

Was he telling her the truth, or telling her what she wanted to hear? He made her feel so divine, at this moment she didn't care.

He stroked her hair. "What we have is rare." He drew in a harsh, shuddering breath as her long, silky legs touched his. Compared with other women she was like a fine crystal goblet among thick glass jars.

She stirred against him languorously, not wanting to move from the lovely cocoon for the rest of the day and night. His hands caressed her belly where his children would grow. His brows drew together. If he kept at her like this, his seed would take root before it should.

"I told you to stay in Ireland until week's end, then meet me at Edenwood. Why did you come to Half-Moon Street alone?"

She suddenly remembered her stupendous news. She turned in his arms to face him. "I came to tell you something fantastic."

His mouth covered hers and she gave herself up to the lingering, melting kisses they'd had no time for in their hot passion. He finally allowed her to draw a breath. "My brother Anthony is alive!"

He sat up. "Is this a joke?"

"No, no. He's alive. He didn't drown. We have his letter, isn't it wonderful?"

"Wonderful indeed. But what the hell has he been playing at all this time? Taking his place put your life in jeopardy."

"Oh, Adam, don't be angry. We don't need to worry about Bernard

Lamb any longer. I'm safe, Lamb Hall is safe, and Anthony is safe from him. Tony's in Ceylon with Mother!"

"Jesus Christ, I don't believe it." Savage swore. "The reason I left you in Ireland to attend to pressing business was Bernard Lamb. I've taken great pains to spirit him out of the country. My self-esteem is a little bruised that you don't need my protection any longer."

She went on her knees to him and lifted her arms about the thick column of his neck. "Adam, I shall always need your protection."

He grimaced. "It will be a full-time job protecting you from yourself."

"What the devil do you mean?" she demanded.

"I mean that you shouldn't be here. You are courting scandal, have been for months. Your reputation is important to me."

"If my reputation is so important, why did you bed me as soon as I walked through the door?"

"If you come here alone, that's inevitable."

She was hurt and annoyed. She decided to hurt him back. She shrugged a shapely shoulder and swept aside the filmy emerald curtains that floated about the bed. "If you don't wish to be my lover any longer, I shall have to find another."

He was suddenly beside her, grabbing her with rough hands. She looked up into icy cold eyes. The scar on his mouth made his dark face threatening. "I'll drown him in his own blood. I was first and I shall be last! You belong to me, Tony. What is mine, I keep." His hard mouth crushed down on hers, branding her as his woman. "We can only be together on weekends at Edenwood. My servants keep my secrets. No one in London will know. In fact, I'd much prefer it if you went home to Lamb Hall. London is no fit place for a young lady."

She looked at him in disbelief. "What the devil is wrong with London?"

"It's a cesspool!"

Her eyes narrowed. "And who knows better than you? You're up to your bloody neck in it, while I'm to be packed off home to be a good girl all week, then as a reward you'll let me be a naughty girl on the weekend. You're nothing but a bloody hypocrite!" she shouted. "I have no intention of leaving London until I put my cargo aboard the *Red Dragon*."

"The *Red Dragon* sailed for Ceylon yesterday with your precious cargo aboard."

"You bastard!" she cursed, raising her hand to slap him full in the face.

He caught her wrist and squeezed it painfully. His eyes fastened on her mouth, then moved lower. "You are angry again. Are you doing it on purpose to arouse me?"

She could see that indeed he was aroused again. As he reached for her, her other hand came up with a stinging blow to his face.

He raised his hand.

"Go on, knock me down. It wouldn't be the first time." Violence was ready to erupt in both of them when a low knock came upon the bedchamber door.

"Mr. Baines is below, sir. He says floodtide is early tonight."

Antonia began to dress. She was seething inside. So, he was off on the *Flying Dragon* smuggling God only knew what.

He watched her in brooding silence. She buttoned the lovely yellow pelisse and picked up her parasol.

"Have a care, Savage. If I open my mouth about you, I could have you swinging on the end of a rope!"

Adam Savage threw back his head and his laughter rolled about the room. By Satan, he'd taught her well how to threaten a man. "I'll see you at Edenwood," he said firmly as she swept from the room.

Tony almost choked on her anger. The liveried servant looked askance at her wildly disordered hair, but she'd be damned if she was going to try to tuck up the curls as Georgiana had done. She tossed it back from her shoulders. "Keep your damned eyes to yourself!" she snapped.

Chapter 38

The *Flying Dragon* made its familiar way into the mouth of the River Somme toward St. Valery. Savage picked out the signal light that told him it was safe to dock, and the moment the plank was let down his crew began to transfer the cargo. They had done it so often, they were actually becoming so proficient that little time was wasted.

Savage knew all he needed was calm confidence to lull the fears of those he had to deal with. The money changed hands quickly and the clipper was out in the Channel again on a steady course for Gravesend.

Savage stood at the wheel, his mind thousands of miles away. Thoughts of Ceylon filled his head. Young Anthony Lamb was safely out of harm's way, reunited with his mother, Eve. Suddenly a fertile oath dropped from Savage's lips. What if Bernard Lamb took a ship from Madagascar to Ceylon? They were almost three thousand miles apart, but both were in the Indian Ocean. By now it would be clear to him that it was Savage who'd had him shanghaied aboard the *Red Dragon*. A premonition touched him. Deep down he suspected Bernard the Bastard would take his revenge by making his way to Ceylon. How ironic life was. Because of deliberate interference on his part young Anthony Lamb's life might be in jeopardy. He had no choice but to return to Ceylon. Antonia would never forgive him if anything happened to her twin now that he had been restored to her. Antonia! He closed his eyes, knowing her image was ever before him.

How she had complicated his life. He had known he must return to Ceylon eventually to make a clean break with Eve before he married Tony, but, coward that he was, he had pushed the dreaded confrontation into the future. Now that her twin's life might possibly be in danger, he would not delay. Above all things Savage hated having his hand forced. He was a man who liked being in control. His greatest challenge in life had been learning to control himself. Once he had achieved that goal he had worked twenty hours a day for eight years to make his plantation thrive and accumulate enough wealth so that he could control his destiny. His life had been unfolding exactly as he had planned. The stately home had been built, its chatelaine chosen. He had returned to his homeland with enough power to have a say in the running of the country. Then a green-eyed, long-legged female, with more guts and passion than any woman had a right to, had scattered all his carefully laid plans to the four winds.

He wanted her with every fiber of his being. He wanted her for his mate, he wanted her for his wife, and he wanted her to bear his children. He intended to do everything in his power to have her too. But the problem was he wasn't in complete control. Tony was a bloody genius at upsetting the apple cart. He created order; she created chaos. She had stretched his patience to the limit when he had thought her Anthony, now she almost drove him to violence in his attempt to control her.

If she learned the unsavory details of his past, he ran the risk of losing her. Finally he faced the crux of the matter. If she ever found out he'd been involved with her mother, losing her was more than a risk, it was a probability.

He squared his shoulders and filled his lungs with the salt sea air. What the hellfire was the matter with him? Brooding and worrying weren't his style. Life was a challenge! Lady Antonia Lamb was a challenge! The dice were not yet cast. He'd play the bloody game and he'd win!

Antonia decided to go to Edenwood after all. But she wasn't going at week's end and she wasn't visiting the Marquess of Blackwater. She was going to have a cozy little chat with John Bull. If anyone knew what skeletons rattled about in Indian Savage's checkered past, it would be his trusted friend and manservant.

She smiled as her wicked juices began to bubble. John Bull still thought she was young Lord Lamb. She wondered what he would make of her transformation.

Antonia felt decidedly guilty when she concocted a story of homesickness for her grandmother's benefit. She had always had a passion for truth until lately and hated liars above all people. Now as she kissed Roz good-bye on the pretense of leaving for Stoke, she silently laid the blame at Savage's door. When she was on the outskirts of London she told Bradshaw that their destination was Edenwood, not Stoke. She felt guilty as sin when he winked and informed her cheerfully that Mr. Burke had already told him to drop her off at Edenwood, then return to London.

When the carriage arrived at Adam Savage's stately home, a welcoming committee of servants was led out onto the driveway by John Bull.

"Welcome to Edenwood, memsab. Excellency told me to expect you. All is in readiness. I am John Bull, Excellency's majordomo."

"John Bull, it's me, Tony!"

He bowed formally, his blood-red turban almost touching his knees. "Yes, memsab. You are Lady Lamb, twin sister to honorable Lord Lamb. May I say the likeness is very marked indeed!"

"It's marked because I'm him! I simply took off my pants and put on a skirt."

John Bull turned imperiously to the curious servants and dismissed them. "Are you trying to tell me Lord Lamb has been defrocked?"

She giggled and took his arm. "I am trying to tell you that I am my brother Tony."

He shook his head in admiration. "The disguise is perfect. You look exactly like a female!"

Antonia gave up. She squeezed his arm. "John Bull, I adore you. I only hope I don't have to sleep on the floor this time."

"Indeed not. Excellency bade me prepare the adjoining bedchamber to the master's suite for Lady Lamb."

"I'll bet he did." Obviously Savage had been back to Edenwood since he returned from Ireland.

"So, you may have your sister's chamber until she arrives. Confidentially, Tony, I am betting your sister will be the chatelaine of Edenwood."

Tony made a rude noise. "Indian Savage will never saddle himself with a wife."

"Oh, indeed, young sir, you are wrong. Excellency has been seeking a wife for a very long time. He seeks a titled lady to be a leader of fashionable society. Someone who will be a perfect hostess when he entertains his political friends. Edenwood is the setting he has created for this priceless jewel. He needs many children. He intends to found a dynasty!"

"John Bull, you are a gold mine of information. My mouth is watering for one of your curries. After I have viewed my room, or rather, my twin sister's room, I'll come to the kitchen so we can have a talk."

The chamber was indeed lovely. She realized she had chosen every piece in the room herself, save the priceless silk Indian carpet. She wondered if Adam Savage had furnished it by design, and decided he had. She must never make the mistake of underestimating him. She heard a faint rustle of silk and her nostrils detected an exotic fragrance.

"Kirinda, how are you?"

"I am very good, memsahib. Are you wishing me to unpack for you?"

"It isn't necessary, unless you are curious about my clothes."

"It would give me great pleasure to see your dresses. I never knew how you had the courage to be wearing men's clothes," Kirinda said softly.

"How did you know I was a woman?" Antonia asked curiously.

"The way you looked at the master. I, too, love him, memsab."

Antonia caught her breath. Lecherous swine! His conquests were legion. Well, he could strike the name of Antonia Lamb from that endless list.

After they had unpacked, Tony went down to the kitchen. John Bull eyed her with open curiosity, then dismissed the other servants from the spacious room. He tapped his forehead. "At last the sun has risen upon me."

She puzzled for a moment, then murmured, "It has dawned upon you."

"Dawn, sunrise, what is the difference?"

"At the moment it escapes me," she answered softly.

"I am shrewdly thinking you are not a man dressed as a woman. Oh, no, you are not as simple as you look."

"I hope not," she said faintly.

"Make your confession, you were a woman all along the way."

"You have guessed my secret."

"No one is pulling the wool over John Bull's ears for long, not even Excellency."

"I imagine you know everything about his clandestine activities?"

"Ah, yes. He is making the run across the Channel thrice weekly. He had a dock built right here on his own property for the *Flying Dragon*. The Greek temple down by the river is really a warehouse where the stuff is stored. There is going to be a resolution in France."

Antonia felt sick. She had refused to believe Savage's smuggling activities were harmful, but she could pretend ignorance no longer. Her own common sense told her the illicit cargos that made money in wars or revolutions were guns, weapons, explosives. Killing people for profit. Savage had told her that she hadn't the stomach for it, and he was right. It was mercenary, corrupt, conscienceless. Part of her cried out that Adam Savage would not do such a thing, but another part of her decided to see with her own eyes what was being stored in the large warehouse.

As she watched John Bull's deft fingers crush the chili peppers and carefully wash the rice, she probed for information that would condemn Savage. "You are the only one who knows the shameful secrets of his past."

"Ah, memsab, he has done things that blackened his soul. He is needing a good woman to redeem him." He looked at her with speculative eyes.

"If redemption is what he seeks, he has a strange way of going about it," Tony said dryly.

"Strange and wonderful are the ways of the Leopard," John Bull said, touching his ruby reverently.

Tony thought grimly, *The wages of sin are supposed to be death, but obviously they are jewels, gold, castles, and titles.* She sighed heavily. "I wish he wasn't such a bastard."

"I am thinking his parents were married. He is not baseborn," John Bull defended.

She smiled tightly. "No, just base," she said with deep regret.

While there was still light left in the sky Tony went outside on the pretext of viewing the gardens now they had been completed. She walked down to the Grecian temple with its graceful columns and lingered about its portico, but there were many gardeners and groundspeople about whose eyes were upon her. She suspected them of being guards. She could clearly see there was a stout lock upon the temple door.

The beauty of the garden made her heart ache. The lake, with its black swans and the woods beyond filled with deer and game birds, made it seem like Paradise, but Edenwood, as its name implied, possessed a serpent who dwelled therein. She loved Edenwood with a passion that bordered on what she felt for its owner, Adam Savage, but her heart told her she must give up both.

At dinner she insisted both John Bull and Kirinda join her. She was entertained by the barbs they shot at each other as they played out the age-old battle of the sexes, yet as she listened and laughed with them, she detected no cruelty in their thinly veiled hostility. They had been together so long and knew each other so well, they were like a comfortable pair of slippers. Not a matched pair, but not far off.

When Tony retired for the night, she had no intention of undressing for bed. Around midnight she intended finding out what Savage had warehoused inside the Greek temple. She gathered a dark cloak, an oil lamp, and a heavy brass candlestick to break the lock. If she couldn't get in the door, she would break a window. They were very high, but climbing had never deterred her before.

To pass the time she took her journal from her traveling case and poured out her heart onto its pages. Without her even realizing it, her words formed their usual pattern. The first page poured out her anger at Savage; the second catalogued his sins; and the third was filled with wistful longings for what might have been. What she had felt was a grand passion. Adam Savage was the love of a lifetime. Thoughts of him had a drugging effect upon her senses. He was like a narcotic, like the evil substances he'd smuggled. Now that she had tasted him, she craved him. When he was far away she could resist his fatal lure, but when they were together he could wipe away her resistance with his wicked attraction. She drifted off to sleep with Savage filling all her senses.

Tony awoke with a start and wondered what the hour could be. It must be way past midnight considering the amount of oil the lamp had burned. She wrapped herself in the dark cloak, turned the lamp down low, and picked up the heavy candlestick. It would make a formidable weapon if anyone accosted her.

The house was very quiet as she made her way downstairs and through the French doors that led out to the gardens. She moved slowly through the shadows of the trees. At first it seemed pitch dark, then gradually her eyes became more accustomed and she discerned the faint light of the predawn sky. Only when she heard the river did she turn up the wick of the lamp. Her footsteps quickened now that she could see the path that led down to the temple.

When she got to the door she put the lamp on the ground, then hesitated—not because it was padlocked, but because of what she knew she would find beyond the door. Why was she doing this? If she went back to bed and pretended ignorance of his smuggling, Edenwood and its master might still be hers. She made her decision. She would confront him with the evidence. He had such a facile tongue, turning lies to truths so that she wanted to believe whatever he told her. She needed proof of his perfidy.

As she raised the heavy brass candlestick, intending to smash the lock, she was grabbed from behind and the weapon forcefully wrenched from her hand.

Adam Savage wrenched the weapon from the dark intruder in the shadows of the temple. He was stunned when he looked down into the face of Antonia. A muscle in his jaw twitched. He had almost felled her with a brutal blow.

Tony stared at him aghast to be caught red handed.

His voice was as icy as his eyes. "Wouldn't it be easier to use the key?" He took the lock, inserted an iron key, and unlocked the heavy door.

She held her breath at what would be revealed as he picked up the lantern, but he did not swing back the massive door. Instead he thrust the lamp into her hands. She imagined both his cold contempt and his hot anger.

"Seek your room, mistress, we have work to do here."

She heard the footsteps of his approaching men and fled back to the house before he could shame her further. With trembling hands she removed the dark cloak and paced the room. She dreaded what he would do to her. The last words she had flung at him had been a threat. "Have a care, Savage. If I open my mouth about you, I could have you swinging on the end of a rope!" Now he had caught her trying to gather evidence against him. She was tempted to flee. The stables held scores of horses, one was even hers. But dawn had arrived. Servants would be awake. She would be easily apprehended. And where would she go? Lamb Hall would be the first place Savage would seek her. She swallowed hard, trying to gain courage. She'd stay and face him. If he began to brutalize her, she would scream for John Bull.

Tony caught a glimpse of herself in the mirror. She picked up her brush to try to improve her appearance. The girl in the mirror stared back at her defiantly. What was the matter with her? She was a woman, wasn't she? She would fight him with a woman's weapons. She would seduce him! She bit her lip, wondering just how she would go about it. In Venice she'd had the tempting gold tissue bodice that displayed her breasts so beautifully, to say nothing of the transparent gold pantelets. The best she could do was a nightdress. He'd never seen her in one. In Ireland they had come to each other naked every night. She took off all her clothes, then donned the white cambric nightgown with its dozen tiny buttons at the neckline. She took the brush up again, stepped before the mirror, then sighed heavily. She thought with envy of the exotic veils that Lotus Blossom must possess.

She brushed slowly, noticing the silken mass now reached her waist. She saw her cheeks blush at her intimate memories. They were so abandoned when they made love, Adam always became entangled in her hair, as if the black tendrils reached out possessively to bind him to her, while tendrils of his long black hair wound about her throat.

When she heard a noise at the door her breath became short and her pulse speeded up crazily. She almost jumped out of her skin as his voice came from behind her. She whirled to face him and saw that he had entered from his own bedchamber.

"I'm sure you have a logical reason for being at the temple in the middle of the night. Why don't you share it with me?" His voice was deceptively soft, like dark velvet.

Tony decided to confess all and throw herself on his mercy. If she became a supplicant she would be able to close the distance between them and touch him. Always before, one touch had been enough to ignite his hot lust.

"I—I was trying to see the guns . . . the weapons you have been smuggling into France," she whispered, taking a tentative step toward him.

"Guns!" His voice rent the very air, stopping her in her tracks. His gaze swept over her as if he were seeing her for the first time. How unbelievably young she looked. The prim white nightdress with its tiny buttons made her look virginal, and in truth she was touchingly innocent. What the hell must he look like to her? Dangerous, sinister, frightening! She actually believed he was gunrunning.

She caught her breath as her eyes fell upon her open journal on the chair beside where he stood. He picked it up immediately.

"No! You cannot read that. It's personal, private!"

He quickly scanned through it. "My name is on every page."

"They are my private thoughts about you. In all conscience you cannot read something so personal. You cannot violate my privacy!"

"You know me to be conscienceless. You're afraid I'll violate you, not just your privacy. Pray be seated, Lady Antonia, while I learn your innermost thoughts."

Tony wanted to fly at him to tear the journal from his hands, but she dared not. She knew the brute strength of those hands. She sat down upon an elegant Hepplewhite chair she had chosen with loving care and watched with flaming cheeks as he dropped into its identical mate. He stretched out his legs, then withdrew his ice-blue gaze from her as he began to read.

The journal was a revelation. Each entry started out hating, cursing, and reviling him, but ended up loving, almost worshiping him. The thing that startled him was the evil deeds she laid at his door. His character was so black, he became amused. He did not offer her the indignity of laughing aloud at her words, however. No hope of keeping his drug smuggling from her. She knew all that and suspected worse. Some pages labeled him an opium addict, others an assassin or just plain murderer.

He was the whoremaster of all time. He kept a concubine and had fucked his way through London's society matrons from Georgiana,

Duchess of Devonshire, to Lady Melbourne and her daughter, the exquisite Countess Cowper. Only the fact that he'd been out of the country for years saved him from fathering Lady Bessborough's illegitimate children, he had no doubt. Yet in spite of the fact that he spent every afternoon anointing his conquests with the honors of his manhood, Antonia obviously adored him. She was madly in love with him and cursed him as ten kinds of villain because he hadn't asked her to marry him.

Tony had romanticized him into some sort of dark archangel who was wicked as sin, and totally irresistible because of it. Poor Antonia, she was in for a devastating disappointment. He was a reformed man who leaned decidedly toward good these days, rather than evil. He hated to burst her bubble but he intended to do just that. She had led such a sheltered, restricted life with no outlet for her passionate nature. Repressed to the point where she craved adventure, no wonder she had jumped at the chance to act out a male role. She had been allowed the freedom to enjoy herself for the first time in her life. She had taken to adventure as a bird takes to flight, spreading her wings and soaring until she touched the heavens.

Trouble was she had become almost addicted to larger-than-life adventures. She had fought a duel, then escaped with him aboard the *Flying Dragon*. As a reward she turned the Carnival of Venice into a living fantasy for him as well as herself. In Ireland they had fallen in love, but had Tony fallen in love with the nabob, Indian Savage? Or the Leopard with its scarred face and wild, untamable nature? Or the nobleman, the Marquess of Blackwater? Could she love the man he really was? Could she love Adam Savage?

He put the book aside and came toward her. A small scream escaped her lips as he swept her up into his arms and held her high against his heart. The scream told him she was enjoying this new adventure. He boldly carried her to his chamber. The domed bed sat upon a pedestal, draped in sheer crimson panels. Thrown across the wide bed and spilling down to the black silk carpet was a cover of leopard skins.

Savage laughed at his own folly. He, too, indulged in fantasies. He gently placed her upon the bed, then pulled off his thigh-high boots and his shirt. Without removing his tight black breeches he lay down beside her. Her lovely green eyes were wide as she tried to anticipate what this dangerous devil would do to her. She gasped as his bold hand reached beneath the hem of her pristine nightgown, but he was content to let his hand caress her long, slim leg while he talked to her.

His husky voice sent shivers along her spine. "Tony, you know I've led a dangerous, corrupt life. No, let me finish. According to your journal you know that I lie, cheat, thieve, and smuggle. The things I do are unscrupulous, unsavory, and immoral. My activities are illegal, even criminal. I violate every law known to God and man." He felt her stiffen. Imperceptibly she shrank from him.

"You know I am venal and mercenary, but I can see that excites you, Tony." His hand moved up to her silken thigh to work its wicked magic.

"No! Please don't do that," she cried, trying to pull away from him.

"Tony, I enjoy being a villainous bastard, but more to the point, you enjoy it." He took his hand from her thigh and began to unbutton the row of tiny buttons at her throat.

"No! No, I do not!" she cried emphatically.

"We both know better." He laughed deep in his throat and Tony heard the evil intent in it. He had the entire row of buttons undone now, allowing his hands free access to her breasts. He pulled aside the cambric and his calloused hands encircled her slender throat.

"It arouses you to know these same hands that touch every intimate part of your body have killed men."

Her green eyes were liquid with loathing and apprehension. "Savage, stop this!"

"Savage," he repeated silkily. *"Nomen est omen,* the name is the destiny! My very name thrills you to the core." He slid her nightgown from her shoulders, revealing her breasts. His pale blue eyes licked over her like the flame of a candle. "The scar on my mouth is so sinister, it makes you wild with desire when it brushes across your nipple." He demonstrated for her.

A moan escaped her lips and she was instantly horrified at herself.

His palm cupped her breast and she felt the heat flood from his body into hers. His lips brushed across her cheekbone and came to rest beside her ear. "I believe the thing that arouses your passion most is the fact that you imagine I am a rake. *You* imagine I am incapable of being faithful to one woman. *You* think me profligate, dissolute, carnal . . ."

Antonia began to tremble. He was aware of her slightest tremor.

"You've always had to be such a good girl. So virginal, lying here in your sweet little nightdress. But when you are in bed with me, you live out your fantasy of the angel and the devil.

The fact that I'm a libertine allows you to be promiscuous. Because I've had mistresses, you had to become my mistress. Because I've used whores, you want to become my whore."

Antonia's hand slapped him full in the face. She pulled her nightgown back up to cover her breasts and tried to flee from the bed. His strong fingers snaked out to encircle her wrist. "Tony, what's wrong?"

"You lecherous swine." She panted, anger almost choking her.

His intense blue gaze held hers. "Tony, you don't want a dull devil of a husband who never breaks the law."

"I do! I most certainly do!"

"God's balls, you don't want a husband who hasn't the guts to commit adultery."

"Yes, I do! That's exactly what I want!"

"Look about you. All this can be yours in return for your sexual favors," he tempted.

Antonia's fury exploded. "You can take your bloody ostentatious Edenwood and shove it up your waistcoat. You are the most self-indulgent, arrogant male I've ever had the misfortune to know. You think your wealth can buy you anything, but it cannot buy me! My God, you are nothing but a Sybarite, decorating your servants with rubies, sleeping on a throne, buying yourself titles."

"You actually prefer a man with morals?"

"I could love no other!" she avowed passionately.

He let go of her wrist. "Get dressed, Tony. I'm taking you back to London."

She fled to the adjoining chamber. It was all over. She had had a narrow escape. She was the luckiest girl alive. The angels must be looking after her. Tony threw herself upon the bed. The floodgates opened and she began to sob. "S-sod the bloody angels!"

Chapter 39

When she left her chamber she was wearing a tasteful cream linen walking dress with matching kid shoes. Her dark hair was twisted into a classical knot that lay simply on the nape of her elegant neck. From head to toe she looked every inch the well-bred Lady Antonia Lamb.

Adam Savage was waiting for her at the top of the magnificently curved staircase. His dark clothes were impeccably cut, his linen snowy. His bow was both polite and formal. They descended together and entered the immense kitchen.

"Women should be seeing and not hearing," John Bull admonished Kirinda.

"Women should be seen and not heard," Savage corrected him quietly.

"See? Excellency agrees with me," John Bull said smugly.

Antonia swept him with a look of outrage that changed to contempt as it also swept over Savage. "Then Excellency is a bloody baboon!"

Suddenly she became aware of voices coming from the dining room. The conversation was in French. She doubted it was the servants.

"John Bull, please see that Her Ladyship's traveling bags are brought down." He turned to Antonia, gesturing for her to lead the way to the dining salon.

Three satin-clad gentlemen got to their feet the moment she entered.

Savage's voice was smooth as silk as he said, "Allow me to introduce our guests, dearest. This is the Comte de Barras . . . his lovely wife . . . his daughters."

The French aristocrat kissed Antonia's hand. "Madame Sauvage, I am honored." His accent was heavy. Clearly he spoke little English. Antonia tried not to stare, but the women dripped Valenciennes lace; all wore ridiculously high, powdered wigs.

Adam Savage introduced her to the other two men. "The Duc de Maine. The Marquis de Saint-Simon."

Antonia wondered if she should curtsy.

"Enchanté," the Duc murmured.

"Beauté du diable," the Marquis said, touching his fingers to his lips.

Adam Savage took a key from his vest pocket. "My sweet, unlock the temple for these two gentlemen. The things stored there belong to them. As soon as the de Barras' finish their breakfast, I shall see them safely back aboard the ship."

Antonia was disconcerted. What in the world was going on? The iron key in her hand was warm from being close to Savage's body. Did he expect her to turn over the guns to these Frenchmen? She wanted to fling the key in his face, but the people in the room had such elegant manners, she felt compelled to act like a lady. Politely, as if she were in a trance, she walked from the salon. The Frenchmen followed.

Outside on the drive stood a dozen wagons. The Frenchmen spoke to a couple of the drivers, so obviously the wagons were theirs. *My God, the arsenal stored in the Greek temple must be formidable.*

Antonia took a deep breath, inserted the key into the lock, then let the heavy door swing open. "Oooh." The word came out on a sigh of appreciation as her eyes beheld the beauty piled before her. Exquisite Louis XIV furniture, gold-decorated Marot pieces, cabriole cabinets, and pier tables stood next to objets d'art, paintings, gilt mirrors, carpets, and other priceless furnishings. It was like Aladdin's Cave.

Cases of Sèvres china and fine crystal sat beside a gleaming mountain of heavy silver epergnes, trays, tea services, silver plate, and the best Georgian dishes in ornate sterling. Why had that devil-eyed Savage let her think the temple held guns?

She sketched a curtsy to monsieur le Duc, then marched back to the house. Thankfully John Bull was still presiding over the kitchen.

"Who are these people?" she demanded. "Where did the priceless stuff in the temple come from?"

"Ah, you are living under a stone. You did not know French aristocrats are being herded into prison like rats? These are the lucky ones. Others are being murdered in their beds by mobbers." He inclined his head in the direction of the dining room. "Excellency brought that family across last night. He has been making three runs each week. They are bringing all their worldly goods before the mobbers smash or set fire to everything."

It dawned on Tony that the Duc and the Marquis had been brought over earlier and had come to collect the treasures Savage had stored for them.

"France is a most unhealthful place to be these days. These mobbers roam the streets screaming for 'equality' for everyone, but that can never be because everyone is not equal." He shook his head. "We Englishmen will never understand the French."

Savage's broad shoulders filled the door frame. "Come, Lady Lamb, we are ready to sail."

Her cheeks flushed. Why had she assumed the very worst of him? She was thoroughly annoyed. Why did she suspect he was amused?

"I've had no breakfast," she said pettishly.

"McSwine's culinary magic awaits you."

A wave of nausea caused her to swallow rapidly. He *was* amused, the evil bastard!

She stayed away from him on the short voyage to London. Mr. Baines sailed the *Flying Dragon* so that Savage could look after Count de Barras's family.

Tony felt seasick and she remembered the Bay of Biscay. She also remembered Adam Savage's clandestine activities along the French coast. Why had it never occurred to her that he was risking his life to help people?

When she arrived back at Curzon Street, Roz took her to task for her sly behavior. "I see you've had a rapid recovery from your homesickness!"

Tony inwardly groaned. She was definitely suffering from some kind of sickness.

"Why did you go sneaking off to Edenwood? I'll tell you why, Antonia. I believe you've formed an infatuation for your guardian. It's a good thing Mr. Savage packed you straight back home. What you need is a husband. Someone with a firm hand and strict morals who will put a stop to all this racketing about. I shall speak with Mr. Savage about it."

"I'm sorry, Grandmother, to have caused you worry," she said contritely, but on the inside she wanted to shout and scream and throw a big, stinking tantrum. When she was in the sanctuary of her room she walked a direct path to her commode, took out her washbowl and was violently sick. She dipped the end of a towel into her water jug, then wiped her face. Her eyes met those reflected in her dressing-table mirror. Could she possibly be with child?

Part of her immediately denied it, but another part of her knew it was more than a possibility. Roz's words still rang in her ears. "What you need is a husband." Antonia began to laugh. "What I need is a husband. I shall speak with Mr. Savage about it," she told the girl in the mirror. But the girl in the mirror wasn't laughing. Her face was tragic. Silvery tears traced their path down her cheeks.

The next morning nausea again assailed her before she even opened her eyes. The thing that triggered it was the smell of bacon wafting up from the kitchen. Antonia was well versed in the signs of pregnancy. Whenever women gathered for a social function it was ever a prime topic of conversation. Within the hour, however, she felt right as rain and was most grateful that the telltale affliction disappeared as quickly as it came.

Roz was off for an open carriage ride in the park with a gentleman caller. Before she left she extracted a promise from Antonia to attend Almack's on Wednesday evening. Frances Jersey was a walking encyclopedia on eligible bachelors.

Tony prowled about the sitting room like a caged animal. Needing an outlet for her terrifying thoughts, she ran upstairs for her journal. She went back to the sitting room, sat down at the secretaire, and opened the diary. Instead of writing, she made the mistake of reading. God in Heaven, she had poured her heart out onto these pages. Adam Savage knew without a doubt that she was hopelessly in love with him. How humiliating! She flung the small journal across the room.

When Tony heard the doorbell, her heart sank. She was in no condition to face anyone. When Mr. Burke came to announce the caller she would tell him she would see no one. It wasn't Mr. Burke, however, who entered the room, it was Adam Savage.

Conflicting emotions raged within her. She was torn between banishing him from her life forever and running into his arms. She did neither. She was distracted by the way he was dressed. He wore a shabby coat with no shirt beneath it. He was unshaven, his boots had seen better days, and he twisted a cloth cap in his hands.

"Tinker, tailor, soldier, sailor; rich man, poor man, beggar man, thief," she said whimsically. She did not feel whimsical.

"Tony, I want you to come with me. Wear your bother's things. Nothing fancy, an old riding jacket will do."

She wanted to laugh in his face. Here he was, larger than life, issuing his orders. He had not the slightest doubt that she would obey him without question. She searched his face. His eyes as always compelled her to do his bidding.

When she came downstairs she caught her breath as he came close to tower above her. When he touched her, she jumped as if she had been burned. Savage quickly gathered her lovely hair into a knot and pulled the cap over it.

He had a carriage waiting. She sat quietly as it turned into the Strand and headed toward the city. She didn't question him. She knew he must have his reasons. Adam Savage wasn't like other people. He lived by his own rules.

The carriage halted at London Bridge. They alighted and the carriage departed. They walked across the bridge to the far side of the river and suddenly they were in another world.

"You once asked me where I lived when I was a lad. I'll show you," he said cheerfully. The buildings were dilapidated. There were no houses, only hovels. Dirty, stinking, overcrowded slums. Row after row of these hovels like rotting teeth were inhabited by men, women, and children dressed in rags.

The gutters ran with sewage. A mangy dog fought two large rats for a piece of offal. Tony clamped her teeth together to keep her gorge from rising. She saw that all the women and children were barefoot. Only the men wore shabby boots.

Businesses thrived. The people might be raggy and dirty, but they were not idle. At street level and down stone steps at cellar level were shops or holes-in-the-wall that passed for shops. They offered everything from gin to barley water, from fish heads to sheep's heads, from lice-ridden wigs to dead men's boots.

The very air was dank, the cobbles wet and slimy this close to the Thames.

"When the tide rises, most of these places are flooded," Adam pointed out.

"I had no idea it was like this on the far side of the river."

"Oh, it's not just this side," he said matter-of-factly. "I'll show you Whitechapel."

The narrow streets and alleys were every bit as squalid and filthy. Every corner housed a boozer, every boozer had a collection of drabs standing about outside in their tattered finery.

"Poverty isn't always the result of idleness. The poor are paid starvation wages."

"Some of those prostitutes don't look any older than twelve or thirteen," she said with dismay.

"Don't waste your pity on them, darling. Save it for the little children. In St. Giles's, close by the London Wall, there are several flash houses that sleep four to five hundred children. The older boys are trained to be thieves and the girls prostitutes, but the little ones are sold. Boys as young as four are sold to chimney sweeps to become climbing boys. Half of them burn to death, the other half are crippled. Little girls are made to stand barefoot in the snow selling matches. Little blue feet momentarily wring the hearts of fashionable ladies and gentlemen. The taste for children in bed, however, has spawned a thriving business."

Tony looked at him bleakly, misery tightening her chest. How could she think about these things? How could she not think about them?

In Smithfields, behind the Tower, Antonia had to hold her sleeve over her nose because of the insupportable stench. They walked through ankle-deep cowshit left by droves of cattle being driven to the great slaughterhouse. Nearby butchers' shops piled guts and offal directly into the street. "They wonder why typhus is rampant," Savage remarked ironically.

Antonia didn't know if she could take much more, but she doggedly followed where Savage led. "London's population is one million. The poor make up three quarters. They are faceless, anonymous, illiterate. Thousands of them end up in workhouses. Parliament allows workhouses to be built, then lets them to a manufacturer to supply him with cheap labor. All he has to do under the law is keep them alive. Poverty-striken parents contract their children to work in mills from the age of five. If they try to escape, they are manacled. They never see the light of day. They are undernourished and work fifteen hours a day and they die like flies. Fortunately the poor breed prolifically."

Antonia's hand moved protectively to her belly, thinking of the child she might be carrying. Savage glanced down at her and saw her tears like silver jewels. He was instantly contrite. "Sweetheart, you've had enough."

With his strong arm at the small of her back he propelled her in the direction of St. Paul's, where there was a hackney stand. When she sat down she realized how weak her legs felt. She leaned back against the scuffed leather seat and closed her eyes.

"Those who don't go to the workhouse end up in there."

She opened her eyes to see they were passing Fleet Prison.

"The wardenship is bought and sold for profit. Lord Clarendon just sold it for five thousand pounds. The governors and jailers grow rich extracting money from the inmates. Those who can't pay are rewarded with brutality, manacles, thumbscrews, and starvation. They don't suffer too long. The cells and dungeons are over a common sewer. They die of jail fever or smallpox."

They didn't speak again until the hackney stopped outside Curzon Street. Savage took her hand. "I'm speaking in the House tomorrow. I'd like you to be in the gallery, to give me moral support. Now you've got something to write about in your journal other than me." He pulled off her cap, allowing the silken mass of her hair to fall down about her shoulders. He brushed his lips across her brow before he opened the carriage door.

Naturally she had nightmares. They were not nearly as horrific, however, as reality. In one of them Georgiana had a monkey on a golden chain. She continually fed the monkey sweetmeats. When it changed into a little boy, Georgiana didn't seem to notice. She patted it on the head, popped a sugarplum into its mouth, and laughed. "What a droll little man you are. I must buy one for the Prince."

In another nightmare she relived taking her bath to scrub off the grime of London's slums. The dirt came off but not the stink. She scrubbed her skin raw, then in desperation submerged even her head beneath the water. When she came up for air, however, she was in the sea, desperately battling the high waves that prevented her from climbing back aboard the *Seagull.* This time she had her unborn child to think of as well. She awoke in a tangle of bedsheets, wet with perspiration. She offered up a prayer to St. Jude that it had only been a bad dream.

When Antonia opened her wardrobe it seemed to her that she had twice as many gowns as she'd thought. Her hand reached out to touch the rustling taffetas, the whispering silks, and the soft velvets. They were far prettier than she'd remembered, in shades that took her breath away, either exquisitely pale or brightly bold. She realized how lucky she was.

What a spoiled child she had been to cry out against having to wear female attire. It was a privilege to be a woman and a luxury to have an extensive wardrobe. She decided to wear the most vivid color she owned so that she would be easily seen from the Strangers' Gallery of the House of Commons.

The burnt-orange gown, banded in dark brown velvet at hem and sleeve, was stunning. She took great pains with her hair so that small curls framed her face and one long ringlet fell over her shoulder. She would never wear a wig again, not after having seen the ridiculous white monstrosities Madame Barras and her daughters had worn. To compliment the outfit and frame her elegant coiffeur she wore a wide straw leghorn trimmed with orange ribbons.

Frances Jersey called for Roz in her carriage for what had become their ritualistic ride in the park.

"Antonia, darling, you are a positive stranger. Do tell me all the latest gossip from Bath. Is that insufferable Beau Nash still ruling the pump room as if he were the Queen? Wags call him Folly behind his back, you know!"

Since Antonia hadn't a clue about Bath, she deftly changed the subject. "You know everything, Lady Jersey. What time do the speeches in the House begin?"

"Lud, is that where you are off to? They should be in their seats by nine, but certain members like James Fox and that disreputable Sheridan lie on the benches and sleep off their night's debauch. Who's speaking?"

Antonia glanced at her grandmother, hoping she wouldn't refer to her "infatuation." "Adam Savage. He asked me to give him moral support."

"Oh, Roz, let's join Antonia. Women absolutely fawn over him. The gallery will be packed. No one can figure out who his mistress is, but rumor says he has several."

Roz said dryly, "I was only remarking the other day how foolish it would be to become infatuated with a man like Savage."

"Oh, Roz, if you have an ounce of blue blood in your veins, how can you help it?"

Antonia ignored Lady Jersey's remarks, but when they arrived at Westminster she realized with dismay that Frances had the right of it. As they climbed to the Strangers' Gallery her heart sank to see so many ladies. She stiffened with outrage as her eyes swept over the fashionable gathering. Every female who had visited Half-Moon Street was present. London's most wealthy, elegant, and beautiful society hostesses eyed each other's outfits and chatted politely.

When Georgiana, Duchess of Devonshire, arrived, she caused her usual stir. Frances Jersey looked at Antonia with raised eyebrows and whispered behind her fan, "The odds-on favorite."

Tony muttered between her teeth, "At least she didn't bring her damned monkey." Angry green fire shot from Antonia's eyes as she leaned forward to study the men below. Someone was talking, probably the Speaker of the House, but he was constantly interrupted by rude remarks from both sides.

Tony's eyes had no trouble locating Indian Savage. Everything about him was unique, his hair, his clothes, his powerful frame. She forced her gaze away from him. He was conceited enough. The arrogance of the man was astounding. To actually have invited all his conquests to give him *moral* support. There was nothing moral about the lecherous swine!

"Gentlemen, I turn the floor over to the honorable member from Gravesend."

As Savage stood, a hush fell over the House and a collective sigh whispered across the Gallery.

"Mr. Prime Minister, Speaker of the House, Honorable Colleagues. First, it gives me a great deal of satisfaction to announce that the wives of the honorable members of this House have achieved something we have not. Both Whig and Tory wives have been able to set aside party differences in a worthy cause. Their generosity has astounded me. Their fundraising efforts have set a precedent. Subscriptions are pouring in for the establishment of London's first foundling hospital. I propose the government support this project." Savage stopped speaking. He raised his eyes to the gallery and bowed to the ladies. As one, they stood and applauded him. Tony found herself on her feet with the rest of them.

Below, the Speaker had to call for order before Savage could proceed.

"If I were to read the entire list of reforms I intend to propose, we would be here until doomsday, so I shall be as brief as possible. First I would like to introduce a bill to levy a house rate to pay for the paving and lighting of Westminster. Sanitation in the City of London is nothing short of appalling. Gentlemen, wake up and smell the raw sewage! Other cities will follow London's lead and our town will be the envy of the Continent. A second bill proposes we establish a Society for Bettering the Conditions of the Poor. Dispensaries should be opened for the poor. If they are taught the rudiments of hygiene and cleanliness, I guarantee the incidence of typhus will drop."

As Antonia watched him she felt the compelling magnetism he radiated. She saw that everyone present felt it also and her heart began to sing as she realized she was no longer jealous of these women.

"The policing of London is ineffectual. We presently have a hodgepodge of parish officers, beadles, watchmen, and street-keepers. They cannot bring law and order to one million people. I propose another bill to establish an effective police force of constables and marshals. When you walk the streets of London you risk life, limb, and property. Who among you hasn't been robbed, who hasn't been diddled by a lawyer or dodged a brick thrown by a rabble-rouser? Only last week a foreign ambassador's coach was overturned. Mobs must not be allowed to gather or we shall find ourselves no better off than the French."

This brought thunderous approval from the benches below. Antonia was startled to see that the honorable members of Parliament were banging their shoes on the tables.

"Few of you have much sympathy for prison reform. *Let the criminals rot* is the general consensus. But the entire system is rife with bribery and corruption. Slum dwellers go to jail, slum landlords go to the bank. The rich are pardoned, the poor are brutalized. Last week a boy of seven was publicly hanged for stealing a spoon."

The House was unusually silent. Antonia felt a lump in her throat. Beside her, Lady Holland's eyes filled with tears.

"You have been most generous to allow me so much time when we have a mountain of pressing business before the House, but my conscience would not rest easy if I didn't touch on one last subject: child labor. The factories and mills have come to depend upon the labor of children as young as five or six who are forced to work up to fifteen hours a day. Gentlemen, that is all day and half the night. They don't just fall asleep at their machines, they die standing at their looms. I expect this Parliament to pass an act that states no child under nine shall be employed and no child under fifteen shall work more than twelve hours a day."

There was much dissenting on the floor, but the ladies of the gallery were on their feet applauding.

Tony picked up her skirts and hurried down the stairs that led from the Strangers' Gallery. She did not know how long it would be before he emerged, but she wanted to be the first person he saw when the doors of the House were thrown open.

Chapter 40

"Adam, I had no idea," Tony said softly as he walked toward her. Her face was absolutely radiant, filled with awe. The suspicion of a tear made her green eyes sparkle.

He took her hands in his. "Don't bestow sainthood upon me, darling." His dark head dipped to touch his mouth to hers, then he realized they had attracted a crowd. Young ladies did not allow gentlemen to kiss them in public places. "I want to take you to bed," he murmured low. "Come to Half-Moon Street."

Like one mesmerized she moved with him to his carriage. He closed the curtains against the curious stares of the crowd. He unfastened the ribbons of her leghorn and threw it on the seat opposite, then pulled her against him. "I must balance all this selflessness with a little wickedness."

"Adam Savage, you are a fraud. You are not wicked at all, probably never were."

He looked deeply into her eyes. "Ah, love, don't delude yourself." His eyes half-closed sensually. "I'm going to take you to bed and prove you wrong, several times."

Tony's heart was singing. Her instincts had been right about this man all along. She was deeply in love with him, knew she would never feel this way about another, knew she would love him forever. She was so proud of him, her heart felt it might burst with joy. He was noble, forthright, committed, and the most physically compelling man in London. She wanted him today, she wanted him tomorrow, she wanted him forever. He was all males rolled into one, father, guardian, friend, lover, husband—

Tony caught her breath and sobered. What if he didn't want her for his wife? He must, he must, she was carrying his child! All she had to do was tell him. John Bull said Adam wanted children, that he intended to found a dynasty.

Today she had learned he had a deep concern for all children. His own child would be precious to him; the mother of his child would be cherished. And yet Antonia could not bring herself to reveal her secret. She laid her head upon his broad chest and closed her eyes.

Beneath her cheek she felt his heart beating slowly, strongly, and she hoped that it beat only for her. She made a wish that there would never be room in his heart for another woman.

Adam raised her chin with his fingers so he could see her lovely face. He saw her silver tears. He sat up immediately and lifted her into his lap. "My sweetheart, whatever's wrong?"

In the security of his embrace she almost blurted out her fears. He felt as solid as the rock of Gibraltar. All she needed to do was confess her problem and he would solve it immediately. She took a deep breath and heard herself say, "Nothing, I'm just so happy."

Tony would be guided by her instinct. She was a woman, not a girl. Adam Savage was the sort of man who needed a woman. She wanted his love but she also wanted his respect. Even more important was her own self-respect.

Tony threaded her fingers through his long black hair, then whispered, "Your eyes are as blue as the Bay of Biscay." She lifted her mouth for his kiss, knowing the passionate response these words always incited. She felt him harden beneath her. Even his thighs turned to marble. Nay, marble was cold. Rather, she felt she was sitting upon rock heated by molten lava.

His kiss was fierce, scalding. "I'm burning for you," he growled.

She knew he spoke the truth. She felt the searing heat of his loins through her gown. Suddenly she couldn't bear the separation of so many layers of material. She lifted her bottom, swept aside her skirts and petticoats, then sat back down upon him.

"Christ, you're hotter than I am." She was the most sexually responsive woman he had ever known. To respond instantly to one touch, one word, or even just one look was the most flattering and exciting thing a man could ever experience.

The carriage was slowing. "Can you wait till we go upstairs?" he whispered huskily.

"Can you?" she panted. His swollen bulge was pressing exquisitely into her cleft. Neither of them knew if they could hold on or if they would spill. They held their breaths as they alighted from the carriage, then slowly, stiffly, with great dignity entered Half-Moon Street. They nodded to the servants, solemnly greeted Jeffrey Sloane, then with careful, deliberate steps ascended the stairs.

The split second the bedchamber door closed, they whooped with laughter, flinging off their clothes with wild abandon. He lifted her high so that her mons was level with his mouth, then pretended to bite her. She screamed playfully, then moaned as he slid her body down his until she rested on his upthrust sex.

His hand moved down between their bodies, his fingers spread her open, he flicked her bud, felt it pulse, then positioned the swollen crown of his cock on it. Taking a silken bottom cheek in each hand he drew her down over his engorged length.

Her sheath began to rhythmically flex and relax, flex and relax. When their mouths came together she opened her lips and offered him her tongue. He took all of it, sucking hard in a rhythm that matched that of her tight sheath. Adam walked to the high bed. His thick man-root deepened with every step he took.

Tony had no idea how he sustained so long, but she offered up thanks to the goddess of love that he did. When his knees touched the bed, he unwound her arms from about his neck.

"Lie back," he commanded with a roughened voice.

She obeyed. He had positioned her on the bottom corner. He did not come down with her, but stood between her thighs, still impaled. He reached down very deliberately, placing his strong, calloused thumbs on the pink flesh just where the cleft peaked. His downstroke was as violent as a lightning bolt. As he withdrew, his thumbs stroked in circles on either side of her bud, multiplying the sensations.

She writhed with pleasure as his hard thrusts made her build, but the gentleness of his manipulations made it possible for her to sustain without spending. Tony now realized his sexual experience with the women of his past was what made him a superb lover. She was the lucky one who would reap the benefit of a long and varied sex life. His intimate knowledge of female sexuality gave him more finesse than other men. Thank God he had initiated her. He had taught her well. Taught her to yield, to give endlessly, to her last shuddering tremor. Taught her to take, to demand, to drain him to his last delicious drop.

Adam did not withdraw but towered above her, savoring her shivers, worshiping her with his eyes. By God, she was so much woman, she'd have him staggering on his legs by dawn. Whenever they were alone together they were so aroused that they always had to make sex before they could make love. The amazing thing was that they enjoyed both equally. Usually the male preferred sex, the female love. This couple was different. They gave vent to their darker passions. His animalism brought out her carnality. Her natural eroticism brought out his unquenchable sexual appetite. They gloried equally in love-making, kissing, touching, stroking, whispering, embracing, molding, caressing, fusing, nestling, melting, brushing, murmuring, hour after languorous hour. The fury of their storm was spent in the first hour. Their slow, serious act of love lasted two more hours.

At last Adam was ready to talk. Their intimacy was almost complete. They had never been closer or more attuned in body and spirit than they were at this moment. He lay supine. She sat straddling him with her silken thighs. It was Adam's favorite position for talking. His gaze could caress her hair, her mouth, her breasts, while the back of his fingers could stroke the inside of her long, slim thighs.

"I took you to those terrible places yesterday so that you would understand what drives me. When poverty killed my father I was powerless to do anything about it. I loathed being powerless and vowed to accumulate enough wealth to allow me to fight London's poverty." He grimaced. "I'm afraid I blackened my soul in my relentless pursuit of wealth, so now I occasionally try to redeem myself."

"Your speech in the House today did that," she said softly. "The Child Labor Act alone will guarantee your ticket into Heaven."

"Holy Mary, sometimes I think you are too innocent for me after all."

Her eyes met his, "Meaning?"

"I know I'm a cynical swine, but we are a society of barbarians. Child labor laws likely won't be passed for another twenty or thirty years."

Antonia's face fell in disappointment, her shoulders drooped in defeat.

He held out his arms. "Come to me."

She nestled beside him and he drew up the covers about them. He took hold of her hand, threading his fingers through hers. "It's a never-ending battle and I need your help. I love you, and that works out just perfectly for me because I need a chatelaine and hostess for Edenwood. I realize it's a bit of a comedown, but would you consider swapping your English title for an Irish one?"

She held her breath in disbelief. Had he actually asked her to marry him?

"Lady Blackwater." She tested the sound of it. She closed her eyes and offered up a prayer of thanks, weak with relief. When she opened them he was looking at her intensely, his ice-blue eyes compelling her to answer him. A bubble of laughter escaped her lips. Did he really think she might refuse him?

He stiffened at the sound of her laughter. "Perhaps Edenwood is too ostentatious for you." He swept her with a look of cold contempt.

Antonia drew up her knees and began rolling about with laughter. She had just had a revelation about the man she adored. That familiar look of icy contempt was a protective mask! The mighty Adam Savage was vulnerable, especially where she was concerned. The thought thrilled her to her fingertips.

Tony sat up and leaned over him. She was so close, she could see herself reflected in his dark blue pupils. "You haven't the vaguest notion how long I've wanted you for my husband."

His natural arrogance returned instantly. "How long?" he demanded.

"Since that first night you tried to make a man of me and made me spew on brandy and cigars."

"You are such a romantic."

"No, I lie. I wanted you for my husband before I ever met you."

His brows drew together.

Tony smiled into his eyes. "It was when I first laid eyes on your ostentatious Edenwood. As a matter of fact I was the one who made it ostentatious. I must have had a premonition it would be mine someday. I talked Mr. Wyatt into all sorts of expensive improvements that must have cost the earth."

"Such as?" Adam demanded, his words dropping like icicles.

"Mmm, let me think," she said, tracing her finger along his top lip. "I suggested he extend the west portico into a terrace and instead of using Norfolk stone I persuaded him to import veined Italian marble."

"How did you persuade him?" Adam again demanded.

"Oh, it was easy, he was half in love with me. I decided we should have a conservatory, and in the bathing room I suggested the wall of Venetian mirrors and the hand-painted tiles." She took her finger from his lip and replaced it with her mouth.

He immediately lifted her hips so that she lay full on top of him. "I have fantasies about you and me in that bathing room. I'll bet bloody Wyatt had a few too."

"James and I enjoyed fabulous intercourse," she punned. She felt him lengthen and harden against her thigh and moved her body lower to capture him between her legs. "He explained to me about power houses and I believe it was at that point I decided to spend just a little more."

"A little more?" His eyes narrowed in warning.

"Mmm, yes, please," she said, rubbing her mons across the throbbing head of his erection.

"You are a wicked little bitch." He reached down to cup her buttocks, then kneaded them firmly, molding her against his shaft and his heavy sac.

"I told him to let Adams carve the fireplaces and Verrio paint your ceilings. Ah, yes, I also suggested he use fourteen-carat gold on the giltwork. Oh, dear, did that cost a lot more?" she asked innocently.

"A lot more," he confirmed.

"Mmm, yes please, I thought you'd never ask!"

"You're insatiable. Tony, I'm trying to be serious."

"Mmm, I can feel that you are, my lord."

"I haven't finished talking. We have a lot of things to settle," he said firmly.

Suddenly she surged up onto her knees and impaled herself upon him. "You talk. I'll keep you hard, no matter how long it takes."

Their bodies were musky from too much lovemaking, yet still she knew how to keep him hot and hungry for her. He lifted her off his jutting erection. "Listen to me, damn you. You cannot fuck and listen at the same time."

Tony exulted in the power she had over him. She marveled at the fact that she had feared him in the beginning. In the early days she had been desperate for his approval. Now that he had asked her to marry, she was utterly sure of him. Every vestige of apprehension had vanished.

"We cannot marry for a few months." His words hit her like a bucket of cold water, dissolving all her fine self-confidence.

Her lips formed the word *why* but she couldn't utter it because they began to tremble.

"I must return to Ceylon. There are certain matters I have to settle, certain things I must take care of. The moment I return, we'll be married."

She found her voice. "No! That will be too late." Panic flared up like a flash fire.

"Darling, I don't relish the separation, either, but I must make this trip."

Her green eyes narrowed. "Why?"

He offered her a half-truth. "I must inform your mother of my intention to marry you."

Her eyes softened. "Oh, Adam, how delightfully old fashioned and formal but totally unnecessary."

"You won't be of age for another year. You need her permission."

"My mother won't care a fig. She's never concerned herself with me in the past, so I'm sure she's not going to start now."

Guilt ate at his gut. "Your parents appointed me your guardian. That responsibility isn't solely a financial one. Your moral welfare is in my hands. A fine bloody job I've done. I couldn't keep my hands off you." Adam desperately hoped she would swallow the "guardian" explanation. None of his guilt was for Eve. He had never told her he loved her. They'd both been brutally honest with each other. It wasn't a real engagement, more a business agreement actually. He had wanted an ornament for Edenwood, she wanted his money. She'd made it plain she wouldn't even consider marrying him unless he procured a title.

Antonia was torn. Adam had such a strong personal code of honor. She knew if she confessed her condition, the child would take priority. She decided she could wait a couple of months. They would go to Ceylon together, get formal permission from her mother, then marry immediately. She would not force him to compromise his integrity. "I've decided to come with you. I've always wanted to see Ceylon. You can do your noble duty, then we can have an exotic tropical wedding and Anthony can give the bride away."

Adam groaned.

Antonia's confidence crumbled further. He obviously didn't want her along. She felt trapped. She couldn't wait until he returned from the Indies, it would take five or six months! Tony was on the verge of swallowing her pride and begging him. Then anger came to her rescue.

She flung off the covers, stepped regally from the bed, then swept aside the emerald panels that enclosed them. "If you can wait six months for me, you can wait forever. Bon bloody voyage!"

The filmy panels, the same brilliant color as her eyes, drifted about like jewel-colored smoke. Her hair was in magnificent disarray. Her breasts and her lips were love swollen from his savage mouth. He knew in that moment it would be impossible to wait six months for her.

He moved to the edge of the bed slowly, like a leopard stalking its prey. Then he pounced, dragging her on her knees until she was imprisoned between his thighs. His mouth came down to brand her as his. "I won't wait six minutes for you."

She clawed at him and bit him, but he subdued her in minutes, not by his strength, but by his animal magnetism.

When she yielded to him, he enfolded her possessively against his heart, his calloused hand stroking her wildly tangled hair. "Honey love, there is another reason I have to go to Ceylon."

She raised questioning eyes to his. "I left you safely in Ireland so I could dispose of Bernard Lamb. I shanghaied him aboard the *Red Dragon* with orders to drop him off on the island of Madagascar. The ship sailed one day before I learned Anthony was alive or I would never have sent Bernard to within three thousand miles of him."

She was aghast. "Surely you don't think he will go to Ceylon?" But she knew how dangerous Bernard Lamb could be and what a formidable enemy he made. "It's my fault! If I hadn't come sniveling to you, begging you to rescue me, Anthony wouldn't be in jeopardy."

"Stop it," he ordered. "I should have gutted the bastard instead of sparing him. Good deeds as well as evil ones always come back to haunt you."

"When do we sail? I'll stow away if you refuse me!"

She was a stubborn little wench, ready to pick up the gauntlet of any challenge life tossed her way. He wouldn't change one disheveled hair on her beautiful head.

Chapter 41

"Absolutely not!" Roz said, outraged.

"I'm old enough to make my own decisions. I'm sailing to Ceylon."

"It's the most scandalous thing I've ever heard. Bad enough you were seen kissing on the steps of Whitehall, now you want to go running halfway around the world with him!"

"Roz, Adam has asked me to marry him."

Her grandmother's gaze swept her from head to toe, taking in the crumpled gown, the wild tangle of hair, the beestung lips.

"God be praised, for it's apparent you've just come from his bed." Roz sighed. In spite of her years she did remember what it was like to be young and in love. "So, this trip is to be your honeymoon?" Roz said, regaining her composure.

"Well, no," Tony answered with a blush. "We plan to marry in Ceylon. Adam insists on asking mother's permission, since I won't be eighteen for almost a year. Because he's my guardian he thinks my moral welfare is in his hands."

Roz almost choked on Tony's unfortunate choice of words and she watched the blush deepen on her granddaughter's cheeks.

"What if you're with child?"

Antonia flinched.

"Ah, that little complication never entered your head, did it? Well, that settles it. I shall have to sail with you as chaperone."

"Chaperone?" Tony's fantasies of a two-month shipboard romance dissolved like snow in summer. "Grandmother, I wouldn't dream of putting you through such an ordeal."

"Grandmother now, is it? Are you suggesting I'm too old for adventure?"

"Of course not," Tony said weakly.

"A man like Savage won't abstain voluntarily and apparently you can't be trusted. With him in rut and you in heat, somebody has to play dragon."

Roz rang the bell. "Ah, there you are, Mr. Burke. You've been looking a little peaked lately. How would you fancy a little trip?"

At Edenwood, Adam Savage discussed the voyage to Ceylon with his own servants. "I'm taking the clipper, it should take less sailing time than the *Red Dragon*. I shall leave the choice to you. Edenwood will benefit from your steady hand, but so would I, no doubt. If you wish to return home, speak up."

John Bull was offended. "Home is where the heart beats. England is my home, Excellency."

"Kirinda?" Adam Savage gave John Bull a warning glance that told him not to interfere. Lotus Blossom must speak for herself. Her lashes swept to her cheeks.

"If John Bull is staying, I am staying."

"Then it's settled," Savage said with relief. Edenwood was precious to him and he needed to leave it in hands he could trust.

Kirinda followed the Leopard on silent feet. He knew she was behind him, realized she wished to speak with him in private, so he stepped into the conservatory. The scent of jasmine brought memories of Leopard's Leap.

"Sahib, I wish a question."

"Ask me anything," he said simply. There were no barriers of race or class between Savage and his native servants. They knew every detail of his unsavory past.

"Will you marry in Ceylon?"

"Yes. I shall marry Lady Lamb a few days after we arrive."

Kirinda's face fell and she made a sign to ward off evil. "Forgive me, sahib, but the widow will not bring you happiness."

Adam's brow cleared as he took her meaning. "I am not marrying Eve. I am returning to Ceylon to tell her so. I have chosen Antonia."

Lotus Blossom's face broke into a radiant smile. "John Bull told me she was the one he had chosen for you. Why is the wretched man never wrong?" Her dusky beauty was incomparable.

"He possesses the wisdom of generations of an ancient civilization. When are you going to put him out of his misery and marry him?"

Kirinda dimpled. Here was another wretched man who was never wrong. "Soon, sahib, very soon now."

Adam Savage's face broke into a rare smile. "Let's fill Edenwood with babies."

When the large black carriage halted on the driveway before Edenwood's portico, Adam Savage came down to greet its three occupants. In the previous week two of them had paid discreet visits to Half-Moon Street; the other had paid a most indiscreet visit.

A mountain of baggage and steamer trunks were quickly unloaded from the carriage and taken directly aboard the *Flying Dragon.* The clipper's cabins had been fitted out luxuriously for its passengers. The dozen nautical craftsmen Adam had hired were still adding the finishing touches, but the long ship looked a very fine lady indeed these days.

Tony and Adam soon learned to communicate with their eyes, for they were never alone no matter how they tried to slip away from the others. In the late afternoon Adam poured Roz a brandy. "I'm taking Antonia for a stroll around the lake." He had a difficult time keeping his amusement hidden. "We will be visible the whole time through the French windows."

They set off sedately, her long slim fingers resting lightly on his arm.

When they were out of earshot she groaned loudly. "Adam, I'm so sorry about this."

His other hand covered hers warmly. "My love, it rather pleases me that they are guarding you. This is the way it should be, you know."

She looked at him in disbelief.

"Mr. Burke called and made me promise that I would not shock Lady Randolph's sensibilities."

"Roz doesn't shock easily. She said with you in rut and me in heat, she was coming along to play dragon."

"She was much more to the point with me, darling. She told me flatly she didn't want you swollen with child before I got you to the altar."

Tony's wide green eyes scanned his face, looking for a hint of suspicion.

"She has a point, you know. Besides, abstinence is good for the soul," he said lightly.

"Hah! Tell me that when we've been at sea a month and you're stiff as a ramrod. You'll think rigor mortis has set in."

"What about you?" he teased. "McSwine will start looking good to you."

She slapped him. "Wretch! I'll keep my hands off him if you will."

They both sobered. They stopped walking. Their hands clung to each other, their eyes glittered with suppressed desire. "You need me to kiss you," he murmured intensely.

She shook her head and said breathlessly, "I need you to fill me."

"Trust me to find a way," he promised. "I love a challenge as much as you do."

She took some deep breaths until her shudders passed.

They resumed their stroll. "I didn't tell Roz about Bernard Lamb."

"I don't want you to worry unduly," he said firmly. "The *Red Dragon* won't make port too long ahead of us. The clipper has much faster speed. *We* know Anthony is in Ceylon, but your cousin doesn't know. He thinks Tony's in London."

"Perhaps he'll never find out. Perhaps he'll immediately take passage back to England."

Adam squeezed her hand, but in his gut he knew fate was a crafty old bitch who'd never let him off the hook before.

A month into the voyage they were halfway to their destination. The *Flying Dragon* was indeed living up to her name. Mr. Baines was a dependable captain who ran a tight ship, cutting through the ocean in a silent, steady glide.

Mr. Burke personally looked after the needs of his two ladies, keeping them isolated from McSwine and the rest of the unspeakable riffraff who crewed the ship.

Adam had rigged an awning on deck for the ladies' comfort on the second day out. Sometimes Tony basked in the sun, soon turning a lovely golden brown, but at other times the sun was so fierce, she was glad to recline beneath the awning, spending lazy hours wafting a huge fan made from palm fronds.

From the long, warm days of inactivity her body was becoming less slim and more beautifully rounded. Adam couldn't take his eyes from her. Her breasts were fuller, her whole body had a ripeness about it that sent his blood surging through his veins. Her looks were heavy eyed and languid, promising him paradise at their next stolen rendezvous.

They managed many stolen moments for kisses or intoxicating love words, but they could never spend hours together as they would have liked, except in the company of others. Adam often took the wheel from midnight until dawn. These were the hours they spent together. Sometimes they thought darkness would never arrive, but finally the sky traded its blue for pink and then black. Past midnight their voices were instinctively soft, not daring to trespass on the stillness.

He could not really make love to her while he was at the helm, but it was an intimate time when he enfolded her against him with one arm, while keeping the other on the wheel.

"This indolent life suits you," he murmured, slipping his hand beneath her cool cotton camisole to cup a ripe breast. "I love the way you look these days, the way you feel, the smell of the sun on your skin, the taste of salt when I lick you."

In bare feet she was not nearly as tall and had to go on tiptoe to twine her arms about his neck. In the tropical night he wore only loose cotton breeches. In the darkness he slipped them off knowing she wore nothing beneath the loose petticoat.

Tony began to rub her body against his. The hot sliding friction of their naked skin was silken torment. "Christ," he rasped hoarsely as her sleek heat scorched him, then became a wet slide as she wrapped her legs about one of his thighs and rubbed herself up and down him until she convulsed with hot shuddering. She moved in front of him between his body and the ship's wheel. She slid to her knees. Her arms wrapped around his iron-hard thews. Her fingers slid into the cleft of his buttocks. Her hungry mouth sheathed the swollen head of his phallus, then her lips sought the ridge three inches below the engorged crown. The tip of her tongue made circles until it found the tiny opening at its center, then she flicked it in slow rhythm with the friction of her lips.

His deep growls of pleasure made her wild for the taste of him. "Tony, I'll spill," Adam whispered fiercely.

"Promise?" she purred.

They clung to each other silently for the next hour. The calm after the storm. Slowly her head slipped to his shoulder and he knew she slept enfolded against him.

The long weeks at sea gave them many opportunities to talk. Roz and sometimes Mr. Burke were included in their discussions. Tony loved to listen to Adam's deep voice talk of Ceylon, its climate, its customs, its people. When he described Leopard's Leap, she heard the pride and love he obviously felt for his plantation.

At other times they spoke of Edenwood. It was plain to the listeners that both Adam and Tony felt deeply about the home they would return to after they were married.

"I feel very guilty that you are being dragged away from your important work in Parliament," she admitted.

"By now they are in summer recess. When we return, be prepared to become a political wife. Mr. Pitt has very ambitious plans to reorganize his party. He has generously asked me to play a major role."

"Do you think the Regency Bill will finally pass?" asked Roz.

"Not if I can help it," Adam replied, "at least not yet."

"Poor George," Roz said, beginning to laugh, but a rather poignant thought prevented it. "Poor Maria," she murmured.

"What does Mr. Pitt hope to accomplish?" Tony asked with genuine interest.

Adam teased, "I'm not sure I should let you be privy to the Prime Minister's plans until you are my wife. Can you keep a secret?"

"Better than any woman breathing." She smiled inwardly, cherishing her knowledge.

"Pitt, with my aid, plans to strip the Whigs of their power. The new party will be Tory."

"How will you accomplish it?" Tony asked.

"Politics is based on patronage. Whig nobles and landlords have made dynastic marriages for themselves and their children. They control votes by bribes or threats. William Pitt will promote Tory interests by filling every office with our own. The civil service, the army, the navy, colonial appointments, church preferments. You create a network of power from the top down. Merchant princes, as men like myself are now called, represent the commercial interests of the country and money talks."

"The poor Prince of Wales will be in his dotage before he becomes Regent," Roz lamented.

"Not so," Adam contradicted. "George is much more shrewd than people think. When he abandons the Whigs and comes over to the Tories, we will pass his Regency Bill."

"But the Whigs are his dearest friends, Fox, Burke, Sheridan," Mr. Burke pointed out.

Savage smiled and spread his hands. "Exactly, and who better would know their character flaws?"

"Oh, dear," Roz said with pretended pity, "all those Whig hostesses who rule society like lionesses will have their noses pushed out of joint."

"Well, that should improve their looks, if not their tempers," Tony said, laughing.

"I predict the lovely Lady Blackwater will become the leading Tory hostess," Adam said, drinking in her dark beauty.

"Yes, darling, you'll become the envy of the ton. The nobility will kill for an invitation to Edenwood."

Adam added, "Our sons will be brilliant enough to attend Eton."

"What about our daughters?" Tony demanded. "Surely you believe in equal education for females?"

"That won't be a problem. We'll simply dress them in their brothers' clothes and send them off to Eton," he said with a straight face.

"Will you never let me live it down?" Tony demanded.

Adam raised his eyebrows to Rosalind and Mr. Burke. They all three looked at her and solemnly shook their heads.

The *Red Dragon* had been almost three months at sea when it dropped anchor in Madagascar. However, it had only taken Bernard Lamb three hours to conclude that it was Adam Savage who had given the orders to kidnap him. At first he thought he'd been removed because he was a rival for Angela Brown's sexual favors, but common sense soon asserted itself. To a man with Savage's wealth and power a trollop from the stage would mean nothing.

No, this little caper involved his pampered cousin, Lord Anthony Lamb. Savage must have finally realized Bernard's intent and removed him from England.

Bernard thought back to the last time he'd seen his cousin. It had been the foggy night he had stalked him at Vauxhall Gardens. With his own hands he had pushed him beneath the horses of a hackney carriage. Bernard had been sure Tony could not survive the ordeal, yet no body had been found, no death notice had appeared in the newspapers.

Bernard smashed his fist into the heavy door of the hold as a thought gripped him. His cousin must have lingered before he died of his injuries. He was probably the rightful Lord Lamb and Savage had disposed of him so that he could not claim the title and the property!

The lure of the sea could become a powerful addiction to some men, but Bernard Lamb found it an abomination. Kept in close quarters as the days stretched into weeks and the weeks into months made his hatred fester. Now, however, the focus of his hatred was Adam Savage.

Whenever the half-naked Lascar took him up on deck for a daily airing, Bernard was on his best behavior. The size of the Lascar's muscles were terrifying and his dark eyes seemed to be watching for an excuse to toss him overboard.

In the hold, however, his revenge against Savage had already begun. In the dim light he had discovered boxes of Paris fashions. One by one he removed the gowns, slashed them to ribbons, then carefully repacked them in their boxes. When he discovered the expensive Venetian talc for powdering hair, he took particular pleasure in pissing in the barrels.

By the time the damage was detected, Bernard intended to be carrying out his plans for further destruction against the bastard who had sentenced him to three months of living hell aboard this hot, heaving hulk.

Chapter 42

The *Red Dragon* freed its prisoner the moment it docked, but when Bernard Lamb realized he was on the island of Madagascar he almost went mad with frustration. All his plans had centered on Ceylon and he would not know a moment's peace until he reached that fatal destination.

On the streets of Cape Amber it took Bernard Lamb less than an hour to learn that ships sailed every day for the Port of Colombo in Ceylon. It took him until nightfall, however, to acquire the money he would need for the journey. By morning he had enough funds to purchase a stylish tropical wardrobe, a gun, and transportation to Ceylon. The hapless sailor he had robbed lay in an alley with his throat cut.

Bernard Lamb had learned at an early age how deceptive appearances could be. When he reached Colombo, his expensive clothes coupled with his polished manners and air of supreme confidence would get him anything he needed from these colonials. He bought a passage on the most impressive ship in port. It took only days to sail to Colombo, and when he disembarked he appeared to be a man of business. Without hesitation he walked into a small government office to hire a guide to take him to Leopard's Leap.

The official was most impressed, however, by his name.

"You must be related to the late Lord Russell Lamb who administered the East India Company."

"Yes, indeed. He was my uncle. As a matter of fact I am here on family business. Could you also supply me with directions to their plantation? My aunt, Lady Lamb, has begged me to come to her aid. It cannot be easy for a woman left widowed and alone here in the Indies."

"I should say not," agreed the government clerk. "When Lord Anthony arrived recently, it was a most touching reunion for mother and son."

"Lord Anthony?" Bernard said doubtfully.

"He, too, needed directions to Government House, so I took him myself. Their plantation is the next one to Leopard's Leap."

"How very convenient," Bernard said silkily. "My cousin Tony is in for quite a surprise." *So, the young swine still lived and breathed. He had more lives than a fucking cat.* He had no idea how his cousin had reached Ceylon ahead of him, but it couldn't have worked out better! Now he would be able to revenge himself on Savage and rid the world once and for all of the present Lord Lamb.

Bernard immediately agreed to accompany the two sepoys who carried dispatches between Colombo and Government House. The horse he bought for the journey took the last of his money and he was obliged to rely upon the sepoys' hospitality.

Bernard Lamb hated everything about the tropics with a vengeance. He hated the heat, the insects, the food, the smells, but mostly he hated the natives. The sepoys' food and drink he was forced to consume were hard enough to swallow, but the thing he found almost intolerable was sharing their drinking cups and utensils. The men sensed his repugnance toward their color. They remained impeccably polite, but they silently marked him as another white bigot.

When Government House came into view on the third day, it was debatable who was more relieved, Bernard Lamb or the sepoys. They bade him good-bye once they passed through the front gates. As his covetous eyes took in the pale pink palatial house a seething resentment gripped him. Why was it some were born to luxury while others had to conspire with the devil himself for every crumb that fell from his table?

As he stood gazing at the splendor he was suddenly filled with a sense of destiny. He knew that his fate lay before him; all he had to do was seize the moment and take it into his own hands. It had been predestined that he come halfway across the world to confront his enemies and forge his future. Bernard Lamb felt fortune take his hand.

A groom came forward to take his horse. A servant bowed low and carried his new traveling bag up the steps. A guard on the front entrance opened the door for him. The turbaned majordomo inquired whom he wished to see.

"I am Lady Lamb's nephew." The words were like magic. He was ushered into an opulent receiving room. Two young wallahs in native dress entered the room. One offered a cool drink, the other worked the punkah fan. Both servants lowered their eyes, then bowed their heads in abject obeisance. Like clockwork, the moment he finished his drink, an inner door swung open to admit a small blond woman. She

had a cool elegance that easily made her the most self-possessed female he had ever encountered.

A trick of the light filtering through the jalousies prevented Eve
from seeing the young man's features until she was directly in front of
him. Suddenly her coolness evaporated. "You must be Robert's son.
You are the image of your father!"

Bernard experienced a surge of power. For an unguarded moment
her emotions had been transparent. Lady Lamb had clearly loved his
father. He took immediate advantage. He stepped close, raised her
elegant hand to his lips, and said huskily, "My father was madly in
love with you until the day he died. Now I know the reason why."

"Flatterer!" she reprimanded him playfully, but Bernard knew he
held her in the palm of his hand. He felt potent enough to step into
his sire's shoes and resume Robert's relationship with this woman
where it had left off.

"My name is Bernard."

For Eve the years fell away; she was sixteen again. She linked her
arm through his intimately, as if they had known each other forever,
and drew him into the inner sanctum. "It's almost time for luncheon
and I know how partial men are to food."

A wallah appeared as if summoned by thought alone. "Put the sahib
in the peacock suite."

Bernard Lamb saw that the luxurious suite had got its name from
the cool tiled floor decorated with a magnificent peacock in full display. Three more servants appeared. One drew his bath in the adjoining bathing room, another began to unpack his clothes, a young native
girl brought a silver tray with a wine decanter and a crystal goblet. The
manservant who had brought him upstairs made obeisance, murmuring, "If there is anything more you are desiring, sahib, please use the
bellpull."

Bernard pointed a finger at the female. "Her," he said with authority. The men withdrew, the girl stood motionless with downcast eyes.

"Look at me," he ordered.

Slowly she raised her eyes. They were liquid with apprehension.
Bernard licked his lips. She fulfilled a longtime fantasy. She was a
slave girl to do his bidding.

"Take off the sari."

With reluctant hands the girl obeyed. His gaze slid over the slim
body, noting the budding breasts, the tiny mons. She was only just
coming into pubescence. He beckoned her with an all-powerful finger.

The look of dread upon her face increased with each slow step. When she was directly in front of him, he lifted her long black hair and wrapped it once about his hand. Too late she realized she was trapped. The fear in her eyes turned to terror as his hand went to his belt and he withdrew his gun. He did not touch her directly, but used the gun as if it were his hand to trace along her cheek and down her throat. Her body began to tremble uncontrollably as he circled her budding breasts with the pistol barrel. When he trailed it down her belly, she pulled away from him in desperation, but he wrenched her back by her hair. She opened her mouth to scream, but the look he gave her made stark fear wedge in her throat, paralyzing her vocal cords.

Her mons was the gun's final resting place. Bernard inserted the tip. Her eyes went glassy. He pulled the trigger. The gun clicked. It took an endless minute before she realized the gun was not loaded. Bernard began to laugh. When he removed his hand from her hair, she collapsed onto her knees in a huddled heap.

He looked down at her with glittering eyes and took the bullets from his pocket. "Little wog, I wouldn't soil my prick with you, but that doesn't mean we can't enjoy fun and games."

Eve gave instructions that luncheon must not be served until her guest came downstairs. Anthony arrived in the dining room at lunchtime and sat scribbling notes in a journal he had begun. The plantation's crops fascinated him to the point where he had begun their serious study. Almost an hour elapsed before it dawned on him that no food had been served. He arose from the table to seek out his mother.

"There you are, Anthony. I have a wonderful surprise."

At that moment their guest descended the stairs, heard Eve's voice, and came into the salon.

"Your cousin Bernard has just arrived from England. Bernard, this is my son, Lord Anthony."

Bernard's eyes smiled at the familiar face before him. Everything about the tall young man was acutely familiar, from the clubbed-back dark curls to the wide green eyes, yet Bernard knew he had never set eyes on him before in his life.

Anthony stuck out a welcoming hand. "This is an unexpected pleasure. How ironic we meet halfway around the world."

"It must be destiny," Bernard replied smoothly. He was fascinated.

Even the husky drawl was the same, yet not the same. "Forgive me for staring. Do you have a brother?"

"A sister," Anthony replied, "a twin sister. People insist they can't tell us apart." It was a family joke, of course.

Bernard shared in mother and son's friendly laughter, but his mind flashed about like quicksilver. Was it possible that the Lord Lamb he had stalked with the nine lives was a bitch impersonating her twin? He could only conclude that it was a distinct possibility. Women were devious enough for any deception. He added another name to the growing list of enemies he would take pleasure in eliminating.

"What brings you to Ceylon?" Anthony asked with genuine interest.

Bernard had had three months to weave plausible tales of why he was in the Indies. He had a facile tongue and quite enjoyed piling one lie on top of another. Living by one's wit provided both excitement and satisfaction. "I'm thinking of investing in a plantation. A friend of mine, Adam Savage, has a place called Leopard's Leap, on the market."

"Oh, Lord, I wish *I* had the resources to buy the place. I'm over there nearly every day. It covers over twenty thousand acres and I swear every plant flourishes. The crops are abundant because it's been nourished with love and care for a decade. It's not just the things that are grown, even the people thrive at Leopard's Leap."

The expression upon Eve's face did not change, but her mind raced about. So, Savage was selling the place after all. Obviously he must have decided his future lay in London. The question was, would he return for her? Actually, the longer he stayed away, the richer she became. In the months since he had departed she regularly used his ship to sell valuable cargoes in Canton. Her connection with Raja Singh and his whole household had proved invaluable. They were so addicted to hunting, they had five hundred beaters.

Eve found a ready market in Canton for almost anything they captured dead or alive. The jackal had a small horn on its skull covered by hair. It brought a high price because it was considered a magic charm that restored men's potency. Birds, too, were a good source of income. Toucans and parrots were caged, peacocks and egrets were valuable only for their feathers. Even snakes brought in money; pythons for their exotic skins, cobras for snake and mongoose fights. Civet cats provided musk glands and leopard provided exotic spotted pelts. She did not hesitate to take ivory tusks from the Raja's emissary. She simply marked the shipping crates RATTAN.

On a recent visit to the mainland Eve had been introduced to Sir
John Macpherson. England's Prime Minister Pitt had appointed him
to India after his invaluable service in America during the War of
Independence. She had had him eating out of her hand and had invited him to come for a visit to Ceylon. She knew he would come. He
was the sort of man who really appealed to her. He was predictable,
he was also an earl. Eve smiled a secret smile. Second Earl Cornwallis.
He had surrendered to Washington at Yorktown, and if she chose, he
would surrender to Eve at Ceylon.

Her mind came back to her present guest and she found herself
wondering what he would be like in bed. Not easily controlled, she
thought shrewdly.

Anthony and Bernard were making plans to ride over to Leopard's
Leap.

"The man the Company put in charge is called Denville. I'll introduce you to him. He's really a decent fellow. He admitted freely I
couldn't learn much about tea and rubber from him, that it's the
Tamils who have the expertise, so I learn by watching them. It's absolutely fascinating."

Eve caught Bernard's eye. "Enthusiasm is quite out of style, but my
son doesn't seem to care. One day I expect him to take up residence
over there."

"Well, I must have caught his enthusiasm. I can't wait to explore
this legendary Leopard's Leap and learn the secrets of its success."

"It will take weeks to see it all, and then beyond the plantation
there is the jungle to explore," Anthony explained.

"This time, be sure to take your gun along, darling," she reminded
her son. She put down her napkin and a servant was at her elbow
immediately, holding her chair so she could arise. She glanced at Bernard. "A man isn't much use in the Indies without a loaded gun." The
sexuality implicit in the remark was lost on Anthony as he gathered up
his notes.

Chapter 43

Only a week had elapsed between the time the *Red Dragon* docked in Colombo and the *Flying Dragon* reached that port. If Bernard Lamb was there, Savage hoped to catch him by surprise. If he was not, there was no need for alarm.

When Savage boarded his East Indiaman he was pleased for once that the *Red Dragon* had taken a full three months to make the voyage. He was less than pleased, however, when he learned the prisoner they transported had ruined the cargo in the hold where they had secured him. Savage cursed, wishing Bernard the bastard had met with a fatal accident on the long voyage. He decided not to tell Antonia of her ruined French fashions; she had taken such delight in choosing them. He told the *Red Dragon's* crew to keep their eyes skinned in Colombo, as he wouldn't be surprised to see Bernard Lamb turn up.

When Lady Randolph saw that their baggage would have to be transported by buffalo wagons she apologized profusely to Adam for having brought so many trunks. What a fortunate inspiration it had been to include Mr. Burke, for without his strong helping hand she doubted she would ever make it to the foothills and the Lamb plantation.

Antonia treated the whole thing like a great adventure, and looking at her granddaughter, Roz had to admit she was absolutely flourishing. The long, indolent sea voyage had made her blossom, or perhaps it was simply because she was in love. Anyone looking at Adam and Antonia knew they were in love and that they had already mated. She had done her best to keep them apart, but as a result they shamelessly devoured each other with their eyes. The sooner these two were married and got on with the business of making babies, the better for everyone.

Antonia's languor disappeared the moment she arrived in Ceylon. Everything here was completely different from England, the people, the trees and flowers, the insects, the fragrant warm air. She was filled with the anticipation of seeing her mother for the first time in over ten long years and she couldn't wait to be reunited with her twin. But mostly she knew her excitement came from the awareness that very, very soon now, she and Adam would be man and wife.

She could hardly wait to see Leopard's Leap, because she knew how much it meant to Adam. His plantation had been a labor of love for a decade and she knew it had become a part of him. She hoped that his adopted country and its people would find a place in her heart.

Antonia hummed and sang as the little mare Adam had bought her trotted along beside a buffalo cart, where Roz sat beneath a large parasol. Adam Savage rode at the head of the small cavalcade of wagons. For two days Antonia had only seen his wide shoulders and broad back, but it was enough to make her the happiest woman alive. She would willingly follow him to the ends of the earth.

Adam rode at a steady pace, alert and watchful for any danger or even discomfort that might befall the small party in his care. He was not looking forward to the confrontation with Eve. The situation would be awkward from the outset. He wished he'd had the luxury of seeing her before the others arrived to settle matters so they knew where they stood, but that was impossible. The best he could do was deliver his charges to Government House, then withdraw to Leopard's Leap so they could enjoy a family reunion. He must discreetly let Eve know he needed to see her in private.

Finally, Savage decided that in all decency he must send a dispatch with a runner to Government House to give Evelyn a few hours' notice that her daughter and her mother were about to descend upon her. As he penned the note he thought how easy it would be to write her a letter explaining in detail why their relationship was over, but that would be the coward's way out. He must tell her face to face, take all the blame, somehow soften the rejection. He must find the words that would save her pride. Savage did not agonize over what he had to do. They had certainly never loved each other.

Adam Savage chose the place to rest and water the animals because of its beauty. At this time of the year a waterfall made a deep pool not fifty yards from the road. In the daylight it attracted thousands of colored birds, and the wild orchids and flowering shrubs were covered with butterflies.

Antonia brought her mare to the pool's edge so she could stand beside Adam. The sound of the water would drown out the private words they shared. "It's like Paradise. Oh, I wish we were alone so we could bathe together."

"Water attracts beautiful things, but it also attracts dangerous ones.

Especially at sunset when wild jungle animals come to drink. Never go near water alone, darling." He took off his shirt, dipped it in the cool water, then put it back on. "Ah, that feels so good. How are you standing up to the heat, love?"

"I don't really mind it. I learn from you. I wear only drab cotton for traveling and tie my hair back with a leather thong as you do. I never felt less glamorous even when I dressed in Tony's clothes, but I feel disgustingly comfortable." She glanced back at Roz and Mr. Burke, then slipped out of her cotton shirt. When she bent forward to dip it into the cool water her lovely ripe breasts almost popped from her cotton chemise. It took every ounce of willpower Adam possessed to keep his hands from her. It had been a long time since he had been able to make love to her. When she put her wet garment back on, his desire was inflamed further. It clung to her wetly, emphasizing every luscious curve. His gaze became so intense, she knew he was fully aroused. She swayed toward him. "Your eyes are as blue as the Bay of Biscay," she whispered sensuously.

"Stop it. Behave yourself. A young bride should be chaste."

"You should have thought of that in Ireland when you took my innocence," she taunted.

He reached out to lightly caress her cheek. He felt so very protective of her suddenly. "It will take me at least a year to strip you of your innocence, my beloved."

Lady Lamb read the note twice before she allowed a small frisson of triumph to lift the corners of her mouth. So, Savage had returned for her after all. If he had obtained a title, his signature on the note gave no indication of it. Even if he had managed to get one it would certainly be of lower rank than an Earl of the Realm. She tried to compare him with Cornwallis, but it was an impossibility. There simply was no comparison. She sighed, knowing if she chose Savage she would never be able to control him, but she simply couldn't resist the man.

The thing that puzzled her was why on earth he had saddled himself with an old woman and a young girl. Probably some misguided impulse prompting him to think she'd like her family present at their wedding. Eve wasn't best pleased. Her mother had always disapproved of her, and as for Antonia, what woman in her thirties needed a seventeen-year-old at her side, glowing with youth?

She tapped the note with a long fingernail as she calculated how much time she had. When they arrived they would be hot, tired, and begrimed from the rigors of the journey from Colombo. Sleeping in a tent did nothing for a lady's disposition or appearance and the dust of the road ruined one's complexion, coiffeur, and wardrobe. She rang for her women and ordered a lotus-scented bath.

Bernard Lamb had ridden over every inch of Leopard's Leap that week. He had viewed the thousands of thriving tea bushes and the four-story tea factory. He knew the exact location of the smokehouse that held a fortune in molded sheets of rubber latex, and he knew the workers' schedules.

Anthony Lamb's future hung by a precarious thread. As he rode before his cousin pointing out the crops at various stages of harvesting, he had been a tempting target for Bernard's pistol. Bernard managed to restrain himself, however, because of their location. He did not want the body to be found at Leopard's Leap. When his bullet found its mark, he wanted his cousin Anthony to fall to the floor of the jungle, where the evidence would be naturally disposed of as soon as darkness fell.

"Well, I think we've exhausted the plantation. How about exploring in the jungle this afternoon?" Bernard suggested.

"I've always had a native Tamil with me before, but I suppose we'll be safe enough if we stick together," Anthony replied. "The flora and fauna are so uniquely exotic, you've never seen anything like it. There are scores of different types of palmetto, bamboo, and rattan, all covered with flowering vines and orchids in shades you never dreamed existed. There are monkeys, macaques, flying foxes, and sloths all picking fruit from the high branches of breadfruit trees, Indian dates, pawpaw, pomegranates, and plantain. I followed a path where the leafy canopy blocked out the sunlight so well, moths a foot across sat on the rough bark of the tamarind trees."

"Do you think you could find that exact spot again?" Bernard asked eagerly.

It was with great enthusiasm Eve greeted her family when they arrived at the plantation. Anyone witnessing the touching reunion might have been hard pressed not to shed a tear. Mr. Burke was such an observer, but the glitter in his eye was not from tears, it was from cynicism. Eve's clothes, manners, and demeanor were impeccable, yet Mr. Burke wondered how many hours she had spent before her mirror? How many of her maids had been punished for their clumsiness while dressing her hair?

Eve welcomed them exactly as etiquette dictated, acknowledging her mother first out of deference to Lady Randolph's age and station. It looked the perfect picture of filial affection, but Mr. Burke knew looks were deceiving and it was usually the ear that picked up the true feelings beneath the surface.

Roz made up her mind to start out on the right foot this time around. Perhaps in the past the animosity between mother and daughter had been her fault. Eve presented her cheek and Roz kissed it gently. "My dear, I am so sorry about Russell. I can see your strength has brought you through it. You look marvelous."

"I detect your disapproval that I'm out of widow's weeds," Eve said sweetly. "How I've missed your mothering me."

Eve turned to her daughter. Antonia stepped forward to embrace her. "Mother, you are just as lovely as I remembered. I'm so thrilled to be here."

The flawless creature in blue chiffon clearly wished to avoid any physical contact. She put up a small, beringed hand as if warding off an invasion and said, "Antonia dear, you're so tall. Why, I believe you must be as tall as your brother." Her gaze swept over her daughter's dusty and disheveled appearance. "You must bathe and change at once."

Antonia's joy began to dissolve. Her mother made her feel as she had when she was six; inferior in every way. Still, there was no denying Eve was a great beauty, and Antonia wished with all her heart that she hadn't been such a disappointment to her mother.

Eve's cool gaze fell upon Mr. Burke, whom she had known most of her life. She acknowledged him with one word, "Burke."

Up to this point Adam Savage had only been an observer, but what he witnessed made him realize what a fortunate escape he'd had. Evelyn Lamb was not cool at all, she was cold blooded as a reptile.

At last Eve was free to turn her attention to the object of her desire. Her lips widened into a smile, she laid her hand on his arm possessively, and she looked up into his face. "Adam darling."

Savage's blue gaze was glacial. "Lady Lamb," he said formally, taking her hand and removing it from his arm. In that moment Eve knew irrefutably that Savage did not want her. How vastly amusing. Too bad! She had him firmly hooked and she intended to reel him in.

Savage bowed to the ladies. "I extend the hospitality of Leopard's

Leap to all of you." His gaze came back to Eve. "I will intrude no longer, but perhaps we could have a private talk tomorrow?"

Eve inclined her head, then turned her back upon him, dismissing him from her presence, if not her thoughts.

Antonia blushed, knowing Adam would inform her mother that they intended to marry.

Eve saw the blush, saw the radiant look upon her daughter's face, and experienced a stab of jealousy she'd never felt for any other female.

"Where's Anthony?" Tony asked eagerly.

Eve waved her hand irritably. "Where he is every day, off at Leopard's Leap. I believe he covets the place!"

Roz thought the word *covet* that dropped from Eve's lips was most apt. It was clear as crystal that her daughter coveted the wealthy nabob. It was also obvious, at least to Rosalind, that they had been involved. Now she understood why Adam Savage had insisted upon returning to Ceylon. His personal code dictated he make a clean break with Eve before he could honorably marry Antonia. Roz didn't like it one bit. Someone was going to be hurt, perhaps deeply, perhaps even permanently. Thank God she had decided to accompany her granddaughter. Roz didn't believe Antonia was any match for Eve's vitriol.

The next hour was a blur of activity as a dozen servants scurried about carrying luggage, plenishing rooms, providing refreshments, drawing baths, and unpacking for the newly arrived guests at Government House.

The small native girl who attended Antonia while she bathed knelt quietly in a corner with downcast eyes. Tony was used to bathing in private, but this child was so self-effacing, she did not make Antonia feel uncomfortable.

Beneath the warm, scented water Tony's hand stole to her belly. It was no longer a silken hollow, but mounded slightly without actually protruding. She smiled over her secret knowledge. Adam would never have permitted her to make this long voyage if he had known about the child. Her thoughts drifted to her mother. The baby would make Eve a grandmother. Antonia stifled a giggle. Her mother would consider that a fate worse than death. She had seen Eve place a proprietary hand on Adam. Her mother had never been able to keep her hands off men. Even as a child Antonia had noticed that Eve touched all her father's friends with intimate invitation. Now that Antonia was a woman, she realized it was just her mother's way of affirming her attractiveness.

Antonia stepped from the bathwater, then dried herself with a thick Turkish towel. Immediately the little maid came forward with the white cotton camisole and petticoat Tony had picked out. The child had wanted her to wear a formal silk gown, but instead Antonia had chosen a simple white batiste, embroidered with scarlet hibiscus blossoms.

Antonia had just begun to brush the tangles from her long black hair when her mother floated into her chamber. She offered up a quick prayer of thanks that Eve had not caught her naked.

"Antonia, we have a guest staying with us. You will have to wear something a little more formal for dinner."

Tony bit her lip. Her mother had a knack for making her feel awkward and gauche. "Adam assures me cotton is acceptable anywhere in the Indies, but it won't take me a moment to change. I hope Anthony will be here for dinner."

"He and Bernard always return at sunset."

"Bernard?" Antonia repeated the name, hating the very sound of it.

"Yes, your cousin Bernard Lamb is staying with us. A most attractive young man."

"Holy Mother of God!" Tony cried. "He intends to kill Anthony!"

"Don't be absurd."

"It's true, Mother. I must tell Adam." She turned to the young native girl. "Please find my riding boots."

"Antonia, I forbid you to go running off to Leopard's Leap, and stop calling him Adam! Mr. Savage and I are to be married. He will shortly become your father!"

Chapter 44

The blood drained from Antonia's face until it was ashen. She felt herself slipping away into unconsciousness. She flung out a hand to grasp hold of something that would keep her on her feet. The dusky female thrust the boots into her outstretched hand.

"The evil one has a gun, memsahib," she whispered.

Antonia blinked two or three times to banish the dizziness and the nausea that threatened to overcome her. She wanted to scream a denial. Her mother and Savage; she simply couldn't bear it! Any other woman would have deeply wounded her, but Eve? In that moment Antonia believed her wound would prove fatal. She felt as if her mother had plucked her heart from her breast.

Then she realized her mother was just as much a victim as herself. Savage had seduced her and made love to her, knowing Eve waited in Ceylon for him to return and marry her. Antonia recoiled from the vile deception. His treacherous duplicity made her sick at heart. She realized she had started the dishonesty between them by misrepresenting herself, but how could any man be so cruel, so vile, as to seduce both a mother and daughter? It was vicious and morally contemptible.

"Russell Lamb is the only father I will ever have." She pulled on her boots. "I must find Anthony. Bernard Lamb is a cold-blooded killer, in spite of the fact you find him so attractive. I am afraid you are a lamentable judge of men's characters."

Eve stepped back at the searing look of contempt. Even as a child her daughter had been incorrigible. So be it. Let her run off into danger. Ceylon wasn't England, but the headstrong girl would have to learn that lesson for herself!

Tony found the stables and startled a uniformed sepoy by taking his saddled mount. She knew Leopard's Leap was the next plantation, but she also recalled it was spread over twenty thousand acres. Though the task of finding Anthony would be difficult, she refused to think it impossible. Twins had an invisible thread that connected them somehow in mind and in spirit.

She rained a hundred curses upon the head of Savage. Thanks to his cunning plot Bernard Lamb was once again stalking his prey. Antonia was blind to the exotic paradise that stretched before her, blind to the tropical sun that turned the sky to saffron shot with brilliant gold as a prelude to setting. She urged the horse to thunder through the rows of strange-looking trees as she cried out her twin's name over and over. She was gripped by such a sense of urgency, her mind blotted out everything save her beloved brother.

At that moment Anthony was on foot, leading his horse so he could get a closer look at the exotic fungi that covered the fallen trees on the jungle floor. Some were brilliant orange with black spots, others were dark purple on top, pale mauve beneath. Even the shapes were unlike any he'd seen before. Some were like frills on a fop's shirt, others looked like painted gnomes' stools from an illustrated fairy tale.

Anthony looked up at Bernard, who hadn't bothered to dismount. He realized he was boring his cousin to tears. "I guess we'd better get going. By the dimness in here I can tell the sun is going down. The jungle comes alive after dark. It's not a healthy place to be."

Bernard smiled. "Not a healthy place at all," he agreed, pointing his pistol at his companion.

Anthony thought his cousin was aiming at some jungle creature that threatened them until he felt the searing pain explode in his chest. He felt himself knocked backward, then everything went black.

Anthony's horse bolted the moment the gun discharged. As Bernard looked down at his cousin's body, a surge of power swept through him. He watched the crimson spot on his white shirt spread and unfurl until it looked like an hibiscus blossom.

It was the hour when the Tamils of Leopard's Leap ceased their labor. As they streamed in from the far reaches of the plantation they stared with superstitious dread at the apparition riding wildly, like some glorious goddess. They feared it was Hakshasa, the Hindu myth made manifest. She was here to warn them of impending disaster. Their voices rose in panic and they began to run. Mothers sought their children then took refuge in the huts.

Adam Savage heard the commotion from the verandah where he sat talking with Denville. He sprang to his feet immediately, then began to run swiftly in the direction of the upraised voices.

Antonia, astride a black stallion, galloped toward him at a furious pace. Her skirt was pulled up, baring her lovely long legs, her knees pressed into the horse's belly. When she was only yards from him he saw that she did not rein in but intended to ride over him. With one powerful, lithe lunge he grabbed her bridle, bringing the animal to a flailing halt. His icy blue stare bored into her. "Are you trying to kill me or yourself?"

"I don't much care!" she flung the words at him, wishing they were weapons. He knew instantly that Eve had revealed what he had desperately hoped to conceal. "Tony, we have to talk!"

His earlier words came flooding back to her. He had warned, "Don't bestow sainthood upon me." She wanted to laugh, but her blinding tears prevented her. "Let me go, you black-hearted devil. If I had a gun, I think I would kill you!"

A shot rang out somewhere in the jungle. Tony clutched her breast. "It's Anthony—he's out there with Bernard Lamb!" She dug her heels into the belly of the black stallion and it surged forward with a tremendous burst of nervous energy.

"Wait!" Savage thundered, but Tony was deaf to everything except the shot she had heard.

Silently, Bernard Lamb turned his horse to lead it from the jungle. The power pulsed through him, urging him on to the next step of his revenge. The anticipation was akin to desire, yet it was far more intense than mere sexual desire. He recognized the emotion as blood lust. He needed only one more element to reach a state of ecstasy. With the blood he needed fire!

He urged his mount to a trot, guiding it to the southern slopes of Leopard's Leap where the priceless tea bushes stretched upward, acre after fragrant acre.

Antonia, driven by instinct alone, galloped in the general direction of the gunshot. Perhaps she had only imagined it. She fervently hoped so, but an inner voice told her Bernard's bullet had at last found its mark. She had lived for both of them for so long, she imagined she felt his wound in her chest. They were still connected by a tenuous thread. If it broke, he would die. Hope burned bright within her, she did not dare to let it dim.

Antonia saw a riderless horse come out of the jungle and instinctively knew it was her brother's mount. Though the sun was sinking fast and the green shadows of the jungle were turning dark, she did not hesitate.

When Tony galloped away from him, Adam Savage knew he could not take the time to get a horse. He loped along through the trees, silently, steadily, at a pace that would conserve his energy. All his senses were alert for danger. His eyes missed nothing, his ears were cocked for every sound, his nose scented peril.

He could not catch her before she plunged into the jungle, but her white-and-red dress fluttered before him like a banner, marking the path she rode.

The thickness of the foliage slowed Tony's horse to a walk and she noticed for the first time how menacing the dark shadows were inside the jungle. All about her things were rustling furtively. A scream gathered in her throat. Panic rose up in her, telling her to turn and flee. Then suddenly she saw the white and red.

She slipped from the horse, not daring even to whisper his name in case he was beyond hearing. She fell to her knees beside him, gasping with fear. The black stallion, scenting what Antonia did not, rolled back its eyes, flattened its ears, and bolted the way it had come.

Though her eyes were blurred with tears, she saw the crimson blossom upon his breast. With trembling fingers she reached out to touch his cheek. She could not tell if he was breathing. "I'm here. Everything will be all right now." She murmured the promise to comfort both of them, but she was in total panic, wondering how she would get help.

Savage didn't slow his pace as he reached the thick canopy of the jungle. A wave of relief swept through him as he saw her horse coming toward him, then a foul curse dropped from his lips as he saw its saddle was empty. He caught the frightened animal by its trailing bridle and quieted it down with a firm, soothing hand. It was reluctant to go back into the jungle, but he gave it no choice. Savage's heart pounded loudly in his ears. He had a damn good idea what the horse had scented.

A pair of green eyes watched the scene with infinite patience and cunning. The leopard, crouched motionless on the low-hanging limb, could smell the blood of its prey. As the girl came directly beneath it, the two-hundred-pound kill splayed its forelegs, unsheathed its claws from its pads, and sprang. Antonia screamed and rolled away from the beast that dropped from above onto her brother's body. It watched her warily as it licked the blood on his breast, growling a warning deep in its throat.

Antonia grabbed up a fallen tree branch, then thrust it at the leopard with all her strength. The big cat immediately retaliated. It had her on her back in ten seconds, its bared upper canines ready to sink into its victim's body to gut it.

For one split second fear paralyzed Savage before he ruthlessly quashed it. He tethered the horse, then reached for his gun, but he could not take the chance of shooting. By the time he sprang, his knife was snugly fitted into the palm of his hand. He rolled with the animal, both of them growling, snarling.

Savage kept his head down between his shoulders to keep his jugular from the cat's deadly fangs. In spite of his great strength the leopard soon had him on his back. He had known it would be so. He plunged his knife into its underbelly and ripped upward, toward its heart.

When he got to his feet he was covered with blood. The fear that had threatened him earlier came back with a vengeance to claim him now. Antonia lay sobbing. She, too, was covered with blood, but he knew it was her blood, not the leopard's. He could do nothing for her here; he knew he must get her to the bungalow.

First he lifted Anthony's body, laid it over the saddle, then slapped the horse's rump to get it moving in the right direction. As gently as he could he picked up Antonia in his strong arms and lifted her against his heart, murmuring softly to soothe her fear. She deliberately turned her face from him. Though she was the one who was wounded, he was the one who suffered the greater pain in that moment of rejection.

He moved swiftly, his long strides taking them from the jungle, which was now cloaked in total blackness. As he emerged from the confining foliage he saw the eerie red glow that was beginning to light up the sky. He knew immediately what it was, where it was, and who had done this evil deed.

There was a great babble of voices as word of the fire spread. The plantation workers were gathering at the mustering grounds for instructions. As Savage came into view a cry went up, then he was surrounded by his native people, who were willing to lay down their lives for him.

"It is the tea, sahib, the tea!" his head banion wailed.

"I know. Go, do what you can, but don't put the workers' lives in danger," he shouted. "Remember, fire will always spread upward!"

Denville came running, a dozen armed guards at his heels. One of the men led the horse that carried Anthony's limp body. "Let me help you!" Denville shouted as he lifted his pitch torch high to reveal a blood-drenched Savage.

"Bernard Lamb did this. I know how he thinks. Get the guards to the smokehouse and the rubber trees. That's where he'll strike next!" He jerked his head at the guard leading the horse. "Fetch him to the bungalow."

Savage's house servants, who had been trained by John Bull, were both competent and efficient. At the back of the bungalow was a field infirmary set up especially to deal with workers' accidents, which occurred on a regular basis. The two young men who worked there were trained to handle everything from severed fingers to snakebite. Savage left Anthony in their hands with only one admonition. "Keep him alive." It was an order they dared not disobey.

He carried Antonia to his own chamber. Two female servants stood by silently awaiting the Leopard's orders. "Boiling water, bandages," he bit out, wasting no words. He stripped off his blood-soaked shirt, dropped it to the floor, then used his knife to cut away what had once been her white dress.

Antonia's beautiful silken skin was torn from beneath her breast to the top of her thigh. The wounds were not too deep, but infection was almost a certainty. His ice-blue eyes gazed down in disbelief at the rounded mound of her belly, then his gaze flew to hers in silent accusation. She veiled her green eyes immediately and turned her face to the wall.

One female brought the water and bandages, the other brought ointment mixed from jungle plants and silently offered up a vial of poppy juice. Savage hesitated long seconds. Finally he knew he could not bear her to be in unnecessary pain.

"Drink!" The order was so forceful, she did not dare to defy him.

The powerful, calloused hands were capable of infinite gentleness. He washed the wounds, silently willing her eyes to become heavy before he poured on the disinfectant. Her eyes were still flooded with tears, the lids not closing. "Anthony?" she whispered hopelessly.

"Alive," he said firmly.

Her eyelids closed with relief, but the tears still seeped from beneath them.

He gripped the bottle of antiseptic. "Tony, this will hurt like hell."

She raised her lashes to look at him. It told him plainly he could not hurt her more than he already had. She did not even cry out as he flooded her torn skin with the antiseptic, but he saw her bite her lips until they were blood raw as he coated her with the ointment, then bound her.

When her eyes finally closed in blessed drugged sleep he called in the guard from the verandah. "I want you to ride over to Government House with a note." Savage scribbled the words quickly. They were brief and to the point. *Both twins are hurt. Come immediately. Bring the chaplain.*

Savage stared curiously at the face before him. The resemblance to Antonia was uncanny, yet the jaw of the young man clearly sprouted dark whiskers. The infirmary team had stripped the wounded man to the waist and thoroughly cleansed both him and his wound. He lay on spotless linen, his lips and face pale beneath the tan.

"He is shot, sahib."

"I know that, Adjit. Did you remove the bullet?"

"We dare not, sahib. You ordered us to keep him alive. You are bleeding. We must tend your wounds."

"Just scratches," he insisted. Savage lifted the gauze pad to inspect the wound. He doubted it had touched Anthony's heart or lungs. If it had, the rough ride across the saddle would have finished him. Savage probed the oozing hole with his finger. He felt nothing and probed deeper. At last he made contact with the lead ball. It was imbedded in the pectoral muscle, which may have prevented any bones from being shattered.

Adam decided against using his knife, but worked away with his finger until he was able to dislodge it and pop it out. The blood welled up afresh in crimson profusion. He covered it with a clean pad of gauze and pressed his whole weight down on it. Suddenly he found himself gazing into wide green eyes fringed with black lashes.

"Are you trying to kill me or cure me?" Anthony gasped with humor.

"You've as many lives as your sister, I think," Savage said with heartfelt relief.

Anthony closed his eyes from the pain, then opened them again after a minute. "You know my sister?" His look was quizzical.

"I do. I'm Adam Savage."

"My guardian?" he asked incredulously, once more gasping at the pain.

Savage nodded. "Soon to be your brother-in-law."

Anthony laughed, then grimaced. "Christ, that hurts!"

"I just took a bullet out of you."

"That bastard shot me!" Everything suddenly came back to him.

"That's what I call him, Bernard the Bastard. I think the bleeding has settled down enough to bind you up, but I want your pledge you'll lie quiet. If you don't, you'll set it off again. I can't waste any more time playing nursemaid. Your cousin has put the torch to my tea factory and my precious bushes."

Anthony was horrified. "I'll kill the son of a bitch!"

"You will lie quiet. I give the orders here." He turned to Akbar. "You'd better prepare some burn dressings. Casualties from the fire will be arriving any minute."

They heard voices. Anthony said, "I think I'm hallucinating. I just heard Mr. Burke."

Savage nodded. "Roz is here too. You'll be in safe hands."

He met them in the spacious living room. Their faces were ashen. He reassured them immediately. "They will both recover. Antonia was clawed by a leopard. I've dressed her wounds and given her a sleeping draft. I'm afraid Anthony was shot, but he's awake and quite lucid. He's back in the infirmary."

"When your note asked for the chaplain we thought someone was dying," Eve gasped.

"I'm sorry." Savage turned to the churchman. "I sent for you to solemnize a marriage, but it must wait. Leopard's Leap is ablaze."

Bernard Lamb was almost delirious with joy as he stood in the shadows of a banyan tree watching the brilliant display before him. The flames would lick teasingly at a tea bush, then suddenly, when he thought it would never catch fire, it would blaze up in a frenzy. One sizzling fireball after another, spreading steadily outward and upward. The stupid wogs were so busy wailing and running about like ants in a futile attempt to save the precious tea bushes, he was able to climb to the second story of the tea factory to set his next fire.

He almost lingered up there too long, mesmerized by the flames and the smells he was creating. It was better than the pyrotechnical display at Vauxhall Gardens.

When he crept back to the massive banyan tree his horse had managed to free itself. He cursed the cowardly dumb beast, swearing to put a bullet into its brain if he caught up with it. Now he would have to get to the rubber trees on foot. It was almost a two-mile trek, but he knew exactly where they were located. He knew how many rows there were and how many trees in every single row. A rubber tree should make an even more spectacular display than a tea bush when put to the torch.

Bernard stared in disbelief when the smokehouse came into view. It was surrounded by armed guards. That fucking Savage was almost as clever as he was, anticipating where he would strike next. He circled back and around, hoping to come into the rows of rubber trees from their farthest reaches. Christ, the stinking Indians were here, too, patrolling every row. He got down on his belly, watching the guards, seeking a pattern as they paraded about with their rifles at the ready. Bernard lay motionless, waiting, watching for the opportunity he knew would come. He felt omnipotent. He had eliminated the obstacle that stood between himself and Lamb Hall. Now he would destroy the thing that was most precious to his enemy: Leopard's Leap. Once the latex was ablaze, he would finish the job by firing the spacious bungalow.

When Bernard calculated there was no one closer than a hundred yards, he crawled on his elbows toward the back row of trees. He cursed as he came upon a narrow irrigation ditch filled with water. He hadn't seen it in the dark. He knew he would have to get beyond the ditch to set the fire, yet he could not bring himself to crawl through the water. He hated this stinking, infested country as much as he hated its pathetic natives. He was being eaten alive by mosquitos and the water undoubtedly attracted snakes as well. He got to his feet, still crouching, then slipped unnoticed across the ditch. Perhaps this was close enough. If his luck held, and he was certain it would, he would only need to ignite one tree. He reached for his long, sulphur matches. The moment he struck it a sepoy saw its flare and cried out an alarm.

Bernard reached for his gun, but it was gone. It had fallen onto the soft, rich earth as he had crawled toward the trees. He did not panic. His mind was sharper, his senses keener, than they had ever been. He leapt the ditch and ran in a zigzag pattern. The thick-skulled, clumsy fools were no match for him.

The sanctuary of the jungle closed its warm darkness about him. As he ran he felt his foot come down between two fallen tree trunks. He heard the sickening snap of his anklebone, but before he could scream out in pain, his head smashed against something that knocked him senseless.

Chapter 45

Savage ran toward the tea slopes, which were over a mile from the bungalow. When he reached the tea factory he saw that the top three floors were gone. Only the concrete foundation, protected by water that continually ran down its walls, remained.

A long line of workers formed a bucket brigade all the way from the lake. He had to shout to make himself heard over the roar of the fire. The lower slopes of tea bushes were destroyed and blackened. The fire raced ever higher. The slopes were dotted with men and women risking their lives to save the bushes on the higher ground.

Savage cursed. He took off up the slopes, ordering everyone he encountered to get back to safe ground. Sparks and soot flew everywhere, dancing in the air like swarms of fireflies. The smell of the burning tea bushes was pungent, acrid almost. It was a smell that insinuated itself into nose and throat and lungs. Savage knew the scent of destruction would be with him forever.

When he got the last workers off the slopes he joined the bucket brigade, salvaging what they could of the long row of storage sheds that held tea chests. Before he returned to the bungalow, Savage loped off toward the rubber trees almost two miles away from the tea slopes.

Denville met him at the smokehouse. "Were you able to save any of the tea?"

Savage shook his head. "Most of the fire is out, except on the high slopes. What remains won't spread this way even if the wind changes. Any sign of the mad bastard who set the fire?"

"Yes! One of the guards saw someone among the rubber trees. He shot at him, but he ran west toward the jungle."

"They didn't get him?" Savage demanded with disgust.

"They wouldn't go into the jungle at night," Denville said apologetically.

"Well, I can't fault them for that," Savage admitted. "I'll get him, never fear, but I think morning will be soon enough. Keep the guard posted. He might try to creep back."

Five hours had gone by before Savage was able to return to the bungalow. It was three in the morning when he slipped into Antonia's room. She was still asleep. Her grandmother, too, was sleeping in the big chair beside the bed.

He discovered Eve pacing restlessly in an adjoining chamber. He held a warning finger to his lips and she followed him back to the spacious living room. "How's Anthony?" he asked.

"Mr. Burke is with him. He assures me there is nothing to worry about." She stared at him in fascinated revulsion. He was naked to the waist and filthier than any man she had ever seen. The smoke and soot had blackened him. His sweat had streaked the dirt into black runnels.

His face was caked with dried blood. Undoubtedly he would have more scars. He was too primitive, too savage for her.

"Eve, it's not going to work between us."

She hesitated, almost afraid to let go. She gave a nervous little laugh. "Did you ever get that title?"

"No. No, an English title proved elusive."

She shuddered with relief. "Adam, I'm extremely sorry about Leopard's Leap. It's a cruel tragedy to come all this way only to see your plantation destroyed." She shrugged helplessly. "You won't even be returning with a wife."

He looked at her with compassion. "I'm in love with Antonia. I'm going to marry her tomorrow."

When Bernard Lamb regained consciousness he felt the agony of his ankle radiate all the way up his leg into his belly. He imagined he could feel the pain searing his brain. It throbbed in rhythmic waves with each and every heartbeat.

He willed the pain to cease and when it did not, he decided the only way to overcome it was to separate his mind from his body. He was able to concentrate his mind so well that he was partially successful, but when he tried to free himself from the vise grip of the tree trunks the agony flooded back to rack his whole body.

He realized his ankle must have swollen to an alarming degree. Fear began to seep into his bones and travel through his veins with the pain. He tried to keep the fear at bay. Hadn't destiny taken his hand tonight? Was he not the new Lord Lamb? Had he not put Leopard's Leap to the torch? Somehow he would survive this nightmare.

Adam Savage soaked in the sunken bathing pool, easing the fatigue that engulfed him. Ten years of backbreaking labor had been wiped out in hours. He closed his eyes, letting go of the tension that bunched his muscles.

Gradually it dawned upon him that he was not cursed, he was blessed. No lives had been lost in the devastating fire. All who had received injuries would recover. He still had the land, nothing could destroy that. He would rebuild the tea factory. Best of all, Antonia slept safely beneath his own eaves. A great joy welled up in him. He was going to be a father. He knew he had been blessed by the gods.

* * *

Bernard's ankle was numbing to the point where he could now bear the dull pain. His whole focus had been centered, so that he had been unaware of anything else for hours. Now, however, he became aware of a creepy, crawling sensation. His imagination was working overtime. His skin felt so cold and clammy, he began to shiver. He gathered his wits and told himself he should get some sleep. When dawn arrived, giving him enough light to free himself, he must have enough strength to get far away from this place even if he had to crawl.

He closed his eyes, feeling dizzy and weak. Even his breathing was becoming faint and jerky. He dozed a few seconds at a time, his skin spasming convulsively every once in a while. As dawn broke, the blackness of the jungle receded.

Bernard jerked out of a doze and tried to struggle to a sitting position. He could not move. He had no strength in any of his limbs. He looked down at his body, then screamed, horror stricken at the loathsome things that covered his entire torso. Hundreds of black, blood-engorged leeches, some as long as ten inches, were feeding on him as he lay helpless. The ones that were replete fell off him, but there were countless others to take their place, irresistibly drawn by the smell of his blood.

Suddenly he looked destiny in the face and realized that his destiny was death. A bloodcurdling scream erupted from his lips as he felt the leeches attach themselves to his throat. As he opened his mouth they slid inside and Bernard lost his last remnant of sanity.

Adam opened his eyes wide just before sleep overtook him. It was fortunate the animal cry had alerted him to his surroundings. He climbed from the water feeling refreshed and ready to meet the new day. It was strange how human a simian's scream could sound.

His left cheek had been deeply scored by the leopard's claws. He realized if he shaved, the gashes would bleed, so he put down his razor and shrugged. At least one side of his face was unmarred.

He encountered Mr. Burke and invited him to join him for breakfast. "What sort of a night did young Anthony have?"

"Not bad at all, considering you removed a bullet from his chest. The change in him is absolutely amazing. The last time I saw him he was just a boy. Now he's a man. I don't just mean physically, though his back is twice as broad as it was. I mean he has matured."

"Working your passage on an East Indiaman isn't exactly a Sunday-school picnic. It broadens the mind as well as the back."

"I would have given my eyeteeth to see Antonia's reaction to him, but I knew the twins would like a private reunion. Never saw children closer than they were, but the separation has done them both a world of good."

"Keep tabs on that chaplain for me," Adam said, winking at Mr. Burke. "We'll need his services today."

"He has finally gone to bed. He was helping in the infirmary all night, and a hell of a night it was for you and Leopard's Leap."

Adam grimaced. "Hard work built the place; hard work will rebuild it. This exotic land has a way of renewing itself no matter what destruction the white man wreaks upon it."

"Anthony said you would rebuild. I believe he's fallen in love with Leopard's Leap."

At that moment Anthony was sitting on the end of Antonia's bed, relating his miraculous rescue. "The *Earl of Abergavenny* was the name of the ship. It had all hands on deck watching a pod of whales that had been driven off course by the storm. In the last rays of light someone spotted the yellow oilskin.

"They told me later what a coordinated exercise in ingenuity it took, to say nothing of courage. It must have looked like a dramatic water ballet. They lowered a gutsy seaman on a rope into the sea until he finally hooked me with a gaff. It took a dozen hands to pull me aboard. I was half-drowned and unconscious. It was my lucky day, Tony. The Indiaman was outward bound for Bombay."

"Oh, God, Tony, you'll never know what we felt like, thinking you had drowned. We concocted a scheme to keep Lamb Hall from falling into our cousin's greedy hands."

"It never dawned on me that you would lose the Hall. What the hell did you do?"

"I took your place. I became Lord Anthony Lamb."

Anthony was appalled.

"Don't look so shocked! Confidentially, I had a hell of a good time playing bachelor, sowing my wild oats. Remind me to tell you about it someday when you're feeling stronger."

"Catty little bitch, are you implying you were more of a man than I was?"

"I gave it a bloody good try," she said, laughing. "We don't look much alike any longer, though. You're sprouting a beard and you've filled out unbelievably."

He eyed her softly rounded cheeks and the lovely curves evident beneath her nightgown. "You've filled out a bit yourself. You're positively blooming."

Tony blushed beneath his close scrutiny. A low knock interrupted them. The door opened to admit Adam Savage. Anthony was on his feet immediately. "Were you able to save any of the plantation?" he asked anxiously.

"The tea is gone, but we saved the rubber."

"When you rebuild, I want to help," Anthony said firmly, hoping Savage wouldn't remind him he was wounded.

"Thank you," Adam said with genuine gratitude.

Anthony looked at his sister, but she had turned her face to the wall. He could clearly see these two had unfinished business between them, and he left the room as he was damned if he was going to be caught in the crossfire.

When they were alone, she kept her face stubbornly to the wall.

"I've come to change your dressings, Tony."

She faced him immediately, her green eyes brilliant with defiance. "Don't even think of touching me," she spat.

"I must see that those gashes don't become infected."

"I've been mauled by a leopard before!" she flung at him. "If I can survive you, I can survive anything."

"Tony, this morning I told your mother that I loved you; that we were being married today."

"There will be no wedding! You lying swine. You deceived me all along, playing your seductive games of conquest. Be honest for once. What is between you and my mother?"

"Whatever was between your mother and me happened before we met and quite frankly, Tony, none of your business." His ice-blue eyes held hers mercilessly. "While we're speaking of honesty, have you examined your own? You say and do exactly as you bloody well please, simply to get your own way about absolutely everything!"

"That's not true," she cried. "The deception I played was necessary."

"I'm not talking about that one." He abruptly sat down on the bed and laid his hands on her belly. "I'm talking about this deception. This is my child. How dare you keep it from me? We should have been wed months ago!"

"Child or no child, I won't marry you," she vowed furiously.

He got to his feet, looming above her. He put a finger beneath her stubborn chin and raised it until they were glaring into each other's eyes. "You can change your mind, or I can change it for you. The choice is yours," he said flatly. He strode from the room more frustrated than he had ever felt before in his life.

Tony was the most maddening, most exasperating creature he'd ever encountered. She knew he loved her with every fiber of his being. What the hellfire did she want from him? The impossible, that's what she wanted! How could he change the past? He decided he needed help.

Adam found Roz in the breakfast room. She came to him immediately.

"Adam, I am so very grateful. You saved both their lives. I thank you from the bottom of my heart."

"Roz, you've got to talk to her. She'll have nothing to do with me."

"Have you settled things with Eve?"

His eyes searched hers. "Of course I have. As if I could marry Antonia without informing Eve of my intention."

"Adam, Antonia believes you were in love with her mother. Even as a child she had to take second place to her mother's great beauty."

"That's ridiculous! Antonia is twice the woman Eve will ever be. I didn't love Eve. I simply believed she'd make a good chatelaine for Edenwood, and Eve certainly never loved me."

"I know that, Adam. I think Eve is only capable of loving herself."

"I should have told Antonia, but I didn't want to hurt her. I was a fool to think I could keep it from her."

"Yes, your vast experience with women should have told you Eve would make sure Antonia knew." Her eyes were filled with amusement that men really knew so little about what went on in a woman's mind. "Give her time. I know Antonia loves you desperately. In a few months she'll come around."

He ran a distracted hand through his long black hair. "Roz, we don't have a few months. Tony has conceived. I had no idea until I tended her wounds last night."

Roz put her hand on his arm. "You must have a hundred things to do. Leave this one to me."

Savage nodded. "I have a jackal to hunt down."

Lady Randolph entered her granddaughter's bedroom with a female servant carrying water and dressings. "I've come to assess the damage."

"Roz, no. I'll do it myself," Antonia said firmly.

"Fiddlesticks! Stop behaving as if you were the first woman ever to have a child. I was the first!"

Antonia said, "Oh, Roz, you always make me laugh. I mustn't laugh; my world is coming apart."

"Antonia, in this world if we don't laugh, we cry. In any case a child is something to celebrate, not mourn. It's flying in the face of convention, of course, to have a child without marrying. You'll really set the gossips on their fannies if you produce twins!"

"Ohmigod, don't say that!" Tony cried. Why had the possibility never occurred to her?

"Let's have a look at you."

Antonia lay down and helped Roz remove her bandages. The gashes were ugly, but whatever Savage had put on them had already begun its work of healing. They were now not much worse than heavy scratches. There was no sign of infection.

Roz gently washed them and patted them dry. "They've already begun to scab over. I think we should let the air at them. What do you think?"

"I think you are right as always," Tony replied.

"In that case I think you'd better marry Indian Savage. He's far too wealthy a catch to let him escape."

"I don't love him for his money!" Antonia flared.

"Then you do love him?" Roz asked.

"No! The answer is no! I don't love him and I won't marry him."

"Have it your way, darling. You usually do," Roz said lightly.

When she left Antonia's room, Roz went in search of Eve. She found her bedchamber easily by the steady stream of house servants running to and fro. Her daughter was propped up in bed with a breakfast tray across her knees. "Could I have a private word, Eve?"

Her daughter banished the servants with an imperative hand, then glanced at her with cool condescension.

"You do that so well. You must have had slaves in an earlier life," Roz said dryly.

"Don't be tiresome, Mother," Eve said sweetly.

"Tired, my dear, not tiresome. I hope you're ready for a few home truths. Eve, I'm tired of shouldering your responsibilities. Motherhood didn't suit you very well, so you cast the twins aside like so much unwanted baggage. I don't believe you loved Russell, and I don't see any evidence you ever loved the children, because you have always been totally wrapped up in yourself. I venture to say that up till now you've been a wretched failure. But, Eve, you are one of the most fortunate women in the world. You have a second chance. How many of us have the chance of redemption?"

"What do you mean?" Eve's cheeks were flushed a dull red.

Roz's face set with determination. Her voice was harsh and implacable. "You will go to Antonia and you will convince her that you and Adam Savage were never intimate."

A low knock came on the door. Roz opened it to find Mr. Burke. He had very thoughtfully returned to Government House to bring everything the ladies would need.

"Paddy Burke, I love you." Roz squeezed his hand in gratitude.

"And I love you, too, ma'am," Mr. Burke said sincerely as he lifted the trunk into Eve's bedroom.

Chapter 46

Eve stared at the closed door for five full minutes after they had departed. *So, they think they have a monopoly on love, do they? How dare they accuse me of not loving my children?* She flung open the lid of her trunk to search for something that would make her look motherly.

There was nothing, of course, but after much deliberation she ignored the silk chiffon and chose a plain linen morning gown. It took her an hour to do her face and hair, then she slipped along to Antonia's chamber.

Her daughter was standing at the window with unseeing eyes. She wore a loose calico wrapper whose brilliant native pattern of blues, greens, and gold showed off her dark beauty to perfection. Eve finally admitted she had never shown her daughter affection because she knew her beauty would one day far surpass her own. That day had arrived.

As Tony whirled to face her mother, her hair spread out in a silken cloud of black curls, her generous mouth formed into a lovely O of surprise, and her wide-set green eyes sparkled with unshed tears.

"Are you feeling recovered?"

"Yes. Thank you."

"Are you up to a mother-and-daughter chat?"

"Not really, Mother—"

"Antonia," Eve beseeched, "give me another chance?"

Tony brushed her hand impatiently across her eyes. "Come and sit down, Mother."

Eve fiddled with her silver bangles. "I've not exactly been the best mother in the world, but believe it or not I do love you, Antonia. When you were a little girl you were so pretty, so precocious, I was actually jealous of you. Twins, you know, have a knack for stealing everyone's attention. You were Russell's darling and he never tired of showing you off."

"I admit I loved the limelight, but you were always the beauty of the family, Mother. I felt I could never live up to that. I'm so sorry I didn't get to see Father again."

"When your father died, Antonia, I turned to Adam Savage for financial aid, but when I told you we were going to be married I'm afraid that was just wishful thinking on my part. My hopes along with my vanity were quite shattered yesterday when Mr. Savage came to ask me for permission to marry you instead."

Antonia searched her face. How much courage this must be taking.

"So, my dearest, if you accept his proposal I want you to be married from Government House. We'll invite all the planters for miles around and I'll be able to show off my beautiful daughter."

Antonia smiled through her tears. "Thank you, Mother. That is so very generous of you, but Adam and I don't need any of that. All we need is each other."

Adam Savage stood grim faced as he looked down at what was left of the corpse. The giant leeches had drained every drop of blood from Bernard Lamb's body. His lingering horror must have been unspeakable. An obscene death for an obscene man, Indian Savage thought with satisfaction. He would have the body buried where it lay in the jungle, not on any part of Leopard's Leap.

Savage knew he must report the death to the family who waited back at the bungalow. A great weight had been lifted from his shoulders now that the twins' lives were no longer in jeopardy, but his heart still felt heavy. He didn't look forward to another confrontation with

Tony, but he was prepared to use force if force was necessary. He tethered his horse to a post in the shade of the bungalow.

Antonia was sitting in his big chair on the verandah, watching for his return. He walked toward her slowly, drinking in her dark beauty. When she saw him coming, she stood up and took a tentative step toward him. Then suddenly they were in each other's arms.

Tony began to sob and Adam enfolded her against his heart.

"Oh, Adam, I'm so sorry about Leopard's Leap. I know how hard and long you labored over your tea groves. I know the pride and passion you feel for this place."

"Hush, love, hush. The only thing that matters to me is that you are safe." Incredibly it was true. His heart was singing. His senses were dizzy from her close proximity. "Leopard's Leap hasn't been destroyed. I'll rebuild, replant."

She pulled from his arms, looking into his face to see if he was just saying the words to comfort her. "Adam, is that really possible?"

"If you want something badly enough, nothing on earth can keep it from you." He kissed the tears from her eyes, then he kissed her mouth, realizing he was starving for her. "Come on, I'll show you."

He took her by the hand, then lifted her before him into the saddle. Her arms clung to his powerful body as he pressed her close, urging the horse in the direction of the tea slopes.

When she saw the blackened devastation stretching acre after acre, it was worse than she had dreamed. But her eyes followed Adam's finger as he pointed out things she hadn't noticed. His lips, murmuring his plans, brushed her ear, sending a delicious shiver down her spine. His head bent over hers lovingly, sharing his thoughts and ideas. Already the workers were clearing the slopes of the blackened clumps of charred tea bushes.

The debris of the factory was being carried away. "We'll build bigger and better," he told her with enthusiasm. It was a good thing he had such boundless energy, he would need it.

"What about tea plants?" she asked softly, hearing his heart beating beneath her cheek.

"What? You think me so shortsighted I don't have tea seedlings? I'll show you tea seedlings!"

They rode at least two miles until they came to a banana grove. Adam pushed aside the wide, flat leaves and there, in the protective shade of the plantains, delicate tea plants thrust their green leaves through the rich soil.

She laughed happily, lifting her mouth for his kiss.

"I want you in my bed tonight. Shall we get married?"

"Yes, please," Tony begged prettily, rubbing her ripe breasts against him until he groaned.

"Of course," she whispered teasingly, "we won't be able to make love until my wounds are healed."

He traced her love-swollen mouth with the tip of his tongue. "Trust me to find a way . . . or two."

They exchanged vows in the spacious living room of the bungalow. Anthony gave his twin into the very good care of the master of Leopard's Leap. It was a most solemn occasion. Lady Antonia Lamb became Mrs. Adam Savage of Edenwood and the Marchioness of Blackwater.

Eve and Rosalind were both weeping, as became a mother and grandmother of the bride, and when Mr. Burke came forward to congratulate the groom, Tony saw the suspicion of a tear in his eye as well.

"Please don't feel sad, Mr. Burke," Tony admonished him.

"My dear, 'tis relief I feel. Savage is the poor devil who'll be fetching the bucket for you from now on."

Savage murmured, "A firm hand applied regularly to the backside will put an end to her drinking and carousing about in trousers."

The household staff of Leopard's Leap had outdone themselves. When dinner was served in the long dining room, it was more like a banquet. It was ten at night before Denville proposed the last toast. Roz lifted her hands for silence.

"I think we should continue this party at Government House and let the newlyweds have their privacy."

When the two carriages pulled away from Leopard's Leap, Adam swung Tony up into his arms and carried her back into the bungalow. "You are an outrageous baggage. Did you wear bright yellow to shock them?"

She moved against him sensually, brushing her hand provocatively across the bulge at his groin. "They'd be shocked if they knew the effect bright yellow had on you. It arouses you to madness. The first time I wore it you took me across your desk!"

"You exaggerate."

"*Exaggerate* means to enlarge or increase beyond the normal. I plead guilty, milord." Tony deliberately touched his swollen erection once again. "Take me to bed."

"To hell with bed. I've waited an eternity to take you to my bathing room." His gaze was so intense, she blushed at the things she knew he would do to her.

"Your eyes are as blue as . . . a baboon's bum," she whispered wickedly. Then she screamed as his teeth bit down on her earlobe.

Anthony was back at Leopard's Leap at the crack of dawn. Adam and Tony had slept only about two hours. They awoke in each other's arms with strands of black hair entangled about their naked bodies.

The lovers clung to each other, whispering, kissing, touching, tasting. They ignored Anthony's cheerful voice as he talked with the house servants. As their passion mounted everything faded away until there were only two, alone in paradise. Their bodies fused, becoming one.

As always it was a wild, erotic love ritual, burning, thrusting, surging, pulsing, throbbing. Savage was all rippling muscle, all rampant, driving male. Antonia was all silken, liquid heat, all scented, sultry sensuality. At their mutual, bursting implosion, lust melted into delicious, overwhelming love.

He cradled her against him with one powerful arm, while his fingers brushed the clinging tendrils of hair from her temple, then traced the lovely curve of her cheek and throat.

"He won't go away, you know," she whispered.

"Anthony? No, I can hear him pacing out there."

"He's worse than a plague of locusts. I wanted us to have a long, lip-licking breakfast in bed, then a warm, scented swim in the bathing pool."

"I'll lick you tonight," he promised, recalling last night's lovemaking in the pool. The wet slide of skin, the liquid tremors, until they were love slick and almost drowning in need. "By tonight your scratches should be all healed over and I won't have to be so gentle with you." He groaned as he ran his calloused palm down her tempting leg. "When your long legs swoop up into the curve of my back, I want to lie like that forever."

Adam and Anthony spent the first of many days together. He got to know his wife's twin brother well. Anthony was so enthusiastic about everything, Adam could tell Leopard's Leap was already in his blood. He recognized the symptoms. Ceylon had had the same effect on him when he first arrived. It was still a part of him, of course, but his future and the future of his children now lay in England.

They began the tedious, backbreaking work of replanting. Adam noted with satisfaction that Anthony's enthusiasm did not diminish with hard work.

"Will you be returning to England soon?" Anthony asked his new brother-in-law.

Adam nodded. "If Tony would like to go home and feels up to the voyage."

"Is she unwell?" Anthony asked with concern.

"No, she's not unwell. She's blooming with health. She's redolent with child."

"Oh, I see," Anthony said, laughing. "I can understand why you want to get back to Edenwood. Mr. Burke has already packed grandmother's things for England, and mother's off to Bombay for a holiday, but I simply don't want to leave yet."

"Why don't you stay on at Leopard's Leap? The lease to the East India Company has only a year left on it. If you're a successful planter by that time, I'll make you a partner," Savage offered.

"Do you mean it?" Anthony asked, astounded at his generosity.

"You're a godsend, an answer to my prayers. What more could I ask than to leave Leopard's Leap in your care? I have a vessel called the *Jade Dragon* in Colombo. I use it for export on the China run. Why don't you try your hand at that too? There are only two cargoes I forbid: opium and ivory."

A fortnight later the trunks were stacked at the front door of the bungalow. The factory was being rebuilt and the fragile tea seedlings had been planted up the rolling slopes of Leopard's Leap.

Adam Savage carried his bride from the bathing pool into the spacious bedchamber they would use for the last time. He had let Antonia decide whether they would stay or return to England. She made the decision for them, knowing what was in her husband's heart. Though he loved Leopard's Leap, it was time to found their dynasty at Edenwood.

Adam slid into bed beside her and lifted her onto his hard body. "Sweetheart, I'm so much in love with you. Thank God you finally believed there was nothing between your mother and me."

She raised herself up on her knees above him, poised for the plunge. "Indian Savage, you don't really believe me that naive, do you? I simply came to the conclusion that you were right, as always. It was none of my business!"

She heard a low growl in his throat, before he pounced. Soon, however, they were both purring. Much later, in the still of the fragrant night, they sat propped against their pillows, sharing plans for their future. Savage reached for a cheroot made from fine Jaffna tobacco. He lit it, inhaled deeply, then stretched back luxuriously. When his glance was drawn back to Tony, he was stunned. She, too, was smoking a cheroot.

"What the hell are you doing?" he demanded.

"Something you taught me to do," she pointed out, her lids half closed against the blue smoke. "What's sauce for the gander is sauce for the goose."

"Too goddamn much sauce!" *My God, she is lovely,* he thought. "I suppose I'll have to give it up if I expect you to stop," he conceded.

Tony crushed out the cheroot and slid down against him in the bed. Savage became instantly erect. She rolled him between her hands like a fine cigar. "Mmm," she murmured outrageously, "let's put this on the mantelpiece and I'll smoke it in the morning!"

Author's Note

Tea and rubber were not grown on the plantations of Ceylon until George IV became King. I chose to write about the Georgian period prior to George IV's becoming Regent. I could lie and say the Regency period has been overdone, but the truth is there are too many Regency experts out there!